Weird Tales to Haunt Your Reptilian Brain

Volume One

Edited by Stephen Rhoades

Also by Stephen Rhoades

Anthologies
Inanimate Things: Volume One
Inanimate Things: Volume Two

Novels
The California Butcher
The Paranormal and Normal Investigators

Contents

The Dark Sent Something Back

by Richard J. O'Brien

Joe Lipkin sensed that the cottage owner in Maine wasn't interested in renting the place to a family from Brooklyn. His wife Marcie had emailed the owner over two months ago regarding the lakefront property near the Canadian border. No phone number was provided in the original ad.

For several weeks, the couple had searched for the perfect place to take their children on vacation. Their son Paul, fourteen years old, had, as of late, become enamored with a girl at school named Jessa Coombs. Jessa was all Paul talked about. His father thought it would be a good idea to get his son out of Brooklyn, at least temporarily, until the boy's fever cooled.

Lucie, the Lipkins' sixteen-year-old, had sworn off boys by the time she was thirteen years old. She wore black a lot, perhaps too much for Lipkin's taste.

On Tuesday of the third week, the telephone rang just as the Lipkins finished dinner. Marcie and Paul were clearing plates from the dining room table when Lucie answered.

"Hello?" she said, staring at her father. "Lipkin's House of Mirth. If you're happy and you know it, clap your—"

"Give me that," said Lipkin as he attempted to wrestle the receiver away from his daughter.

"I'm sorry," Lucie said to the caller. "Who were you looking for? Oh, hold on."

Lipkin looked at Lucie. "Who is it?" he whispered.

Lucie cupped her hand over the mouthpiece.

"I don't know," she said. "Sounds foreign."

"This is Joe Lipkin speaking," her father said, after he took the receiver from her.

"Your wife is having a bit of fun at my expense," a voice said. The voice didn't sound foreign; unless, of course, New England had been annexed by Canada.

"My daughter," Lipkin replied.

"Name's Ted Catskill," the man said. "I believe your wife inquired about my cottage up north of Allagash in the County."

"The county?"

"Sorry," Catskill said. "Aroostook County. I forget you're from out of state."

"Yes, we wanted to rent your place—"

"I gathered that from the email. Do you have a honkin' family?"

"A what?"

"How many children, Mr. Lipkin?"

"Two," he said. "There would be four of us."

"Toddlers?"

"Teenagers," said Lipkin.

"Good," Catskill said. "It's not that I don't care much for young-sters. Mine are all grown, of course. It's just that the North Woods can be troublesome for the little ones. Coming up to do some canoeing, are you?"

Lipkin named the tentative dates that his family had in mind for summer vacation.

"I am curious," he concluded, "about the cost."

"Smart man," said the caller. "Five hundred a week ought to do it."

Marcie entered the living room. She held up two fingers.

"My wife says two weeks," Lipkin informed Catskill.

"That's fine," he replied.

"Do we send you a check or—"

"Cash," Catskill said. "On the day you arrive, look me up at Hayford's Market. The market's open until eight in the evening. It's a few miles before you get to the cottage. If I'm not there, just leave the money with Clem Hayford. I'll get it from him."

"Thank you, Mr. Catskill," Lipkin said. "Will Mr. Hayford have a key to the cottage for us?"

Catskill laughed. Then he told him, "There are no locks on the cottage, Mr. Lipkin. Not much use up here, if you catch my drift."

Lipkin did not, but he let the matter go.

"We'll see you in June," he told the cottage owner.

"The good Lord willing," Catskill said before he ended the call.

By the time Lipkin pulled into the gravel lot in front of Hayford's Market, it was already 7:30 PM. Lipkin and his family had driven to Portland the previous day. They stayed overnight in a hotel, saw very little of the city that night, and by the time they left it was already one in the afternoon. Halfway from Portland to Saint Francis, they stopped to fuel the Subaru station wagon. By the time Lipkin found

Hayford's Market, both Lucie and Paul were ready for another bathroom break.

"Hi," Lipkin said as he approached the front counter of the shop. "Could you tell me if Ted Catskill is here?"

An old man sat reading a paperback copy of Caesar's *The Gallic War*. He lowered the book and stared at Lipkin with eyes that looked like deep blue oceans.

"You just missed him," the old man announced. "I'm Clem Hayford. You must be Mr. Lipkin."

"I have Mr. Catskill's money for the cottage," he said.

Hayford waved his paperback at Lucie and Paul, who stood behind him along with Marcie.

"They look as if their teeth are afloat," he said.

"Excuse me?" said Lipkin

"Restrooms are just past the soda coolers."

"Would you happen to know how far it is to Mr. Catskill's cottage?" Lipkin asked.

"Just a piece outside Saint Francis," Hayford informed him. "Don't worry. You'll make it before the dark gets here."

It was near-dark when the Lipkins made it to the cottage. A gravel driveway led from the road to the front of the house. The perennials planted haphazardly in the front yard appeared pale; ditto for the impeccable lawn.

"Dad?" Paul said as he tapped him on the shoulder. "I don't have a cell phone signal."

"Jesus, Paul," his mother said, "will you give it a rest, please?"

"Let's just grab our bags and the food," Lipkin told his family, "and go inside."

From the outside, the cottage looked like something straight out of the Irish countryside. White plaster walls, small windows, the trim and the front door done in Kelly green.

"Do you hear that?" Lucie asked.

"What is it now?" Marcie replied.

"I don't hear anything," Paul said.

"That's just it," said Lucie. "No crickets. Nothing."

The front door, as Catskill had pointed out on the phone, did not have a lock; only a latch door handle. Just inside the front door, there was a small antique telephone cabinet. Lipkin's parents had owned a similar one when he was a little boy. Atop the cabinet, a lit Tiffany dragonfly lamp and an old rotary phone. Lipkin dropped his bag, which brushed against the cabinet's front legs, causing the lamp to tilt. He steadied it before it fell over.

"Nice work, Dad," said Paul.

He was at that age when everything that came out of his mouth sounded sarcastic. This time, of course, it was intentional.

"Why don't you go upstairs and pick out a room for yourself," Lipkin suggested.

Paul's sister beat him to the stairs.

"You look troubled," Marcie said.

"I'm fine," Lipkin told her.

Together they checked out the eat-in kitchen and the back yard. A tree line of ancient maples marked the end of the cottage's property.

"I should put something together for dinner before the natives get restless," Marcie said.

They went back inside the house. Lucie stood in the small living room perusing the old books that lined two floor-to-ceiling bookshelves.

"Where's your brother?" Lipkin asked.

Lucie shrugged.

"Your father asked you a question," Marcie said.

"He took a room in the back upstairs," Lucie informed us. "Probably up there pulling his pud thinking about Jessa Coombs."

"Lucie!"

"What?" she asked. "That's what he does."

"Come to the kitchen and help me get some dinner ready," Marcie commanded.

"I'm not hungry."

"It wasn't a question."

"Dad!"

"Do what your mother says," he told his daughter.

Alone now in the small living room, Lipkin looked over the books that lined the shelves there. None of the titles appeared to be recent. He pulled down a copy of Hemingway's *A Farewell to Arms*. A standing lamp in the corner provided light enough to read by when he sat down on the small sofa. Lipkin read the first couple pages, listening to Marcie and Lucie in the kitchen. There was something unnerving about the cottage, the way the outdoors lacked familiar summer sounds. Though he'd never admit it to his children, Lipkin doubted his decision to drag them so far north.

"Joe?" Marcie appeared in the kitchen doorway. "Where's Paul?"

"Upstairs," he answered as he kept reading.

"Well, go find him," his wife said. "We're having sandwiches."

An old-fashioned push-button light switch at the bottom of the narrow stairs worked the light at the top. The steps creaked as Lipkin made his way upstairs. There were three rooms and a small bathroom on the second floor. Two of the bedroom doors were open. Lucie had chosen a small room on the left that faced the front of the house. The master bedroom, just past the bathroom on the right side of the short hall, also had a push-button switch. He turned on the overhead light. When he did, the darkness retreated like smoke being sucked out of the room. A queen bed with a dark wood headboard and a single dresser were the only pieces of furniture in that room.

The door to Paul's bedroom was closed.

"Paul?" he called out.

His son did not answer. Lipkin knocked again. After that, he opened the door. The bedroom light was on, but Paul was not there. There was a dresser identical to the one in the master bedroom along with a single bed. Paul's bag sat atop the dresser, unpacked.

A closet, built into the far corner of the room, stood with its wood door slightly ajar. When Lipkin pulled the door open, the closet was empty.

Lipkin left the second floor without turning the lights off. Downstairs, he fished out his cell phone from his luggage. No signal.

"Where's Paul?" Marcie asked.

"Not upstairs," he told her.

"Did he go outside?"

"I don't think so," Lipkin said. "I would have seen him."

"Did he crawl out a window and onto the roof?" Marcie inquired.

"The screens don't open in the windows upstairs," Lucie offered. "I tried already."

"I'm going outside to have a look around," Lipkin said.

The front door stuck when he tried it. He gave it another tug, slamming the door against the wall.

Outside the cottage, the night remained silent. Lucie had been correct. All the familiar nighttime sounds of summer, crickets and other bugs, were absent.

Lipkin called for his son several times, but each time he did so it was like shouting into a thick fog, as if the dark itself had muffled his voice.

Marcie and Lucie joined Lipkin outside. His wife and his daughter had their cell phones. Marcie tried dialing Paul's number on hers. Lucie's expression told Lipkin what he already knew. The cell phones were useless.

"Shit." Marcie slapped the side of her phone. "My cell doesn't work either."

Lipkin ran back into the cottage. Atop the telephone cabinet stood the old rotary phone, a relic from the 1950s. The original phone number was typed on a small piece of paper and encased in a clear glass disc. It was one of those decades-old exchanges that used a name in conjunction with a number. GYpsuM-1225.

When Lipkin picked up the receiver he heard a dial tone. He called 911. A three-tone bell rang in his ear before a recorded voice told him to check the number and dial again. He tapped the switch hook in the cradle. When the dial tone returned, he rang 0.

"Good evening, how may I direct your call?" a woman asked on the other end.

"Police," said Lipkin. "It's an emergency."

"One moment, please."

A series of clicks sounded.

"Springhill Police," a man said. "Officer Dekker speaking."

"Hi," he said. "I'm calling from a cottage in—"

"Gypsum-1225," Officer Dekker said. "That's Ted Catskill's cottage. We know where it is. What's the nature of your emergency, sir?"

"My son has gone missing," Lipkin informed him.

He went on to give Dekker a description of Paul.

Dekker asked him how long he'd been missing.

"He didn't just slip out for a walk?" Officer Dekker asked.

Lipkin told him and proceeded to tell the officer how his son had gone upstairs in the cottage and vanished.

"Well, it's after dark now," said Dekker. "We can't send anyone out there just yet."

"So I'm supposed to search the North Woods alone?" he asked.

"Listen, Mr. Lipkin," said Dekker, "I'll see if a unit's available. But I'll be honest with you. Once the dark comes, citizens are on their own."

"What do you mean—"

"Hold on, please."

Lipkin waited. Marcie stood next to him. Lucie paced the length of the small living room, biting her fingernails.

"What's going on?" Marcie asked.

"Mr. Lipkin?" Dekker got back on the line.

"I'm here," he said.

"One of our officers will be around directly," Dekker said. "If your son should come home—"

"He didn't leave the house."

"So he's there after all?"

"No, my son is missing," he said. "Like I said, he went upstairs. And now... Hello?"

The line went dead.

The cottage phone remained out of commission for the rest of the evening. Likewise, so did the Springhill Police. It was early the following morning when someone knocked on the front door. Marcie, Lucie, and Lipkin spent the entire night calling for Paul from the front and back porches of the cottage. Lipkin's worst fear was that Paul had climbed down from the second floor and fell into the nearby pond. He wanted to walk the surrounding woods, but Marcie talked him out of it.

"We can't let anything happen to you," she said.

Lucie managed to sleep for an hour on the sofa in the living room. No matter how many times Lipkin and his wife encouraged their daughter to go to bed and rest, she wouldn't hear of it.

When the knock presently sounded at the front door, Lipkin was torn between feeling relief and dread at the same time; relief in that the police had arrived at last, dread because he feared they had come to deliver the worst news.

A young police officer greeted him when he opened the door. He was tall, bull-necked, an obvious athlete turned law enforcement agent from the looks of him. His name was Stivers. Lipkin invited him into the cottage.

Lucie remained silent as Marcie and her husband gave the police officer the details. Stivers wrote down several notes on a page in his pocket-size notebook.

"Anything else you folks care to add?" Stivers asked.

"Does this happen often up here?"

"People go missing in the county sometimes," he explained. "We'll check with the Canadians over the border, of course."

"What about a search party?" Lipkin asked.

"Slow down, Mr. Lipkin," said Stivers. "Officially, we can't consider it a missing persons case until twenty-four hours have passed. Any chance your son beat it back to Hayford's and caught a Greyhound bus home?"

"Not at all," Marcie replied.

"What about you?" Stivers said to Lucie. "You were the last one to see your brother?"

She nodded.

"We took our bags upstairs," she offered.

Stivers was about to ask something else when another vehicle pulled up to the cottage. He stood up before anyone else did, looking nervous as he did so.

Lipkin went to the front door and opened it. Another police officer climbed out of an SUV. He wore sergeant stripes on his sleeve. He was short, thin, and balding.

"Mr. Lipkin?" he said as he approached. "My name is Sergeant Toomey. I heard your son is missing?"

"Yes, one minute he was upstairs and—" Lipkin began.

"Could you tell Patrolman Stivers to come outside?"

Stivers excused himself as he slipped past Lipkin. He went and joined Toomey in the yard. They had a hushed and, judging from the expression on Toomey's face, heated discussion. The whole time Toomey talked he stared at Lipkin. His eyes looked like two nickels.

Marcie and Lucie joined Lipkin on the porch. They watched as Stivers shook his head several times. Toomey grabbed the young police officer by his arm. When he spoke next, Lipkin heard his words.

"That's the way it is with the dark," Toomey said, shoving the bigger man toward his patrol car.

"What do you suppose they were talking about just now?" Marcie asked.

Lipkin was about to answer when Toomey offered a wave, climbed back into his SUV, and followed Stivers off the property.

"So, they aren't going to do anything?" Lucie said.

Lipkin ushered what remained of his family back into the house. Once inside, he used the old rotary phone and dialed the operator.

"Do you wish to place a call, sir?" an operator said when she picked up.

"State police, please," he told her.

The operator put Lipkin on hold. A few seconds later, the line went dead. Lipkin tapped on the switch hook several times. There was no longer a dial tone.

"The phone's dead," he said.

"What about Hayford's Market?" Marcie asked.

"Good idea. Lucie?"

"Dad?"

"Stay here in case your brother returns," he told her.

"No way," she said. "Don't leave me here by myself."

"You go," Marcie told me. "If Paul comes back..."

"I won't be long," Lipkin said.

Hayford's Market was open. There were several vehicles in the parking lot, among them a Springhill Police SUV. Lipkin recognized the number on the side of it. As he started for the store entrance, Sergeant Toomey exited the market.

"Mr. Lipkin—"

"What was all that about the dark?" he cut him off.

"I beg your pardon?" Toomey said.

"Back at Catskill's cottage," Lipkin reminded him. "When you were talking to Stivers."

"I don't know what you're talking about," he replied. "Do give us a call if your son shows up before nightfall."

"The phone's dead," he said. "I think it was deliberate."

"Why is that? What did you do? Call the state police? Try to supersede my jurisdiction?"

Toomey's breath smelled like wet dirt. He gripped the butt of his pistol as he spoke. His other hand came to rest on a canister of mace on his belt.

"Nothing of the sort," Lipkin told him.

"Good," he said. "I can send an officer around before sundown to follow up. And I'm sorry about the phone situation. Up here, we never went in for cell towers. Better that way. Tourists, of course, can't live without their technology. No offense."

"None taken."

"Good day to you."

Lipkin waited until Toomey got into his SUV and drove away. Then he went into the store.

Clem Hayford was seated behind the front counter. A young woman rang up groceries for a customer at the register. Hayford was still reading *The Gallic Wars,* unaware, it seemed, that customers were milling about his store.

"Mr. Hayford?" Lipkin said.

"Call me Clem," he said as he put down his book. "What can I do for you? Everything's all right at the cottage?"

"Is there somewhere we can talk in private?"

"My office," he said. "Follow me."

The two men made their way to the back of the store. A door marked *Staff* led into a cramped office filled with shipping and re-ceiving paperwork. A few framed photos hung on the walls around Hayford's old metal desk. Lipkin recognized the young woman from the register in one of the photographs. She stood between Hayford and his wife in front of the market.

Hayford gestured to a chair beside his desk. Lipkin sat down.

"What's on your mind?" he asked as he took his seat at the desk.

"Did Toomey tell you about my son?"

"Toomey doesn't say much to me," said Hayford. "Bad blood that goes way back. What happened to your son?"

"He's disappeared."

"Suppose he went out and got lost?"

"That's just it," Lipkin told him. "He never left the house."

"*Cum tenebris spes reliquiere,*" Hayford muttered.

"What's that? Latin?"

"From *The Gallic Wars,*" he replied. "When it was dark, they aban-doned hope."

"What do you know about Catskill and his cottage?"

"Ted and I go way back. He's a good man."

"I don't doubt that," said Lipkin. "Anyway, the reason I'm here is because the old phone at the cottage is out of order. And my cell phone—"

"Don't I know it," said Hayford. "It's like we're stuck in another century up here. Go on ahead. I'll give you some privacy."

Lipkin didn't bother to look at the phone on the desk until Hayford left him alone. It was an old rotary phone, similar to the one back at the cottage. The phone number on it, typed on paper yellowed with age beneath a clear plastic disc, was GYpsuM—2120. He dialed the operator.

"Hi, Clem," the operator said. "What can I do for you?"

It was the same voice on the phone as at the cottage, the one Lipkin spoke to last just before the line went dead.

"State police, please," he said in his best county accent.

"Hold, please."

There were a series of clicks.

"State police operator 4175," a male voice sounded.

"Yes, hello," he said. "My name is Joe Lipkin. I am staying near Allagash on vacation. My son has disappeared."

Silence.

"Hello?" Lipkin said.

A series of clicks sounded. Then the line went dead.

"How did you make out?" Hayford said from the doorway, his voice startling the other man as he spoke.

"Do you always have trouble with the phones around these parts?" Lipkin asked.

"No, sir," he answered. "I admit, it's a bit antiquated. But we like things that way."

"How far is the nearest state police troop from here?"

"Let's see," Hayford scratched his chin as he stared up at the ceiling, "that would be down in Houlton."

"How far away is that?"

"That's a good forty or fifty miles from here. Is something wrong?"

"My son is missing," he told him. "The local police haven't been helpful at all."

Hayford grimaced.

"It won't do you any good to go down there," he said. Hayford stepped into the office and closed the door. "A word of advice, if you don't mind. Wait a day. Sometimes they come back."

"People have gone missing before?"

"Tourists? Sadly, yes. This country up here isn't easy on folks who don't know it."

"I need to get back to the cottage."

"You want I should ring you up if I see your boy?"

"He's about this tall," Lipkin held up his hand to show him, "with dark hair—"

"I remember what he looks like," said Hayford.

He opened the door and exited the office. Lipkin followed him out. Hayford shook his hand.

Outside, Lipkin expected to run into Sergeant Toomey. The parking lot was nearly empty. It was warm and sunny out; a perfect New England summer day, if Paul had not been missing.

An elderly man called to Lipkin from inside his pick-up truck parked next to the Subaru. As he spoke, a truck passed on the road, drowning out his words.

"How's that?" Lipkin said once the truck was gone.

"I said there's a humdinger of a storm coming later this afternoon." He pointed west.

On the horizon, dark gray clouds rose in tall columns.

"Wonders never cease," Lipkin told him.

"Come up the county on vacation?"

"Yes," he answered.

"From whereabouts?"

"Brooklyn," he said.

"Ah, New York. I loved the city as a young man," the old-timer announced. "Plenty of temptation, if you catch my drift. Then I met my wife," he stared straight ahead as he continued his yarn, "and she was from up these parts originally. She wanted to come home and give back something to the community after she finished medical school. How do you say no to love? Am I right? My wife was a pediatrician, long retired now. You wouldn't know to look at me, but I was always good with figures. So, I opened a sporting goods store..."

The old man was still talking when Lipkin got into his vehicle and drove away.

Paul had not returned. Lipkin sensed that Marcie was teetering on the brink of a breakdown. He told her about the failed attempt to call the state police.

"Where's Lucie?" Lipkin asked.

"Upstairs trying to sleep," said Marcie.

The stairs creaked. Lipkin turned to see his daughter descend from the second floor.

"I'm hungry," Lucie announced.

They ate sandwiches in the kitchen. No one spoke a word. Outside the kitchen window, the tall pines at the back yard's edge swayed in the wind.

"Is it supposed to rain?" Lucie asked.

"That's what I heard at the market," her father said.

Marcie barely touched her food. Lipkin could tell that, during his absence, his wife and daughter had been crying. He felt like crying too. But it was important for him to keep it together. If not for his own sake, then for his wife and daughter.

Lipkin was famished. He ate three cold-cut sandwiches and drank two glasses of milk. Lucie nearly matched him. Marcie was content to nibble on a potato chip or two.

"I ran into this old-timer at the market—" Lipkin started to say.

Marcie slammed the table with both hands. "Why won't anyone help us?" she cried.

Lipkin felt hopeless. After lunch, he tried to nap in the master bedroom, but it was no use. He went back downstairs and found his wife and daughter huddled up on the sofa together staring at the old rotary phone. He joined them on the sofa.

A lightning flash preceded a sharp crash of thunder. Lucie sat up-right. Marcie held onto her daughter. Lipkin was going to suggest that he go out and look in the woods behind the house for any sign of Paul, maybe drive around the local roads in the hope that his son was out there wandering around and trying to find his way back to the cottage. As he considered these possibilities, someone knocked at the front door.

Lipkin got up from the sofa. He motioned to his wife and daughter to stay seated. Then he went to the door.

"Mr. Lipkin," Officer Stivers said when the door opened. "I can't stay long. I just—"

"Won't you come inside?" Lipkin asked.

"No, thank you," the young police officer said. "I wanted to come by to tell you that I am filing the missing persons report soon. It's close enough to twenty-four hours."

"Thank you," he said.

"Also, I wanted to give you these." Stivers held out six white candles and two boxes of matches. "We lose power when the summer storms come along. I don't know if Mr. Catskill left anything in the cottage for you."

"You're very kind, Officer Stivers," said Lipkin. "Now, about my son—"

"We're doing everything we can," he cut him off. "As far as search parties go, the chief plans to get some volunteers together tomorrow—"

"Why wait?" he asked.

"The storm, Mr. Lipkin," Stiver said. "In an hour it will be dark. Use the candles if the electricity goes out. I must go. I'm sorry I don't have any good news."

Lipkin watched as the police officer walked back to his cruiser through the pouring rain.

That evening, the Lipkins minus Paul ate chicken and potato salad. Sometime after eight o'clock, Lucie announced that she was going upstairs to sleep. Before she went up to her bedroom, she took a box of matches and a candle.

"Just in case," she told her parents.

Outside, the storm continued unabated. Twice within an hour the lights dimmed inside the house, but the power remained on.

"Why don't you go upstairs too, Marcie?" Lipkin told his wife. "I'll stay down here tonight."

Marcie hugged her husband. Her eyes were puffy from crying all afternoon. She squeezed Lipkin's hand.

"I may come back down later," she said.

After his wife and daughter went upstairs to sleep, Lipkin lit one of the candles Stivers had given to him. He took it into the kitchen, removed a plate from the cupboard, and dripped hot wax onto it. Next he set the lit candle on the plate on the kitchen counter by a window over the sink. He lit a second candle, took another plate from the kitchen cupboard, and returned to the living room. Lipkin left the second candle burning on the plate atop the coffee table.

He lay back on the sofa, listening to the water running upstairs as his wife and daughter readied themselves for bed. Lipkin had every intention of staying awake that night. The falling rain drummed against the windows and lulled him into sleep.

Early the next morning, taking the steps two at a time, Lipkin traversed the stairs to the second floor. The first door he reached was Lucie's room. Without knocking, he opened the door. The bedsheet beneath which Lucie slept last night lay wrinkled flat against the bed, but she was not there. Next, he rushed down the hall. As soon as he opened the door to the master bedroom, his new fear was confirmed. Marcie was missing from that room as well. The door to the room Paul had chosen as his own remained open just as Lipkin had left it.

Lipkin raced down the stairs. He found his car keys and exited the cottage without shutting the front door. The sun was up, the air humid from the previous night's rain. He got into his car, started the engine, and sped off.

By the time he reached Hayford's Market, it was nearly nine in the morning. There were a few cars in the lot. Lipkin exited his vehicle and ran inside the store.

Clem Hayford sat behind the front counter.

"Mr. Lipkin—" Hayford began.

"I need your help," he said. "My family is missing."

"How can I help?"

"I need to get in touch with Catskill," Lipkin said.

"He didn't leave you a message?" Hayford asked. "He leaves a message for cottage guests on the answering machine. Ted used to leave cottage guests these beautifully hand-written notes from his wife, but ever since his wife passed over he uses the machine instead."

"Catskill's wife died?"

"No, sir. I said passed over."

"What does that mean?" Lipkin asked.

"Go listen to the machine," he warned.

Lipkin turned on his heels. He walked right into Toomey as the police sergeant approached the front counter.

"Excuse me," said Toomey.

Lipkin ignored him.

"Mr. Lipkin?" Toomey called out. "Do you have a minute?"

"What is it?" Lipkin asked.

"If it's okay with you," the police sergeant said, "I'd like to stop by and follow up about your missing boy."

"That's not necessary," Lipkin announced. "I called the FBI field office in Bangor last night."

It was a lie, of course. But Toomey didn't know that. The color went out of the police sergeant's face. His mouth moved as he tried to form his next words. That's how Lipkin would remember him, standing there with his jaw muscles working but no words coming out.

Lipkin found the answering machine inside the telephone stand. It turned out Hayford had told him the truth. The light on the answering machine blinked red as he held the device in his hand. Lipkin pressed the *play* button.

"Mr. Lipkin," the recorded message began, "Ted Catskill here. I wanted to remind you that you might want to keep on at least one light in each of the rooms upstairs prior to sunset because the dark—"

Catskill's message ended there. Lipkin pressed the play button again. The message ended again when Catskill spoke the word "dark." Whatever message Catskill had intended to leave had been cut off.

Next, he picked up the old rotary phone and dialed zero.

"How may I direct your call?" an operator answered.

"Could you connect me with Ted Catskill's residence?" Lipkin asked.

"I'd be delighted to," the operator told him.

The phone on the other end rang three times.

"Mr. Lipkin," Catskill said when he answered.

"Why don't you tell me what's going on here?" Lipkin demanded.

"A little bird told me you were chewing on Clem Hayford's ear—"

"Who told you that? Toomey?"

"Toomey's a twit," Catskill announced. "But he does keep everything in line."

"I don't care about that. Where is my family?"

Silence followed. Lipkin thought Catskill had hung up on him.

"It's an old story, Mr. Lipkin," the old man said. "One I don't care to—"

"What happened to your wife?" Lipkin asked.

"She passed over. Hayford told you, didn't he? I love Clem like a brother, but the man can't keep his mouth shut."

"Passed over to where?"

"If you want your family back," Catskill said, "you'll have to wait for the dark to return."

"What's in the dark?"

"Not what's in it, Mr. Lipkin," he said. "It's the dark itself, a living thing capable of taking physical shape. The dark is, after all, the most ancient of all life forces. It existed before light, before the Word—"

"Is that where your wife is now?" Lipkin asked. "Did she get taken by the dark?"

"She did," Catskill said. "And the dark sent something back in her place."

Lipkin went to bed early that night. It was just before sundown when he entered the master bedroom. Once the sun dipped below the maples in the back yard, the room's walls turned blood orange. Lipkin had left the windows open. The dark orange light soon faded into a colorless gloom.

When the true night came, Lipkin was still awake. It was just after 8:30 PM. Turning to his left, he saw the darkness blow through the window screen overlooking the side of the cottage. He felt short of breath, as if a great weight bore down on his chest. The details of the room—the single dresser, the ornamental trim around the windows, the uneven and heavily plastered walls—faded from view.

In the dark now came hushed feral voices, whispers of a language foreign to him. The room fell away. Lipkin remained immobile as he was transported to another place. When he could see again, tall pines with pale gray trunks loomed overhead.

Lipkin sat up. The air was cold, the ground beneath him damp. He stood up, drawing deep breaths as he did, and looked around. In the distance, shapes moved in the shadows between the pines. A hyena-like cackle sounded in the distance. First one, then others answered the call.

The sky colored dark gray loomed low over the treetops. Everywhere he looked, it was the same. Even his hands looked ashen and dull. He called out his wife's name, his son's name, his daughter's name. The air muted the sound of his voice, no matter how loud he shouted.

Patches of fog drifted about him now. The cackling continued deep in the woods. There was no sun, no moon, no stars by which he could find his way. The pines were devoid of moss. Lipkin had read in a book somewhere that moss always grew on the north side of a tree. That knowledge was useless now. So he started walking. He paused now and then to listen. Whenever he did, he called out to his family. No one answered. The shapes concealed by shadow tracked his every move, letting lose their hideous and predatory raucous cries.

Lipkin approached a clearing. The damp air grew colder. He stood now along a row of ancient pines. A woman's muffled cry sounded. He watched as Lucie darted toward the clearing through the trees on the opposite side. One hundred yards or so separated Lipkin from his daughter. He ran over the uneven ground toward her. With only twenty yards between them, Lucie, dressed in a t-shirt and pajama shorts, limped toward him. From that distance, the cuts on her legs were visible. Her bare feet were caked with a dark brown substance. As Lucie reached the last row of trees before the clearing, a dark shape rushed her from the left. Lipkin quit running. His daughter was no longer there.

Moving into the tree line on the other side of the clearing, Lipkin saw what remained of Lucie. Whatever had attacked her had left her torn into pieces. Her right arm was still connected to her torso. Her left arm lay nearby. Her legs were missing. Lipkin removed his shirt and covered his daughter's contorted and mangled face. Next, he gathered up her body parts and placed them together.

As he stood up, wiping his bloodied hands on his jeans, he turned and spotted something in the woods. Lipkin approached what appeared at first to be vines hanging from the lower limbs of a pine tree. Upon closer inspection, he discovered that the vines were adorned with strips of skin. Beyond the hanging hide lay a skinless body. The skull, also devoid of skin, was damaged; the lower jaw had been torn away. Lipkin guessed that the corpse was his son Paul. The sight of the carnage forced Lipkin to purge his stomach of its contents. After that, he dry-heaved several times. When he was able to pull himself together, he dragged the corpse to where he had left his daughter's remains.

Lipkin stayed close to his dead children, waiting for whatever lived in those woods to tear him to pieces as well. He did not know how much time had passed. He felt weak, still sick to his stomach. Looking deep into the woods now, he leaned against a pine tree. Suddenly, a familiar figure appeared.

"Stay there," Lipkin shouted.

Once more, his words became muted in the damp air. His wife didn't hear him. Marcie ran toward him only to suffer a gruesome fate similar to Lucie's.

Three shadows in the shape of hulking two-legged creatures descended on Marcie just as she reached out her arms toward her husband. Lipkin stood less than five yards from her when they clawed Marcie into a mangled, bloodied mess. One of the creatures took off deep into the woods. The other two scrambled up the trunk of a tree and vanished into the dark canopy overhead.

Lipkin dragged what remained of his wife to where his daughter and his son lay. His hands, his arms, and his bare chest were coated with the blood of his family now. Exhausted, he sat on the ground with his back against a tree. Before long, sleep came.

He stirred when someone shook him by his shoulder. Startled, he crawled away from his assailant.

"Father," said Paul. "It's me."

Lipkin paused. Behind his son stood Lucie and Marcie. They each appeared unharmed. Lipkin looked at his hands. The dried blood on them looked black.

"Come, Husband," Marcie said. "There's a way out."

"See the sunlight?" Lucie offered.

Turning, Lipkin spotted sunrays coming through the woods. Slowly, he climbed to his feet. Where his family's remains once lay were depressions in the pine needles; beyond them, dark streaks hinted at drag marks.

His wife and children huddled close to him. When they wrapped their arms around him, their limbs felt cold, like a brass railing on a winter day. Lipkin smelled wet earth on their breath as they coaxed him toward the sunlight coming through the forest.

It wasn't until the cottage came into view that Lipkin noticed something different about his wife's eyes, as well as those of his children. The eyes of all three were identical now: lifeless and colored gunmetal. Lipkin remembered Catskill's words about his own wife.

The dark sent something back in her place.

He considered his new dead-eyed companions, and how they had rescued him from that dark and savage forest. Whatever they were called, they were his family now.

Cassandra

by Tim Boiteau

THE BIGGEST PACKAGE FOR Cassandra under the tree that year was from Aunt Janelle. The size of a child's coffin, it came to us fully wrapped in glossy paper with a candy-cane pattern. I was excited to see what Janelle, who was always so generous, had sent, but when Cassandra pulled the doll out of the box, my stomach dropped.

It was blonde and Amish, which Janelle's note explained accounted for the wooden creature's featureless face. It was also the exact height of Cassandra and came wearing a plain white dress with a blue sash ribbon.

"It's beautiful!" Cassandra exclaimed and proceeded to sit it down by the tree and show it all the other toys and clothes she had received for Christmas.

For Christmas brunch, we had French toast and scrambled eggs, and Cassandra insisted that she bring her new doll to the table. Every one of its limbs had stiff-moving ball-and-socket joints, so it could be postured however Cassandra wanted, but since they were all one type of joint, the fingers and legs and arms could be moved into unnatural bent configurations.

"Dad, can you make Cassandra her own French toast?" she shouted into the kitchen as she was situating the doll.

"Aye aye, Cap'n!"

"Mom, can I have an extra napkin and utensils for Cassandra?"

"Are you calling your doll Cassandra?"

"Uh huh, just like me."

"Sure, sweetie."

Once we were all seated at the table and eating, our daughter spent most of her time trying to manipulate her doll's wooden digits to grasp a fork and knife. "Ha! I did it!" she shouted with triumph once she managed to have her doll holding a fork with a piece of French toast speared in its tines.

James and her high-fived.

Then Cassandra knit her brow. "How is she supposed to eat it?"

The answer to that question didn't come till a few days later, but in the meantime, with little to do during the winter break, Cassandra spent every waking (and slumbering) moment with her new doll. Even when I called various family members to wish them a Merry Christmas, Cassandra would bring the doll over and manipulate its arms and creep out everyone we know. Except for Aunt Janelle, who, despite me calling several times that day, never picked up.

When James went to read Cassandra a bedtime story and tuck her in, she told him, "Cassandra wants you to kiss her too and read her her own bedtime story."

"Oh, does she?"

"Yes, and it has to be one about dolls."

"How about *The Store-Bought Doll*?"

"Yay!" Cassandra cheered, lifting up her doll's hand in triumph.

When I checked in an hour later, Cassandra was sound asleep, her rotating unicorn nightlight casting a rainbow cavalcade of horned equines on the wall, and the doll was propped up against the wall, as if watching over the little girl. As I left, I felt my hackles raise and a shiver run down my spine. The doll, when James had put them to bed, had been lying down supine beside Cassandra. I was certain of that.

Well, maybe Cassandra had sat her up afterward.

The next day was a Monday, and James sequestered himself in his basement office while I wrote upstairs at the dining room table. I was only half-monitoring my daughter as she played with her toys, until Cassandra suddenly burst into tears and ran over to me and began tugging my arm.

"What is it, honey?" I asked, mind slowly reengaging with reality.

"Cassandra's making fun of me."

"Sorry, what?"

"My hair, she's laughing at my red hair."

"Oh dear, umm, I'm sorry." I drew her into my arms and gave her a squeeze. Probably she was projecting onto her doll some negative experience with a bully from school.

"She said it looks like tomato sauce!"

"Well, it does, kind of. My favorite." I rubbed my tummy. "Gorgeous. Just like your father."

"Can you tell Cassandra to stop making fun of it?"

"Sure. Cassandra," I turned to address the doll where it sat blank-faced on the couch, its limbs arranged in a twisted and painful-looking display. "stop it this instant. Leave my beautiful daughter alone."

I went back to work, and in the distance I heard James talking on one of his conference calls, his bass voice carrying through the floorboards. The sound gradually faded as I became reabsorbed in my writing. Then, suddenly, Cassandra was at my elbow again, in tears, yanking me over toward the living room area.

"She won't stop. She's talking about my eyebrows now and says I look like someone shoved my face into a plate of spaghetti."

"Honey, maybe you should play with some other toys."

"I want you to scold Cassandra."

"Cassandra, I've had quite enough of you," I said, gathering the wooden-limbed thing into my arms. "You're getting a timeout, little miss."

Cassandra (my daughter, that is) began to cry, stuffing her fingers into her ears, as I carried the doll into the bedroom, dropped her unceremoniously onto the bed, and shut the door. As I returned, I noticed a flash of pain in my wrist and saw that a long sliver of wood, much thicker than a mere splinter, had pierced my flesh at an angle. Wincing, I drew out all four inches of it, shocked by its syringe-like length, and blood began to trickle down my arm.

Cassandra, meanwhile, was in hysterics.

"Let her out! Let her out! Let me out!" she was screaming.

"Honey, what's wrong?" I said, crouching down beside her, my hand pressed against the wound.

"She won't stop! She won't stop! The screaming. Let her out!"

I rose and went back to the bedroom, opened the door—and gasped.

Cassandra the doll was sitting Indian-style in the center of the floor, its limbs no longer arranged in the twisted pose from before. I dithered there a few moments, debating whether or not to carry the doll back into the living room. My daughter had already ceased crying, so I decided to just leave things as they were and went to the bathroom to clean my arm.

Life was calm the next couple days. I forgot all about the strange incident with the doll, having convinced myself that I must have set it down on the edge of the bed, and after shutting the door it must have fallen onto the floor and rolled into the position I found it in. But then the voices started, and my attention returned to my daughter's bizarre manner of play with her new doll.

In the intervening days, Cassandra had started dressing up her toy in her own clothes, which fit the doll perfectly. Thus, James and I had seen it wearing familiar-looking skirts and sweaters and stockings, and today, the day it started talking, it was wearing a pink sweater with snowflakes on it, a rainbow-striped skirt, and rain boots. Most startling, however, was the hole in the center of the doll's face, about one inch in diameter.

"What happened to your doll, dear?"

"She couldn't speak very clearly before, because she didn't have a mouth. So I gave her one," my daughter said, smiling up at me. Doll and child were seated in her room, at the little tea table we'd gotten her last year, which she was already almost too big for. Both of them had plastic teacups full of tap water and rubber *petits fours*. I remembered having heard the drill yesterday when I was working, but I had assumed it was James doing one of his little home improvement projects. Later that night, when I mentioned the hole in the doll's face, James had admitted having heard the drill too—admitted that he'd assumed it had been me using it. At this moment though, when I was looking down at my daughter playing with her doll, I guessed that James had helped her drill the hole into the doll's face, which peeved me a little, because Cassandra hadn't had the doll but three days and already it was ruined; if she wanted a mouth, we could have painted one on.

"*This cake tastes like shit,*" Cassandra said in a deep, unsettling growl, a voice I had never heard her make before.

"Hey, little lady, we don't use that language in this house."

"Don't get mad at me. It was Cassandra," she said, pointing at the doll sitting across from her.

She had placed the teacup in her doll's hand, even going so far as to arrange its pinky finger in a dainty, curved extension. She had also used some lipstick, drawing a messy crimson circle around the drilled portal into the doll's skull.

"Well, please tell your friend not to use that word anymore, okay?"

"Okay, Mom."

"*Okay, Rita.*"

Both Cassandras came to dinner that night. Chicken Marsala, asparagus, linguine—my daughter's favorite. The doll seemed to approve too. Cassandra chopped the food into very tiny pieces and pretended to stuff them into the hole in the doll's head.

"*More,*" she kept saying. "*More, more, more.*"

I was concerned that my daughter wasn't eating her favorite dinner.

"I'm not hungry, Mom, but Cassandra is starving. She hasn't eaten in hundreds of years."

"Well, go easy," James said, addressing the doll. "A wooden digestive system probably doesn't handle poultry very well."

The next evening was date night, and James's mother came over to watch Cassandra. As I was applying lipstick, there was a flash of pain and a flush of warmth as blood trickled down my chin. A tiny gash had been torn in my upper lip. The culprit? A little splinter sticking out of the angled head of the lipstick. I rushed out to the living room, where my daughter and her doll were playing poker on the floor, my mother-in-law reading her book behind them.

I pointed toward my bloody mouth. "Cassandra, look at this."

"You look pretty," she said.

"My lip's bleeding."

"Oh."

"Do you know why?"

Cassandra shook her head.

"Because you used the lipstick on that doll of yours."

"Oh... Sorry."

"Please, don't do it again."

"Okay, Mom."

"Thanks, sweetie."

I was heading back to the bedroom when I overheard Cassandra say in the doll's low growl, "*Rita looks like a fucking whore.*"

I turned and saw my mother-in-law's comically shocked expression. My daughter, too, was shocked by what she had just said, but the doll was placid, of course, the cards fanned out in its hands.

"What did you say?" I asked my daughter.

"N-nothing. Cassandra said it."

I rushed in, yanked my daughter up by the arm, and dragged her screaming into the bathroom. "I didn't say it!" she cried. "I didn't! It was Cassandra. Really, really, it was."

I turned on the water, placed a bar of soap beneath it, got it nice and lathery, then shoved it with some difficulty into my daughter's unwilling mouth. Maybe I was too forceful with it, had shoved it in too deeply, for she began to gag, and her face went purple, then out came a hot rush of yellow, bilious vomit all over me and my red dress.

Then she looked up at me, her eyes still filled with tears, and started cackling in the doll's voice.

When we got home from our dinner and a movie that night, James's mother reported no more strange incidents. Cassandra was in bed with the doll. No, she hadn't spoken in the strange voice or said anything else off-color all evening.

The next day, we were at breakfast as usual, when I noticed a fly landing in my eggs. I shooed it away and watched it buzz over to Cassandra the doll and land on the blank face, which was a little smudged by now from being handled by the grimy hands of a six-year-old, its mouth still colored red with lipstick. The fly walked and hopped across the face, then dipped into the hole. I continued to eat, watching the doll, and noticed more and more flies circling its head.

James had noticed too. "Jesus," he said, going to retrieve the fly-swatter from the closet. When he returned and started whacking them, he paused over the doll, sniffing. Then he bent over and peered into the hole. "Hey, Cassandra, have you been putting food in here?"

"Uh huh."

"Oh, gross."

"It was just pretend at first, but then Cassandra started complaining that she was super hungry and started calling me bad names and threatening to do bad things to me if I didn't really feed her."

"Christ almighty. Is that raw meat?" James asked, then his tone changed. "Hey, this head is hollow. Man, oh man, you really packed this thing full."

"I'm sorry, Dad."

"I think I'm going to have to make the hole bigger to clean this thing out."

"*Get away from me, you little prick!*"

James jumped back, and I did a double take. Just at that moment, I had been looking at my daughter, lost in thought, wondering what kind of threats the doll had made, but when she had spoken in its voice, her lips hadn't moved at all. Indeed, the sound seemed to have come from the doll itself.

"How did you do that?" James asked.

"Do what?"

"The voice, her voice, it was right next to my head."

"It was just...Cassandra...talking," she said and continued to poke at her eggs.

"Honey," I said, reaching across the table and putting my hand on hers. "How did the doll, how did Cassandra, threaten you?"

She gave me a cold look, still mad about what happened last night, but when James prodded her as well, she wriggled her hand free from mine and answered him. "She said she was going to...saw off my arms, then she was going to saw off my legs, and then she was going to saw off my head."

James ended up stripping the doll naked, taking it outside (Florida in winter, it was only seventy degrees out) turned on the spigot, and used the hose to clean out the doll's hollow head. I was watching from the kitchen window as I did the dishes, and it was one of the most surreal things I've ever seen James do, the way he held it up from behind, letting it vomit out the dirty, chunky stream of water through the little hole in its face, almost like he was practicing the Heimlich maneuver on a dummy.

And all this while, Cassandra was on the floor, her lips completely immobile—maybe they would quiver slightly or maybe I was just imagining it—and she was making this awful gargling sound and would occasionally let out a, "*Get your hands off me, you creep.*"

The doll was left out in the sun in the back yard, and James reentered the house nursing his finger, which had been sliced open by a jagged edge of wood when he had been trying to scoop out a bit of the refuse inside the hole.

After putting a band-aid on it, he threw his hands up in the air and said, "I've got work to do. Cassandra, no more doll today."

Cassandra looked at me, shocked and hurt. "But she's my friend!"

"I agree with your dad, hon. This has all been getting a little too crazy. I think you could use a break from her."

Cassandra came over to me and whispered, "But she's not going to be happy."

"Cassandra, it's just a doll."

"I know, I guess, I mean, I don't know." She was still whispering, afraid the doll would overhear her.

I gave her a big hug and said, "How about I take a break today too? Let's go to the park. Westmore Park, the one with the giant tire castle."

Cassandra's eyes lit up. "Can I wear my princess costume?"

"Duh."

That was the end of the doll. At least for the day.

That night, the Cassandra doll stayed outside, ostensibly drying, but in reality just giving James and me peace of mind, or so we had hoped. In fact, what happened was that all night the motion sensor was tripped and our floodlight in the back yard kept turning on. Every time this happened, James would curse and grab his phone and open the security camera app, then he would curse again, shut off the lights remotely, and try to get back to sleep.

"What is it?" I asked him the second time this occurred.

"Nothing," he grumbled, face in his pillow. "There's nothing moving out there."

I opened his phone and looked at the feed. Indeed, the back yard was empty. It was a sparse sward of navy blue beyond our deck, the pale naked doll lying beneath our one tree.

I tried to get back to sleep, but my mind was too busy, full of book ideas, edits I needed to do in the morning.

The light flicked back on.

"Jesus fucking Christ!" James said, pulling on his pants and striding out of the room. I watched through his phone app as he appeared outside, hands on his hips, then I heard him shout out into the night, "It happens again, I'm calling the cops!"

Then he was back inside, shimmying out of his pants and climbing into bed. I was still watching the feed on the camera. Nothing was moving out there. I deactivated the light, and both of us managed to sleep for an hour or so.

But then the light flicked back on, and James's phone alerted us. He had his pillow over his head by now and, despite his previous threat, refused to be roused. I picked up the phone, and then I noticed that Cassandra was not beneath the tree. Not exactly, anyway. She had moved a few feet out into the yard.

My heart was racing as I deactivated the light and stared at the darkened video feed of our back yard. It must have been a prank, some of the teenagers from the neighborhood. Maybe they had come to steal the doll and panicked when the light turned on, or maybe they were moving it toward our house, just to freak us out.

Well, it was working.

I got out of bed and carried a blanket and pillow to the living room, half-sitting, half-reclining on the couch and looking over the back, out the window, and toward the yard. I lay there, staring out into the night, listening to the deathly quiet, watching for movement. I don't know how long I managed to stay awake, but when I woke up, it was a pale, gray morning, and I heard the coffee maker gurgling in the kitchen. I rubbed my eyes, then screamed.

The doll was seated at the opposite end of the couch, its limbs as twisted as tree branches, the hole in its head gaping at me.

I leapt off the couch and bumped into my daughter, who had been standing in the center of the room, staring at me and the doll on the couch together.

"My god, honey. Did I hurt you?" I said, catching my breath.

"No. Can I put clothes on Cassandra now?"

I closed my eyes and exhaled. "Fine. You brought it inside, didn't you?"

"Yes," she admitted. "She was tapping on the window."

"I need a shower."

"Mom," Cassandra said, "what happened to Aunt Janelle?"

"What are you talking about?"

"Cassandra says she knows what happened to her."

"Umm, she's fine, far as I know."

"That's not what Cassandra was saying while you were asleep. She says her arms were sawed off, and her legs were sawed off, and her head was sawed off."

"What are you guys talking about?" James said as he shuffled into the room, wearing his Christmas robe, which he usually persisted with until early February. "What happened to Janelle?"

"Janelle is fine, honey," I said.

Cassandra shook her head. "Can we call her? Just to make sure?"

"Ugh," James said.

"I'll do it," I said, looking around for my phone. When I rang her up, Aunt Janelle's phone went straight to voicemail. She did live alone and was known to drink late into the night, so it wasn't a surprise that she wasn't up yet or that she'd let her phone's battery die. Nevertheless, I left a message, thanking her for her Christmas gifts and asking for her to return my call when she was available. I realized while doing so that Janelle had never returned our call on Christmas Day, not even an emoji-laden text.

I had wandered into the kitchen while leaving a somewhat rambling message, and I heard in the background James starting up the shower. When I turned around, there was Cassandra, my daughter, holding the doll's hand. They were both standing at the entrance to the kitchen.

"*Well?*" Cassandra said in the doll's voice.

"Well, what?"

"*Well, her arms are sawed off, and her legs are sawed off, and her head is sawed off, aren't they?*"

"Honey, don't talk that way about your great aunt."

"But it's true."

"No, it's not, and besides, we just don't talk that way."

"Give me breakfast, Rita."

"Cassandra, can we not do the doll this morning?"

"She's hungry, Mom."

"No more toys at the table. That's final."

"Sorry, Cassandra. Come on."

I poured myself some coffee and watched my daughter manipulating the doll's legs as the two of them made their way tediously down the hall to her room. My hand was shaking. I put on the radio and started putting away the dishes.

Then I heard a scream, and I dashed down the hall and found my daughter lying on the ground, her mouth bloody, and the doll, still naked, was looming over her, a painted rock in its hand.

"My god, what happened, honey?"

"Cassandra struck me," she cried.

"Honey…"

"It's true. She did."

I took a breath. "Let's get an ice pack on that mouth of yours."

While we were in the kitchen, I called to James and explained what happened. He shook his head. I knew we were thinking the same thing; I knew there was no need to speak more on the subject of Cassandra.

I turned to my daughter. "How do an Egg McMuffin and hash browns sound for breakfast?"

"Yay!"

I took her out to the drive-thru, not the one around the corner, but downtown, a good ten-minute drive from us, and took my time getting back, a zigzagging route through various neighborhoods ostensibly to look at decorations, which were all unlit and sad, deflated and grotesque in the morning light.

When we got back home, the doll was gone.

"Where's Cassandra?" my daughter asked after looking everywhere.

"She said she had to go back home," James told her.

"Really? But she was my best friend, and she didn't even say goodbye."

"I'm sorry, honey. She was just in such a rush."

A few weeks passed by. School was back in session, and memories of the Cassandra doll retreated into the shadows. Then one Saturday morning my daughter appeared at the breakfast table wearing a blonde wig and the doll's dress, with a messy ring of lipstick on her face that missed her lips for the most part and gave the illusion that her face had two separate mouths.

"Where did you find that dress, honey?"

"*What's for breakfast, Rita?*" she asked in that gravelly voice, ignoring my question.

"Cereal."

"*Cereal blows. I want bacon and eggs.*"

"Hey, language, little miss. And stop doing that voice."

I looked to James for an explanation, but just then his phone rang. He answered it, ducking out of the room, and when he returned to the kitchen a few minutes later, his face was cadaverous, his blue eyes unfocused.

"What's wrong, honey?"

"The police called. Augusta. They...need me to come identify a body."

"Is it your aunt?" We had been so busy with things, I hadn't even realized that Aunt Janelle had yet to return my calls.

He nodded. "I-I-I... Yeah. Aunt Janelle."

Cassandra was eating her cereal and chuckling softly.

James would head there and back in a day, leaving me with Cassandra, who refused to wear anything other than the doll's dress and wig. That afternoon I noticed a smell coming from the attic. While Cassandra was playing in her room, I headed upstairs, and was suddenly struck by the thick stench. There were flies everywhere, big ones, darting toward my eyes and mouth and up my nose. I stumbled around before finding the lights, and as I looked around, I noticed a box in the middle of the attic floor, one flap open.

It was the doll's box. I guess James hadn't gotten rid of it after all.

I don't know why—I had assumed that he dumped it in the trash or even donated it to Goodwill—but I was royally pissed that the creepy thing was still in our house. I strode over and bent down to lift up the box, when I glimpsed the silky red hair inside. I opened the lid. And there was my daughter: her arms, her legs, her torso, her head.

"Rita!" something downstairs screamed out. *"Rita! Get the fuck down here and play with me!"*

Satisfied

by J.R. Graham

MARY CUT AWAY THE twine from the filets. Her new kitchen knife sang as it sliced the white, egg-like fat from the pink meat. The knife was a Christmas present from Daniel—he'd left the price tag on the box so she'd known how much it had cost. Another slice, and her stomach turned. She barely made it to the garbage bin before her breakfast made a reappearance.

Closing the bin, she rubbed the swell of her belly. The little guy was so picky. She straightened her apron. It was her favorite one, with dainty yellow tulips embroidered on the hem. Mary forced down a glass of lemon water before returning to the filet. She dressed it in a dry rub and set it in the fridge.

The rest of her afternoon was spent cleaning the house and setting the dining room. She polished the silver candlesticks and set in each a fresh candle the color of cream just before turning to butter. The crystal wine glasses threw little halos of rainbow across the lace table-cloth. It had been a gift from Daniel's parents on their wedding day. The lace was from Spain and known as bone lace—not for the color, as Mary had initially thought, but named for the little instruments used to weave the lace that were historically made of bone. She smoothed the tablecloth carefully, noting every tiny fray. She remembered how Daniel's mother had smirked when she'd ask if its color was where it got its name.

At half-past six, she lit the candles and drew the curtains. She opened the wine early so it would breathe, knowing if she didn't, Daniel would notice. At half-past seven, she phoned Daniel's office to find that the receptionist had gone home for the day.

At eight o'clock, she cooked the steaks. Then she poured herself a glass of wine and prepared two plates, one for her and one she kept warming in the oven. The filet was cooked to perfection, tender and pink, the potatoes perfectly soft and garlicky, and her stomach rebelled against every bite.

Mary gave up and pushed away her plate. She gagged into a napkin until tears streamed down her face. She sobbed as the candlelight glinted off the silver.

The phone rang. She wiped her eyes.

"Mary, dear." Daniel had to shout to be heard over the din of jazz music and his co-worker's laughter. "We closed the Davis deal."

"Congratulations. You've worked so hard on that account."

Something in her voice must have given her away, because he said, "I'm sorry, sweetheart, I meant to call, but everything happened so fast. How'd the steak turn out?"

"It was good."

"Can you make a plate for me? I'll have it when I get back."

"When will that be?"

"I don't know yet. Tony was going to take us to— Hold on, honey. I've got to go."

Mary hung up the phone and stared at the wall. The tears threatened to return. She ran her fingers through her hair and froze. A great clump of hair fell out of her head just above the nape of her neck. She gasped, and the gasp turned into great uncontrollable breaths; the wallpaper blurred until it was only a yellow smear.

She leaned back against the wall and focused on short breaths, her hands holding tightly to the lost hair. It must be a side effect of the pregnancy. She'd make an appointment with Dr. Schaeffer tomorrow morning, first thing.

She cleaned the kitchen, did her nightly skin routine, and got into bed, but not before carefully arranging her hair to cover the bald spot. She had to lie on her back rather than her side to keep the hair in place, and the pins stuck painfully into her head, but at least this way Daniel wouldn't notice when he came home.

She woke to the sound of him whistling drunkenly as he came upstairs. Her sleep had been sporadic and unsettled, distracted by the growling of her stomach. She would have to ask Dr. Schaeffer for something to treat her nausea so she could eat again. Daniel kicked his shoes off and climbed into bed, shirtless but still in his slacks. Besides the cigar smoke and whiskey, he smelled heavily of some flowery perfume. Mary didn't ask why, but put her arms around him and cuddled closer, as much as her belly would allow. He mumbled something and immediately started to snore.

Mary woke again. But this time the streetlights were out and all was still. It was the time of night when the dark seemed almost liquid. An almost tangible, smothering thing that ate all light and sound, and seemed to challenge anyone to break its silence. The time of night when witches snuck out to dance and sign the Devil's black book.

She was starving. Unbelievably starving. Every cell in her body screamed at her to eat. The hunger gnawed at her stomach, then reached for the rest of her with searching claws. She needed to eat. And for the first time in days, something smelled *good*.

Mary closed her eyes and bit down. Something salty and warm gushed over her tongue. Her meal tried to pull away, but she held tighter and sank her teeth deeper.

"Mary, what the fuck?" Daniel yelled, making her snap back to reality. She released him and he pulled away. Red trickled down his shoulder from where she'd bitten him. She'd *bitten* him.

"I'm so sorry. I don't know what came over me." She reached for him, but he launched himself into the bathroom and slammed the door. The lock clicked into place.

Panic twisted her stomach. She fixed the pins back over the bald spot. What was happening to her? Her hands went to her stomach. What was this child doing to her?

After an excruciating amount of time, Daniel emerged, his shoulder freshly bandaged. He flicked on the light. "What the hell was that?" he said.

Mary wrung her hands. "I don't know. I was asleep and then I was biting you. I must have been having a nightmare and reacted."

She left out her desire and the way he had tasted. Rich and filling—a panacea for the hunger that was consuming her.

He sat by her and took her hand. His voice was soothing now.

"You're lucky, it doesn't look like it will scar. But you should make an appointment with Dr. Schaeffer in the morning and see if everything is okay with the baby."

Mary nodded. He placed his hand over her stomach and rubbed in concentric circles. The baby did nothing to react. Dr. Schaeffer said it was still too early to worry that she hadn't felt any kicking, but that didn't stop her.

"I'll sleep in the guest room," she said quietly as she gathered up her pillow.

"I wouldn't ask you to do that." Daniel slid back into bed. "But I'm not going to lie. I won't sleep very well knowing I could be devoured in my sleep."

A few months before, on a sunny afternoon, she'd finished her house-work and had the chicken defrosting for dinner when she noticed the store-bought rose centerpiece had started to turn, the roses emitting a sickly sweet smell. Without much thought, she'd collected her gardening shears and wandered into the back yard. Most of the yard was a well-manicured lawn, but the back fourth of an acre was an untenable copse of trees. Daniel had plans drawn up to tear it out and replace it with a pool they'd be putting in next year.

Mary cut some roses from the hedge that ran across the fence. They were beautiful late-summer roses, a deep evocative red. She found herself wandering into the trees and was pleased to discover among the wild blue daisies dotting the ground like scattered stars some type of climbing ivy, and on her way back a clutch of wild, snow-white lilies. She brought her haul back to the kitchen, rinsed, trimmed, and set them on the island. She got out her favorite crystal vase, one she'd inherited from her mother, and started arranging.

She ran her hand over the curve of a lily petal. It was delicate but firm, more substantial than the others, a skin-like feeling as if she was caressing a cheek dusted with powder.

"What the hell are you doing, dear?"

Daniel stood in the kitchen doorway, his golf clubs slung over his shoulder, and one dark eyebrow raised.

"Making a new centerpiece for the table." Mary gestured to the flowers, the vase, and the scissors. Daniel seemed annoyed by her tone.

"I can see that. But where did you get these flowers?" He glanced across them. "They don't seem like the regular ones."

"I got them from the back yard."

"In all those stupid trees?"

Mary nodded. He sighed and set his golf clubs against the wall and came over to her.

"I don't want my wife, my *pregnant* wife, much less, foraging around like an Italian peasant searching for truffles."

She opened her mouth to respond when Daniel grabbed her arm.

"What on earth have you done to your nails?"

There was dirt under them, and she'd chipped one.

"We have that charity gala tonight. We're sitting at the same table as the Harrisons, remember?"

"I'll clean them up before tonight." Mary tried to snatch her hand away. Daniel's brown eyes went dark.

"Go clean them now." His tone was decided. His hand squeezed tight on her wrist; it hurt, but it wouldn't bruise.

"I'm going."

When she'd come back downstairs, she found that Daniel had cleared away all the flowers. They were in the garbage cans he'd taken to the curb. "Trash flowers" he'd called them. By the time they were driving to the gala, his tone was one of apology. He wore his wedding tuxedo, her a black-lace gown with the pearls his mother had given her.

"I shouldn't have reacted like I did." He took her hand, the one with the wrist that was still sore. "One of the guys at work, his wife does flower arranging, nothing fancy, just for the house, but she gets her flowers in bulk from the market. We could get you set up with that."

"I want to sell them." The defiance in her voice surprised her as much as him. "I want something that's mine."

"You'll have something that's yours soon enough," he said, his hand moving to her stomach.

Streetlights flicked by overhead.

"Fine, fine. Let me find you your first commission, though. I don't want my wife going around town begging for money."

She nodded in agreement, and by the end of the night she had her first commission from Dr. Schaeffer, who'd happened to be at their table. Daniel had made sure to point out to her the centerpiece, a sterile affair of lilies, all the same size, color, and stage of bloom.

Mary tapped her foot on the linoleum floor of Dr. Schaeffer's office. She glanced again at the great vase of flowers in front of reception and gave a small smile. The arrangement was in a great white and blue porcelain vase from which spilled irises, pink hyacinths, and large yellow roses. It was hers, her first official commission. She'd spent hours agonizing over what flowers, what color scheme, would the porcelain be too much?

"Mary Winstead?" The nurse smiled at her, clipboard in hand.

Mary followed the nurse down the hall into a second room and took her place on the examination table. Dr. Schaeffer came in shortly afterward. He was an older man with salt and pepper hair and a somewhat pudgy appearance that showed his interest in the finer things of life.

"Mary, my dear. How are you?"

"Very well, and you?"

"Oh, you know, Patricia and I just returned from Hawaii. It was lovely, crystal blue water and white sand, until she got a stomach bug from some bad tuna."

"How is she doing?"

"Much better now." The doctor sat on a stool and wheeled it over to her. "Now, what seems to be the problem?"

Mary squeezed her purse. "I still haven't felt any kicking, and I've lost a clump of my hair."

"Ah, yes." Dr. Schaeffer's double chin moved as he nodded. "Hair loss can be a side effect of pregnancy. Some women's hair grows thicker and shinier while others lose some of their hair."

"Should I be concerned?"

"No, no, it's quite common," said Dr. Shaeffer. He jotted down something on his clipboard. "Now, taking a bite out of your husband, we need to do something about that."

A chill ran through her. "Daniel called you?"

"He was concerned about you." He spoke without looking up from his clipboard. "And rightly so. It sounds like you've also been nauseous and not been able to keep anything down?"

Daniel had called her doctor behind her back. Her throat tightened along with her smile.

"That's also quite common," he said. "Some women experience more severe morning sickness than others. I'm prescribing you a medication that should help. There are two options, but one isn't recommended for women prone to light-headedness. Daniel said you tend to get dizzy easily, so we'll go with the other one."

Mary felt her frustration squirming inside her, but she plastered a smile on her face and said, "That's right."

"Well, here you are." Dr. Schaeffer ripped the prescription from the pad and handed it to her. He then had her lay back and did a quick exam. He said the heartbeat was good and she was where he'd expect her at this point, if only a smidgen underweight, but that the medication should help her get her appetite back.

She was gathering her coat and purse when she asked, "Are you happy with the flower arrangement?"

Dr. Schaeffer glanced back at her, his forehead creased briefly in confusion. "Oh, yes, those were yours, right? Lydia at the front desk said they were lovely. Now I'd recommend taking a pill and having something with carbs and protein which should be easier on your stomach. So go home, dear, and take a pill, wait a half-hour, and make yourself a turkey sandwich." He returned his attention to the clipboard.

Mary picked up the prescription at the pharmacy and returned to her car. She ran her fingers over the cool leather of the steering wheel. Her stomach twisted and growled as though it were consuming itself as a last resort.

She meant to return home and do as Dr. Schaeffer had ordered, but found herself by a wrought-iron gate on a dirt path leading to a secluded graveyard. The little collection of tombstones sat in a clearing of imposing oaks and weeping willows. It was a place where mist hung in the air even in the middle of the day and, despite the afternoon sun, the trees cast dappled shadows over the stones. Mary took in a deep breath, smelling damp, earth-filled moss and wild mushrooms. She always found comfort in the place for the dead hidden beneath lichen and loam.

This little cemetery stood in stark contrast to the graveyard in town that she and Daniel would visit to pay respect to his father's grave. Carefully tended grass grew between perfect lines of tombstones maintained by men driving around in zippy golf carts. A white brick reception building greeted them with its trickling water feature. They would buy a flower arrangement from the small shop in the reception building before driving the packed-gravel road to the grave and placing the flowers in the stone vase built into the tombstone before spending a couple minutes in respectful silence and driving back home.

Pushing aside the gate, Mary crossed the springy bed of moss that had been fed by centuries of nutrients from its dead tenants. She picked her way through the scattered stones, naming the sprays of wildflowers as she went.

The stone she sought was in the heavy shade of a great oak tree. The faded script read:

Lydia Maria Byrne, Beloved mother and friend.

"Momma," Mary whispered to the stone, "I don't know what I'm doing wrong." Her hands clutched her stomach. A moment of panic gripped her. She still felt nothing inside.

"What do I do?" Tears threatened to well up, but she blinked them away frantically.

Something caught her attention. Stretching across the base of the tombstone was a silvery spiderweb flecked with dew.

When she was young, no more than eight, her mother had taken her into the woods behind their little house. Her mother's hair was loose, her long blonde hair falling like waxen thread as she knelt with her woven basket to collect the herbs she needed. She had Mary kneel on the forest floor and pointed to a delicate web that stretched from a fallen log to the forest floor. Flecks of dew clung to it, and in its center was a great black spider with a red hourglass on its belly.

"A black widow. Be wary of them, dear. Their bite is venomous."

Mary leaned a little closer to the web. The spider's body was unlike the others she had seen scurrying along the forest floor—usually brown with narrow bodies that blended in with the dirt. This spider's body was made of two perfectly round segments, pitch-black and standing out starkly from the green behind it.

"They don't need to hide," her mother said when Mary pointed this out. "They wear their warnings on their back. The red hourglass means time's up for anything that messes with them or tries to eat them, even their mates."

"What do you mean?"

"The female will eat the male after mating to provide nutrients for her clutch of eggs."

She'd smiled in response to Mary's disgusted face. Her vibrant green eyes, so different from Mary's which were a reserved brown, glittered in the dim forest light. Then she fell silent, her face turning serious.

"Mary, the women in our family make very hungry children just like that spider."

"I don't understand."

Her mother seemed to regret her words, for she looked away, studying the spider once again. A shadow had fallen over her face.

"I don't feel very hungry," said Mary, fearing she'd said something wrong.

Her words seemed to take her mother by surprise, for she laughed, her loud unabashed laugh that Mary had always loved. A flock of crows took flight at the sound.

"That's because I fed you well."

She stared down her challenger. A turkey sandwich on rye bread with a glass of milk. Mary had taken a pill the moment she got home, waited the half-hour, but she'd still gagged the whole time she was making her sandwich. Plugging her nose, she took a bite.

Mary barely made it to the bathroom before her stomach revolted. She spilled her guts into the toilet until she was retching up nothing but yellow-green bile. Once her stomach was completely empty, she fell back and rested her head on the cool tile. Her body was weak, her limbs achy and exhausted.

There was something hard in her mouth. She spit and a tooth hit the floor in a spray of blood and bile. Her tongue found the hole where one of her bottom molars used to be. She bit back a scream. What was happening to her?

She wrapped the tooth in a tea towel and hid it in the ice maker. She rang her dentist, but no one answered, then she rang Dr. Schaeffer with the same result. Where was everyone? Mary glanced at the kitchen clock and saw it was after five.

"Shit, shit, shit."

She hadn't realized how late it was. Daniel would be home in the next fifteen minutes and dinner wasn't even in the oven. She pulled the salmon out of the fridge and did a quick rub of lemon, butter, and herbs before getting it in the oven. The potatoes were just coming to a boil when Daniel walked in the door.

"Mary, what's going on?" He wore dark grey trousers, with the matching blazer draped over his arm, and a white button-up shirt. "Why is the dining room so dark?"

"I'm sorry, honey," said Mary, careful to smile more on the right side of her mouth so as not to reveal her missing tooth. The starchy smell of the potatoes was making her queasy. She pressed a hand to her stomach; that empty feeling was back.

"It was a long day, and I was hoping to come home to a hot meal."

"It'll be ready in ten minutes," she assured him. "Do you mind getting out the tablecloth?"

He grumbled about something under his breath before vanishing into the dining room.

"This thing is going yellow. We should just toss it." He returned with the bone-lace tablecloth and dropped it on the kitchen island. Then he poured himself a glass of bourbon.

"The table, Daniel?" She did her best to keep the edge out of her voice, but her hunger was back, and her stomach was growling like a pack of wolves.

"You'll get to it," he said with a wave of his hand.

He came to stand next to her and watched as she stirred the potatoes. That overwhelming need came back to her, the claws reaching, the hunger screaming inside her. Blood pounded against her temples. Daniel leaned in to inspect the potatoes and her hand reached for the knife on the cutting board.

She leaned in and sniffed his neck. The heady scent of him filled her mind, her body, her being. She gripped his neck and pulled it closer, running up the column of his throat and tasting the salt-laced sweat. It was like finding a well after wandering a sun-bleached desert.

"Mary, what are you—"

The knife's cut was clean.

Mary had dinner late that night. It took much longer than she would have thought to butcher and cut the meat. After the initial frenzy of her first few bites, she was able to slow down. She knew that she needed to divide up what she had in order to ration it out as much possible. With that, she'd decided to set the table proper.

She took her first bite and closed her eyes. She savored the succulent meat infused with a hint of rosemary. The radio warbled in the background. Daniel had never liked the radio on during dinner. With each bite, the candles seemed to grow brighter and more vivid.

There was a soft pressure against her stomach. Her silver went clattering onto the bone-lace tablecloth. She touched her belly. Unmistakable this time.

A kick.

Beyond the Salt

by River J. Myers

WHEN I WAS SMALL, my father drew a circle of salt around the house. "Don't step outside it after dark," he said. "Not even once."

The line was imperfect, uneven, thinning in places, but he said it didn't matter. What mattered was the promise that kept us safe.

"What promise?" I asked.

He looked at me, face shadowed by the lamp, his hands trembling as they gripped my shoulders. "The one I made to keep you. The one that cost your mother her voice."

I looked to where she stood in the kitchen doorway, her throat bearing that strange, silvery scar. She hadn't spoken since my birth.

The night the salt washed away, I was alone. The storm came heavy, wind shoving rain against the house like it wanted in. I sat on the kitchen floor with a candle, listening to the dark, feeling it lean close.

Mother's wind chimes, silent for years, began to sing.

I checked the windows. The circle was gone. The yard beyond was wrong; stretched and wide, endless as water. The trees had vanished.

No grass. Just the outline of something moving slow in the black, too far to see clearly.

But it had arms. And in them, it cradled something that glowed like moonlight.

***

When my parents returned the next day, I was still in the kitchen. My father stared at me like I was already gone. Mother touched her scar and began to hum a melody I'd never heard before.

"You let it in," he said.

"No," I whispered. "It let me out. It showed me what you took."

***

That night, I sat by the door, staring into the yard. I could see it now; the shape, clearer this time. Closer. Arms too long, head tilted. Curious. A silhouette as still as a house. In its hands, my real mother's voice gleamed like starlight.

My father swept a new circle of salt with shaking hands, speaking words that sounded like falling rain.

"It's too late," I said. "The price is due."

Mother—the one who raised me—began to sing.

The knocking began at midnight. Soft, like fingernails against wood. I pressed my hands to my ears, but the sound found its way in, whispered behind my eyes, asked questions I finally understood.

By morning, the salt had turned to mercury, flowing like silver tears.

Outside, the world was still wrong; flat and ceaseless, the ground soft under my feet. I stepped past the threshold. The shape was waiting, arms open, my true inheritance burning bright between its fingers.

It smelled like rain and dirt and ancient promises. It didn't speak. It didn't need to.

I took its hand. The light passed between us like a song.

When my parents woke, the door was open. The salt circle was gone.

My mother screamed—her first sound in seventeen years—as her borrowed time ran out. My father collapsed, the weight of his broken promise crushing him at last.

Out in the yard, I watched them through the window, though they couldn't see me anymore. I pressed my hand to the glass, my skin now gleaming with that same silvery sheen.

It's cold here, on this side. Quiet. But I can sing again, my real voice restored.

I wait by the house, the shape beside me, its arms still open, its mouth a dark line sewn with starlight. One day, they'll step through, when guilt weighs heavier than fear.

And I will be here.

Waiting.

With my mother's voice in my throat, and truth burning bright between my teeth.

Music to Die To

by Ron J. Cruz

HENRY HOLT REINED IN his horse as he rode up to the campsite. His gaze immediately shifted from the gaunt figure lying beside the fire to the fiddle hovering, unscathed, in the flames. His eyes lit up as he watched the instrument float above the red embers and crackling wood, wisps of smoke curling around it as they rose into the night.

Reemus, Holt's trail partner, rode in from the opposite direction, his pistol trained on the man lying by the fire. The recumbent figure remained still.

"Look at it," Holt said, gesturing to the fiddle shimmering in the heat.

"Blazes," Reemus replied, eyes widening. "Ever seen wood that don't burn?"

The man on the ground stretched his bony finger toward the fire. "Been trying to burn it for days," he rasped. "Damned thing won't burn."

"The man in Warren said avoid the fiddler," Reemus said, holstering his gun. "You the fiddler, mister?"

"I swear to god," the man choked out. "Wish I never played a single note."

Holt dismounted and approached the fire, his stare fixated on the instrument, tongue resting between his teeth. He donned a leather glove, eyes never breaking free from his prize, and prepared to snatch it from the flames. Just as his hand grabbed the neck, the man on the ground rolled over, pulled a gun, and shoved the barrel into his own mouth. Before Holt or Reemus could move, the man pulled the trigger and expelled the contents of his skull into the air.

"Now why the hell did he do that?" Reemus snarled, wiping away the spatter that peppered his neck and shoulder.

"Reckon he didn't find you agreeable," Holt said with a smirk.

He'd met his partner in Virginia, both heading west: Holt to marry a girl, Reemus fleeing a pregnant one (and her father). Neither woman liked the men, and it didn't take long on the trail to realize they didn't like each other either.

Watching his partner with the beautiful fiddle, Reemus said, "That's a hell of a piece."

Holt removed his glove, holding it in his bare hands. "You believe it ain't even hot?" he said, running his fingers over the back. "It's cool as a breeze." As he turned it, a low vibration came off the strings, rendering a soft growl that bit into their ears like a dreadful warning.

"Can you even play it?" Reemus asked, flinching from the noise. "Never took you as musically inclined."

"I used to know "The Man from Dry Gulch"," Holt replied, finding the bow and nestling his face into the chin groove. "Listen here."

Their horses grew restless, and a hot wind kicked up. He momentarily paused, then erupted in spasms and jerks, aggressively sawing the bow. Discordant notes screamed from the strings—flats and sharps clashing, forming a dark melody, an unholy opus. Holt's body convulsed and his head rocked about violently as he wrenched out the notes.

"Terrible," Reemus chuckled as he dismounted. "Definitely not "The Man from Dry Gulch"."

Reemus's boots barely touched the ground when his face suddenly went blank, body straightened long and tall as if impaled on a spike. His eyes twitched, his mouth opened, and he began to lurch about. Thick, yellow bile heaved through his lips and bright red blood spilled from his nose and ears. As he choreographically convulsed around, the top of his head split open, and liquified brains and muck rolled out like stew from an overturned pot. Reemus added a grim accompaniment of choking cries and sputters as his flesh melted away, running down his sides, leaving a messy mass of skin on the ground.

Holt continued to play, watching his partner melt away before him. His own ear, above the ridge of the instrument, freely bled, but he could do nothing but continue to saw away like a possessed puppet, reeling and rollicking, kicking up dust as he involuntarily stomped around. When it was over, he fell to the ground, exhausted and out of breath. He fought for air, staring up at the sky as his heart threatened to burst.

Moments passed as Holt slowly regained control. He watched clouds drift across the sky and found a sense of calm. His fingers were raw from the strings and the bow seared an impression into his hand. Once he regained agency over his body, he sat up. Blood had crusted around his ear and mouth, and he wiped it away with his sleeve. The fiddle dropped from his grasp as he dusted off his hat and set it back on his head.

The charred cremains of Reemus's body retained his form, like a fragile statue crafted from dust and ash, his hollow eyes staring blankly into the air.

"Damn, Reem." Holt grimaced as he stowed the instrument in a saddle bag. "Can't do much with your gelding without raisin' suspicions, ya know?"

The spirit of Reemus, as if in reply, drifted free from his burnt cadaver. Embers glowed in his empty eye sockets as he floated upon his horse. Upon his touch, the animal instantly suffered the same fate, its flesh falling away as it bucked and whinnied in terror. The air filled with the acrid stench of scorched hair and sulfur. Now a wraith, Reemus mounted the ghostly steed and rode toward the bluff. Sparks kicked up from the hooves of his mount as they climbed the hill, joining the ranks of a massive army of melted souls, their blazing eyes watching him fall into place.

Holt gasped at the army of ashen apparitions that mustered along the red bluff above him. Shoulder to shoulder, some on horse, others on foot, they lined the hill like a dark cloud, waiting to rain fire and brimstone. They floated like vapor, bristling with scorn, collective gazes fixated on the young man with the fiddle.

His breath quickened and his veins felt icy as he scrambled atop his horse. Holt quickly burst into a gallop, beating along the trail away from the bluffs. He was all spurs and elbows, kicking away as fast as his horse would take him.

He nearly tumbled from his saddle when he looked back to see the horrendous horde had spilled down the steep incline, falling into pursuit. The cadence of his gallop was loud, and he was suddenly aware the army behind him made no sound. They kicked up dust, hooves hitting the ground like flint, kicking up sparks, but they were silent—fiercely quiet and unwavering.

After a couple miles, his horse's breathing grew heavy and gait unsteady, and Holt allowed her to slow down. He looked back as he came to a stop and saw his pursuers also slowed and stopped.

He didn't move. They didn't move, but their fiery gazes tore through him. After a moment, he tore off again, only to find they kept pace. They never closed the distance nor allowed it to grow—they maintained their gap. He recognized them to be nothing more than a shadow, a gruesome gallery of souls cursed to follow him with a relentless gaze.

As night fell, Holt camped off the trail, obscured by a jagged formation of red sandstone hills. He made a small fire, heated up food, and fought through a tide of exhaustion maintaining watch. The cursed horde crowded around him; the constellation of their blazing eyes framed the night like a galaxy of stars. He stared back as long as he could, but eventually succumbed to slumber.

In the morning, he awoke with a gasp. The hope of crawling free from a nightmare disappeared with the sight of the wretched crew crowding in around his little camp. Though they maintained their distance, the air was heavy with the stench of decaying flesh and burnt hair.

Holt attempted to ignore them, working through his breakfast. He stowed his gear, attended to his horse, and even relieved himself—all under their watchful gaze. Saddling up, he decided on Jefferson City. This was the plan before Reemus transitioned, he thought. Do it for Reemus.

Holt scanned the ghoulish crowd for his trail-partner's face, finding him front and center. The slack-jawed vacant stare had been replaced with fire and fury. Holt nodded toward his fallen comrade, saying, "Who you ridin' with these days?" But there was no reply. So onward he rode.

Less than half a day out of town, in the last little stretch of desert, Holt ran across a peddler with a large wagon of goods. He was a graceful man with a golden tongue.

"Hallo, sir," he said, slowing his wagon. He removed his large top hat, stood, and made a bowing gesture. "I'll have my whole stock open in town, but if you're after something a bit...risqué, things a young fella might not want to procure in front of church folks, I can oblige."

Holt peeked back at his army of the damned, ensuring they were still in tow. Catching the quick glance, the merchant thought the young man, intrigued by his salacious suggestion, was ensuring they were alone.

"Now what kind of goods would you have that might interest a young man?" Holt asked.

"You look like a man that'd be interested in the sight of a womanly form." The merchant's contagious smile spread across his face, and he nodded in agreement with himself, causing his tall hat to wobble humorously. "I've got images that'll make your saddle tight. Even oils that would lubricate a tumbleweed."

"Now I quite appreciate that," Holt replied. "But I already got the image of a woman in my mind, my Sarah, and I'm not trying to replace her."

"I see." The salesman pivoted. "Does Sarah like shined stones, jewelry, or music boxes?"

"Well, I have a music maker here that might interest you." Holt pulled the fiddle from his saddle bag and held it up.

"Now, mister, I'm sellin', not procurin'," he replied with an unshaken smile. "I already have violins, harmonicas, and even mouth harpies."

The first pull of the bow wiped the cocksure grin from the salesman, replacing it with an involuntary contortion as every muscle jerked violently. Holt played in earnest, this time taking control of the instrument, while the peddler tumbled from the wagon, landing on his back. His hands smoked, his neck blistered, and he ripped off his jacket as if it were aflame. His toothy smile stretched grotesquely, lips peeling back over his chin and nose, sliding off his head like a gory mask. His frantic eyes shot around before they fell from his face like comets with bloody tails, crashing into the earth and bursting like sacks of pus. Flames lit his empty sockets and his blackened spirit rose, floating upright. His burned-out hat still crowned his head as he let out a final scream before sliding down the trail, joining the cursed company that followed the fiddle.

"Think I'm getting the hang of this thing," Holt said with a smile. Then he turned to the recently departed salesman. "You don't mind if I examine your wares, do you?"

He rustled through the merchandise in the back of the wagon, digging through fabrics, shovels, shears, and other worthless goods. Stumbling upon a large spool of rope made him gasp. The thought of swinging from a noose, shaking and pissing his life away, hastened his search. He found a small box of money in a compartment beneath a bit of hay, and he helped himself. As he climbed from the back, he saw crates of snake-oil cure-all, grabbed a few bottles, and tossed it to the army behind him. "Try this out," he chortled. "Maybe it'll help, maybe it won't."

Back on the trail, the afternoon sun was relentless, but he slowed his pace to arrive in town at dusk. He'd only stay the night—eat some food, have some drinks, play a song or two, and increase his fortune and soulful index.

The horde followed him with increased intensity. Were they closer, or just bigger? Holt couldn't tell. But they were sharper, more vivid—slack-jawed mouths full of maggots, writhing like tongues. Their stench of rot was thick and inescapable. Could he settle down with them always there, following? Make love to Sarah with those hateful eyes always watching?

"Don't slow down now," he yelled, waving them on with his hat. "Almost there."

Holt stopped in the first saloon, leaned against the bar, and sipped whiskey until evening fully settled across its earthen bed. The army of the damned pressed against the doors and windows, their burning stares fixed on him, while town folk passed through the ghouls as if they were clouds, oblivious to their hateful existence.

The piano man filled the air with a festive polka and the smokey atmosphere was cheery. Men filled tables throughout the room, some eating, others playing games. Stairs ran up along the side, and unchaste cherubs, women of comfort, congregated along the banister on top of the landing, smiling sinfully, temptingly tantalizing.

The crowd was a hard collection of ruffians, cowboys, and the devil's own. Holt fought against his nerves and sense of doubt. Scenes played in his head where things went wrong, the fiddle didn't work, and the crowd fed him to his own horde. But then he calmed, picturing Sarah's bare hip in the candlelight, her tongue dancing between wet lips, and he found the necessary resolve to pull out the villainous violin and move to the piano.

Nobody noticed him at all until the first series of notes filled the air. Then tables were knocked over and screams erupted. Nobody died the same way, but death found them all the same.

A woman with a large, ruffled dress danced, kicking around with horrific stomps, flames of hell lighting up her toes. She pulled her dress down and revealed heavy breasts, but the beauty of her heart-shaped nipples was eclipsed by the severe shaking of her long white neck, which she broke with a severe head-snap to the side. Her tongue poked through her lips, then split open like a blooming flower, blood thrown outward. She continued to undress, pulling off her skin from her shoulders as she danced and twirled, shucking herself free from her earthly husk.

The piano man joined the fiddler's tune, smashing each side of the keyboard with bloody fists as he mechanical rocked back and forth, eventually falling backward and instantaneously decomposing as worms cleaned his corpse faster than he could die.

The saloon emptied as, one by one, the patrons exited, eyes blazing as they floated by, heads smoking, and the smell of the saloon being replaced by the smell of the grave. They formed a grotesque parade of painfully disembodied souls, amassing outside in the street.

Holt worked his way through everything they'd left behind, collecting as much money as he could. Eventually he only took large bills and coins, selectively leaving the smaller change behind. There was plenty to pull from the bar and even more from the banker in back who exchanged gold bullion for bills. Holt left with three canvas bags stuffed with loot.

Three days from Sarah's, he pushed his horse as much as he could, but exhaustion caught up to them both. When he found safe places to camp, he slept with his bags under the blanket and a pistol in his hand.

One night out, he fell asleep with a smile on his face. In his dreams he found her, soft eyes casting adoration and lust. They washed each other clean in a deep, warm pond, and she shimmered like the night sky, sparkling with stars she wore like jewelry. There was a daisy in her hair, and flowers strewn around, and they stretched out across a rawhide rug in front of a stone fireplace where the violin splintered and burned. Legs falling open, she sighed, and her sweet breasts cast shadows like tombstones across the white skin of her stomach.

Suddenly, the walls became thinner than sheets and stretched inward with the pressure of hands and contorted faces, the gnashing of teeth and stretched-out fingers reaching for Holt. Sarah screamed, reducing to ash. Flailing, Holt looked up into darkness as he cut through the air, falling into a glowing canyon of flames, a pit of hell. Before he hit the bottom, he shuddered and woke up next to a fire beneath the peaceful desert moon, his horrible horde looking on.

That morning in town, Holt bristled with anticipation. He found a room with a bath. He bought fresh trousers, a shirt, and a leather vest, even fashioned himself with new boots and a hat. The crispness of new clothes camouflaged his moral decay; he was fresh as a mountain spring and strutted like a bridegroom.

Jessup would recognize he had become a man. Holt felt ten feet tall, sparkling like an icon. People tipped hats and nodded with signs of respect, and nobody gave a thought to the musical case he tightly held under his arm.

Halfway down the walk, a blind man with milk-white eyes, no pupils, sitting in a chair in front of the general store bolted upright and turned his attention to Holt.

Holt rode along the ridge toward Jessup's homestead. He'd gotten directions in town and learned it was across a ridge with rolling hills and blooming flowers. His dreadful ranks fanned out beside him, floating in the air like a sea of ghost riders tearing across the sky.

Upon his arrival, Sarah's father was not even home. This was the best scenario that had played out in his fantasies. He'd set things with Sarah before encountering the old man.

"Hello?" she said as she stepped onto the steps of the cabin.

"Sarah Hickenstaff, love of my life!" He was off the horse before it stopped, the momentum of everything in his life propelling him into this moment. "I am here to change your last name and build you a kingdom."

"Harry Holt," she said with a sigh.

"It's Henry," he corrected. "Henry Holt."

Though still pretty, the blush in her cheek was duller than he re-membered. Somehow, she wasn't excited. Her eyes didn't dance, her bosom didn't heave. It was nothing like he anticipated. Instead, she looked like a nervous girl, interrupted from her chores.

"Henry Holt," she stammered. "Yeah, I remember you."

"I've come to marry you," he explained, taking off his hat. "I'm gonna do it right. I'll talk to Jessup and make this whole thing proper."

"Well," she started. "As flattered as I am, I'm not interested in marrying you. I dated a boy in Buck's County, but I'm not marrying him either. At least, not yet."

"I rode out from Virginia with this sole purpose in mind." Holt gazed into her eyes, searching for signs of affection and charm. He looked for his dream girl. "But, Sarah, I'm in love with you."

"I'm sorry," she replied flatly, then started to turn away. "You should go."

"I think I'd rather stay and talk to Jessup," he said defiantly. "I doubt he'll let you pass up a man of my means."

"That's not a good idea," she said, stepping back. "But it looks like you'll be talking to him nonetheless."

She pointed and he turned to see her father fiercely galloping across the expanse of land. His mouth was tight, eyes stern, and his hand held firmly to his holstered pistol as he rode.

"He ain't coming to talk to you," she warned.

"I didn't want to do this," Henry lamented, drawing his gun on Sarah. He pulled the fiddle from the bag and forced it into her hands. "I want you to play me a song."

"You need to go," she said emotionlessly, staring directly into his eyes. "My father is going to kill you."

"I wanted you to love me," Holt said, turning his head as he spoke.

"But I don't," Sarah replied.

"Then play me a song," he demanded, the gun shaking in his hand as he spoke.

"I don't even know how." She smirked.

"Then pretend like you know how," he said gruffly as he cocked his gun.

"Well, I'm sorry, Henry," she said, gripping the bow and neck. "Guess this is as good as any music to die to."

"It is." Henry smiled as he holstered his gun. "But I will never leave your side."

The moment the bow touched the strings, Sarah went into a trance and the fiddle took hold of her soul. She rose into the air as the strings began to sing. Her arm flapped violently with the production of music, but it was clear she had no control. The instrument possessed her as demonic music filled the air, sparks flew up and around her, and smoke slowly rose from the friction of the playing.

Holt felt the immediate stiffness of rigor mortis as his body died instantly, but his nerves lit with the pain of fire and torment as his spirit broke free of its skin. His spine and bones burned hotter than a fanned blacksmith's forge and there was no respite. His jawbone splintered and cracked open, eyes popped from the intensity of the heat, and his heart exploded from the pressure of spontaneous combustion. His skin dissolved, fat pustules burst like pimples, blood mixed with mucous, sliding down his muscles which bubbled and burned away, leaving the bones to splinter like firewood, crackling as they fell to charred dust.

His spirit floated free from its earthly form, seething with a new-found pain he would never extinguish and a hate he would never have to fan. Joining the ranks of the unholy mass, he began his eternal vigil over the fiddle and its musician.

As Jessup rode into earshot, Sarah continued to play, converting her earthly father into a sinister sentinel. Tears rolled down her cheeks as she flailed and fought her own song but couldn't slow the momentum of the music. The old man rolled off his horse, floated upward, and went rigid, starting to dance around like a marionette. He died with a gasp, outstretched hands reaching toward his daughter.

As the song came to an end, Sarah fell back and fought to catch her breath. Any hope to awaken from this terrible dream faded as reality settled in. The gritty ground became more tangible on her hands and the smell of burnt flesh and hellfire filled the air.

She struggled to lean against the steps of the cabin and looked at the massive legion of acolytes she had acquired. Her eyes widened and breath fell shallow as flaming eyes as far as the horizon circled in to stare. It was the largest army she had ever seen, and they would be with her until she took her last breath.

The new additions fell into the ranks, a vulgar man she'd never loved and the only man that she had ever adored. Henry Holt and her father, both eternal companions, would follow her every step forever.

Haint Tree

Melissa Burkley

THE SHERIFF'S TIRES SIZZLE like sirloin on the cast-iron black-top, steel hood so hot you could fry up a few eggs with that steak, have yourself a hearty breakfast. Asphalt gives way to gravel, gravel to packed dirt, as the truck slows, then stops under the sacred shade of a live oak tree. Sheriff Herschel Cobb steps out, all 240 pounds of him cinched with a leather belt straining to do its job. Not yet noon and already damp crescents hang under his arm pits. Old timers said last summer—that'd be the summer of 1947—was the hottest on record for Cokesbury, South Carolina. Herschel could already tell this year's gonna give that record a run for its money.

His deputy, Garvin, arrived on the scene first and is currently straddling a ladder propped against the tree's massive trunk. An oven-door breeze runs its fingers through the leaves, a soft rustle of distant voices, and Herschel catches the scent of it. Strange fruit rotting under the raging sun.

"Who called it in?" Herschel hollers up to Garvin, a paper-white hand shielding his eyes.

"Allen Moore," the deputy yells back, not risking a look down. "Caught sight of it while he was drivin' out to milk his cows this mornin'." Knife in one hand, the other clutching the ladder, Garvin leans over as far as gravity will allow and starts sawing at the rope.

Herschel gives a berth wide as his girth, making sure to stay clear of anything that might fall. "We got any ideas on who's responsible?"

Beads of sweat snake down Garvin's face as he works the knife. The branch gives a groaning creak in protest. "Word 'round town is it was the Beechem brothers." Flies the size of raisins swarm around Garvin's head like a dark storm cloud. He thrashes a hand at them, then starts back at the rope. "But I was waitin' til I heard from you to do anythin' bout it."

Herschel gives a deep-throated sigh. His ancestors had been living in this little corner of South Carolina for over one hundred years, and for just as long they'd served as sheriff of these parts. Somedays it was good to be sheriff—today was not one of them. "After you get this taken care of, give the older brother Walt a call. Tell him to stop by my place 'round two this afternoon. I'll be waitin'."

"Will do, boss." Garvin's knife slices through the last of the rope and the body drops to the ground with a wretched thud.

"That's one down," Herschel says. "Just two more to go."

Come two o'clock, the sun is beating down so hot you'd need potholders to pull worms from the ground. Herschel stands on his front porch, awaiting Walt Beechem's arrival. His eyes train on the dirt road that winds through his soybean fields like a brown garter snake. Used to be tobacco that blessed his land, before that it was cotton, but times were a changin' whether you liked it or not.

Movement fish-hooks Herschel's gaze, drags it to the big tree squatting at the farthest end of his property, out where the Cobb farm ends and the county road begins. Silver beards of Spanish moss drape from the tree's limbs, swaying slightly—odd, since there's no hint of a breeze.

The southern live oak is a massive specimen, stretching nearly 80 feet tall, and—as the old timers like to put it—as old as the hills. His family has been farming this land for generations, but the tree had planted its roots in this soil long before the Cobbs had. Truth be told, that tree was probably older than the country itself, back when there were only red men in these parts as far as the eye could see. When he was a little boy, Herschel's grandpappy, God rest his soul, claimed that in his day there were over fifty live oaks in Cokesbury. But years of drought, lightning strikes, boring beetles, root rot—some say runoff from the textile plant in neighboring Wheatfield—had all conspired to reduce their numbers. When Herschel's daddy went and ran his Model T into the one out on Hangman's Road, killing himself and the tree in the process, that number whittled down to just two: this one here on the farm and the other one on the far end of town—the one Herschel was sweating under just this morning.

A tell-tale plume of dust mushrooms in the distance, finger-snapping Herschel back to the present. When the older Beechem brother pulls his Chevy pickup to the house, he comes in too hot and his braking tires dig gouges in Herschel's well-tended lawn. Walt gets out, dressed in a wide-brimmed Stetson, brown trousers, and a bandana noose round his sun-scorched neck—doing his best to look like a young John Wayne.

"Afternoon, Sheriff," Walt says with a tip of his hat. He's got on a pair of candy-apple red boots that only a cocky boy of twenty or so would attempt. The Duke wouldn't be caught dead in those shit-kickers. "Garvin said you wanted to talk?"

"Sure do. Appreciate you comin' out this way." As he waves Walt up to the porch, an unease crawls up Herschel's back, thin and spindly like the legs of a grasshopper. He feels suddenly exposed standing out here in the open, as if someone or something was watching them. "Let's have our talk inside."

Herschel pours himself a thumb of whiskey, then does the same for his guest and plunks the shot glass down on the table. "Way I hear it, you and your brother got into a bit of mischief last night."

"Hell, you know how it is." Walt runs thick fingers through thick black hair. Herschel used to have hair like that. *Thick as a thicket*, his wife used to say, one piece twirled round her slender pinkie. Now the hair was gone, so was the wife. "Someone's gotta keep them in their place."

Walt leans back in his chair, drink in hand, and props his dirt-caked pansy-assed boots on the table. Herschel wants to reach across and knock those eyesores right off, maybe do the same with that smug grin on Walt's face, but he knows better. The Beechem boys he could handle, but their father was mayor, which made him Herschel's boss. Maybe he would've done something ten years ago, but he was too close to retirement to stir that hornet's nest now.

Instead, Herschel takes a long sip of whiskey, savors the burn in the back of his throat. "I figured as much. So, tell me what happened."

"Started in town earlier that day. I was standin' outside of Pick-wick's, smokin' a cig and waitin' on my brother to grab us a few bottles of pop. Then up hobbles this old negro man and, right in front of me, he uses the water fountain. You know the one, with the clear-as-day sign saying *Whites Only*." Walt's cheeks flush crimson, like they've just been smacked good. "Couldn't goddamn believe it!"

"Course, it didn't help that you and your brother busted up the one marked *Colored* the week before with a sledgehammer."

Walt leans back farther, the wooden chair crying out in pain. He gives a fox-in-the-henhouse grin so wide, Herschel can practically see the feathers poking out from tobacco-stained teeth.

"Oh, sure, there's some truth in that," Walt says. "But I think even you would agree there's no excuse for such blatant disrespect like that. So I hollered at the old man to stop, but he ignored me. So I moved him out of the way. Was just a nudge, nothing more than that, but that damn geezer, why, he took a tumble to the ground. Pretty sure he was fakin', but that's when a group of young ones from across the street came a runnin'. One of 'em picked the old man up while the other puffed up like a tom turkey. Got right in my face, so close I could smell the day-old collards on his breath."

Walt leans forward to demonstrate, treating Herschel to a sour, meaty scent. Like a pot of hammocks and beans left out on the counter overnight.

"I was about to show him the side of my fist," Walt continues, "when Jackson came out of the shop and pulled me back. Said there was a better time and place for this sort of thing. Truth be told, my brother's always had the cooler head in these situations. Momma says it's 'cause he was born in winter, whereas I was born at the height of summer."

Walt's fingers drum a frenzied beat on the tabletop and Herschel wonders if the boy shouldn't lay off the sweets.

"So late last night, I rounded up some of my buddies..."

When he says *buddies,* Herschel knows he means Klansmen. The KKK, or what many around here called the Invisible Empire, is as much a part of growing up in Carolina as shrimp and grits. Herschel was not Klan himself, but he knew most of the townsfolk who were. He had no beef with the Klan, so long as they kept their activities quiet. As sheriff, it was his job to keep things in town settled. Sometimes that meant enforcing the law, but as any lawman worth his salt will tell you, other times, that means turning a blind eye. Old FDR may be running things up north, but down here in Lowcountry, we take care of our own. Whites gotta look out for whites. Five generations of Sheriff Cobbs have been preserving the status quo and, God willing, the next generation would do the same. There was a time when Herschel assumed that birthright would fall onto his own son's shoulders. Not anymore.

"We tracked down two of the young ones and the old one. Took care of things the Klan way..."

In this Southern pocket of God Bless America, "Klan way" involved a couple barrel-chested men to do the heaving, a good strong rope to do the hauling, and the bough of an old live oak to carry the payload. Any other type of tree—your sweetgum or your pecan—was likely to snap under all that weight, but not a live oak. Guess that's why Grand-pappy jokingly called 'em dead oaks instead. Irony is, Granpappy died from a lightning strike while taking cover under the awning of one of them very trees—dead oaks indeed.

"You know how it is," Walt continues. "Once your dog turns on you and tries to bite, ain't nothin' you can do but put 'em down." He drains the rest of his whiskey, then shoves the empty glass aside like it's just let him down. "So, have we got a problem, Sheriff? Do I need to get my father involved here, or are we good?"

Herschel empties his own glass, then wipes his wet upper lip with the back of his hand. "Now, Walt, I know you did what you had to do. I don't take issue with that. I take care of my own, same as you. But what I do take issue with is the fact that you and your buddies left them bodies hangin' for all the world to see. Why, that's somethin' that could land our town on the front page of the *Charleston Post*. We wouldn't want that, now, would we?" Herschel sits up straight, does his best to stretch his six feet to match Walt's six and a half. "Do we have an understanding?"

The vein at Walt's temple pulses, throbbing out a warning in Morse code. "We had no choice. Had to send a message to all the rest of those coloreds. They need to know disobedience will NOT be tolerated in our town. Every year they's gettin' more and more ornery. Forgettin' who they are. Forgettin' their place." He sucks in a deep breath. "But I understand your point, Sheriff. I do. I promise, Scout's honor. I'll keep it in mind for next time."

"Good. Then I think we're done here." Herschel stands up—chair legs screeching like the midnight cry of a barn owl—and offers his hand. Walt swallows it within his own leathered baseball mitt.

On the porch, Herschel gratefully watches those gawdy boots disappear into Walt's truck. "You make sure to tell your mama I said hello and that I missed her pecan pie at the last church gatherin'."

"Will do." Walt gives him a two-fingered Army salute, then steers his truck down the driveway and out onto the county road.

Once again, Herschel throws a stone-skipping glance at the old oak.

Once again, the tree's moss drapery rustles even though there is no discernable breeze.

That damn tree, it's a dark blight on Herschel's heart. He'd dropped to a knee and proposed to Mellie under it. And when she said yes, he was happy as a pig in slop. Couldn't imagine being any happier than that moment, and truth is, he probably never was. But what the good Lord giveth, he taketh away. Or in this case, the tree taketh. Seven years later, their only child, Thomas, was climbing in that tree, despite Herschel's many directives not to. Boy took a tumble, broke his leg in three places. But that fall broke something else too: their marriage. Thomas got a bone infection, and by winter, he'd passed away. Mellie was so distraught, she left to live with her sister in Beaufort. That was five years ago. Herschel hadn't heard a word from the woman since. On more than one occasion, stumbling in a drunken stupor, he'd grabbed the axe and thought about chopping the cursed thing down, turning it into firewood, burning those memories into ash.

A deep thirst churns in Herschel's gut, a thirst only whiskey can quench. With a heavy sigh, he turns his back on the world and heads into the house. Before closing the door, he takes one last glance at his only remaining legacy. The sun is just starting to set, its dying breath kissing the tops of the soybean leaves. A sea of gold-leafed filigree. He pushes the door shut, that gilded light switching off like one of those new-fangled light bulbs all the city folk are raving about these days. As he maneuvers through the living room, hands searching for the kerosene lantern, a thought itches like a dog at the back door of his skull.

Probably just his tired eyes playing tricks on him—sure, that had to be it. But the tree...he could've sworn it looked closer to the house than usual.

A drumroll of thunder, and quickly on its heels a cannon fire of lightning. Herschel startles out of his chair, kicks the table leg, and sends the half-full whiskey bottle clattering to the floor. It had been early evening when he cracked the seal on a new bottle of Glenlivet. Now, in the flickering light of the storm, his watch reads 3:31 a.m. Wasn't the first time he'd fallen asleep at the kitchen table, cheek steeping in a puddle of drool, tongue a dried-out slug in his mouth. Since Mellie left, it was a regular occurrence.

A crack of lightning snaps the air in two. Head spinning, Herschel stumbles to the window and pulls back the curtains. Nothing but pitch black. He holds his breath, waits…

A bolt of lightning whip-cracks across the sky. A banshee cry as the wind lashes the leaf-packed boughs of the oak back and forth, an angry head-shaking motion that reminds him of Mellie, the last time he saw her.

The world plunges headlong into dark, and once again, that strange sense that the tree is somehow closer to the house than it ought to be. It's a sensation he feels less in his head and more in his bones. Same ache he gets when he's out deer hunting and senses his prey is hiding in the trees, tasting his scent with its pink tongue, plotting its escape.

A movie-projector flicker of light against the sky, and in between those strobes, Herschel can see it now. The tree is coming closer.

Fifty feet from the house—

Darkness, flash.

Now forty feet—

It's the whiskey, he tells himself. *Just overdid it is all.*

Another flash.

The tree now twenty feet away—

Back to black.

Clawing, scratching, something pawing at the front door. Hollow, scraping sounds like branches (*fingers*) raking their tips (*fingernails*) into solid wood—the sound of a frantic dog begging to be let in.

A mule-kick of panic thuds within Herschel's chest. He presses a hot cheek against cold glass, straining to see anything in the gloom. When at last the lightning singes the sky, his whiskey-soaked brain refuses to believe what his eyes are seeing. The massive oak is squatted just beyond his porch now, its roots freed from their prison and undulating like brown-skinned tentacles. Branches weave through the railing, greedy limbs splitting spindles, prying back nails, uprooting floorboards. Moss-draped fingers press flat against the windows, hold closed the door, block any means of escape.

Herschel clamps a trembling hand over his mouth, smothers a newborn scream as his eyes land on the things hanging from the thickest bough of the tree.

Haints. Three of them. Dark, withered forms that dangle at the end of ropes. Hard-pitted peaches left to rot in the summer sun.

Their dead eyes bulge from shriveled sockets.

Their bloated tongues loll from scream-stretched mouths.

Their bodies sag at the end of cotton cords, swinging back and forth as fiercely as the whiskey sloshing in Herschel's belly.

The sight of them squeezes a starter pistol in his gut, releasing a panic that gallops down his bowels like one of them racehorses in the Kentucky Derby. Herschel knows these three haints; not their names, but their faces. Saw 'em just this morning, swinging in the boughs of that other oak tree.

But it ain't the haints stalking him tonight. Herschel knows this with a steely certainty that bypasses the wires in his brain and plugs right into his quivering bowels.

It's the tree itself.

His gaze is nailed to the oak, to the trunk, to the bark that is writhing and twisting like a pit of snakes. In that swirling maelstrom, echoes of a human form appear, dissolve, reappear somewhere else. The ragged notch of a screaming mouth. The bulging burr of a nose. Two furious knots for eyes.

It's angry, a voice calls up from the dark well of Herschel's mind. *Angry for the way its sibling was used in last night's lynchings. Angry for all its Southern cousins who've been used in the same way—to torture, to terrorize, to kill.*

Get the goddamn axe, another voice says, this one louder than the last. *It's by the fireplace. Cut that thing down before it has a chance to cut you down.*

Herschel spins on his heels, readying to obey the command, as a cymbal-crash of thunder clangs overhead. No, not thunder, not this time. With numbed shock, Herschel watches the tree crack the roof in half. His legs buckle, and for the second time in his life, he takes a knee under the old oak.

The first thing that goes through Herschel's head is how much he hates this fucking tree.

The second is a 200-pound branch of authentic Southern-grown live oak—bayou-bred, roots fed off blood-stained soil, sweat of nameless slaves, generations of unmarked graves, heartwood hardened by colonization and horrors of the plantation. That thigh-thick bough cracks down on Herschel's skull and opens it as easily as a sun-warmed watermelon.

Grease Paint

by B.L. Daniels

LARRY PUSHED OPEN THE door to Swanson's Antiques. The tinkling of a small brass bell announced his entrance, and the air inside was a bouquet of dust, old clothes, and tarnished metal.

"Afternoon, Larry." Mr. Swanson peered over his spectacles. "How's work?"

"It's a paycheck." Larry shrugged. "The parts come in, I put them someplace, then they go out."

"Exciting," Swanson replied with a smile.

"It's not my true work anyway. Can I see the catalog?" Larry pointed to a large, colorful book. It lay atop the glass case full of smiling ceramic animals that also functioned as Swanson's counter.

"Ah yes." Swanson flopped the catalog open in front of Larry. "How did last weekend's performance go?"

"Terrible." Larry scowled. "Kids have no appreciation for art. They didn't pay attention to the dancing or juggling. Not even shadow puppets. One of them threw up, and it splattered on my shoes."

"Ooh. Sounds rough."

"Then I asked the teenager working there to shut off the animals, and he just called me a creep and walked away."

"Animals?"

"Yeah. A band of singing animal puppets. My finale was interrupted by a beaver with a ukulele singing 'Dixie Land.' The kids laughed at *that*. Imbeciles."

Swanson chuckled. "Well, Larry, they *are* children, and you *are* a clown."

A twinge stung Larry's right eye. "Lorenzo isn't a clown," he said. "He's a harlequin."

"Oh, right." Swanson drew his hands back across the glass.

"Clowns are buffoons. They elicit pity. Harlequins are mischievous and sophisticated. They're astute and bring wonder and fancy to people's imaginations. Not cheap laughs." Larry snatched a pen from the yellowed *World's Greatest Grandpa* mug that sat next to the register and ticked three checkboxes on the page. "I need white, red, and yellow."

"You should get extra if you can afford it." Swanson tapped the page. "It's getting tougher every month to get those tins of grease paint from my distributor. It might be time to think about acrylic."

"It's not right," Larry deadpanned. "It's not traditional, and it doesn't even cover well."

"Larry, have you ever heard that old saying about separating the art from the artist?" Swanson rubbed a chin full of stubble.

"No," Larry replied.

"It's about setting expectations, Larry. About being able to create something without...well...without getting so wrapped up in it. Am I making sense? I just think you might be happier if you tried that."

Larry stared momentarily. "Get me an extra tin of white. You know I'm trying to save up. Have you thought more about my offer?"

"I have, and I'm sorry, but I just can't part with it for that cheap. It's an antique."

Larry gazed up at the vintage harlequin costume hanging on the rear wall of the shop. Its black and white checkered pattern was offset by delicate lace embroidered at the collar and cuffs. It was magnificent. "Don't let anyone else take it. I'm going to find the money."

"It's been here for a long time, Larry. I doubt anyone else is going to buy it."

"Just promise me." Larry jabbed the pen back into the coffee mug.

Swanson glanced at his wristwatch. "Larry, it's 1:15. Isn't your lunch break over?"

"Oh crap." Larry turned and dashed out of the store, the brass bell sounding as he yanked the door open.

"I'll just put that order in for you," Swanson said to himself.

"You're late," Carl said from behind the register.

"I know. Sorry." Larry stared at the floor. *Carl's Cut-Rate Car Parts* was just over a block away from Swanson's, but it may as well have been a mile. Larry was late, and knew he was going to hear about it.

"You're seventeen minutes late," Carl said, sticking his tongue into the hole where one of his front teeth used to be. "You know one o'clock's my hour, Larry. Were you dickin' around in that old man's junk shop? You'd better have brought my books."

"Yeah, here you go. I stopped at the newsstand." Larry handed Carl a brown paper bag.

Carl greedily snatched it and slid out issues of *Hustler*, *Barely Legal*, and *Juggs*. "Yeah, there we go." He licked his lips. "Ooh, look at the set on her, Larry." He shoved the issue of *Juggs* into Larry's face.

"Yes. They're, uh, ample." Larry averted his eyes.

"Alright. Get behind this register. I'm headed to the can. Slow Mike is packing an order of brake pads in the back. Don't bother me. If you or that dullard needs to take a piss, do it out back. An' if you need to take a shit, well, here's a paper bag." Carl shoved the crumpled bag into Larry's hand, then grinned and headed for the bathroom.

"You shouldn't call him slow," Larry murmured.

"Excuse me, boy?" Carl spun around, face wrenched up. "He's slow. Ain't he?"

Larry immediately regretted his comment. "Uh, yeah. A bit."

"Yeah." Carl tilted his head and sneered. "That's why I call him Slow Mike. Now, just do as I tell ya, and I'll give you something to spend on your weird little puppet shows."

"Got it," Larry replied, seething inside at the condescending old pervert.

"Good." Carl nodded and headed back toward the bathroom.

"Mmmmhmm, look at that set..." Carl mumbled to himself before the door slammed shut and the lock clicked.

Carl's ritual may have been crass, but there was something about it that Larry respected. Pornographic magazines—or "titty books," as Carl referred to them—were his art. He didn't care for pictures on phones or websites. He needed something tangible, something real. Larry admired that, even if the magazines ended up wrinkled and water-stained next to the toilet on the bathroom floor.

"Mike? You back here, Mike?" Larry peeked through the open doorway that separated the front of the store from the stockroom. Rows of gray metal shelving units lined the walls and divided the floor into narrow aisles. Larry made his way back, and a potpourri of cardboard, rubber, and motor oil filled his nose.

"Yup," a voice replied.

"Hey, did you see a box of ceramic brake pads back here? I need to bring some more up front," Larry asked.

"Ummmmm, I thought I saw 'em somewhere." Mike turned away from the box he was unpacking and lifted his ballcap to scratch a head full of unkempt black hair. He towered over Larry at about six foot three. His hands were like grizzly bear paws, but a soft face gave him the appearance of an overgrown child. "They must be around here somewhere." He shrugged.

"We'd better find them, those things are expensive." Larry moved and shuffled boxes, searching for the pads.

"Nope. Not under here." Mike looked under a workbench.

Larry noticed a shipment labeled *pads* on the outbound table. He snagged a thin silver box cutter off the bench and sliced the taped box open.

"Hey, I already packed that," Mike whined.

"Yeah, with the ceramic pads." Larry hefted the expensive brake pads from the box.

"What? Oh..." Mike recoiled with a sheepish look on his baby face. "You're not gonna tell Carl, are you? He's gonna yell at me."

Larry sighed. "No. I won't tell Carl. You just... You need to be more careful and pay attention."

Mike nodded. "Hey, Larry?"

"Yeah?"

"Do you have any balloons?"

"No, Mike."

"Do you...do you think someday you could make me another animal?" Mike stammered. "I...I could even give you some money for the balloon."

"I told you that was a one-time thing." Larry huffed and adjusted the box of brake pads into his chest.

"Okay." Mike got quiet. "I just really liked the dog you made me. He really looks like a real dog. He's lost some air, but he still looks like a real dog, and I keep him in my room. I thought maybe he'd like a friend. Like a cat, or a giraffe."

Larry sighed again. "Okay. Maybe. But you have to promise you'll pay more attention when you're packing orders."

"I will!" Mike grinned. "Thanks, Larry. You're really nice. It's no wonder kids like you to be at their parties. If I had a birthday party, I'd want you to come and be the cl— Wait. What's the big word you use? I know you don't like the c-word."

"Harlequin," Larry deadpanned. "And the kids don't always like me, Mike." Visions of sneering children filled Larry's mind. Their faces smeared red with marinara sauce, belittling him while they guffawed at the moronic performance of an animatronic rodent.

"They don't? Well, that's not nice."

"No. It's not." Larry dug his fingers into the cardboard box, cutting tiny indentations. "Most people aren't like you, Mike. They're not nice. Most people are mean and self-centered, and they don't care about anyone else or their happiness."

Mike's eyes widened a bit. "Yeah, that's not very nice at all. Hey, Larry, I think I'm gonna finish packing the boxes now." He turned back to the workbench.

The lock on the bathroom door clicked once more and jarred Larry from his trance. "Shit," he whispered to himself.

"Where the hell are you?" Carl yelled from the front room.

Larry spun to make his way out of the stockroom, but Carl was already in his face before he could breach the doorway.

"What the hell are you two doing back here? Jackin' each other off? I come out to get a soda and there's no one at the damn register!"

"Sorry, Carl. I came back to bring up some pads..." Larry tried to step forward, but Carl slapped his hand firmly on the box.

"If ya needed pads, yell to the dimwit to bring 'em up front to ya. But ya *don't* leave my damn register alone with all the money in it."

"Got it."

"Do ya?" Carl glared at Larry over top of the box.

"Yup." Larry swerved through the doorway into the storefront while Carl berated Slow Mike. The old man unleashed a swarm of profanity that buzzed in Larry's ears like angry hornets while he maneuvered the box behind the front counter.

This place was hell. It strangled his creative soul. He'd been at this for too long, and it was time to make a move. For his own sake, and Lorenzo's.

Carl emerged from the back room and grabbed a bottle of Moxie from a blue plastic cooler. He twisted the cap off and sucked at the dark brown syrup.

The thick gulping noises from Carl's throat made Larry's lip curl. "Hey, Carl?"

"What?" Carl ripped a belch that reeked of Moxie and bologna sandwich.

"Can I have my next paycheck today?"

"What?!" Carl burst out laughing. He tugged at Larry's pants. "You got a pair of brass walnuts danglin' in there? Jesus, lemme hear 'em knock together."

"I'm serious." Larry smoothed the leg of his pants.

"Yeah," Carl chuckled. "Me too. You come back late, leave my register alone, then you ask me for your paycheck three days early?"

A flicker of rage burned inside Larry. It sparked in his brain, and the heat crawled down his spine and tingled through his ribs. He stared at Carl's unkempt, bushy eyebrows. They offended him. Carl and his eyebrows didn't give a shit about his art, and they never would. They only wanted him to show up for soulless drudge work five days a week until his muse was smothered.

"I saved you a bunch of money. Mike almost shipped these out." Larry pointed at the box of pads.

"What?" Carl seethed.

Larry felt a twinge of regret through the anger, but it quickly faded. He envisioned the suit hanging in Mr. Swanson's shop. The embroidering was exquisite, and he needed to feel that lace slide between his fingertips.

"That's why I was in the back. I couldn't find the ceramics. I cut open one of the boxes and Mike had mixed up the shipments."

"That goddamned retard." Carl chucked the bottle of Moxie on the floor. Brown sludge fizzed and flowed across the laminate floor. He stomped toward the back room.

"Wait!" Larry grabbed Carl's shoulder. "Don't fire him."

"Why the hell not? I should smack his goddamned thick skull with a tire iron. Maybe that'd knock some smarts into him."

"No. It was a mistake. I fixed it. You'll never find anyone else who will work here for next to nothing. Do you think there's anyone else at the group home who can lift boxes that heavy?"

"Mmmph." Carl snorted.

"If you fire him, they're going to ask questions. That lady from the state will come around. You know, the one with the glasses."

"Mmmph. That skag's got a face like a vulture. She thinks those glasses hide it… They don't."

"And if Slow Mike says anything, they could accuse you of abuse. You could have to pay a fine, and they'll definitely kick you out of the program."

Carl took a deep breath and blew more bologna stink into the air. "I ain't payin' them shit."

"No, you're not," Larry replied. "And if you can give me this week's check early, you don't have to pay me either. I'll come in and work the next four Sundays…for free."

"Excuse me?" Carl's eyes grew wide.

"You heard me," Larry said. "It's a one-time offer."

Carl marched over to the cash register. He pushed a button and the drawer popped open with a clang. He lifted a black plastic divider and pulled a fat white envelope out from underneath it. "I'll give you the key on Friday night. You show up early on Sunday. Seven o'clock. Full day. Four o'clock. No lunch break." He rifled through some twenties in the envelope, then pulled some out and shoved them at Larry.

"Got it." Larry snatched the money.

"You lose that key, it's your ass."

"Got it." Larry nodded.

"Good boy." Carl smiled and wiggled his furry eyebrows.

Larry shoved open the door to Swanson's shop and rushed inside. The tiny brass bell clanked from the force.

"Larry. You're in a hurry, eh?" Mr. Swanson peered over his spectacles.

"The suit," Larry said, huffing to catch his breath.

Swanson shook his head. "Larry, I'm sorry. We've gone over this so many times, I just can't let go of it for that cheap."

Larry pulled a thick wad of bills held together by a rubber band and slammed it on the glass counter. "The suit."

Swanson's eyes grew behind his spectacles. "Oh, um. Larry, where did you get this money?"

"Work. Carl gave me an advance. I've been eating lots of ramen noodles...when I eat."

"Well then, I suppose it's yours." Swanson reached behind the counter and grabbed a metal pole adorned with a rubberized hook.

Larry's heart raced in his chest. His palms dampened while Swanson deftly retrieved the harlequin costume from the wall. "Here you go, my boy."

Larry's breath shuddered when he finally grasped the suit. It was even softer and smoother than he'd dreamt it would be. He caressed and turned the fabric in his hands, then raised it to his face and took in its musty velveteen scent. He gently worked the lace embroidery between his fingertips and let out a tiny groan as he became slightly erect.

"You have a show this weekend?" Swanson asked.

"What?" Larry came to, ecstasy interrupted.

"I asked, do you have a show this weekend?"

"No. Lorenzo has a performance. *The*...performance," Larry replied.

"Ah, yes." Swanson chuckled. "Well, then, I suppose *Lorenzo* will be needing these for the big show." The old shopkeeper produced three small silver tins and set them on the counter. "They had black and white. I hope you've got some red left at home."

"I do." Larry snatched the grease paint and shoved it in his pocket.

"Alright then. I'm sure there's enough here to cover those too." Swanson unbanded and smoothed the crumpled pile of bills. "Good luck this weekend, and don't forget what I said, Larry...about art and the artist."

Larry stared into one of the ivory buttons that adorned the costume's chest. Gold thread snaked through four perfectly carved holes, binding it to the material. Then he gazed up at the old shopkeeper. "Everyone wants to tell me how to entertain. What I should and shouldn't do. They think they know art, but they just want to put me and Lorenzo in a box so they can feel safe in their mundane lives. I'm not going to let that happen, Mr. Swanson. They're not going to put us in a box."

Larry turned and shuffled out of the antique shop, head down, again focused on the suit. The tiny brass bell tinkled when the door swung shut behind him.

Larry was home by dinnertime. He tugged the frayed brown cord that dangled in the entryway of his tiny one-bedroom apartment, and a bare light bulb came to life overhead in its ceramic socket. Cockroaches scattered under the worn floor moulding, back into the walls.

The smell of musty laundry and week-old lo-mein noodles permeated the living room. Piles of clothes and empty white boxes littered the floor. No matter. He hugged the costume close and rubbed his nose in it. It was soft, and the musty funk of Mr. Swanson's shop still clung to it. He rushed through the tiny galley kitchen, where a sink full of dirty pans endured water torture beneath a dripping faucet. He flung open the bathroom door and flipped the light switch.

The fluorescent bulb over the sink flickered and buzzed. It cast pale light across the black and white tiles, the pink porcelain bathtub, and the mold stains that crept from the corners of the ceiling.

Larry smelled the costume again. He breathed deep and committed the scent to memory. Then he dropped to his knees and laid it in the tub. He shoved a black rubber stopper in the drain and reached for the red plastic can that sat next to the pink porcelain toilet. Its contents sloshed as he pulled it across the floor. The black cap clicked and clicked until it finally came loose. Fumes wafted up and filled the tiny bathroom while Larry bathed the costume in mid-grade unleaded. He snatched the plunger from behind the toilet. Gripping its crusty rubber bell, he used the handle as a stir-stick. The costume snaked and writhed in the amber fuel. Larry watched it cruise through tiny rainbow trails, guiding it with the plunger handle. His eyes and nostrils burned. He nearly fell over, but caught himself on the tub's edge. He carefully stood and opened the tiny window next to the tub.

It was ready. He yanked the black stopper and the fuel gurgled down the drain. The costume lay soaked, and Larry carefully picked it up and draped it gently over the shower curtain rod to dry. His head was spinning, and he stumbled back into the kitchen, clinging to the doorframe.

He swung open the fridge door and light cascaded across the tiny apartment. He grabbed a carton of milk and sniffed. All he could smell was gasoline. He took a swig and discovered it had barely turned from what little he could taste. He pulled out two small red and white boxes by their wire handles and found a plastic fork in the sink. He turned on the faucet and let the water run from brown to clear. The dirty pans shifted and clattered, making just enough room for his hands. He scrubbed with a bar of *Lava* soap until his knuckles felt like they had been sand-blasted. He raised his palms up and took a whiff. Not gone, but better. The fumes still permeated the tiny apartment though. Grabbing his Chinese, he flopped on the brown couch that dominated the center of the apartment. A small glass table stood beside it, along with a thirty-two-inch flat-screen television he'd found at the thrift shop. Some of the colors were off, but it was still watchable.

Suddenly, there was a knock at the door. It made Larry's heart jump, and his pork fried rice tumbled to the floor. *Who the hell would be visiting me?*

"Larry? Larry, are you in there?" an old woman's voice came from the other side of the door.

It was Mrs. Osterman.

"Damnit," Larry grunted and scooped rice off the floor back into the tiny box. "Hold on, Mrs. Osterman, I'm making dinner. I'll be right there!" he shouted at the door. He ran over and cracked the door open. Mrs. Osterman was on the other side. She was all white hair and concern, in a plaid nightgown.

"Larry, there's a smell in my apartment. It smells like a gas leak. I think we should call the fire department."

"No!" Larry blurted out. "No, there's no gas leak, Mrs. Osterman. We don't even have gas in the building. Everything is electric."

"Oh. It is? Well, I suppose you're right, Larry. But then what is that smell? I was sitting and looking through my magazines and it's giving me a horrible headache. Maybe I should just call the landlord."

Larry's fingers dug into the door edge and the pit of his stomach knotted. Mrs. Osterman lived alone. She had no one but her collection of porcelain dogs. She once told Larry they were "art." But they weren't art. They were garbage. They were garbage that she stared at and talked to while she watched the evening news and the banal sitcoms she nodded off to at a blaring volume that kept Larry awake. Many of those nights, he wondered why death seemingly forgot to drop by her apartment each week.

"No, Mrs. Osterman, don't call the landlord. It was me. It's my apartment."

"What?" She raised her hands to her chest.

"It's my dinner. I microwaved some old Chinese food. It must have been bad. It smells terrible. I was trying to air out my place when you knocked."

"Oh, Larry." She shook her head. "You shouldn't eat the ethnic food."

"Excuse me?"

"The ethnic food," she repeated. "No one knows what they put in it. It's horrible for the indigestion. If you're hungry, I can always make you a nice casserole."

"Casserole?"

"Yes. With tuna." She smiled.

"I have to go now, Mrs. Osterman. I'm going to open the windows and get the smell out. Everything is fine. Goodnight."

"Goodni—"

Larry shut the door, cutting her off.

"Nosy old bat," he mumbled and grabbed his "ethnic food" containers. He flung open the windows, then sank into the couch and flipped on the *Mummenschanz* DVD he had borrowed from the library. It was three months overdue, but no one ever came calling. It no longer mattered. Larry watched the strange mimes perform on the discolored TV screen, and shoved pork fried rice into his mouth. His imagination raced with flights of fancy; Lorenzo would finally become one of the greats. No more pizza parlor gigs. No more wretched drudgery at Carl's shop. He would finally exist in the eyes of the world. This was going to be a consummate performance.

Larry's Kia Rio halted and backfired in front of a fancy mailbox. The address he'd received led him to a massive new housing development. He peered out the passenger window through the dried bird shit and wrinkled his nose at the gargantuan house looming above a paved driveway. It was garish, with stone facades, and bold wainscoting over the windows. The vinyl siding was a slightly different tone of beige than the house next to it. It was a soulless monument that stood on a tenth-acre of grass, among twenty-seven other soulless monuments on their own tenth-acres.

Unwilling to perform hungry, Larry dug into the stained paper bag in his passenger seat and pulled out a chicken sandwich. He unwrapped it and took a bite. It was salty, and a bit of grease ran from the corner of his mouth. He carefully dabbed it with a napkin, checking for traces of paint. It was clean, and that made him happy. He took a swig of diet soda, and tossed the sandwich remains atop a small mountain of wrappers and plastic bags that had entombed the Kia's passenger floor mat. He adjusted the rearview, and a painted face stared back at him. "Fi-diddle-da-dee. Time for Cayden's party."

The car door slammed shut, and Lorenzo pranced up the driveway.

"Tim. Tim! Where are the organic juice boxes?" Cindy called out. She was elbow-deep in the big blue cooler, sifting through ice and bottles of Perrier.

"I dunno, Cindy, did you look in the basement? I'm putting out the *veggie* snacks you asked me for. Do kids even eat these? They look like cardboard." Tim scattered small bags on a folding table adorned with a plastic tablecloth. "I think we have some Kool-Aid in the pantry I can make."

Cindy marched over to her husband and grasped his wrist. "Kool-Aid?" she whispered through clenched teeth. "Kool-Aid? Tim, nobody lets their kids drink Kool-Aid. I'm not dealing with that kind of judgement today."

"Okay." Tim yanked his hand away.

"No, it's not okay," Cindy continued. "I invited the moms from my book club. I have to see them every three weeks, and I'm not going to be labeled with that kind of reputation. This party has been enough of a nightmare to put together. People are arriving and we're still setting up. And I thought the clown was supposed to be here already."

"Wait. You hired a clown?" Tim scoffed.

"Yes. Why?"

"I think Cayden and his friends are a little old for clowns. Besides, they're irritating. Couldn't you get that video game truck or something?"

"No!" Cindy turned bright red. "No, I couldn't. Tim, do you realize how goddamn hard it was to find *anything?* Nobody even had birthday parties last year, and now it's impossible to find anything without reserving six months in advance. Jessica is bringing Brayden today. Do you know what she had when we went to Brayden's party, Tim? A bounce house. A fucking...bounce house."

"Yup, sounds like quite the arms race."

Cindy huffed and rolled her eyes. "You don't get it, Tim. But what I *need* you to get are the juice boxes."

"Jesus Christ," Tim replied.

"Don't argue."

"No, Cynthia. I think your clown is here." Tim pointed behind her.

Cindy turned and saw a pudgy clown in a frilly black and white costume skipping across her back yard. He looked about six feet tall, and slightly too large for his outfit. His ankles and wrists peeked out from the cuffs, and his face was painted black and white, with slightly smeared red lips. Her guests kept their distance as he advanced. She stood, paralyzed, until he was a few feet from her. "Um, Laurence?" she asked. He smiled a mouthful of yellow teeth. "Hi, I'm Cindy, and this is my husband, Tim."

"Lorenzo! Harlequin extraordinaire! At your service to be sure, madam." Lorenzo bowed and rolled his wrists with flourish. "Now, where is the young master?"

"Oh, Cayden. He's over there with his friends." Cindy pointed to the circle of kids congregated at the far end of the yard. "Why don't you introduce yourself? I'm sure he'll enjoy it." Her voice stammered a bit.

"Yeah. Maybe some clown tricks will get their faces unglued from those screens," Tim quipped.

The smile vanished from Lorenzo's face. "I'm a harlequin. Not a clown. Sire."

Tim chuckled to himself. "Okay...Lorenzo. You look like a clown to me, but whatever you say."

"We're different. You'll see." Lorenzo nodded at Tim, his tone ominous. Then he pranced away toward the children.

"Where the hell did you find that guy? He smells like he slept in a junkyard," Tim whispered at Cindy, incredulous.

"Craigslist," she replied.

Lorenzo made his way across the perfectly manicured lawn, smiling at the vapid families who paid more attention to their phones than one another. They were completely unaware a true artisan was in their midst, but they'd see soon enough. He carefully approached the circle of children and listened to their conversations about video games and social media. Cayden, with his angular haircut and expensive clothes, boasted about the number of likes on his latest skateboarding video.

Tween opulence curdled Lorenzo's blood, and it was time to set the stage.

"Hello, children." Lorenzo smiled and twisted his head.

"Eeew. Cayden, your mom got a CLOWN!" a girl in rhinestone sunglasses jeered.

"Mom. Mom!" Cayden stood with one hand on his hip. "You hired a stupid clown for my birthday? Lame. I wanted the video game truck!"

"Video games rot brains." Lorenzo flashed his teeth, and watched some of the kids jump back. "I'm not a clown. I'm a harlequin. And you're in for a treat."

"Oh yeah, clown? What kind of treat?" Cayden crossed his arms and projected false bravado.

Lorenzo put a hand on his shoulder. "You kids want to have some *fun* with your parents? See a shocking performance they'll never forget? You can put their faces on your little screens for posterity." He snatched another boy's phone and hurled it into some nearby bushes.

"Hey! My mom just got me that!" the boy cried and ran off to retrieve the device.

Cayden smirked. "Okay. Let's see what you got." The rest of the kids smiled and nodded along.

"Very good, young master. You're about to witness true art." Lorenzo patted Cayden's shoulder. "Now, follow me."

Lorenzo marched back toward the house with a spry gait, Cayden and the other children a few paces behind. They were in for the show of a lifetime, but like any master performer, he knew the audience had to be warmed up. Their tiny brains required cajoling from the electronic trance they had grown accustomed to. Perhaps some juggling? Shadow puppets? No, this wouldn't be a repeat of the pizza parlor. Animatronic rodents weren't going to steal his thunder today.

"Gather round, children, and witness the mystery and merriment of harlequin!" Lorenzo announced, arms over his head.

"Ooh, the clown show is starting. Everyone, the show is starting!" Cindy called to the guests, and ushered them into carefully structured rows of white plastic folding chairs.

Lorenzo stood motionless and silent. He surveyed his audience. More opulence. Some stared expectantly, while others compulsively checked screens as their offspring did. He was about to awaken them from their entitled slumber, and demonstrate how a true artist could change lives through spectacle.

First, the dance.

Lorenzo engaged his body in the lithe motions he had rehearsed so many times. His limbs moved effortlessly within the velveteen confines of the suit. They were as one, and each pirouette and adagio told a bittersweet story of lost love and redemption.

"What the hell is this?" a dad in a pink golf shirt said to his wife, and snorted. "He's just flopping around on the ground and waving his arms. Is he having a seizure or something?"

Paunchy detractor, I'll impress you yet. Lorenzo contorted and twisted his body harder, staring at Cindy. *Yes, she is mine now.* He could see the dance had enraptured Cayden's mother. Her eyes darted frantically back and forth at the other guests. A bead of sweat ran down her face and dissolved into the pearls clasped around her neck.

Now, the temptation of lust, and the transgression of desire.

Lorenzo snatched a handful of apples from a bowl labelled organic on the nearby table of snacks. He again locked eyes with Cindy. He could feel their connection. It radiated across the yard, and sent a burst of heat through his body. He polished each apple on the crotch of the costume in slow deliberate motions. Gaze fixed on the mother, he saw Cayden and the other children laughing, phones raised, in the corner of his eye. *They're all mine now. I've captured their fancy.*

"Dude, Cayden. Are you recording this? He's totally perving on your mom!" a boy shouted.

"Recording? Bro, I'm *live streaming it.*" Cayden snickered and turned the phone on himself. "What's up, fam? Cayden here. Check out this weirdo. Clown creeper is freaking out my mom and all these parents. Make sure to like and subscribe!" Cayden put the focus back on Lorenzo as the harlequin rubbed apples on the crotch of his suit in a crass display. He moaned and stared, slack-jawed, at Cindy. The parents in the audience whispered to one another, their faces twisted in disgust and confusion.

"What the hell is going on here?" Tim stepped through a sliding glass door into the yard, his arms filled with more snacks. He approached the performance, small yellow bags cascading from his arms onto the lawn.

The husband returns. The lovers are found out.

Lorenzo grinned at Tim and juggled the apples, still warm from his loins.

"Hey! I saw what you were doing. Get the hell off my property!"

"But, sire." Lorenzo could feel Tim's breath on his face, and continued juggling. "I am but a simple mischief maker. If I've offended or upset the lady of the house, you have my deepest apologies."

"Get the hell out! Otherwise I'm gonna knock your teeth down your throat." Tim slapped the apples to the ground. Cindy rushed into the confrontation.

Lorenzo's eyes narrowed, and he tilted his head, sheepish. "Alas, I've apologized. And yet the master of the house says I must depart before the grand finale."

"Dad, what are you doing? Get out of the shot!" Cayden yelled.

"Tim, wait." Cindy grabbed her husband's shoulder. "We don't need a lawsuit."

"No, Cindy. This freak has got to go."

"C'mon, Dad! My viewer count is going down. You're ruining my birthday stream!" Cayden whined.

"Just let him finish. Cayden and his friends like it. Please. We're having cake in a few minutes anyway."

Tim shook his head and huffed. "Fine. Whatever. I'll go get the cake out of the freezer." He stomped back toward the house, muttering to himself.

"The lady of the house prevails," Lorenzo grinned. "Your feminine wiles have given renewed life to this performance."

Cindy glared at him. "Whatever. I just want my kid to not hate me. Please do the finale and wrap up. I'll pay you out front after we have the cake." She headed back behind the folding chairs.

"This performance may be brief, but we are heartened by a finale none of you shall forget!" Lorenzo announced to the remaining parents. "Where is the young master on his birthday? Prince Cayden. Come forward."

"You gonna go up there, Cayd? Maybe he's gonna grab your ass," Brayden mocked, eliciting laughter amongst the kids.

"Pfft, whatever. I'm not scared of him. Here, make sure you keep streaming. If he does something weird, I'm gonna kick him *in tha' nuuuuuuts. WAAAAAH!"* Cayden stuck his face in the smartphone camera, waggling his tongue for his anonymous viewership.

Cayden sauntered up to Lorenzo. "Okay, what are we doing? This better bring the hype for my stream. You pranking my mom was pretty sick, but I want people to go *crazy*."

"Oh, it will." Lorenzo chuckled. "Come this way. I'll explain the finale so you're ready." Lorenzo walked Cayden farther into the lawn out of earshot.

"I brought a very special guest to your party, Cayden. Would you like to meet her?" Lorenzo asked.

"Where is she?" Cayden smirked.

"Right here." Lorenzo drew a length of green bungee cord from the sleeve of his costume. Delicate rainbow-colored kerchiefs were tied at various lengths on what seemed like an endless cord that he fed from somewhere in his suit. "This is Minerva, my pet snake."

"It looks like a rope with some napkins on it."

Lorenzo sighed. "Cayden, don't offend Minerva. You'll be performing with her in the grand finale."

"Um, I dunno." Cayden hesitated and began a slow retreat.

"You're not afraid of snakes, are you, Cayden? You wouldn't want to disappoint your friends and all your adoring fans. Not at this, the apex of the performance. You don't want them to think you're a coward, do you?"

"No, dude, you're just...you're weirding me out."

"Ah!" Lorenzo smiled and jutted a finger into the air. "Then let me assuage your fears. You shall simply dance with Minerva and I for a moment. Then I'll give everyone a big surprise and we will laugh at the looks on their faces." Lorenzo pursed his lips and touched the finger to them with an impish look. "Do you agree? Your friends are getting impatient."

Cayden looked back at his crew. They watched him through their phones and urged him on with thumbs up. "Okay. Yeah, let's do this. But it better be good."

"It will be so wonderful," Lorenzo whispered.

Cayden and Lorenzo approached the crowd. Minerva dangled lifeless from the suit sleeve, her vibrant colors contrasting against the black and white fabric.

"The moment you've awaited. The finale!" Lorenzo flared his arms once more, Minerva flopping against the grass.

The partygoers were silent.

Lorenzo danced and twirled, and swung Minerva like a lasso. He caressed the handkerchiefs and stretched the bungee cords, feigning motions like a snake. "Dance, Cayden. This is your moment. Do not disappoint Minerva or the onlookers!"

Cayden rolled his eyes and bopped back and forth in an off-time kilter. "This is lame."

Lorenzo danced in circles around the boy, and twirled the bungee cords until the child was wrapped in bright colors. The guests stared puzzled at the bizarre scene unfolding before them.

Suddenly, Lorenzo stopped.

"Is that it?" Cayden asked.

"Oh no. Now it's time for the surprise." Lorenzo shook his head, his mouth stretched into an oversized, demonic smile. "I forgot to tell you what kind of serpent Minerva is." He watched a look of terror wash across the child's face.

"What kind?" Cayden gulped.

Lorenzo leaned close and whispered into Cayden's ear, "She's...a...*boy constrictor.*"

The harlequin grimaced and yanked the bungee cord tight. Cayden screamed, and Lorenzo tightened his grip. He dragged the struggling child back from the frightened audience.

The party erupted into confused panic.

"Oh my god, what is this?" Cindy shouted. "Tim!"

Tim maneuvered a large sheet cake through the door and dropped it at the sight of his son captured by a maniacal clown. White and blue frosting splattered the gray patio stones.

"Now for the moment of transformation!" Lorenzo bellowed. He turned his gaze on the father. The look of horror in the man's eyes was magnificent when the Zippo lighter appeared from the pocket of the costume. Tim broke into a sprint, but he was a second too late. "SURPRISE!"

Lorenzo felt the heat when the lighter ignited his suit. Cayden shrieked when the flames engulfed them. He clutched the boy tighter to his chest and whirled. They danced together, the oxygen from their swift movements feeding the blaze. He heard the parents scream, and saw guests frantically tap their phones. Cindy cried out to God, but Lorenzo knew he wouldn't answer. The children just stared in disbelief, still pointing their phones at the fiery spectacle. Their reactions were exquisite.

Exquisite also was the pain. The flames lapped at Lorenzo's painted face and ignited the grease. He closed his eyes and the fire engulfed his head. Cayden thrashed and squirmed, but was no match for his strength and the serpent's coils. He smelled their flesh cook. Soon they would be fused together as one and transformed. Only then would the performance be complete. A work of pure art.

A loud hiss erupted, and Lorenzo was wracked with pain when cold smoke billowed over his scorched body. "Cayden! Cayden!" Tim screamed and threw the fire extinguisher to the ground. Lorenzo's back hit the ground, and he cried in anguish when Tim ripped away the scorched elastic and peeled the boy away from him. The warm afternoon air stung bone and raw flesh. "You fucking freak! What did you do to my son? Cayden? *CAYDEN?* Jesus Christ, somebody help us!"

No! The performance isn't over. You've ruined everything. Give me back the boy. Give him back!

Tim watched the clown writhe on the ground and reach for them. Most of his face was gone. His left eye had burst in its socket, and his exposed jaw gnashed in what looked like some horrific attempt to speak. The black and white suit was scorched to his flesh, and what remained of it clung to him like melted black cellophane. Tim clutched onto Cayden, the boy was in shock, and Cindy howled in anguish next to them.

Lorenzo heard sirens approaching, and the father's shoe rushed at his face. Then nothing.

Lorenzo opened his eye. Everything was blurry, and he couldn't move. A white room came into partial focus. There were periodic beeps and the thrumming pulse of machinery. A television squawked in the distance.

"Goddamned freakshow. They should have let him die in the ambulance for what he did to that boy."

From the corner of his vision, Lorenzo made out two dark blue forms—men—standing just outside a doorway.

"You know they can't do that, Dan. They gotta try to save him.."

"So he can spend the rest of his life in a nuthouse, eating three meals a day with basic cable on our tax dollars? They should have made an exception."

"Those poor people. That kid was in surgery for five hours, and he's gonna need more grafts. His mom was just crying out in the hallway the whole time. Inconsolable."

"Now a follow-up on the bizarre tragedy that took place yesterday at a local child's birthday party…"

The television wrenched Lorenzo's attention away from the men outside the door. He could just barely make out a picture of himself on the TV behind an anchorwoman in a red dress.

"Police are guarding the suspect, known only as Lorenzo The Clown, who is in critical condition in the Bayview Memorial ICU. It's still unknown why he set himself and a 12-year-old boy on fire yesterday at a gathering. The horrific scene went viral last night after some guests uploaded videos to social media. Be advised, the following footage we're about to show you is graphic and may be too disturbing for some viewers."

Yes! YES!

Lorenzo vibrated with excitement as his performance played on the television. The flames, the screams. The father had tried to stop it, but now his art was forever memorialized for all to behold. Lying on the ground, smoldering, he feared everything was for naught. But the transformation *had* taken place! The boy, the family, and himself.

The clip ended, and Lorenzo's eyes teared up from relief.

I hope you were watching, Mr. Swanson. Do you see now? You were wrong. You CAN'T separate the art from the artist.

Amidst the wires and equipment, beneath a fogged plastic mask, a grin crawled across Lorenzo's face where his lips used to be.

Mr. Giggles

by Carson Fredriksen

CATHY HAD LEFT THE home of her cruel father for the last time over three hours ago. Cathy's father, Norman, found himself not caring in the slightest.

He was too preoccupied with the task of going through her room. He was planning on either selling her leftover possessions for what measly little money they were worth or simply piling them into his pickup truck and burning them all in a huge bonfire out in the woods.

With beer in hand, Norman sauntered down the heavily stained carpeted stairs towards the room he tried to avoid whenever possible.

It was never his idea to have a child. If reality ever came with a reset button, he'd be the first one in line. He'd travel back to his college days and tell himself to never talk to a woman while he was under the influence. It'd only lead to an accident nine months later.

"Although," he spoke to himself, now relishing the ability to do so without fear of looking like a lunatic, "I did luck out by keeping custody of her after the divorce proceedings."

Not that it helped much. For the past 10 years, she would always spend time with her mother or find some excuse to accompany her when she went to get her hair done or headed to the shop for a single carrot.

He never laid a hand on her though. When people saw marks, they talked. Someone could only say they fell down the stairs or ran into a wall so many times before it became suspicious.

On the other hand, if you ignored your daughter when she scraped her knee or told her that no plastic surgeon in the country could make her beautiful, there was less to prove. The whole thing just became a "he said, she said" situation. And considering that no one from her school or the police came to his door, it seemed his gambit had paid off.

"Bet she's already on the phone crying to mommy and moaning about what a terrible person I am." Norman finished off the rest of his beverage before he chucked the bottle down the darkened hallway. He didn't feel like doing much more today than going through his daughter's room. A simple broken bottle could wait.

As he turned towards the door, Norman realized that he hadn't heard the shatter of broken glass. In fact, he hadn't heard anything at all. He turned his head to the left and stared down the narrow, darkened hallway. He stared for so long that his eyes slowly made out the forms of the rusty washing machine and the pale orange laundry basket waiting nearby like a loyal servant. Making sure he didn't look away for a second, Norman reached out and flicked the light switch.

The bottle lay in front of the laundry machine without so much as a scratch on it. Norman felt his arm drop limply to his side. He had never had a problem coming down to the basement, but now it seemed like invisible eyes were watching him from the walls.

"N-Never realized how quiet this place is." Norman tried to laugh off his worries, but that creeping sensation of being watched remained.

He shook his head in a frenzy, wondering if he should've brought a case of beer down there instead of a single soldier, before he flung open the door and stepped inside.

Norman certainly wasn't expecting to find anything that could make him set for life in terms of riches. But based on what he read about how much certain nostalgic toys were going for these days, he figured there'd be at least something he could exchange for some extra beer money.

All he could see was the small single bed in the corner, a plethora of horse pictures plastered on the walls, and several stuffed animals all lined up against one side of the room. Their black glossy eyes stared him down. Even when he moved over to the bed, he felt like their lifeless eyes were following his every move.

His field of vision suddenly came upon an old-fashioned easel in the corner. He couldn't recall ever buying Cathy one, nor could he recall his ex begging him to get one for her. But these questions were soon halted when he saw what was drawn on the front.

A figure's wobbly form nearly covered the entirety of the board and was colored in a purple kind of chalk, although no such instruments could be seen anywhere. It possessed the usual shapes of arms, legs, and a head, but it was missing any distinguishable features that made up a face.

All it had was an army of smiles covering its body.

While all the smiles were comprised of normal-looking teeth, the figure's actual smile was made up of what looked to be tightly packed rows of razors.

A single purple line spewed out of its mouth and made its way to the top, where a single name was present.

Mr. Giggles.

"Man! That kid must've been fucked in the head to make something like that!" Norman sneered as he grabbed the easel with both hands and dragged it around. The shrill screeching drilled harshly into his ears, but it was a small price to pay to not look at that thing for much longer.

But when he finally had the foul thing out of his sight, Norman soon found himself staring at something that was equally baffling.

Eight pieces of lined paper decorated the majority of the space. Four were taped together in one line while the others were taped in the next line as if they were a part of the same bizarre chorus line. As if he were reading a novel, his eyes found their way to the first page and began reading the slightly skewed scribbling.

It's been three hours since Mom drove away from the house. I never realized how much she mattered to me until I walked into the living room and saw how sparse it was. Dad's gone out of the house. He'll stink of cigarettes, sweat, and beer once he comes through the door. You may forget a lot of things, but smells are pretty much forever.

I also can't shake the feeling that someone's watching me. It's always been that way since we moved in here two years ago, but sitting alone in my room has made this feeling stronger. I'm facing the closet because I can't bear to turn my back to it.

Norman felt like a colony of insects was crawling on his back as he turned his gaze toward the closet.

The doors were open, exposing a lone hanger swinging gently by itself.

"Goddamn kid," he muttered to himself, now wishing he had a glass of scotch in hand. "Even when she's gone, she still has to get to me."

He turned his attention back to the first page. Realizing that nothing else new had been written, he looked at the adjacent scrap of paper. Now even more text was added while strange black dots covered the side of the page and appeared to have dripped downwards as if the shapes were bleeding.

I hear laughing, or is it more like giggling, coming from the closet at night. I don't know how I missed it these past years, considering I'm not much of a heavy sleeper. But last night I awoke to hear the strange noise which was definitely coming from across my bed. It didn't sound like one kind of laugh though. It was almost as if there were a whole crowd of people stuffed into my closet and laughing up a storm.

But there's no way anyone can be in there. I have a hard enough time fitting into it with all my clothes and toys packed in there.

I can't recall how long I stared at the two closed closet doors, almost expecting one of them to open slowly at any minute. But the next thing I knew, it was morning and a single piece of paper was at the foot of my bed. I knew for sure I hadn't written it.

It was then that Norman noticed the adjacent page stood out for two reasons. The first was that the font was extremely neat, as if it were stolen straight out of an 18th century nobleman's handbook. The second was the color of the text.

All of his daughter's entries were written in a light blue color that came from the head of a pencil crayon. The text on this page was jet black, again looking like it had been written with a feather and a bottle of ink.

And he sure as hell didn't keep anything like that in his house.

"*DO NOT BE AFRAID.*"

Norman didn't know much. Hell, he'd gladly admit his IQ was below average. However, he knew that someone or something writing something ominous like that would certainly make him afraid.

The fourth page was the last one in the row. But now it looked to be a conversation instead of a journal entry.

"What do I call you?"

"YOU MAY CALL ME MR. GIGGLES, BECAUSE I AL-WAYS WEAR A SMILE ON MY FACE AND UP MY SLEEVES."

"What do you look like?"

A series of black dots decorated the next line as if Mr. Giggles was at a loss for words, or had a massive case of writer's block.

"I'M AFRAID I CANNOT SHOW YOU."

"Why's that?"

"BECAUSE THEN YOU WOULD EITHER DIE OF FRIGHT OR GO COMPLETELY MAD. SURELY YOU DON'T WANT THAT AT SUCH A YOUNG AGE, DO YOU?"

"Can you at least draw yourself on your easel? Would that be okay?"

There wasn't anything else written after that, though based on the image on the back, it was safe to assume that Mr. Giggles worked on his end of the bargain. Norman could still feel those smiles float through the papers and lock onto his body.

"I'll just read a little more," Norman said, noticing his voice breaking slightly, "then I'll burn this whole damn thing right in this room."

The next page was written in the same conversational style as the previous one. Now, though, his daughter's words were written with a blue pen and had the penmanship of a high school senior.

"TELL ME, CHILD, WHY DOES THAT BEAST THAT YOU CALL 'DAD' TREAT YOU SO BADLY?"

"Because he still sees me as an accident. My parents got together basically because my mom got pregnant with me. My dad thought he could make it work. But soon he realized that he wasn't a settle down and raise a family kind of man. But somehow he got custody of me after the divorce, and now I only get to see her on holidays and every other weekend."

"DOESN'T IT SEEM CRUEL THAT A MAN CAN TREAT YOU AS BAD AS HE WANTS AND YET ISN'T LOCKED UP IN A CELL OR HANGING FROM A NOOSE?"

"Once I graduate, though, I'm out of here! He can try to guilt trip me all he wants, but I won't let him control me anymore!"

"WELL I'M HAPPY FOR YOU, CATHY. YOU DESERVE BETTER AND I KNOW YOU'LL FIND IT SOMEWHERE OUT THERE."

"Are you coming with me?"

"I'M AFRAID NOT. I'VE HAUNTED THIS HOUSE EVER SINCE IT WAS CONSTRUCTED OVER FORTY YEARS AGO. I'VE HELPED MANY CHILDREN WITH ANY WISHES THEY WANTED."

"I just want to be with Mom again."

"YOU WILL BE. I DON'T NEED TO DO ANYTHING ABOUT THAT. BUT TELL ME, WHAT ABOUT YOUR FATHER?"

"As bad as he is, he does provide a roof over my head. I can't have anything bad happen to him now."

"WHO SAYS IT NEEDS TO BE TODAY? WHAT WOULD HAPPEN TO HIM ON THE DAY YOU FINALLY MOVE OUT?"

Norman suddenly felt all the heat being sucked out of the room and the walls seemed to have a thousand eyes pouring into his stout figure.

"S-She's just pathetic," Norman whispered, feeling his chest constrict so much he thought his heart was going to give out from exhaustion at any second. "H-Having to resort to imaginary friends to do someone's dirty work. Pathetic! She could've just come up to me and said it herself."

The next page soon followed with a single sentence in the middle.

"WHERE WOULD THE FUN BE IN THAT, NORMAN?"

Now Norman was sure that a heart attack was imminent.

"YOUR DAUGHTER SURELY IS CREATIVE," the text on the next piece of paper read, still situated in the center as if it were begging for attention. ***"BUT WITH WHAT I HAVE PLANNED FOR YOU, I DON'T THINK SHE'D HAVE THE STOMACH TO WATCH."***

No other text was on the final page. There was only a face, one with a giant smile and two smaller smiles where its eyes should've been.

For the briefest of moments, Norman was fused to the floorboards. Then he found himself grabbing the easel with both hands and flinging it across the room. Specks of plaster fell from the walls while the legs of the easel broke in two.

He raised his right leg and stomped on every square inch of the easel that hadn't been damaged. The pages became crinkled and dirty from the soles of his shoes while more and more wooden pieces flew around as if he were trapped in a wooden snow globe.

Norman was about to turn around and run back up the stairs to get his hammer when he caught sight of the other side of the easel.

The chalk illustration now showed a man staring at a broken easel on the wall, his mouth drawn in a scowl. Behind him, a figure stood in front of a closed door. It towered over the man by a good foot and its body was covered with jagged smiles.

Norman's mouth hung open. His rage had been completely extinguished, leaving nothing but an empty shell that didn't dare turn around.

He was so focused on his thoughts that he failed to notice an empty beer bottle roll into the room and stop by the back of his feet. Nor did he hear the door shut behind him, even though no wind was present.

Wall to Wall

by J.L. Royce

THE FURNITURE HAD BEEN relegated to the dumpster; the baseboards were haphazardly piled in the hallway. Fred stood poised at the threshold of the living room floor, slapping a crowbar in his gloved hand, surveying the expanse of worn, filthy carpeting. He strode to the far corner of the desolate space.

"Let's do this." Fred grinned at Beth, alien in her respirator and yellow rubber gloves.

"My hero," came her muffled response.

She was the adventurous one, hiking the Aztec Trail to Machu Picchu and bicycling to Alaska. But Fred was the dreamer, and his latest dream was this old Midwestern house.

The carpet was twenty-something and badly aged. Once a bland beige, the years had left it a muddy mustard mess. The structure was old enough to have finished wood floors beneath the carpet, not just a rough subfloor. Beth remained unconvinced, lobbying for modern flooring instead of refinishing.

"Moment of truth," said Fred, working the sharp edge of the bar under the tack strip at the wall to loosen it. "Hidden hardwood beauty, or not..."

Locking his fingers under the fabric, he leaned back and heaved mightily, ripping away a four-foot-wide strip of carpet, the thin wood edging giving way with a shriek of nails.

"That's right, you bitch…" Fred grunted and waddled backward, tugging as he went. As he strained to expose the disintegrating under-pad that lurked beneath, a miasma of mildew wafted out.

"It's not the house's fault," said Beth. She sat down beside the exposed area. "This *is* awful—and I think I see some stains under here."

She methodically pulled up strips and chunks of foam crumbling away from its net backing. "You work so hard at this…painting the walls, stripping the wood trim, and all. I'd be perfectly happy with vinyl plank."

"We can do better than that!" Fred squatted beside her, tearing away the pad to reveal a patch of honey-colored maple flooring.

"Yeah!" He eagerly picked away at the remaining bits, brushing aside the mess. "Traditional oak. This could be beautiful again."

The garbage bag beside Beth slowly filled as she cleared away the debris. "It just feels like this house is taking over our lives."

"Careful with that scraper," Fred warned. "Don't want to ruin the wood!"

Her eyes narrowed and she said in a muffled voice, "You've got all those tack strips to pull up, and all those little holes to fill. Then there are staples and carpet tacks everywhere—"

"No…vinyl…flooring!" Fred ripped away another strip of carpet, then sighed and looked at Beth. "I just want this to be the best possible home for us, for…our family."

"It will be." She smiled. "One step at a time."

"Right." He locked a Vise-Grips on a protruding carpet staple and tugged it out. "See? Easy."

Beth pleaded, "If we just re-carpeted—"

"Wall-to-wall carpeting is awful." Fred confronted his wife. "The average human sheds a *pound and a half* of skin per year. So, in twenty years, the family of four who lived here dumped enough skin to make a whole 'nother person! Then there's all the other filth that settles in. Why would you want more carpeting?"

She snorted into her mask, wiping a strand of brown hair away from her sweating brow. "They didn't spend *all* their time in this room, you know."

"From what the realtor said—and the aroma of this place—I'd say they didn't get out much."

On hands and knees, Beth resumed picking out the remains of the padding, not pausing until she had caught up with Fred's carpet removal.

"I'd hoped to hear some history of the house," she said. "That realtor was pretty vague."

Fred grunted. "Nobody left to talk to. It was sold by the estate—a good deal for us—because everyone in the immediate family's dead."

"Wait—weren't the children still young?"

Fred shrugged. "Beyond that, I didn't ask. Can we get back to work?"

With the passing hours, the atmosphere became stifling despite the open windows. Beth sat up, panting in the heat (having abandoned her mask), and turned to find Fred staring.

"What are you doing?" she asked.

He took a swig from a sweating long neck and offered her one.

"Just admiring the view." He smirked. "You look good in cutoffs and a wet tee."

"This isn't college." She accepted the beer with a surreptitious glance down at the telltale nubbins beneath her damp shirt. After a long swallow, she murmured, "Well, I don't feel very sexy."

"What do you say to a break? A nice shower, then..."

Beth scoffed. "We just have one corner left—if you stop daydreaming, we can finish before dinner."

"Well, you can't fault a guy for respecting beauty." He dropped to one knee and stroked her cheek. "Agreed: finish tearing out the carpet and pad before we stop. Then the union-mandated break for dinner and sex."

Beth sighed. "Who says romance is dead?"

They kissed, then set to work. Fred humming a pop song about booty, ripping carpet to the rhythm. As they worked, they shared plans and dreams, how they would make the old house their own. Her office, his workroom, their bedroom, and perhaps—someday—a nursery for a baby, a cautiously discussed possibility.

"Looks like the wood's ruined over here," Beth said, as they cleared the last of the old carpet away. "It's all black."

Fred set aside the latest load of stripping and nails he had painstakingly removed. Dropping the pry bar, he massaged his aching hands.

"Water damage? Lemme see." Fred knelt beside her.

Beth duck-walked back, pointing. "If the wood was badly stained it could explain why they covered it..."

He scraped away the padding and frowned at the exposed hardwood. "I thought you said it was damaged. There's no sign anything soaked through."

She ran a hand over the floor. "I could have sworn... Maybe a shadow?"

Fred stood. "Maybe you need another beer?"

"No—and neither do you. Let's bag the last of this junk so we can wrap up and make something to eat."

"Just wash up—I'm taking you out to dinner."

Beth sighed. "Oh, that sounds really good. I need a break." She staggered to her feet. "This place...is getting to me."

He frowned down at her bare legs. "You need a shower—your knees are black."

Beth examined herself. "Ew!" She pulled off a glove and rubbed unsuccessfully at the discoloration. "This is awful! You don't suppose they covered the floor because..."

"What?"

She shook her head. "I don't know. It looked like mold...or dried blood?"

"The Cursed Carpet!" Fred laughed. "Come on, it was nothing."

Beth glared at him. "Go get the shower started—let's see how much hot water this place has—I'll be there as soon as I dump this trash."

"Can't wait." Fred winked and strolled away, whistling.

Fred stood in the spray, water sluicing the sweat from his body, and considered the bathroom. The water heater was producing an acceptably hot shower, but the tub he stood in and the vanity beyond were certainly in need of an update. With that much work invested, a new bathroom floor made sense too.

He was studying the mildew on the shower ceiling with mild disgust when he saw the bathroom door open through the translucent curtain. A vague figure entered the room.

"Come on in, babe—the water's fine!" Fred called over the hissing spray. When she didn't respond, he pulled the curtain aside to peek out. Beth drifted past, naked, ignoring him.

"Hey, aren't you coming in?" He leaned out and saw her facing the far corner of the room. She slowly turned to face him; her knees were clean, but a dark discoloration covered her belly.

The stain *moved*: swirling, changing.

Fred blinked and rubbed the water from his eyes, peering without his glasses. The shape on her belly resolved into a man's face, unshaven, his beard merging into Beth's bush.

"What the *fuck*?" When he spoke, the eyes on Beth's belly focused and wandered the room until they found him. The twisted suggestion of a mouth squirmed into a leer.

Beth tottered toward the shower, her face blank. She clumsily lifted one leg and stepped over the edge of the tub to join him. Fred's eyes were drawn to movement on her chest.

Shadows emerged from her cleavage to cover her breasts: children's faces. This was no stain, for the spray of water had no effect on them. Beth raised her other leg, and with a jerk of her hips, stumbled into Fred, clutching him. Her empty eyes locked on his, and her mouth opened, revealing more darkness. Her lips blackened as the shadow spread like spilled ink across her face, animating it with a mask of female features.

"*Hello, dear.*" The voice had been Beth's once, though never before had it filled him with such dread. The mask smiled, and the arms rose to draw him in.

"*I want you so badly.*" The body pressed him, and Fred could feel the children clawing his chest, the male imago working his crotch. "*Are you ready for me?*"

The lips that were no longer Beth's pressed his, her tongue introducing a foetid chill into his mouth. To his horror, it only fueled his arousal. He clawed at the thing's back, hands finding no grip on the wet flesh.

Fred pulled futilely at Beth's hips; but even as he did, some*thing* moving in his groin gripped him, drew him inside her.

The stranger's face drew back from his, dusky lips parting, and smiled.

"*Be mine.*"

Escapism

by Megan Diedericks

DOES THE TREE TRAP the bird, or does the bird trap the tree—making a home of it and taking until there is nothing left to give? Existential questions only lead to crisis, and Willow had enough words swirling around and causing havoc as hurricanes in her mind.

The library had always been her greatest comfort, but since she moved out of her childhood home, it looked foreign. It's a place that is familiar to her, but the shadows are deeper and the edges are sharper. It's the same place her mother taught her the value of words and writing—but her mother was dead now, and the house belonged to her.

Willow walked along the shelves, pulling her fingers over the dust-riddled spines of the books. Her black lace sleeves went along and came back painted brown.

"Hardly anybody ever comes in here anymore."

The unfamiliar voice felt so close to the back of her neck, Willow flinched. They remained standing with their arms behind their back, suit neatly tailored and pressed. They watched intently as Willow turned on her heel, her red eyes smoothing them over.

"Who are...?"

"Wren." They extended a hand. "Your mother hired me to take care of the library."

Willow shook their hand, and her thoughts intensified. The dust on her fingers, now transferred to theirs, pulled her attention back to her crumbling surroundings.

"I hope you don't mind my saying, but I do not believe you are doing a very good job."

Wren's dark eyes smiled at her, the lifted corner of their mouth betraying a pearly, sharp tooth.

"Am I not? Take a closer look."

The settled dust no longer drowned the books. Each bundle of bound pages looked fresh from the printing press. Her hands were also clean, and she knew not which sight was more hallucinatory—the vibrant library or the innocence restored to her hands.

Wren was gone when Willow lifted her head. A slight lacerated breeze cut through the silence, and just when she thought she was alone again, a bony hand rested on her shoulder like it was meant to be there. It was Wren.

Though inclined to pull away from any touch, Willow waited until Wren decided to let go. They gently nudged her to turn, and Willow saw that Wren had a book in their other hand.

"I think you might enjoy this one."

Willow accepted the offering—her second mistake.

"What's it about?"

"Murder, but aren't all books about murder in one way or the other?"

"Not a romance novel," she reasoned.

"Would those *characters* not *kill* for love?"

The way Wren pronounced the words stirred something in the pit of Willow's stomach, and their gaze did not falter until she could think of something to say.

"I suppose they would."

"Give it a read." Their voice was commanding, yet draped in softness.

"Right now?"

"Why not? Do you have something better to do?"

Funeral arrangements and readings of wills along with scornful, watchful eyes was definitely not something better.

"No."

"Wonderful." Wren clapped their hands, and the gas lamps flickered on. "Have a seat."

Willow plopped down onto a sofa, red and velvet—a chair that looked so in place within its out-of-place nature that she began to wonder if it had always been there. She opened the book and read the first sentence.

"I will see you when you get back."

"Get back from..." Willow lifted her head; she was no longer at home. "...where?"

The hardback-book clasped around her wrist, squeezing until no blood could go to and fro—it was a harsh, willful hand. Willow pulled her body away from the grasp; trying to free herself proved to be a nearly impossible task.

Hateful red eyes were burning through her skull, devouring every dark thought and warm memory she ever had. She felt starved and empty, her survival instinct was defeated. She went along with the razors pulling her into the unknown.

Hot liquid showered over her outstretched hand—at first she thought she was bleeding, but when it continued to drip from above, she knew better. She lay alone on barren and dry grounds. The heat boiled her skin, and no amount of saliva was enough for her shriveled autumn-leaf tongue. Her soft features were mirrored with a drooling, feral wolf.

She remained perfectly still, a panicked outcry and a lump of breath caught in her throat. The wolf's growling grew more vicious—it wanted her; she was the little piggy put out to keep the big bad wolf satiated.

In its eyes, she saw the only monster she ever truly knew: herself.

She could not look any longer. She hoped her eyes would see a brighter horizon when she turned her head away from the inescapable danger. As soon as she moved, it was feeding time.

The wolf leaped forward, and its jagged teeth bore into her neck. She felt hot liquid again, and this time she knew she was bleeding.

Horrific screams crescendoed against the library walls when Willow tossed the book across the floor. Her hands instinctively found her neck, wanting to cover up the gaping holes that were not there.

Wren spoke beside her. "Did you like it?"

Willow swallowed the lump in her throat. "I... What just happened?"

Wren shrugged behind the desk they were tapping their black fingernails on. Willow wondered if the beaten-up piece of wood was there when she had walked into the room.

"You read the book in one sitting. You would not even move for a pesky fly."

"What time is it?"

Wren pulled out a golden pocket watch that was safely hidden inside their jacket.

"Night time," they snickered.

"I...I lost the whole day?"

"Night is more fun anyway."

"I have to..."

Wren was standing in front of her, obstructing the space she needed to rise. She did not see them move, nor hear their chair screech against the laminated wooden floors.

"Read this one." Wren placed a new book in her lap.

Willow stood and the book fell to the ground; her face was mere inches from Wren's. Their chests were one forced breath away from touching. Wren tilted their head to the side, and Willow's pangs of hunger forced her to sit back down. Wren crouched down and held the book up for Willow to take. Reluctantly, she did.

"I need to eat."

"That is what my literature is for—to feed."

"You wrote this?" Willow opened the book.

"Every story is mine, whether I wrote it or not—I am always there."

Willow watched Wren walk over to the first book she had tossed like it was a pot of scalding water. They picked it up, placed it under their arm, and walked away. Willow was perplexed by the last thing they said to her, but the pages were calling her name.

The book weighed heavy in her right hand. At the back of her mind, there was a broken record stuck on the same part of knowledge: *Something is wrong.* But she was wielding a righteous weapon and running toward the enemy.

The blades slammed against each other, one trying to turn the other into an ashen piece of paper. Willow's sword slashed an arm, successfully forcing her enemy to relinquish their weapon. She bent over to pick it up, her chainmail uncomfortably hugging her body. When she rose, among the blinding smoke and licking flames she saw what she had been running from.

The red eyes drew closer—a stumbling figure who held a wound on their stomach together was their owner.

"No..." Willow whispered, dropping both swords in her two-left-footed attempt at escape. The figure was looming over her, gargling words that did not make sense to her ears. She turned on her stomach. Willow scathed her arms as she crawled, and the iron left imprinted patterns on her flesh. The clumsy footsteps never stopped following her, but they did not have to tread for long.

Willow's body froze—she suddenly thought she knew the answer. Flipping herself over onto her back, she forced down the vomit that bubbled to the surface as she looked into the bleeding eyes of that decaying face.

"I'm sorry, I'm so sorry. Please forgive me."

The rotting flesh resembled the fabricated movement of a smile. It shook its head and dug its fingernails into her ankles. Willow's agony was heard among all the repeating and never-ending war crimes.

The monster pulled her back into the middle of the aftermath. Willow tried to weaken its grasp with kicking feet, but nothing can lessen guilt. She accepted the nightmare, and turned her head to the side, hoping that reality was waiting over the horizon.

She saw the two swords she had lost laying in a cross that was not pointing at her. The creature swept one of the blades off the ground; it hissed while being dragged across the grain. The clawing skeleton-arms of her memory lifted the sword above its head and plunged it downward—first, Willow's chest was penetrated. Parts of her heart clung to the double-edged sword as it went through her stomach.

No amount of strong, healthy vocal cords could give voice to her pain. The blood welled up in her mouth, threatening to dribble down her cheeks. Her world was painted red when she slammed the book shut. Once again, she tossed the horrors away from her grasp.

Wren caught it this time. Their other hand had another book ready to be forcefully glued to Willow's hands.

"No...no, no, no." She was crying—knowledge of your transgressions is a heavy burden to carry. "I don't want to read anymore."

"This is the last book," Wren promised. "One more, then you can leave if you wish to."

They took a step closer, the book pointed right at the villain.

"Is this Hell? Am I in Hell for what I have done?"

Her cheeks were drenched in crimson.

"More of a Purgatory, if you believe in that sort of thing." Wren darted a look towards the shelf where Willow's mother always kept a Bible.

"That is quite an inspiring read. It's packed to the brim with ideas for torture and ways of murder. But this..." Wren put the book on the sofa's armrest, "...is all yours."

Willow's glazed eyes stared at the black book until it felt like the world died outside. There was a knife, which she recognized, illustrated on the cover—this was something she did not want to face, but Wren's ever-present, ever-lingering existence made her know she had no choice.

Willow's shaky hands, bathed in dirt both of this world and of her sin, held the book to her chest. Wren watched her, waiting for her to forgive herself or for her to succumb.

Willow steadily opened the book. She wanted to plead with Wren once more, but they were not who she saw in the library.

Willow's mother, Maya, was giggling over a page in a book she always read when her spirits were lower than the core of the Earth. Willow watched her every move, and Maya was completely oblivious to what lay ahead.

Maya placed the book down on a desk Willow recognized as Wren's, before it became splintered and weathered. Willow followed her mother out into the hallway, every step like there was a shard of glass slowly slicing through the soles of her feet.

Willow noticed her mother pause at her bedroom door; she did not move until Willow took another step. Maya turned the doorknob and entered the room where Willow was waiting for her.

"Oh! I didn't know you were home. Come and give your mother a hug." Maya opened her arms and offered a warm smile.

Willow was painfully frozen in the doorway, and could only stand and watch herself commit the worst of crimes in the name of...vanity.

The kitchen knife tore through Maya's flesh like it was nothing, and only the soft look of forgiveness that faded as her mother's life did was able to tear Willow away from the page.

Silently, she closed the book and kept it on her lap. Her knuckles whitened as her grip tightened around the folds of her mourning dress.

"Why did you show me that?" Her tone was cold and distant.

"Why did you do it?" Wren tried to take the book back, but Willow pried it from their deadly hands.

"Why did you do it?" they repeated, and pushed their hands into their pockets.

They slowly tapped their foot, waiting for her honest answer.

"I...I don't know."

One of the gas lamps gave way, pulling darkness closer to her.

"Try again."

"It's the truth! I just... For money."

That was the answer she convinced herself of, but the truth was, Willow knew her mother would give anything to her—evidently, even her life.

Another pulse of darkness threatened to swallow her.

"One more chance." Wren was holding the remaining lamp.

"I..." She shook her head. "Please don't make me say it."

The glow of the lamp began to fade.

"You said I could leave if I read the book!" she yelled.

"That is true, but if you truly wanted to leave, this would not be happening."

"What happens if the lamp goes out?"

"I think you know."

Wren's shadow stretched out behind them, betraying horns on their head—a shadow Willow would live beneath if she did not confess to her first mistake.

"What happens if I tell you?"

"I will present you with a choice."

"Life or death?"

Wren shook their head. "Those might be the stakes you are used to reading about, but I cannot offer you life. You forfeited that right when you decided to take a life."

Willow remained silent. The wheels turned in her head and the lamp faded more; darkness seemed imminent and insistent.

"Why did you do it?" Wren asked for the last time.

"I wanted to know what it felt like to kill."

The lamps were given new light.

"What did it feel like?"

"Like power, and...I liked that power."

The floorboards cracked, pulsating like they had a heartbeat, and sent splinters flying toward the ceiling. The room tore open, allowing flames to reach into earth. In the distance, wolves were howling—they were threatening to take her away.

Willow pulled her legs to her chest. She was still on the couch and trying her best not to let her withering frame be taken away.

"What are my choices?" she demanded.

"You can go with the wolves and live within the flames, or stay with me and do what I do."

"What exactly is it that you do?"

The howling grew quiet.

"I bring justice to people like us, or..." Wren looked down into the hellfire, "I take them home."

The floor slowly stitched itself back together. Wren did not have to ask to know what Willow's answer was. They gave her the lamp, and she followed them into the darkness of the library.

There, she waited until the walls bled in guilt and a sweaty man ran through the cobwebs. He was hiding behind a bookshelf, rocking himself back and forth. The man's body jerked when he saw her figure standing beside him.

The bird had made a home of the tree, and she would bring others to their knees at her disintegrating roots; her false sense of power could bring horror to life.

Willow leaned down, extending a book toward the man's bulging eyes.

"I think you might enjoy this one."

Fool's Gold

by Elijah M. Newton

"ANOTHER ELIXIR, M'DEAR." SHULTS pushed his glass toward the bar woman.

She poured another whiskey. "Why you still here?"

"Same reason you're still here." He shot his glass. "Where else would we go?"

He was a man, after all. Men are industrious, ambitious, and filled with avarice. There was a time, a very long time ago, that Shults had two silver dollars to rub together.

Traces of his former self remained; ambition and greed, those are things that the endless march of time can never take away from a man. The days when he would bring his wagon into town laden with precious ore and see every face light up with envy were beyond him. Indeed, they were beyond this dying one-horse town. All the young men had left town years ago, heading east for the factories sprouting up like weeds or west to meet their fortunes on the wagon trains.

If Shults were a few years younger, he would have made the trip with them.

"The mountains been good to me. Why forsake them now?" He pushed his glass forward once more.

"Leaving ain't the same thing, dearie." She poured another whiskey. "This one's on the house."

Nowadays, he'd be lucky if he could scrape enough silver from the recesses of the Smokies to afford a shot of the cheapest rot gut. His luck had run out. Shults sighed. He cast his throbbing eyes across the saloon. There were only the typical old drunks, drowning their sorrows only to find them at the bottom of yet another empty bottle. Shults didn't want to be like them. He didn't want to die alone, sitting on the same stool. He'd once been offered a farm and the hand of a functional woman, but the allure of the mountains had been too strong. Or was it his ambition?

A sudden racket disturbed his thoughts. A wild whoopin' and hollerin' came from outside, and before anybody could wonder what it was, a young man blasted through the swinging doors like a firestorm and slammed the largest nugget anybody'd seen in these parts in near a decade onto the bar.

"A bottle of your finest, my dear!" The crust of grime across the young man's face broke as he grinned. "And a round for all these sad sacks!"

"Is that real?" The bar woman eyed the nugget. "I ain't trading booze for painted rocks."

Shults looked down at the bar. He knew all too well exactly what she was referring to.

"It's as real as you or I!"

The bar woman pocketed the stone. Either way, it was good enough to tender. The young man took three deep swigs of the liquor. "C'mon, you geezers." He pranced around the card table. "It's time to celebrate!"

"Where'd you get that gold, boy?" inquired the rustiest of the old men. "Mountains tapped out for the better part of a decade now, eh, Shults?"

"Better part of a decade," Shults murmured.

"Fool's gold, most likely." The second man nodded. He tossed his chips into the pot. "Always fool's gold."

"Not my claim it ain't!" The young man slammed down his empty glass. "A source as fresh as a sixteen-year-old whore."

"Like you know the feel of a woman!" A third man laughed. "Barely got stubble on his chin and a few nuggets of fool's gold and he thinks he's a man!"

"Ever killed before?" The first geezer chortled.

The young man flashed his six-shooter. "You want to be my first?"

"Naw, put that thing away," said the second man. "We was only playing."

"Ah, leave the poor boy alone," the bar woman said. "The nugget's real enough for me. Let him think he found a spot, might do the town some good."

"Enjoy it while it lasts, boy," the third man warned. "Things always dry up around these parts."

The young man tossed another handful of nuggets onto the bar. "By this time tomorrow, you'll all know the name of Jim Maynard!"

He sauntered out of the saloon, no doubt headed toward cheap tricks and trouble.

Shults couldn't lie. He was jealous of the youth. Maynard. He missed the days when it was him bursting through those doors to throw a coin or two. Or did he? Those were the dangerous days in his profession. Days when you could be loud with your gold but had better be quiet about where you'd found it. He'd been a quick draw in his time. He'd had no choice. Too many men had challenged him for his claim or for his haul.

A man's only as good as his draw hand, and Shults had been one of the best.

Not anymore. Not with these hands, shaking from the wear and tear of decades of leaning over a pan in a creek. He didn't have the privilege of being loud anymore. These days when he found anything, he was quiet. Real quiet.

He picked up a chunk of the boy's gold. It was nearly pure. Maynard hadn't just been barking like a young pup. He'd found a fresh vein to tap, the kind of lode that could make a man's future.

Shults returned the nugget to its pile. The frigid coals in his belly stirred, all that remained of a fire he'd long thought dead. He swallowed his last drop and got to his feet. He nodded to the bar woman. He hadn't the strength to stake another claim. But he could still do what needed to be done.

Shults secreted himself among a copse of giant ferns. He'd never seen them grow this big. Everything in this part of the mountains was massive and overgrown. He'd heard stories of the deep woods, ancient woods, up here in the Smokies, but never anything quite like this. Maynard had pitched his camp on the shore of a lake so clear and unnaturally still that Shults could see all the way up from his hiding place that its gravel bed sparkled with gold flakes.

The boy puttered around his camp, tending his fire and settling in for the evening. The sun dipped behind the towering behemoths, casting deep shadows across the forest floor. Shults couldn't help but be amazed at the sight of it all. A beautiful and peculiar country. Silence blanketed the tops of the pines all the way to the soft loamy bed of their needles. Aside from the boy himself, there wasn't a single hint of life. No birds chirping. No deer grazing. No fox hunting. Not even a mosquito. It was perfectly quiet. Perfectly peaceful.

This is God's kingdom on Earth, Shults thought to himself. He bit off a piece of tobacco. There wasn't an ounce of malice toward Maynard in his old heart. Either Shults did this and died, or did this and lived. The only other thing he knew was that spending another season on that bar stool wasn't living.

The sun's golden light deepened to orange, then blood red, and finally to shades of blue and purple. The black of night came swiftly in the mountains. This was the hour of the wolf. The sounds of the boy jawing off on his mouth harp floated over the hill. It was a low, mournful note that trailed off into bittersweet silence. There was no need for a flashy end. It was simple and said everything that needed to be said. It was a good last song.

Shults stole closer to the camp. The fire had smoldered to red-hot embers, just enough to cast a faint glow. He crouched. His knees burned, pain shooting up his back like lightning, a reminder that he was no longer a young man.

Only a few more feet.

Maynard had built a wicker barrier around the perimeter of his camp. Animal skins and cured meat dangled from the trees. A pot steamed over the fire. A rifle lay across a jumble of burlap sacks loaded with supplies. But what caught Shults' eye was the gold: piles and piles of it. The nuggets sat out in the open air as if they were no more valuable than the sand he was standing on. It was a hell of a haul. The Devil's haul. The kind of load that gets an unwary man killed.

For a moment he contemplated only taking a little bit. Just what his old arms could carry. But something in him said no. If he was going to rob the boy, he was going to do it like a man.

Shults peered at the lean-to. It was surprisingly well built. Maynard had dug it out from the soft topsoil, unusual for a young man. It was designed for comfort and longevity, not something Shults would have bothered with in his youth. Maynard must have spent a great deal of time here.

Shults slid his knife from his boot. It sang for blood. The shot would have been easy for Shults to make if his eyes were but five years younger. Or maybe ten. In his younger days he could thread a bullet through a needle at a hundred paces, but these days he could barely hit a deer a yard out. Besides, there was no need to do this loud if he didn't have to. Maynard didn't need to know what hit him. It was easier this way.

Shults gripped the smooth leather of his knife. It had gutted countless deer, and now it would split this boy open. He crept over the wicker barrier. He was four feet from his prey. The glade was quiet, the lean-to dark. Three feet and his steps were weightless. Two feet and his heart was cold. A foot away and he raised his blade.

The bedroll was empty. Maynard's clothes were folded neatly next to his freshly polished boots. A pistol and a knife lay nearby.

Shults froze. A sharp sound, familiar and strange, pierced the silence. An animal maybe. A second time, a bark like a fox. A third time, and Shults recognized it for what it was.

A man's voice. Down by the water's edge.

Shults crept through the shadows. The dark pool of the mountain tarn held a darker shape within it. Naked. Unarmed and unaware, Maynard stood on the shore with his arms outstretched. He bent forward and splashed water on his head and back. He jerked upright and flung his arms out once more. His voice rose and fell. He bent again, rhythmically, compulsively. His limbs dangled. His posture was rigid, unnatural, like some demon had entered his body and was figuring out how to work it for the first time.

Shults crept closer.

"Goosey, goosey, gander..." Maynard folded and splashed water on his head. "Where shall I wander?"

Shults was only a few feet behind the boy.

"Upstairs, downstairs..." Maynard dipped and rose. As he disturbed the lake, a pale glow rippled across the water. It vanished a moment later. "And in my lady's chambers."

The water flashed again.

"There I met an old man..." The lake returned to supernatural stillness. "Would not say his prayers..."

Shults couldn't take his eyes from Maynard. Water ran down the smooth skin of the young man's back. It trickled in rivulets over his muscles, washing away dirt and grime, the nude man growing younger and more beautiful with every handful of water.

"Take him by the left leg..." A flash of golden light. Maynard stumbled over his words. "Take him by the...take him by the...take him...take..."

The boy's voice shook as he struggled with the proper ending to the rhyme. Faintly, underneath the sound, Shults picked out the presence of something else, something he couldn't name.

"Take him by the..." Maynard's arms drooped. "Goosey, goosey..."

Sorry, kid.

A wink of silver and Shults sank his knife into the base of Maynard's skull. The boy gasped. Shults stabbed him in the brain twice more. Hot blood sprayed from the holes. Droplets hit the water and sank. Shults wiped his eyes with a trembling hand as the globules of blood disappeared one after another, the lake itself consuming them like ants feasting on the corpse of a salamander left to bake in the sun.

Maynard sank into the hungry water. A golden outline illuminated the crumpled body as it drifted away, drawn by an unseen current toward the center of the lake. A trail of blood followed in its wake, tiny red droplets vanishing one by one. Shults wasn't sure what to make of it, but he didn't have time to wonder. The lake and its bounty of gold was his. He'd taken it as a man should. He'd bested Maynard and claimed it as his own. In these parts, that was as good a claim as a bond with the government. Nobody knew the boy. Nobody would be looking for him.

Shults slogged back to the beach. He stumbled in the dark as he followed the dim glow of the coals. The day had taken too much. He had nothing left. He crawled into the lean-to to sleep in another man's bed. The blankets still smelled like Maynard. A smile crept across Shults' face.

Daylight revealed the bounty he'd earned under the cover of night. The rusty stain of dried blood reminded him of the evil committed in its acquisition. Shults wasn't a religious man. He'd committed too much sin to be accepted into God's house. But this was different. He'd crossed an invisible line. Maynard had been unarmed, unaware. Shults wasn't ashamed of how he'd bested the boy, but he knew nobody should go that way. He understood it. He kept it in the forefront of his mind even as he reached out to touch the first nugget.

There was more gold than he knew what to do with. Piles and piles of it. He tried to take stock of it all. He picked up a nugget and hefted it, turned it over and over, estimated its value, pressed it against his lips.

It was damp with dew and soft. Real soft, like nothing he'd ever held in his hand before, and heavy. A pick, a shovel, a pan, and a few other odds and ends lay in a pile along the beach, but Shults already knew where Maynard had found the gold.

He stripped as he walked toward the beach. The smooth surface of the lake reflected the sun like a perfect mirror. Not even the ripple of an insect disturbed the water. Calm. Beautiful. It should have been inviting.

His sudden fear was irrational. Cowardly. He knew how to swim. The longer he stared at the water, the easier it was to see the gold glittering in its depths. All he had to do was take one step. And what was one step when he'd already committed a mortal sin?

He dove into the water. It was cold and clear. He kept his eyes open despite the sting. Moment by moment his vision improved, revealing the great depth of the lake beneath the shafts of sunlight that stabbed straight down to the gravel bottom.

A tingling sensation ran up and down his limbs, chasing itself across every inch of his skin like a million pinpricks, like a million invisible creatures massaging his muscles, easing the stiffness of age from his joints. He kicked his legs just to feel the supple strength of his knees. He was only minutes in the water and yet so refreshed he might have shed ten years from his age. Not even the best yaupon tea could make him feel this good. It was as if he was a younger, stronger man.

He burst from the water. He drew a great lungful of air and laughed. He splashed his way to the beach and ran back to Maynard's camp. He emptied a burlap sack, showering the trees with corn, and sprinted back to the lake. Without hesitation, he dove into the cool water, spangling the sky with glittering droplets. He grabbed handfuls of gold in every size and shape, from chips and flecks to nuggets the size of his fist, and stuffed them into the sack. The water remained tranquil and clear however much he disturbed the sediment at the bottom. He hauled his load to the surface and dumped it onto the beach.

Strength and vigor flowed through his body. Whether it was the lake itself or the gold, it didn't matter to him. Nothing could bring him down, not so long as he had his claim.

Shults carried on with his labor until the sun sank behind the tree line. A chill settled over the glade. He emptied his sack one last time and tossed the burlap aside. Even this early in the evening, the ripples from his final swim had left golden trails across the water. There was so much gold in this lake that even the tiniest particles winked back at him in the last of the day's light.

His camp was cheerful that evening. He feasted on a hot stew of salted pork and beans, filling his belly with the food of another man. Full to bursting, he jawed merrily on Maynard's harmonica, playing the one tune he knew, "Camptown Races," and singing aloud in between.

He carried on in this manner for days. He hauled gold from the lake, drank its water, and cooked his stew from Maynard's supplies and the bounty of the glade. When he grew weary, he slept. When he grew hungry, he ate. But as each day came and went, those needs withered away, leaving him with restless thoughts, idle hands, and one thing more that shook him night after night.

Bad dreams.

Images of Maynard haunted him. Shults saw the boy walking on the water's surface, naked, his hands outstretched. The water remained undisturbed as he strode toward the center of the lake. A trail of blood marked his path, staining the water as it hadn't done the night of his death. Blood ran from a crown of thorns on his brow and stigmata on his hands. He looked back only once. He beckoned to Shults to follow.

"Come, my son." Maynard's voice was deeper than it had been in life.

"I'm sorry, Father." Shults was gripped with panic. "I can't."

Shults woke. He was naked, standing in the water. Droplets trembled along his outstretched arms. He took a step back, stumbled. He fled back to Maynard's camp, but could not sleep.

Daybreak brought a strange revelation. Gazing into the water to shave, he no longer recognized his own face. Every wizened wrinkle had been smoothed, every crease and line, the crow's feet, the pockmarked cheeks. He looked instead at his own self from thirty years before, a fresh, young face.

Fear kept him awake that night and the next. The third night he slept, but woke once more to find himself bending over the water's surface. He'd been whispering, his throat raw. To whom, or what, he couldn't have guessed.

A deep emptiness grew inside him. There was no telling how long he'd been in the glade. The nip in the air foretold of summer's end and the mountains were no place to winter without proper supplies. It had been days since his last meal. Or had it? The piles of gold on the beach had multiplied. Each one spilled into the next until he couldn't tell them apart, the beach becoming one long glittering carpet of gold.

There was something happening to him. Nothing that Shults could place. Time acted strangely. Some days were moments and others could have been weeks. It had been early summer when he'd taken the claim, but it was getting colder. Fall must have come and gone in favor of an early winter.

There was some invisible presence in the glade, in the lake, the beach, the mountains. When he worked, it worked. When he dove, it dove. When he slept...it ate.

Shults felt it. He knew it. This thing took a piece of him every night. It grew stronger the longer he stayed. Instinct told him to leave that place and never come back, but something far more ancient compelled him to stay. The piles of gold, the endless gold, still made him happy. But no matter how much he hauled up from the lakebed, it wasn't enough. There would never be enough. The thing told him there was plenty to be had, all he needed to do was claim it.

He made up his mind to abandon the camp. He packed his few belongings, his knife, Maynard's harmonica. He loaded a sack with gold nuggets, and then a second and a third. He stuffed them into every bag and box, into his clothes, his boots. He worked through the morning and that afternoon, emptying his own things onto the ground, abandoning the knife and the harmonica, unable to leave a single piece of gold behind. Darkness found him with tears streaming over his youthful cheeks, his fists clutching silky smooth nuggets of gold, surrounded by gold, gold spilling from every bag and sack and box.

The vision of Maynard returned that night. His nude, bleeding body walked along the lake's icy surface. He beckoned to Shults, and once more Shults refused.

He woke to find himself standing at the water's edge. His sharp eyes caught sight of a shadow, a figure, out in the middle of the lake, its head bowed, sinking into the water's golden light until it disappeared.

How had Shults gotten there? Why was he naked? Had he fallen asleep?

He stood on the snowy shoreline, no longer able to tell the difference between the real and the unreal, the wish and the dream. Maynard had left a trail of rusty footprints limned in gold. Shults cursed the boy. He cursed the day Maynard had blown open the doors of the tavern, cursed the gold the boy had slapped onto the bar. Cursed moreover himself, his weakness. His need for the gold.

He sank to his knees. His legs had the springy lightness of youth, but his soul was twice that of the old man he'd been, an empty husk. He wasn't a prayerful man. He wouldn't ask God to forgive him, or even to spare him. But he made one vow. Today's had been the last haul of gold.

He stepped onto the icy surface of the lake. He followed the trail of blood. His heart was light now that he'd yielded. The force that guided him no longer pulled, but seemed to walk with him. It was the lake, it was the gold, it was Maynard, it was loneliness. His foot broke through the thin crust of ice. He let the lake take him, without struggle, without regret. The water closed over him in silence. He sank into the crystalline lake until he came to rest on the soft golden bed.

And there he rested in Maynard's gilded arms until he, too, turned to gold.

The Vigil of the Heretic and the Thief

by J.L. Royce

THE OLD MONK STRUGGLED under a heavy pack, wending his way northwest across the harsh Turkish countryside. John watched and waited from his vantage behind a boulder, assessing the opportunity and risk.

What could be in that pack? Gold from Jerusalem? John had traveled to the Holy Land with Richard; some of his fellow Englishmen had found riches along the way, but many more had found death by the sword, or disease. John had found neither wealth nor death—yet—though both options remained open.

The ex-Crusader absently rubbed his stump, glancing at the spiderweb of white scars across the tanned skin as he considered: *Ambush or befriend?* With a deep breath, he chose and stepped into view.

"Ho, brother," he called in his native English.

The old man froze in his tracks, swaying as though he might tumble over like a cornered mouse.

John raised his arms. "I mean you no harm." A calculated gesture, revealing his loss.

In the several years he spent wandering the East after the embarrassing treaty that ended the Crusade, John had picked up a smattering of several languages. He repeated his greeting in Greek and French.

The monk cleared his throat and spat before replying in passable English, "I am old, and have nothing of value."

"Then perhaps you'd share my fire and bread tonight. I would welcome the company." John displayed the loaf he had stolen in the last village. It was to be his dinner; now, it would serve as bait.

The old man glanced around as the lengthening shadows consumed the trail. "Well met, then. I have wine."

"I am John of Cornwall, son of Edward the farrier."

"And I am Brother Gavur."

John stepped closer. "You know England?"

"My Order has gathered men from many lands, though I've never visited English shores. How do you come to be so far from your home?"

"I took up the cross with King Richard, at our Holy Father's urging." He gestured off the trail to a clearing he had spied earlier. "We can rest here."

Gavur nodded. "Your king is long gone." He shuffled after John, clutching his pack tightly.

"I fell ill," John lied. "I'll fetch the wood."

He gathered deadfall, tucking the sticks under his truncated left arm, and soon had a small fire burning. The monk brought out a wineskin and several crude bowls.

"Your illness." Gavur nodded at him. "Is that how you lost your hand?"

"No, it was in battle; then came the sickness in the blood. Many die that way, not from losing their blood, but from the taint growing in it."

The monk grunted. "This is true."

"Many months I lay...immobilized." A charge of theft in Antioch had resulted in John's imprisonment, mutilation, and exile.

Satisfied with the fire, he joined Gavur. The old man stank of traveling many days unwashed.

"I am bound for Mersin," said John, "whence I hope to take passage, perhaps to Italy and from there to England."

He drew his knife. The plan required gold, and John had none—yet. "I may offer to work off my passage."

"You will find it difficult to sign onto a ship like that, less a hand."

John waited. He braced the loaf with his stump, cut a slice, and passed it to Gavur.

"You should know," said Gavur, "Mersin sees few seagoing vessels." The monk swirled the crust of bread in his bowl of wine and gummed it noisily. "You can reach Cyprus, and thence Candia, and onward. My Order's house is in the hills above Mersin; you would be welcome to rest there, while you seek passage."

John's smile of gratitude was honest at least.

"I thank you, brother. Gavur..." He studied the monk. "Not a Christian name." John had heard the epithet, however, uttered by the Turkmen.

The monk's wrinkled face creased into a knowing smile. "It is an honor to be called a *heretic* by the Moors."

John poked the fire. "I have no coin to repay your hospitality, but I would gladly relieve you of your burden on the walk."

Gavur frowned, and the ex-Crusader feigned indignation. "I may have lost a hand in God's quest, but my back is still strong!"

Chastened, the monk said, "I tire." He removed a small book, embossed with the cross, from his robe.

"I would pray my compline now. We will talk further in the morning."

The night was cold and clear, the moonless sky awash in stars. The Englishman stared into the heavens, waiting. In his mind, he wandered back to Cornwall, its cliffs and streams, a beautiful country. He recalled trudging across that country, usually hungry, scrabbling in the streams for nuggets of tin: a miner. The Crusade promised glory...

A sound: the old man was stirring, as expected. Peering into the bowl of darkness, reading the stars, John reckoned it was around midnight. He waited for Gavur to stumble through the bushes to relieve himself.

John crept carefully over to the monk's dusty pack. Reduced to embers, the fire still glowed, and by its dim light, he managed to loosen the leather straps and peer inside.

He cursed silently: a *book*. Handsomely covered in leather, nonetheless a mere book. John ran his hand over the cover, hoping to feel jewels or the cold touch of gold sheathing, gold buckles at least, but felt only...skin. The touch was oddly electric, warm, and soft as a woman's thigh. John rocked on his heels, breath quickening, and pulled the book out far enough to reveal the cover. He recognized Arabic script, and was pondering it when he realized, with a start, that the old man's stream had ceased. He quickly dropped the pack and turned to fuss with the embers.

"I heard you rise," he said when Gavur returned. "It's damnably cold—pardon—I'll build up the fire."

The monk stepped past him to grab the pack, flinging open the flap. "You touched this?" he demanded.

"I took nothing," John said.

"Did you touch it? *Read* it?"

"I've not had book learning like you, cosseted in a warm monastery. I could barely read battle orders." He had learned a smattering of Arabic from the knaves and whores of Jerusalem but did not admit it.

"Good." Gavur placed the pack behind him. "Don't touch it."

"Why—is it valuable?"

"Leave it be," warned Gavur. "I say this for the salvation of your soul!"

"You shouldn't travel alone with such a priceless—"

"The head of my Order tasked me with retrieving this book from the Moors before it could fall into unscrupulous hands, those interested only in profit. It is more valuable—and dangerous—than you could know."

"Then we're well met indeed," said John. "I may lack a hand, but I've not lost my fighting skills. I'll see you and your treasure safely to your destination. I'll be of use."

"Yes, you may...you just may..." Gavur's eyes narrowed.

John gestured at the sack. "What will you do with it?"

"I shall translate it from Arabic into Greek for further study."

"Though the book is dangerous? Why not destroy it, if it is wicked?"

Gavur scowled. "It is not unlike a sword, useful or dangerous depending on its owner's skill."

"And intent."

They lapsed into silence, soaking in the warmth of the renewed fire. John expected the old man to nod off soon; his knife lay concealed behind him, ready to be employed at the first opportunity.

Gavur rose with a grunt. "It is a new day; join me in the vigil." He bunched up the hem of his robe and knelt, drawing his prayer book from his robe.

When John hesitated, the monk said, "You may find prayer soothing," and waited, book in hand, until John went to his knees.

The mumbled Latin did nothing to reduce John's avaricious intent, merely inducing an ache in his joints. But he would play the part until he could secure the treasure. As the fire died and the cold wrapped John in an unwelcome caress, he grew introspective.

His life had been one of predictable drudgery until the call to the Crusade; then came the march to the Holy Land, the battles, the careless thievery, and his downfall. As John bemoaned his life, Gavur's Latin chant melted into an indistinct drone dulling his mind.

John drifted into a hypnogogic state. Gavur's words—at least some of them—were no longer Latin or Arabic. Nature's voices joined the monk's: the wind, and the insect life of the surrounding wilderness. Whether it could be called *speech* was unclear, but John felt the once-meaningless sounds shaping into a message, hissing and ominous. The hideous murmur rose in volume as insects swarmed, joining the chorus.

He started and looked around. The monk had shed his robe, shadows dancing over his sagging flesh. He no longer held his little breviary;

rather, he chanted from the large black volume open in his naked lap. His frail voice had grown into a demanding snarl, the words a guttural tongue the Crusader had never heard: not Christian nor Moorish, but frightful in tenor.

John found it impossible to rise from his stiff knees. He made to reach for his knife but could not lift his hand in defense. The sounds from the darkness were no longer the innocent susurration of life, but the clamoring voices of insanity, horrific in their insistence.

Gavur's eyes gleamed as he rocked in place, hips thrusting beneath the book as if mounting a woman. The monk noticed John's struggle to flee or attack.

"Well met indeed! You can aid me, as my lamb, to sacrifice! For I shall be reborn, in the spirit *and* the flesh, in Her service!"

The fire flared at his words, collapsing, then erupting afresh, coiling and rising. John gawped as the sparks swirled up into a writhing, incandescent spiral.

"It begins!" Gavur laughed in delight, the corybantic chorus joining him in aroused anticipation. The air grew thick with insects, plummeting into the flames and rising again, alight, feeding the inferno.

"That...that sound!" gasped John.

"The *al azif*," replied the monk. "The voice of the desert. Nature longs to join with me. She is a whore, ever ready to couple in the inseminating dance, the mindless orgy..."

Gavur's words trailed off, his eyes on the glowing whirlwind as it rose above their heads.

"The gods who ruled our world before Man crawled from the mud await us at the interstices, beyond the stars...await our worship...and I know the way."

Higher and higher the spiral rose, until it seemed the stars themselves would join the conflagration.

"Behold!" The monk set aside the black book, pointing a writhen hand at the dome of night.

The stars wavered; John thought at first it was the smoke from their fire. Peering steadily, he shuddered as the stars *moved*, patterns evolving: words, beasts familiar and bizarre, gods in majesty.

John struggled against the invisible restraints, desperate to grip the knife beside him and end the heretic's mad chant. But he could only watch the fire spout grow in height and intensity.

With a shout, Gavur stood, naked, arms upraised.

"Life for life; death for death—accept this offering and grant my request—youth and vigor, with the power to do Your will!"

The insectile chittering peaked as the tower of fire quivered, and its base moved slowly away from the fire ring to a position between the men.

"Yes!" cried Gavur. "Take him!"

But despite his frantic gestures, the swirling flames danced toward the monk.

"No! I command you!" Gavur screamed. The droning shaped itself into laughter, echoing off the rocks, then words.

"*You have done well...*"

The old man screamed in agony as his flesh seared and peeled away, hands reduced to bones as he beat at the flames consuming him.

The incorporeal bonds abruptly vanished, and John tumbled to the ground. He hid his face as the flames of Gavur's pyre singed his hair, awaiting his demise with the resignation of a soldier facing an implacable foe. The monk's screams faded as the charred body collapsed into bones and ash.

When the hellish flames failed to consume him, John dared to raise his head. The inferno had abated, shrinking to human size. As he watched, the flames assumed a human form, a female form, supple, crowned with a fiery mane writhing in the breeze. The *al azif* shaped itself into a woman's voice and spoke.

"*Join me,*" came Her offer, with beckoning arms. "*Be my creature, or die.*"

John struggled to his feet and tottered toward the effulgent being. Her arms encircled him, engulfing him with flames, not of destruction but passion.

"*You will carry me west; I will guide you, teach you—and reward you.*"

The thief convulsed in pleasure at Her touch, eyes drifting shut.

"*Imagine our consummation...my creature.*"

Her laughter hung in the air, tenuous as a morning mist, and then was gone. When John opened his eyes, he was alone.

"No!" John cried. Her absence pained him more than the loss of his hand.

The fire was mere embers. At John's feet lay the smoking remains of the monk, and beside them, untouched by the flames, the book. As he reached to retrieve it, John stared in shock at his left hand, restored. He turned it, flexed it, then used it to pick up the book.

John clutched the volume to his chest as jealously as a lover, curling on the ground. The dead monk's cloak, befouled with age and abuse, lay nearby, and he pulled it over them. Murmuring his thanks and devotion to the Goddess in his arms, John kept the vigil until he drifted into a dreamless sleep.

On the morrow, he would resume his journey. With the Goddess walking beside him, nothing would stand in the way of their return.

Nativities

by Rob Francis

SOMEONE HAD HUNG DOZENS of Christmas lights across the old house. Salman gazed at them from his bedroom window, all hope of sleep abandoned. The three-storey monstrosity of rotted brick and wood that stood opposite his family home was derelict. In the six years Salman had lived here, he'd never seen anyone enter or leave. The house had just sunk into greater dishevelment and decay.

Yet someone had put up three long rows of lights across the frontage in a zig-zag pattern. The bottom row was green, the middle white, the topmost red. Classic Christmas colours. He listened to Mum and Dad talking downstairs, knowing he should be sleeping – Dr. Colgrove had said that rest was very important for a boy like him – and watched the flickering lights well into the night.

There was a pattern in their flashing. The green row would flash seven times, white once, and red three times. Then all the rows would flash together. After thirteen minutes of this, each light would flare once before the sequence started again. It was soothing. Restful.

Salman cupped the lighter he'd taken from Mum's purse, his thumb resting on the wheel. Every few minutes he flicked it, satisfied at the roughness of it against his skin. He didn't need to see the flame bloom. Its heat was enough.

He was certain there was a message in the lights, if only he could understand it.

The nights were cold, but it had yet to snow this winter. Just clear, open skies or intermittent rain. Only the festive lights hinted that Christmas was coming. Salman could summon little joy at the prospect.

A man stood outside the old house. Salman had seen him before, walking a little mongrel dog, though he was alone now.

It was late. The man should have been sleeping. Salman thought his name might be Peterson, or something like that. He was facing the old house, head tilted to the lights. Their radiance shrouded him in shifting colours. The lights began their individual flashes.

Salman pressed his forehead to the cold windowpane. It made everything outside seem closer, even if his breath did fog the glass.

The lights completed their sequence. The door to the old house opened, just a little. Mr Peterson stumbled to it, shoved it wider, and vanished inside. Then the door closed.

Salman sat back and wiped the condensation away. His parents snored in their bedroom down the hall. Apart from the lights, all was still.

There was a face at an upstairs window of the old house. It looked like Mr. Peterson. Salman fetched his little telescope, which wasn't much more than a toy really, but it made things a little clearer. Yes, there was

Mr. Peterson, staring from the dirty glass. His face was illuminated by the Christmas lights, still flashing out their message. There was movement in the shadows around him, and it seemed to Salman that something bulbous and stick-legged was in the room, a hulking shape amongst the gloom. The old man's eyes were open, though his face was slack. Salman knew Mr. Peterson was awake, because every time the bulbous thing moved, his eyes would roll and his head would tremble.

This was something he should talk to Mum and Dad about. Except they didn't seem in much of a mood to listen to him of late. Not since they'd found the matches in his drawer. It made them assume the worst of him. What would they think if he told them about the old house and the lights? What would they do? Dr. Colgrove would certainly be informed.

He raised the telescope again.

There were two children standing before the house. Both were swaddled in thick jackets with furry hoods, and each held the other's gloved hand. They were motionless before the lights. A coldness spread through Salman's gut. He swatted the window-sash open so that freezing night air crept into the room.

"Hey! You two!"

The children didn't move or give any indication they'd even heard. Salman craned his neck, looking up and down the street for their parents. It was after nine on a school night; they shouldn't have been out. The lights began their individual flashing.

"You two! Stay away from there!" Salman hurried to the closet to grab his trousers, pulling them on as he searched for a hoodie. But Mum and Dad were still awake. If he went downstairs, they'd want to know what he was doing. He hesitated. Stole back to the window.

The door was closing. The children were gone.

Salman flicked the lighter to life, holding the flame against the window until a spot of glass darkened.

Salman couldn't stand to look at the old house. He couldn't remember the last time he'd slept. He'd been to school but had no recollection of what he'd done there, who he'd seen. The pattern of the lights was ever in his mind.

Eyes burning with exhaustion, he hauled himself to the window. It was past his bedtime, though that meant little anymore. Somewhere downstairs, Dad was washing the dishes. The clatter of plates and cutlery made Salman's heart stutter.

Mum was standing before the house. Just like Mr. Peterson and the children, she was motionless, looking up. Her hand gripped a shopping bag. Salman grabbed the telescope. At the upstairs window, the old man and the two children were standing, eyes wide, pale faces shivering as something moved behind them.

He opened the window. "Mum!"

The shopping bag dropped to the ground. The door cracked ajar.

Salman ran downstairs, almost slipping in his haste. He burst into the kitchen. Dad was wiping a mug with a tea towel, whistling softly.

"Dad! Mum's in trouble."

"What are you doing up? You know it's important that you get some rest."

"Dad, never mind that! Mum's outside the old house over the road. There's something wrong."

"She's just popped out for milk. She'll be back soon."

"No, Dad, come on! We have to get her before she goes in. There's something living in there."

Dad hesitated. He never listened to Salman, not really, but something in his son's urgency must have reached him. He placed the mug on the draining board and rubbed his eyes.

"Fine." He took his phone from the worktop and tapped the screen. The call tone jingled for endless seconds before going to answerphone. Dad sighed.

"I'll go look. Go to bed, Sal. You need to sleep. I'll be back soon." Dad grabbed his coat from its hook in the hall.

Salman ran to his room and peered from the window. Mum had gone. The old house was dark.

Dad passed down the street, coat zipped to his chin. He paused at the old house. Shuffled on the spot as if unsure what to do. Looked up at Salman's window. Glanced at his phone again. Then he carried on, away from Salman. Away from the old house. Salman groaned. He was going to have to find Mum himself.

He got dressed and looked for his pocket torch in the bedside table. Satisfied that it worked, he hurried once more down the stairs. He was just pulling his trainers on when the door opened with a gust of frigid air and Dad stepped in, supporting Mum on his shoulder.

"Mum!" She was white and slick with sweat, hair bedraggled and clothes rumpled. Her eyes rolled as she tried to focus. "Dad, what happened?"

"She was lying on the street, Sal. I think she's had a bit of a fainting attack. She's been under a lot of pressure." He avoided looking at Salman as he spoke. "Sometimes when people faint, they go like this, all pale with a cold sweat. I'll get her to bed, she'll be fine in half an hour." He moved her towards the stairs. "You get off to sleep now."

Salman followed them up and waited while Dad led Mum to their bedroom. "Don't worry, son." He nodded and closed the door behind them.

Salman lay still, listening. The wind was picking up outside. Neither of his parents had emerged from their room. The clock read 03:57. Perhaps they'd both fallen asleep. Except Salman was sure he could hear Mum moving around, making little gasping noises and short, pained moans. Dad had been speaking to her after they first went in, his low murmurings carrying to Salman in the quiet. Now he was silent.

Mum gave a cry. Salman slipped from the bed. He caught a glimpse of the old house as he did so, the lights glaring bright, the door wide open. He rushed down the landing to his parents' bedroom.

The room was lighted by a sliver of moon through the open window. Shadows were moving across the bed and floor. Dad was motionless, prostrate on the carpet with the pale moonlight bathing his face. His eyes and mouth were open, though his face seemed swollen. On the bed, Mum was naked, spreadeagled, two great folds of skin and flesh to either side of her and a great cavity where her gut should be. Eviscerated, like a deer he'd once seen butchered on TV. Her face was covered by one arm, thrown up as if to shield herself.

Something small flashed bright green in the blackness. One of the shadows moved into the light, and Salman shivered at the furry, many-legged thing that was revealed. It was heading to the open window, and now Salman realised that all the shadows were doing so, a dozen bulbous, furry creatures with bony legs. As they moved, their abdomens briefly glowed white, or green, or red. There may have been a pattern there.

He knew where they were headed.

Salman ran back into the hallway, slamming the door behind him.

None of this could be real, and so nothing was happening to him. The world was all nonsense, and perhaps always had been. Let them tell Dr. Colgrove whatever they wanted. None of it was real, and anything he did now didn't matter.

He ran to his room and grabbed an armful of dirty clothes from the floor. Pausing only to collect the lighter, he jogged down the stairs and out into the night. Snow was falling. It was almost Christmas, and finally the weather was matching the season.

The boy in the furry-hooded jacket sat against a lamppost across the street. His face was pale and wet. The front of his jacket was dark with liquid, undulating as something tried to break out. A moment later, several dark bodies plopped to the ground around him. Salman turned away.

Farther up the street, Mr. Peterson stumbled away into the night, clothes torn and trailing like loose skin.

Lights were still flashing at the old house, but he ignored them and the shadows they cast. Only fire could banish the darkness now.

He stuffed the clothes through the rusted letterbox, holding back one thick, fluffy sock. It took only a second to light it. He held it a while to make sure it was ablaze, as flames licked around his fingers. Then he dropped it through the letterbox and stood back in the road to watch the beautiful, burgeoning glow envelop the door.

Something big moved upstairs, making the house shudder. Smaller shadows slipped around the windows and around Salman. He didn't care. None of this existed. Only the fire.

Flames and smoke leapt from the house. The lights flashed. The snow fell.

And the shadows crept closer.

Assorted Testimonies

by Dylan Freeman

Kent, Ohio

October 2007

This happened my freshman year of college. I was getting snacks after a stressful midterm, and someone asked a question. I didn't hear it at first, and figured it was someone in the next aisle having a conversation. I heard it again at the register: "May I borrow your mind?"

On instinct, I answered, "Yes."

I woke up in the hospital a day later, after standing at the register unresponsive. Doctors diagnosed it as a mini stroke, but I still wonder.

What was borrowing my mind?

Nationwide

March 2020-December 2022

It became a lot easier for *them* to blend in with everyone wearing masks. Normally, you can tell them apart from actual people when they talk. Their mouths don't quite sync up to the words, like someone didn't dub the lines properly in a movie. When they smile, they have too many damn teeth.

That's why I'm against masks—I know they help, I know the damn plague is real, but I can't stand the thought that anyone I talk to who wears one could be one of these...*things*.

Superior, Wisconsin

Recurring

About once a year, when it storms during the summer, we get a really thick fog coming off Lake Superior. I mean five-feet-of-visibility bad. It usually burns off before noon, but people keep on seeing weird stuff in the fog.

Only one I've personally encountered is the Caddy. Drive down 35 southbound when it's foggy, and you'll hear its horn blaring, and then see a red Cadillac barreling out of the fog the wrong way. When I tried swerving to avoid it, I just...went *through* the damn thing. I've seen it three times now, and it's always startling.

Alaska

Throughout 1993

When I was younger, the entire wilderness around Nome sang. I don't know how else to describe it; there was a sound out in the woods, in the ice, throughout the Iditarod Trail. You can hear it on coverage of 1993's race if you listen closely enough. Sometimes, people would try singing along to the music, idle humming or whistling, and then they'd keel over. They'd wake up a few days later, but their hair would fall out, or they'd get nosebleeds or have birthmarks and moles slough off.

The explanation the government gave was geological activity caused by permafrost thawing, but I don't buy it. How does permafrost cause that kind of physical damage?

Centralia, Pennsylvania

October 2002

I attempted to shoot a found-footage film in Centralia with a few friends. *The Blair Witch Project* had been out for a couple years at that point, and the town was mostly abandoned. The few people who still lived there, despite the eternally burning coal fire, actually agreed to be in the film as extras.

I ended up having to scrap it due to something going wrong with the physical film. The footage of the chase scene at the end of the film, where the characters are trying to escape the monster in their car, is overexposed when they're moving down the road, and it looks like there's something crouched on the hood of the car, looking in, whenever the camera swings to the front. I don't like the look of that thing, and I don't remember seeing it when I was shooting. So, I've never so much as looked at it in the cutting room.

Baltimore, Maryland

September 2011

When I was younger, I'd end up in the ER with a migraine once a week. Only one drug cocktail would help; prescription-strength opioids, over-the-counter painkillers, and everything in between did nothing. After almost six months of this, I told my dad, "I'd give anything to never have another migraine."

A few seconds later, I felt a sharp pain in my left eye, like a hot poker was stabbing it. I was dragged to the hospital screaming and delirious with pain. The eye was removed after nothing else could alleviate the pain, and a nurse got fired after they couldn't find it in the medical waste, but...I haven't had a migraine since.

New Orleans, Louisiana

May 2010

There was a public pool I used to visit that got wrecked by Hurricane Katrina. It finally re-opened after five years, but I never went back after my first visit. The water felt wrong somehow. At first, I thought it was just that they had messed with the chemical levels and the chlorine was off, but when I tried going off the high-dive, I saw...*something* in the water below me. I don't know how to explain it. It almost...it almost looked like the pool was getting ready to swallow me whole. I climbed back down, and the next person to dive off the board didn't come back up.

Since it reopened, two or three people drown in that pool every year, even with a lifeguard on every side of it.

New York City

Recurring

So, there's this alley on Park Avenue that doesn't appear on any maps. Some people use it as a shortcut, because it goes straight to Madison without you having to mess with the light on 97th. You gotta be careful though, because the alley doesn't *always* lead to Madison.

A family of tourists took it once on the advice of a local. The parents ended up on the other side just fine, but their kid vanished. Whole city was swept, and they eventually found him on Coney Island. He said he looked away for a second and ended up in one of the fun houses there. One of my co-workers at my old firm went through it and somehow ended up over at JFK. But I got something that tops that—I went through it back in 2009 and ended up on the Brooklyn Bridge. I looked over at Manhattan, and I swear, the first time I looked? The Empire State Building was on fire. Freaky as all hell.

Peoria, Illinois

[Date Withheld]

I was hired as a security guard at the local cemetery. There were reports of disturbances on the gravesites, gouge marks in the dirt. I figured it was probably some coyote or something else looking for food. I didn't want to shoot the damn thing unless it was rabid.

About three weeks in, I saw what was doing it. It wasn't a coyote. It was like...it was like an earthworm, but it...couldn't be. It was like the earthworm was this thing's *tongue*. I know that doesn't make a damn lick of sense, but... I just didn't know what to make of it. I couldn't see the top of its head.

I got hired at a mall a few miles away after that. Feel sorry for the poor fool who got my job.

[Location Withheld]

December 21st, 2012

I remember thinking the 2012 apocalypse was going to happen. I was a dumbass kid, sue me. But I stayed up all night on the 21st, wondering if the world would end right before Christmas, and I...saw something.

I was looking out my window around midnight, and I swear I saw what I thought was...another moon. It was full, which didn't make sense; it shouldn't have been bigger than slightly half that night. But there was this big white orb in the sky, just next to the moon, completely circular and perfect. I stared up at it for about ten minutes, wondering if this was Nibiru or some kind of meteor or... I don't know what.

Then, as I was about to call the police about this thing, seeing if anyone else saw it, it *blinked*.

Random Mark

by Ian Klink

THE MARK ON JIMMY'S hand had grown since he slept with her. As he walked toward the bar in the pouring rain to try to find her, he couldn't help but scratch at it again.

What was her name? Was it Cara? Cynthia? It ended with an E. It most assuredly ended with an E.

It became an impulse to scratch at it by now. It did not hurt, throb, or anything that would cause anyone alarm. It was just the fact that the strange dot that was tiny when he first noticed it a few days ago was now the size of the bottom of a coffee cup across the back of his hand.

He first noticed it when he woke up the next morning, surprised and relieved she had already left. He never usually went for one-night stands, but it had been quite lonely the past few months since Erica left and he needed the friendship, even only for two or three minutes. He pulled sheets off his rank body, the smell of sweat and aggressive sex caked on his skin, and went straight to the shower to wash the night before off. It was when he turned the knob warmer that he noticed the mark, no more than the size of a pea. He scrubbed as hard as he could and eventually just felt it was a mole or the start of a wart.

It eventually grew to the size of a quarter and Jimmy started to worry, and scratch.

The doctor at the walk-in clinic said it was a rash and wrote him a prescription for steroids, but that was when it was the size of a nickel.

He scratched. When he stopped scratching, he scratched more.

His thoughts repeated the same words more and more as he got closer. *What the fuck is this?!*

"Hey, mister. Change?" some random street urchin asked, holding up their used cup, reeking of lost gin.

"Fuck off!" Jimmy yelled, never looking away from the black mass covering the knuckles of his right hand, scratching at the rough surface.

"Screw you!" the drunkard said and looked around for another source of help.

"Jesus Christ," Jimmy softly muttered to himself, scratching. Even though it did not itch, he hoped, like most desperate souls, for the easy solution. His mind said if you keep scratching it might just come off, the desperation many souls have fallen prey to in times like this.

At this point, he had been scratching for over three hours. The grayish-dark skin never cracked and no blood ever left, except for the blood underneath his mangled fingernails.

"She has to be there," he whispered. "She just has to be there. She better fucking be there!"

Did she have it? Was the mark there and I never saw it?

As a car drove past, he scratched, even when the water splashed on him.

"Asshole!" Jimmy yelled at the car. He looked around to see if there was something to throw. Near his foot was a dead beer bottle. Jimmy grabbed it with the marked hand and threw it. As the glass smashed into tiny shards in the road, missing the car entirely, he began scratching hard at the mark, not even realizing he was doing it.

The little bell rang as Jimmy opened the door to Dante's Tavern, where he had met her three days before. Although not a regular customer, Jimmy had been there a few times, enough to know it was easy to find company at such a place. As the door closed behind him, he immediately started scratching at the mark.

The bartender noticed him come in, nodded politely, and continued his conversation with the older customer drinking.

Jimmy walked a few steps in and looked around.

She was not there.

Maybe she's in the bathroom?

He approached the bar, still scratching. "Excuse me?"

The bartender looked in his direction. "Yeah?"

"I need your help. Do you remember me?"

The bartender shrugged. "No. Am I supposed to?"

"I came in a few nights ago."

"Woopty shit." The bartender was very proud of this, living for the chuckle it gave the older customer.

"Is there anyone else here?"

"Listen, pal—"

"Is there anyone in the bathroom!" Jimmy yelled, scratching his hand harder.

"None of your business, bud."

"Hey, man, look—"

"Unless you're a cop, I'd prefer you leave now."

Still scratching. "Look, I'm sorry for yelling. I need to find this girl I left with."

The older man laughed, sipping the foam of his beer down his wrinkled gullet.

The bartender looked at him and then back at Jimmy. "My job is to serve drinks. I don't keep tabs on people."

"She was blonde and about six feet tall," Jimmy started and stopped scratching long enough to show him her height with his marked hand, then scratched again. "I need to find her."

"Buddy, you just described every lady who comes in here."

Jimmy was boiling to the top. He closed his eyes and said, "Just fucking tell me wh—"

"Hey!" the bartender yelled. "I think you best just turn back around and—"

From the kitchen door, a waitress came out, holding a towel in her soft hands.

Jimmy stopped scratching.

It was her, and she was just as shocked to see him.

"You!" Jimmy yelled, pointing at her with his marked hand.

The bartender felt this might not go the right way and started to move.

"It's okay, Jesse!" she said, holding her hand up to stop him. "It's alright. Please."

Jesse eyed Jimmy before nodding at her. "You sure?" he asked.

She nodded. "Can I take a smoke break?"

Jesse breathed out. "Sure."

She smiled and then looked at Jimmy. She pointed toward the door, set her towel down, and walked toward him.

Jimmy started scratching again as she got closer, knowing she was looking at his marked hand.

She lit her cigarette, took a huge drag, and spit near the trashcan in the alleyway as she looked down at his hand. "Did you see a doctor about it?"

Jimmy was scratching as he nodded.

"They didn't think anything was wrong, did they?"

He stopped scratching for a second, puzzled by her remarks.

"I did the same thing," she said through a puff of smoke. A rain droplet fell on her bangs, and she looked up, smiling a bit. "They said the same thing to me."

"So you did have it!" Jimmy yelled, his voice bouncing off the brick walls.

Her smile left. She drew another drag, held it in for a long time, and let it out while she spoke. "Yes, but I put some makeup on it so you couldn't see it."

"Show me."

She lifted her arm and there was a mark the size of an apple on the inside of her arm.

Dark, gray, and unafraid. It stared at him like a target, innocent of the horrors it produced inside those it formed on.

Jimmy started scratching his hand. "You fucking bitch!" he yelled, out of control of his natural rage.

She held her hands up, flicking ashes from the cigarette on the shoulder of her uniform. She backed up a few steps before taking a deep breath to say, "You have to give it to someone. If not, it will just keep growing."

He heard her, but nothing of what she was saying made sense, and yet, inside his mind, he knew very well she was telling the truth. He knew nothing about her until the night they went back to his place, but he could see in her eyes the truth behind the fear of her confession. "The fuck are you talking about?"

"I don't know why, but you must give it away. Don't ask me."

He scratched hard. "That makes zero, *fucking zero* sense!"

Tears formed behind her eyes and she wiped them away.

He could only focus on the dark circle on his hand, scratching.

"Stop scratching at it. It does nothing."

"Fuck you," he softly whispered, ignoring her as his fingernails dug across his skin. "How do I get rid of it?"

"I told you how."

"Bullshit. Is there a cream or something? Like a steroid or whatever?"

"No," she whispered.

"Does it just stop growing?"

"I don't know. Mine did as soon as I...as I..." She tried to finish but yanked into her purse for another stick of relief. Her hand was trembling as she tried to light it.

Jimmy rushed over, smacking it out of her hand, and threw her against the brick wall. "What did you do to me!" he screamed, covering her face with his saliva.

"I'm sorry!" she cried. "I'm so... I'm so sorry."

Jimmy couldn't believe his ears. "Yeah. You're fucking sorry! You fucking gave me some disease and you're fucking sorry?"

"Look, just give it to someone, okay? That's it and you'll be fine! It won't grow or anything. Just give it away."

"Why me?"

"I don't know?"

Jimmy reached his marked hand back to strike her and came close when the back door opened.

Jesse stood there with a baseball bat. "Go away," Jesse calmly spoke.

Jimmy looked between the two of them. Knowing he was out-matched, he slowly backed away.

"Get in here, Connie," Jesse said, finally giving Jimmy her name.

Connie looked deep into Jimmy's eyes and slowly walked toward to the door.

"Start walking or I'll fucking break this across your head," Jesse gladly offered, spinning the bat in his hand.

Connie walked a few feet before turning around.

Jimmy stood taller, hoping she'd have something of comfort for what he needed to do.

She thought long and hard before she spoke. "Just give it away. That's all." She paused for a few seconds before adding, "I'm sorry." She turned around and walked through the door past Jesse.

"You fucking kid—" Jimmy started, but stopped when Jesse held the bat tight.

Jimmy threw his hands in the air and began walking as he heard the door slam behind him. He started scratching at his mark again.

A few weeks later, it was all over the back of his hand, and even spilled a little into his palm. He tried the bar again, but Connie had left, and already having been threatened with a baseball bat, he did not want to try his luck by asking the bartender where she was. Too afraid of what they might do, he would not return to the clinic. Desperate times called for desperate measures.

He pulled the utensils drawer with such strength, the front broke, spilling all the sharp knives onto the broken kitchen tile. "Shit!" he yelled to no one. He shifted through a few till he found the sharpened knife his mother had loaned him a few years back. She had ordered it online and it was guaranteed to slice and dice with precision or your money back.

He set his marked hand on the counter and held the sharp knife in the other. He pushed the knife into the dark skin.

Do it! Go on! Do it!

Jimmy took an exhausted breath and pushed the blade deeper.

It did nothing.

"Jesus Christ!" Jimmy screamed. He sliced the blade across the dark surface and it chipped away the metal.

He threw the knife across the room, scraping some of the cheap faux wood flooring with its sharp edge. As Jimmy sank to the floor, cupping his watering eyes in his normal hand, the fear overcame him.

What do I do? What's happening to me?

A ding on his phone brought him out of his funk for a second. He pulled out his phone and opened the app.

The algorithm of the site wanted Jimmy to know his ex-girlfriend had just posted several pictures of an office party they had the previous day.

She's the one who should have this. Not me!

Jimmy took in another long breath, knowing what he had to do next, and with a deep breath started texting her while scratching his hand.

Although he waited for more than an hour at their favorite Chinese restaurant, part of him was convinced she would not show up. After all, it would be typical behavior and one of the thirteen thousand reasons they broke up. He wore gloves and a jacket. How to leave the gloves on while he passed the mark would be a problem.

If I can even get to that point. Probably won't get through dinner, knowing her.

His thoughts betrayed him, hearing that deep part of his mind telling him this was wrong.

Just remember what she did. Just focus on what you saw that night and remember... She deserves this.

"No one deserves this," he spoke out loud. When it dawned on him, he looked around to see if anyone noticed, but no one was around. It was a decent establishment, but most orders were taken out nowadays. Great if you want to eat in privacy. Amazing if you do not want anyone to hear your inner thoughts.

She deserves it. And even if it sucks, just tell her right away. Just tell her to give it away. She was always screwing around, so what difference would it make?

She walked in and looked around. It took a few seconds, but once she saw him her eyes narrowed.

He had seen the look before. It was the same look she gave when she walked out a few months ago. It was a mix of love, hatred, fear, and desire. Only those who have fallen hard in love can understand the stew of all these emotional flavors together.

She slowly walked up, nervously scratching her left ear lobe.

All he could think about was how great it would be to scratch the mark.

"Hello, Jimmy," she said softly, the feelings behind the words timid.

He tried to stand up, but clumsily hit the table, making his almost empty water glass spill.

She smiled.

"I'm sorry," he said, regaining his embarrassment.

"You don't have to get up," she said, sitting down and pulling her hair behind an ear. "How are you—"

"How are—" he said, interrupting her.

They both laughed, and for a brief moment when they looked into each other's eyes, they forgot all the bad.

Until he remembered what she did and the smile slowly left.

They sat there for a few moments in complete silence. She looked around, waiting for him to speak. He kept looking at his hand, the flash of hurtful memories flooding back.

He couldn't take it any longer. "I'm glad you came."

Then she glared. "I'm not sure why."

"What does that mean?"

"Jimmy. We haven't spoken in months. Why now?"

He took offense to this. "What the shit, Julie?"

"This was a mistake," she said, bolting up.

"Wait!" he said. "Please. Just wait. Hold on."

She slowly turned around. "I knew it. This is a fucking mistake."

"It's not. Just sit, please." He hoped she would.

I need her to.

"Please, sit," he asked, giving her a look of hope to help persuade.

Julie looked at his eyes and turned her head toward the door. "Fine," she finally said, giving up and walking over to sit in the booth.

"Thank you," he offered.

"Don't thank me yet. You've got five minutes before I bolt. What do you want?"

She deserves it.

He smiled seductively and called over the waitress. The urge to scratch the mark was killing him.

When they got to her house, she could not open her door fast enough before he had his hands all over her. She playfully smacked them away and the latch moved, but his embracive kisses continued. Even till the very end of the break-up, their sex life was powerful and amorous, something only two people who truly loved one another could emote.

"I missed you," she whispered through his lips.

"Me too," he said, sliding his hands under her shirt.

She stopped. "Not yet."

"C'mon!" he said a little too aggressive and feared the concern in her eyes. "I mean, I just… I missed you so much." He softly touched her lips. "I need you again."

"Maybe," she playfully answered, all the concern washed away.

He nodded his head to the bedroom.

"You go in. I want to just... I'll be in there in a second."

"No, right now," he demanded, pulling her in for an aggressive kiss.

"I said wait, Jimmy."

He pulled her forcibly closer, feeling her body rubbing against his rising heat.

"No. Stop!" she demanded, pulling away from him. "What the fuck is wrong with you? Seriously. What is the matter!"

His mind was blank. All he could do was scratch at his gloved hand.

She looked at him with disgust. "I knew it. I just... I fucking knew it."

He scratched the itch, needing to scratch a deeper one. He lunged for her.

She spun around screaming, and as he grabbed her dress they fell to the floor near the couch, smashing a designer vase full of beads. Some ran across the floor and others rolled onto his back as he pinned her down.

"Jesus Christ!" she yelled, struggling beneath him.

Jimmy smacked her across the face with his hand. As he reached with his marked hand for the zipper, he heard her crying.

It made him stop and he started crying too.

Stop it! Stop it! Stop it!

As if waking from a horrid dream, Jimmy looked across the room and saw his reflection in the mirror behind the door.

It was not the man he once knew. He was a marked man.

He looked down at Julie, fear stoic on her face, with tears rolling onto the broken shards of glass.

"I'm sorry!" he yelled, jumping off of her and running out the door, kicking the spilled marbles across the dark living room.

He ran through the streets, his mind confused. As his thoughts cleared, he came to a stop to catch his breath.

How can you be this stupid? How could you believe her bullshit story!

The worst part was his realization of how much he still cared for Julie. He knew then he would get her back. Just as soon as he got rid of the mark.

Across the street, he saw the *OPEN* sign at the walk-in clinic.

The bell above the door rang for a while as he stepped up to the nurse behind the counter.

"How can I help you?" she asked.

"I, uh...um, well... I have a, a, a...mark of, uh, some kind."

"There's a little bit of a wait. Just fill these out and bring them back."

Jimmy nodded his head, grabbed the forms with his gloved hand, and walked over to the waiting area. He sat down, pulled off his glove to write, and began to fill out the form until his stomach sank in horror.

Across the room was a homely, barefoot man, looking directly at Jimmy with eyes of comradery. The man's body was covered with the mark, from head to what Jimmy assumed were his toes.

Jimmy scratched his hand so hard he finally broke through the skin, bleeding onto the grimy linoleum.

The Virgho Method

by Nicola Lombardi translated by Joe Weintraub

AT FIRST HE DOESN'T realize how the sounds of those hurrying steps—barefooted, undeniably small—had crept into his consciousness, initially like an intruder, then little by little, clearer and clearer, until the indistinct voices that must have belonged to the world of dreams gradually retreat into silence, disappearing entirely. And when the small footsteps stop, right there, at his side, by the bed, Karl can't help but open his eyes again.

"Milius," he groans, his tongue still half-glued to his palette.

"Papa," the boy says right away, urgency in his voice. "Papa, there's a woman in my room."

The man feels something crumpling in his stomach, something rough that in a few moments clambers up inside him until it wraps itself painfully around his heart.

"A...a woman," he repeats, feeling a little stupid, his head bloated with fog.

He looks deeply into his son's eyes, or as much as the faint yellowness of the light streaming from the hall will allow him. It's the middle of the night. Three-fifteen. He does not have to look at his clock to know that. The boy continues to stare at him. Fear alternates with expectation in his pale little face.

Instinctively, Karl turns to his left where Hanna is continuing to sleep, her back to him. She had heard nothing. He is tempted to wake her, but he realizes at once that he could spare her that. His wife is very tired. Better to let her rest.

He turns back around, and a scattering of words begins to drift out from between his lips. "Milius...I think...don't..."

But the boy is already running down the hallway in anticipation, as would an anxious little puppy. Karl drops his bare feet down from the bed. The freezing chill of the floor immediately bites into him, but he ignores that discomfort as he struggles instead to gain his balance, while the blood flows sluggishly from his brain, leaving him vaguely disoriented.

Moving with care, he reaches the door of his room and yields to the haziness of the light that awaits him with a slight, intermittent droning. "Milius?"

His son's room is open. Inside, a dim glow partially illuminates the bed.

Karl slows his pace as he moves forward. Milius said that there's a woman in that room. Of course, it's possible. Or maybe not? And where has Milius gone now? All questions will be answered very soon, but in the meantime, they are drumming insistently behind his ears.

Until he reaches the threshold, he persists in keeping his eyes low. *So as not to trip, so as not to get hurt*, he repeats to himself. But in the end, he has to look.

Sitting on the mattress, in the middle of the bed, an elderly woman in a long, white nightgown meets his gaze, and Karl is under the impression that his heart is shifting, ever so slightly, in his chest.

"Again, Mom?" he mutters, physically feeling the bitter taste of his own breath along his tongue.

The woman merely nods. In the dim light, from that face cross-hatched by a thousand wrinkles, all of the distress that must have been steeping inside her trickles out. "Of course, he's came back again," she then adds, her voice barely audible. "Always at the same time..." A fleeting melody of tears punctuates those last words, and Karl is seized by a despondent misery and dejection deep enough to blunt his hearing, almost as if he is descending one heartbeat at a time into the blind depths of the sea.

"He also came to me," he hears himself saying, as if that information could be of some use to anyone.

"We have to put an end to it." His mother then sighs. "We can't go on like this. You, too, can see that very well."

Having said that, the woman raises a bony arm and, vigorously scratching the top of her head, she momentarily ruffles her thinning grey hair. She then stretches her arm back out, showing Karl her fingers now stained in red. That color should not stand out with such clarity given the very faint light of the surroundings, but Karl's mind is drenched in it. Choking back a stony sob, he instinctively shuts his eyes, but at that exact instant he feels two sharp, stabbing pains at his temples. Only in the moment when he again raises his eyelids does the sudden agonizing torment subside. He then goes back, stumbling over his own steps.

And there they are along the hallway. A track of small, bare footprints. Their color—*that* color—is the same. They are heading into the master bedroom. Entering, Karl sees that Hanna is still sleeping. Milius is not there, or maybe he's hiding. Is he afraid of him? But what an absurd thought, why would he ever be afraid? He loves his son, loves his wife, loves his mother...

A hissing, rustling sound, amplified by the persistent impression of being underwater. Hanna is turning around under the sheets. Karl takes a slow step toward the bed, climbs up into it on his knees, and approaches his wife on all fours.

"Hanna? Are you awake?" His heart swells yet a few centimeters more, pounding fists against his ribcage. He attempts to close his eyes once again, but two biting stabs at his temples force him to reopen them wide along with his mouth as he tries to feed air into his lungs.

The woman, little by little, props herself up onto an elbow. Karl groans as he tries to find a glimmer of consolation, of understanding in his wife's blue eyes. But he cannot. There are no eyes. There are no golden waves of hair to trace shadowy curls onto her cheeks. There is no face.

From the darkness, Milius' small singsong voice chants out, "Papa, what have you done to Mama?"

Hanna's head does not rise up with her body. It remains on the pillow.

"What have you done to us, Papa?"

A roar shatters Karl's chest, and a blast of blood and darkness engulfs him.

From the intercom inside the room reserved for the victim's relatives and the representatives of the news outlets and networks, the metallic voice of Dr. Virgho announces, "The prisoner, Karl Oyser, convicted of the murder of his wife, Hanna Volberg, his son, Milius, and his mother, Olga, while under the influence of alcohol and illicit narcotics, has expired today, the 25th of September, 2035, at the time of 17:33, in accordance with the court judgment CM/44S of the fourteenth of this month." Barely detectable in the background of those words is the hissing monotone with which the devices for the electroencephalogram and the electrocardiogram accompany the definitive linearity of their electronic paths.

An electrically operated grey curtain drops, as if in a theater, in front of the glass wall through which those authorized had witnessed the execution. Claudia, Hanna's sister, rises and heads for the side exit, supported by an attentive husband. Her eyes are red, swollen. She holds a handkerchief pressed against her mouth to hide the trembling of her jaw. The journalists remain in their seats, recalibrating their cameras or rearranging their notes in anticipation of the next scheduled proceeding.

In the meantime, in the room behind the curtain, under the supervision of the warden and a government official, two orderlies look after the release of Karl Oyser from the straps that bind him to the cot and then, cautiously, they lift from his head the virtual-reality viewer before conveying the corpse elsewhere.

The Virgo Method is by now tested and proven, with surprises or malfunctions rarely occurring. "The innovative system for the elimination of prisoners condemned to capital punishment," reads a press release issued some months previous by its designer and developer, Anatoli Virgho, "is essentially based on the work of a team of highly skilled computer programmers. Assisted by the utilization of Artificial Intelligence and sophisticated virtual-reality viewers, multisensory episodes are generated to which the condemned prisoner, placed under a mild sedation, is compelled to bear witness, or more accurately, 'to live through.' Such episodes have as main characters perfect reproductions of their victims, incorporated into contexts that simulate the ambient conditions in which the crime was committed, but the circumstances are modified and intensified in such a way as to operate perniciously against the nervous and circulatory systems. Veritable waking nightmares in which the executioners of the sentence are, ultimately, those who would have the greatest right and motive for it." And the journalists, naturally, did not miss the rare opportunity to take apart the luminary's last name, coining the phrase "Death by *Vir*tual *Ghost*," playing on the fact that the deaths of the condemned, as it turns out, are actually caused by the ghosts of their own consciousness. "In the very likely event that the guilty party closes his eyes for more than two seconds to avoid seeing what is being transmitted through the special viewer," the same press release continues a little further on, "instantly there is a sensor that detects it, activating the mechanism that controls the intercession of two needles at the height of the temples."

The curtain rises up again.

A new prisoner in an orange uniform is now seen lying on the cot with a strap restraining his chest and others tight around his wrists and ankles. With a blank expression, he stares at the circular neon light on the ceiling. Dr. Virgho is there personally to apply the viewer over his eyes, a sort of black binocular plate fastened securely to the head so that it cannot slip off in the case of possible spasms.

In the viewing room, besides the journalists who suddenly interrupt their subdued chattering to turn their attention to what is about to happen, an elderly couple and a young woman are sitting like waxen statues, stiff, silent, impassive.

"In accordance with the court judgment CM/45S of the fifteenth of this month," Dr. Virgho announces through the intercom in a slightly pompous tone, "we are here enforcing the execution of the sentence provided by law against Alex Cardona, twenty-four years old, found guilty of raping, strangling, and burning the body of the minor, Lydia Wolke, his sister's friend."

The three waxen figures, in unison, burst out into a fit of prolonged, hoarse sobbing.

The sky is a deep shade of blue, and the sun shines with a force that, with the total absence of clouds, becomes almost unnatural. Alex stands upright in the middle of a seemingly endless expanse of grass, deeply inhaling the afternoon's crisp air. A lively breeze, with cool fingers, ruffles his greased-down hair and swells the grassland into waves of emerald.

Suddenly, a shout. "Alex!"

The young man turns, drawn to that crystal-clear voice. A hundred meters or so away from him, he sees Lydia. The girl, just sixteen, long hair the color of ripe wheat, is running toward him, her arms outstretched.

Alex's heart skips a beat. At that very moment, he has only one desire: to embrace that young girl, to press her close against him, to kiss her...

Lydia comes closer, ever nearer, even if her initial strides are weakening into labored movements, almost as if she were now advancing through an invisible gelatinous curtain. Alex reaches out, ready to greet her. And while the intensity of the sunlight seems to weaken, and the gusty wind becomes less welcoming, the scant, feather-light clothes of the girl begin to unravel, to sheer off and flutter into the air like swarms of crazed flies.

"Alex!" Lydia screams out again, always closer, with a raspy voice that sems to come from everywhere. And her skin—Alex now sees very clearly and he cannot stop himself from trembling—is turning black, splitting apart and peeling off like her clothes that are now no longer there. Her hair, blonde just a little before, is lifting from her scalp in burning clusters and flying away, dispersing into the now leaden sky. By now that wretched creature has almost reached him, just as a thick smoke begins to pour out of her mouth.

And Alex's shrieking heart prepares to explode.

I Am the Body

by Winnie Soldi

HALFWAY THROUGH THE DRIVE, Jason and I stopped at a diner to have my first-ever batch of highway pancakes. Jason said they were the best he'd ever had. I couldn't taste them. I was anxious to get started.

Jason walked me through the stops we would make, running his finger over the map he had been studying for the past couple of weeks. I nodded emptily at his directions, putting on the bravest face I could muster. After washing our food down with some burnt coffee, we hopped back into the car to complete the rest of the six-hour drive. By nightfall we had arrived before the southernmost section of the reserve known as the Greenwoods.

At first, it helped that I was sleeping with my therapist. I felt a closeness and devotion that no other clinician could provide me with. But I believe what truly saved me was falling in love with him.

It was Jason who suggested I should go back home. That the dreams, the paranoia, would never end if I didn't return to see what remained of the New Sun with my own eyes. As much as I repeated it to myself…I never truly believed that still being alive wasn't some horrible mistake.

"You have spent so much time treating your trauma in a room hundreds of miles away from where it all took place, Alicia…" Jason had said. "As much as I want to think myself a capable clinician, there's only so much we can accomplish by talking things through." He had taken my hand at that point. "But, of course, the decision is up to you."

I knew what he meant. Even though I had spoken extensively about my years in the New Sun, I had not banished its influence on me. The place still called to me. *Home* called to me. It wasn't a fully formed voice whispering in my ear any longer. Slowly but surely, I had silenced it—at least in part. I could no longer hear the Brightness's voice; its influence now crept into me through the tangled back alleys of my mind, by way of intrusive thoughts and tics that reminded me I did not belong in the outside world. That I never had and never would. I wanted to prove it wrong.

That first night, we camped just outside the woods, a few feet away from the car. The trees swayed in a gentle breeze. I felt oddly at ease, if a little sad. For I knew that among the things I would encounter in these woods, my family would not be one of them. After dinner, I poked my head out of the tent to look at the stars. I hadn't seen a sky so clear, lights so bright in a long time.

"See, it's not so bad. We'll do it together. One step at a time."

I let Jason hold me. I could have melted right there, as I felt something stronger, bigger than myself shelter me.

"You'll be fine, Alicia. It's just a place like any other. It has no power over you."

But as I heard Jason's breath relax and fall asleep, I knew it wasn't as simple as that. And that places do indeed have power. I knew this was no simple walk in the woods or we wouldn't be here in the first place. In fact, I felt as if my entire family, some fifty or so people, were poking their heads out from behind the trees, watching me undertake this journey through the woods. Not that I *actually* saw them, of course. They were dead and gone.

I shut my eyes, focusing on my heartbeat. On the twitch in my left eyelid. On my own flesh-heat. Feeling this piece of bone-skewered meat, whose sole tenant I am. Sometimes it felt empty, this body. Like a partially vacated house, too big for only me. I've always had a certain squeamishness for my body. I never liked to feel my own pulse, for instance. But I had learned to fear my thoughts more than the ominous ticking of my heart. You could always tell when bodies went missing. But a mind? How could you tell when a mind was truly gone? When an all but invisible tenant had vacated its house?

Knowing I should try to sleep, I followed my therapist's advice and focused on clenching every part of my body starting from my feet up to my neck, then relaxing them one by one, until emptiness swept away all traces of me.

I decided to return home when I saw Jason talking to a woman at a flower shop. She was about my age, and a lot prettier than me. Not that it took much. Just the fact that people can smile made pretty much anyone more attractive than me. I had never been at ease with my life on the outside, and my smile was no exception. Back in the woods, little was expected of me, save devotion. I did not need to dress my manners up by arching my lips or pitching my voice higher to sound nice and sweet. Rehabilitation on the outside consisted of tedious years of behavioral treatments. Even so, my smiles were never successful. They always felt like an unnatural contraction of my face, which caused me to look like an animal baring its teeth. Anyways, it wasn't jealousy or some petty comparison with a random woman that convinced me to make the journey home. I think I just awoke to the realization that just as I had changed (hopefully for the better) during the course of my treatment, so had Jason—Jason, who had seemed so impervious to my dread, suddenly looked starved. Famished of that normal, mundane warmth everyday human contact was meant to provide—something I could not give him. Our relationship had been predicated upon my healing, getting me to that rumored *better place*.

I wished I could be rid of the constant reminder that everything was about me. I wanted Jason to stop having to feel like he needed to keep watch over me. He was my therapist, yes—but he was my love above all. I no longer wanted to feel his gaze narrow across the room when I suddenly eyed a knife or a sharp object, my flesh asking for a sweet release my mind had been conditioned into desiring long ago. But this, of course, was part of the years of manipulation and brain-washing I had endured; therapy taught me as much. Jason had employed love as diligently as any other clinical tool. Years later, I was finally starting to see that I deserved a future on the outside. I had come to the woods of my childhood as a champion of my own future, and I wasn't about to let my past drag me down with it. Failing myself also meant failing Jason and all the time he had invested in me. That seemed somehow more important. How many times had Jason rushed out of bed to wake me up from yet another bout of sleep-walking? Held me as I clawed my way out of a nightmare, only to wake up screaming in a world that still felt foreign to me. Foreign but beautiful. I knew I would only ever graze this world's surface if I did not cut ties with my past...if I did not walk through these woods.

The first day of trekking, we followed an easy path marked by wooden posts slathered in red paint to mark the trail due north. I can't say I recognized the trees, because the New Sun had never wandered on the marked paths. Jason and I spent the time walking, holding hands. Sometimes, we stopped to look at swaths of colorful fungi overtaking the trees or admire the vista of a hidden lake whenever the forest opened up onto a valley.

At night, we ate tinned beans and sausage. We put on phony Southern accents and pretended we were cowboys out in the wild. Jason held me when the sun set and the temperatures dipped. I never slept better.

The trail started descending the following day. Jason stopped to consult the map. I knew this moment would come, I just didn't know if I was ready for it.

"Here?" I asked after about a minute that his eyes had not lifted from the map.

And then I realized that I was not only ready, I was impatient to see this wretched place I once called home and be done with it, once and for all.

A few more days, I told myself, *and the only reason we'll ever be walking in the woods again is because we wanted to take a hike.*

The path steepened once we cut through the trees, leaving the marked trail behind. The ground was more unstable, rugged. We had to climb up and down bluffs, using the map and compass to keep us on course. I found myself hungrily parting branches that snapped backward resentfully as soon I walked through them. Several times they stole a tear from me that had nothing to do with the fresh scratch on my face. At some point, we lost sight of the sky. The trees grew thick over us. Older too.

I only realized I was breathing heavily when Jason convinced me to stop for a water break.

"You don't have to go so fast, you know," he said, passing me the canteen.

I drank, but water did not undo the thickness that had formed in my throat.

"I'm not going fast," I said, panting, wiping my mouth with the back of my hand as I handed the canteen back to him.

"You're almost running, my love."

"Sorry. I just want to get it over with."

He smiled back. "Is spending time with me so horrible?"

"You know what I mean."

"I know."

The first time I researched the New Sun post-extraction, I was in a public library, when I was still living in the halfway house. What popped up on the computer screen were articles written about a death cult in the woods. I didn't like how they used the word "cult."

We weren't just hobos in the forest; I had told myself as I scrolled through article after article. I was taught philosophy, theology, and several different cosmologies by my elders. Our minds were not flooded with electrical impulses and crowded with civilization's fictions. We were taught all the lies so that we might discern the truth. The key was the human mind, only most people did not put it to proper use. We used it to worship the Brightness, which would one day grow to the size of a sun. A New Sun only my family could see, one we would be masters of. Our minds were capable of stirring the very evidence of man's sanctity. Religions, faiths...they all merely pointed to something divine. But we actually experienced it.

Despite my frustration with the media's portrayal of my family, there was one ineluctable fact all the articles shared: a fourteen-year-old girl had been picked up by a highway patrol car. Officers were called to the scene, tracking her back to a death-cult camp. Forty dead bodies found in a circle, each one with a stone stake poking out of their throats. I was the only unwilling survivor. Fear of death had stayed my hand.

At the time, however, I had not come to the library to read up on my rescue or even to discover what the newspapers' warped opinion of the New Sun was. I was still only a couple of years into my recovery. I suppose I just wanted to see pictures of home again. I still very much believed that by refusing to kill myself, I had failed my family. That I was not able to give the Brightness the ultimate sacrifice it had demanded.

As I scrolled through the drivel of news, my eyes fixed on a black-and-white picture of a police officer carrying a girl in his arms toward the camera. I remember staring at the screen until my eyes burned, trying to make out the little girl's face. But it was too grainy for me to recognize her.

"Stay back," Jason warned.

I obeyed.

Jason approached the furry mound between the trees. When he was about two yards out, he put a hand up to cover his nose and mouth. I knew it was safe to approach then.

It was a bear, after all. The fur was slashed down to the muscle in several places. Flies shimmered around it. I spotted the pink teats among the fur, still strangely moist, as if something had only just been suckling on them.

"It's dead," Jason said after a while.

"But how?"

"Look at the cuts on the fur. It might have fallen from one of the cliffs we spotted back there."

But even I could tell that the cuts were too shallow to have caused any real harm. And if it had fallen from a cliff... Well, then what the hell was it doing in the middle of a woodland? The cliffs Jason was referring to spanned a couple hundred feet in height. We had sighted them intermittently, in the rare moments the trees would part for us. Surely, if the bear had fallen from such a height, it would have died on impact.

Then I noticed the thick dark blood clotted on the beast's fore-claws.

I circled around to study it from the front.

"What is it?" Jason asked, reading the fear off my face.

Even he went silent when he saw what I was seeing. A grey mucilage dripped from the bear's eye sockets. Claw marks had raked both sides of its eyes straight down its face. Fur and muscle had been peeled back, the bone glowing white in the morning light.

"Something attacked it," Jason said. I knew he was trying to sound reasonable, logical, in control. "Probably another bear. They go crazy during mating season. Territorial," he went on.

"What do you know about bears?" I sneered.

"I read up on them to prepare for the trip."

Of course he had. I sighed, trying to drain the anger from my body. The familiar feeling of not being understood, of being patronized. I listened to my training, clenching and unclenching my feet, calves, and fists.

I hated myself for lashing out at him. He had taken care of all the logistics, navigation, packing. He had even practiced emergency fire-starting in the back yard with flint and knife. Not only that, he had supplied me with an endless stream of words of affirmation, assuring me that he loved me, no matter the outcome of the trip. If at any point I wanted to turn back, I had but to speak the words. He had taken the burden off me as much as he could, so that I could focus on simply walking through these woods.

"You're right," I conceded. "Unlucky bear. Shall we?"

He nodded. We moved on. I didn't need to look back at the bear to confirm my suspicions.

The blood on the bear's claws. The marks on its face.

It seemed to me that the bear had clawed its own eyes out. As if it had seen or experienced something unbearable. An all-too-human gesture.

Just like how you rake your fingers across your cheeks when your mind becomes too full, I told myself. *As if you were trying to get something out of your head.*

For a moment, I wasn't sure if it was my own voice in my head who addressed me or someone else's.

I think Jason saw me shiver, because suddenly his hand was around my waist.

"I'm fine," I said.

"I know," he answered.

My first therapist was a cunt. Convincing her that I not only saw the world differently, but that the world obeyed me in certain ways, because of the Brightness the New Sun worshipped, was excruciating. Every day I knew I would have to confront someone who would not believe me—who would try to convince me that what I had experienced wasn't real. But I persisted. I went on and on about how people had become detached from the forests they had crawled out of, living in cities that buzzed with electrical impulses that disabled their native mental frequencies. I told her of how we venerated the Brightness.

Opened ourselves up to it. And the Brightness, in turn, filled us with wonders. Allowed us to perform miracles. I can scent fear, taste anger, and even move things with my mind. At least, I could.

The initial stages of therapy felt very much like a recurring nightmare. Every day I tried to explain the purpose of the New Sun; every day the therapist nullified my efforts by telling me I was the victim of a death cult. That my family had manipulated me into thinking that my death would contribute to some cosmic purpose. More effort was put into disproving my statements than in trying to understand me.

Not Jason. He had been my ninth therapist. Jason had believed me. In fact, he had encouraged me to display my powers. Reverse psychology of sorts, I guess. But it had worked. Every time I reached out to the Brightness, I came up short. I could not hear the trees speak to me. I could no longer ask the Brightness to move things for me. It was gone, or it had never been at all.

But Jason did not denigrate my efforts. He encouraged me to get it all out, try all I might to make contact with the Brightness. My failures eventually served as a path to healing. To acknowledge the delusions my family had planted deep within me.

But Jason did not humiliate me with the truth of my delusion. He invited me to share everything about the New Sun and the Brightness we worshipped. He proved himself interested, not just in curing my delusions, but in learning about *me*. So I told him what I had been told by my elders—that I was the body for a greater will to inhabit. That the Brightness was an unfathomable force that could cross into our world from the Outside by way of the human mind. That a secret grandeur used to speak to me. The Brightness spoke to me. With a voice as real as yours or mine. My family would hold hands and chant for hours in a cave, one of the many exercises we did to hone our minds, quieting our wills to a whisper, so that our bodies were clean and pure for the Brightness to fill.

Jason wanted to know everything. He was gracious enough to be curious about what I had lived through, and he allowed me to feel safe enough to open up without suffering yet another person's judgement. At first, I just thought this was the ingenious treatment of a capable clinician, but to my utter awe, it was more than that. Jason wanted to know every part of me because he loved me. To this day, he was the greatest miracle in my life.

I dream of sixty lips moving without sound. I stare at the Brightness's throne, a tangle of reeds and bone with stone stakes spoking out of it. Oh, but the last time I looked at the throne there was only one stake left in it. All the others had been plucked and buried in flesh, when the Brightness's throne had been pillaged by its own devotees.

I wake, sweating, shaking. Jason is sleeping beside me, breathing peacefully. But I can't look at him for too long. I bowl over, holding my head. Something hurts in my skull. Dread has grown in it like a tumor since I last woke. A dread feeling, a *knowing* that something is wrong.

I unzip the tent and poke my head outside. Focusing on breathing. Just breathing. But the forest is too strong for me. It assaults my senses all at once. I hear the trees speak to me. Just like they used to. Their reedy voices singing their ancient sorrows to the wind. The old sounds and scents of the woods draw me forth like a lost animal called back home. I look around. The trees shake. But there's no wind. Something is pounding on the ground far off, causing the world to start and stammer.

THUMP

THUMP

THUMP

Then, I see it. The maggoty carcass of the bear we stumbled upon. Only it's moving jaggedly through the forest like an arthritic creature, a stop-motion abomination in a child's flipbook. I can see the bare bone where fur and muscle have been torn across half its face. The mop of guts it trails as it runs toward me—

I woke up panting like an asthmatic, shivering in Jason's arms. His warmth seeping into me, bringing me back to life. I felt his strong hands plunging into my arm-flesh, reassuring me of the here and now. Pinioning me to my greatest and most sacred possession. My body.

"It's okay. It's okay," he cooed repeatedly. "What did you dream of?"

I told him only of the bear carcass running toward us. I did not tell him of the first dream. Of the chanting in the cave. Reality is always scarier than any made-up monster. I feared that uttering it would somehow break the spell of sanity that had taken over a decade of therapy to cast. Was reality that brittle? I feared Jason would turn to smoke. That I would fall through his arms and end up in the cave again.

I knew this to be a step backward in my mental health. Jason had always pointed out that not being able to speak something aloud was our most reliable diagnostic tool for identifying where trauma lurked. That's why I had told him everything in the first place. By then, Jason knew as much of the Brightness and the New Sun as I ever did.

I suppose I might have told him of the full extent of my dream. But there we were, more than halfway through the woods, and I didn't want to let him down. After everything he had done for me, I wanted to put the matter of the New Sun to rest, once and for all. The little girl might have been carried out of the woods in the arms of a police officer—but the woman, I had told myself, who willingly re-entered those woods, would walk out on the strength of her own two legs.

She was shivering under the rain. *I* was shivering. Someone was speaking. Murmuring something repeatedly. Then the words came in clear.

"I am the body. I am the body. I am the body."

I was clutching my own throat, choking the words down. As if to sever the utterance from their source, which was not me. Could not be me. I looked around.

A halo of flies had gathered over my head, marking me. Unfamiliar trees reached their arms toward me.

No. Not arms. Branches. Just branches.

I shook my head, dissembling the irrational thoughts. I waved my hands, undoing the crown of flies over my head.

You brought him for me, an old voice whispered from the darkest depths of my mind.

Contrary to my first stint with therapy, my extensive sessions with Jason taught me that I should not try to ignore the voices. I should, instead, answer these suggestions with my own voice.

You brought him for me.

"No," I said aloud. "Jason is here to accompany me. Because he loves and cares for me."

Just like that, silence was restored to my skull, leaving only a dull ache behind.

By way of the moonlight seeping through the canopy, I recognized the impression of my own tracks. I followed them back to the tent. I entered, breath shivering, snuggling up to Jason.

"Where were you?"

"I just had to pee."

"I'm so not in the shape I thought I was," Jason said easily, as we climbed over some sedge and weeds growing at the edges of a stream. "Maybe we should make this a monthly excursion, you know? I mean, not here obviously. But some other place."

I could offer very little in the ways of small talk, so I just nodded and smiled, masking as best I could.

My mind was strangely busy that morning. Not thinking, exactly; in fact, I wasn't really thinking at all. Instead, it felt like I was sitting outside a locked door. Behind that door, I sensed all manner of activity. I could hear the slightest murmur and sound without really understanding what was being said. As if something else had locked themselves in a small part of my mind I could not access.

We continued walking, the pressure in my head escalating with each step. Jason was still talking. His voice barely a murmur by then.

And then, it broke. The accumulated pressure was released. My mind suddenly emptied. I bowled over in an orgasm of relief.

I took a moment to breathe before pulling myself up by a low-hanging branch. Then it dawned on me. The forest had gone quiet. Too quiet. Jason was no longer talking.

drip

drip

drip

I turned around. My eyes found him immediately. He was standing a couple steps behind me.

Blood fanned his forehead.

His eyes were all cornea from the sharp angle he was facing. I followed the vector of his harrowed gaze.

drip

drip

drip

Ten or fifteen feet above us, a feathery obscenity was massed on a branch. A ball of feathers and gore. Maybe I could see a beak. I wasn't quite sure from where I stood. Whatever had happened, the bird had been reduced to a mealy mess.

I realized Jason was still standing under the bloody rain. He had been too shocked to move. I ever so slightly moved him out of the way.

In that moment, I knew Jason was afraid. I could see him try to form a justification for such an encounter, a rationalization to speak aloud. Some spell to mend the world back to normal. Not for his sake, but for mine.

For what could possibly spontaneously crush a bird like that?

"I've heard about that happening," I managed.

"What?" Jason turned to me.

"Birds flying into an aircraft engine. They get mangled pretty bad."

"Yeah," he said. "Yeah."

"Come on. I'm hungry."

Maybe I never really got better. Maybe I just got better at lying.

At some point, I may have realized that what had made Jason a good lover had likely made him a bad therapist. Partners were supposed to accept you for what you were, love you for what you were. They may challenge you, but they never invalidated who you are, or they just wouldn't be with you in the first place. Therapists, for all their round-about ways they have of saying things, force you into changing yourself. Make you understand that something isn't right. That it was up to you to adapt to the world, not the other way around. Had the truth gotten lost among the caresses, the kisses, the sweet words whispered to me over and over again like a spell?

You'll be fine. You'll be fine. I love you. I love you. You can do it. One step at a time.

That had been Jason's motto: One step at a time.

And I had believed it.

"Did you hear that?" I asked.

Jason turned toward me, cocking his head. We stood in silence, watching the wind yawn through endless rows of trees.

"I didn't hear anything. What did you hear?"

My voice had been clipped by the full-body pulse traveling through me. It was voiceless, sexless. My body shivered as it received another pulse. A simple sign of acknowledgement too complex, too pure for language to encapsulate.

"Alicia?"

Jason had never had good hearing. Like his father. But I couldn't fault him for not hearing this. Just as he had inherited the habits and quirks of his kin, so had I. Perfect hearing would not have helped him receive this message. A call seated within the very ground we walked on.

"It was nothing."

"Look, I'm not trying to invalidate what you heard. Just talk to me."

Here it goes. A therapist's circular mode of saying that the patient could not trust themselves; that her experiences required an interpreter. I felt myself clenching at the reductive ways in which he was trying to "make things better." I hated Jason there and then for being so simple. For being unaware of the powers our presence was stirring.

I continued walking, but the world was slowly losing focus. The present lost through a murk of the pulses, rising with every step I took. My eyes blurred, my anger dripping over me like so much hot blood.

I hissed through gnashing teeth, as my jaw clenched and my mind released all of it.

A loud sound broke from the canopy. Birds shot into the sky like a spray of black confetti. A moment later, Jason was falling onto the forest floor.

"Are you alright?"

"Yeah. Sorry. I tripped," he said as he unwrapped his foot from the vine.

I was shaking with fury. This time directed at me. Yet another reason to hate myself.

I did what Jason had taught me. *Focus on your body instead of your thoughts.* I took a moment to clench my fists and relaxed them. Clench and relax, clench and relax. Slowly, I pried my attention out from the fetid well of my mind.

"Can you walk?" I asked.

I felt Jason lean more weight onto me than I had expected. He waved away my attempts to help him. But I could see him grimacing.

"Yes. I'll be fine."

I held the map as he pointed to the few thumbs'-worth of trekking that remained to arrive at the New Sun's sanctuary, which roughly translated to another day and half of walking. I let him hold my hand, told him to give me all the weight he needed. He did. And I was glad of it.

He thought I was shaking from withstanding his weight. I did not tell him that the black birds had arranged themselves in the shape of a horrible face when they had shot up from the forest. That that the vine he had tripped over had, in fact, moved to entrap his ankle. This entire place resented his presence.

"Do you still love me?" My voice a mere shiver in the twilight of our tent.

"Of course. Why would you ask that?"

"All of this." I held up my hands to explain but I couldn't. I did my best to stifle a sob. "You're hurt..." I managed to get out the smallest fragments of the truth.

"It's not your fault. I tripped."

I went quiet a while before I spoke again, carefully picking my words. "I'm afraid something bad will happen."

"You think that because of the horrible things that *have* happened here," Jason countered smoothly, even though I knew he was in pain. "You were a victim of some twisted people, Alicia. Nothing more."

His forehead was matted in sweat, and his ankle had swelled to twice its size. He wouldn't be able to walk, and we still had a couple miles ahead of us. The truth was I was responsible for everything. For getting us here. For existing even. If only Jason didn't love me. If only I could have spared him from ever meeting me...

"I just need to get some rest. I'll be fine tomorrow."

Jason could do that. Part my barbed thoughts despite getting stuck with nettles every time. He had done that for the entirety of our relationship. His unwavering devotion made me love him and hate myself more in equal parts.

Old words came back to haunt me.

When the Brightness was displeased, his devotees were sent scampering through the woods in fear. How could I explain all this to Jason? How can a blind man be made to see? That everything that had happened to us had occurred for a reason.

I was just the body. What if the Brightness used me to harm Jason further?

I could not let that happen. I would not let the only thing in this world that loved me suffer because of me.

I realized, then, that I had not come to the woods to prove that all that I had lived through with the New Sun had been imagined. I was here to overcome it.

"I am the body."

I leapt awake, caging my hands over my lips to staunch the words. Leakage from the horrible dream I'd been having. My throat was dry as if I'd engaged in some dark colloquy for hours.

I looked to Jason. He was shivering, sweating. I placed my hand on his forehead. He was hot. Burning, in fact. I pulled up his pant-leg. The ankle had pretty much stayed the same. But I feared what this fever might portend.

I shook him briefly out of sleep. Just long enough to get him to take some Advil in hopes of lowering his temperature. Then I rocked him gently back to the sleeping bag, as tears broke through my eyes.

"I should have never gotten you mixed up in this," I whispered to him. "I felt the woods. Right from the start, I felt them, Jason. They turned against us the moment we stepped foot in them. I ignored the signs. The bear...the blood marking you...you got hurt because of me..."

I held Jason close, just as he'd held me so many times. These weren't random occurrences. They were warnings. Warnings for him to stay behind or else...

Jason had been wrong, I decided. This wasn't simply a test of where I was in my healing process. This was a final stand. If I failed, I wouldn't be able to simply turn around and leave and try some other time. If I could not bear out whatever waited for me in these woods, it would not be worth turning back.

I wove my fingers through his hair, damp from the sweat. More than anything I wanted to wake him again, tell him that he was in danger. That we should turn back.

But how many times had he refrained from telling me how worried he was? When he found me crumpled on the ground, so exhausted I was unable to stand, or staring at a wall pleading to something that wasn't there—how many times had he smiled and encouraged my progress?

I snapped Jason's backpack open, taking one of the torches and stacking most of the food in the corner of the tent, taking just what I would need for the rest of the trek.

Once I climbed out, I gave Jason one last look. I could have stood there forever, watching that beautiful man sleep. Eventually, I turned and walked away into the night.

A couple hours into my march, the wind picked up, ripping the tears from my face. The forest was filled with the awful call of home. The pitter-patter of rain slowly wore away at the edges of my mind. I stuck my hands under my armpits, trying to find some warmth in the crevasses of my own body. The moisture brought old smells to the surface. Somewhere out in the underbrush something had died. Windfallen fruit that had rotted on the forest floor.

I stopped under some thicker-looking pine branches. My hands shook as I piled sticks and kindling just as I had seen Jason do. I lit a match, but the flame was not even close to taking. Everything was wet.

I should have done more than just watch Jason practice fire in our back yard.

I stood hugging myself, rubbing my chest. I realized that I still had the map in my back pocket from when Jason had passed it to me. I hoped he would not try to navigate without it, that he would wait for me in the tent. I consulted it, trying to define my best course across the remaining stand of trees.

You are the body. The words licked at the back of my mind like cold flames. *You know where to find me.*

I nodded, gritting my teeth.

I know.

I lit a match under the map. It took easily, eating away at the dry paper. I quickly threw damp kindling on top of it until I had nourished a healthy flame. Then, I leaned back against the tree to relax a moment. Every now and again I would toss sticks and other windfallen wood on it. I managed to pick at some sausage from one of the tins I had brought with me, while I warmed myself.

It had been day when I sat down. Within minutes, it had grown dark. I did not stop for long. Only long enough to get warm.

Even though it was night, I had walked these woods when I was a girl; I could just as easily walk them as a woman.

I followed a crumb-trail of stairs between the branches. Not that I needed them. It wasn't even that I recognized the way back home. I could tell you the trees told me. Or that the ground gave up its secrets of footsteps long-faded. But you wouldn't understand.

The rain made everything slick like motor oil. The wet leaves brushing my face felt like welcoming kisses.

I parted the last branches before the clearing. Most of the log cabins were still standing. My family knew how to set a good hearth. They did not build something that would not last. What damage had been done to the structures had been caused by the police, the reporters, and eventually the vandals and miscreants in search of thrills who had come to visit the remains of the commune after seeing it on the news.

Before long, I was walking between the log cabins, eager to see the places I had left behind. The communal orchard from which we ate of was overgrown with weeds and brambles. The field I used to play in as a child was soft and shapeless from the recent rains. I recognized my old house. I tried walking inside, but only made it as far as the front door.

And then I came to face the cave. The opening of the chanting chamber was shorn out of the shoulder of a hillock, in a reddish clay carved out of hell's earth, or so it seemed. *So far, so good*, I told myself. A few more steps and I would be done. But I stopped. For a while all I could do was stand.

In front of me lay the chanting chamber, a man-made cave hacked into the earth itself. The entrance stared at me like a dry toothless mouth, beyond which my family awaited me, arms extended. Ten years ago, they had waited for me, but I had not heeded their call.

A pulse forced a shudder through me, returning me to my body. A wet click like an eye opening sounded from the depths of the cave. I clenched and unclenched my fist, reminding my body of its owner.

My fear of the Brightness would only end if I walked the same road it was taking to reach me. If I stepped into the cave, proving to myself that nothing could hurt me there.

"One step at a time," I said out loud, trying to channel Jason's strength through his words.

"One step at a time."

I hoped with all my heart that he was thinking of me. I believed he was.

I made it to the threshold of the chamber. The cave walls were made of a primitive red clay. The shadow fell as heavily as death's cloak on my shoulders. I could feel it by then—could feel it pulsing like heatwaves off a fire. I stood, struggling to breathe the solid air for a moment, steeling myself before taking another step in the darkness.

And then a pulse, stronger than the ones that had preceded.

I could see in the cave. The Brightness filled it with light. I saw its throne at the back of the chamber. A mess of reed woven across a grisly tree of human bones. A stone stake lay buried within. My hands clenched of their own accord, as if in anticipation of gripping my own death; a death I had avoided long ago.

The body is back. Back at last.

The voice thundered in the back of my mind.

The darkness became busy with something. Charged.

Desperately, I tried not to believe. I tried, with every fiber of my being, to prevent my memory from embracing this presence as a reality. I clenched every part of my body in revolt—from my toes to the jelly in my skull—so as not to believe.

And then I felt it lurch into me.

It plunged into my mind, reclaiming its residence. One consciousness, staining, overtaking the other like overmilked coffee. And suddenly my body, my home, was filled with life again. Every room bursting with energy, every window—eyes, mouth, ears, vagina, anus—every outlet bleeding with light. It jostled its way through me, making space for older memories to accommodate themselves.

The Brightness deftly slipped past all the barriers I had erected against it. The safeguards I'd built over the years—CBT and EMDR trauma exercises—seemed now like the superstitious rituals of a primitive. A single beam of black static weaving itself through years of safeguards erected in therapy and all the loving words conjured to control my so-called illness. Here I was, inviting it to taste me again, to use me. My skull just a prophylactic for the Brightness to penetrate into the world. My breath turned to a whinny. Air escaped through a wet nose that was no longer mine, breath pluming into the darkness. I felt the Brightness inside me, a sensation as startling as the first gulp of cold river water. So I sang for it like I had when I'd been a child. I let it suckle on the sweet jelly of my mind, on thoughts of love and yearning I'd harbored for it all those years. The shame I had been made to feel...that something was wrong with me—that I was horribly dislocated from the world everyone on the outside was living in. I offered everything to it until it had had its fill. It had been so long since it had experienced a human mind, and it was hungry. Oh, how it hungered. But I was much too small for it. It was jagged and overlarge for me. It needed more than just one scared little girl. It needed others...others who would not forsake it.

I woke on the ground, breathing in dust. Too tired to do anything other than cough the dirt out of my lungs and lie there, where I'd been left. My thighs and crotch sticky. I had soiled myself. I was no longer in the cave, but just outside, under the forest trees.

The Brightness must have pulled out of me to give me time to recuperate. It would have killed me if it had stayed inside for too long.

I could hardly move. I held up my hands to find a pair of scratched palms caked in mud. I whimpered as I tried to stand.

I did not feel anything stir in the back of my mind. Was it also resting? A long time had passed since the Brightness had last inhabited someone. Too long had it been starved of human contact. It had assailed my mind like a parched man flinging himself at a lush oasis. But in its pursuit of the human, it had not accounted for the exhaustion that followed. For the limits of my body, its mortal playground.

This gave me time. Time to come up with a plan.

But I could hardly cobble together these tenuous notions, let alone formulate an actual plan.

I lost consciousness again. When I came to a second time, my thoughts were sharper, but they came with a mind-cleaving headache. It was no longer dark out, but early morning.

I wasn't too confident I could find my way back to Jason. But I had to make an attempt. Coming here had been a mistake. To succeed here would not signify mastering my past, but to respect it. I saw that now. There was no healing to be done in these hellish backwoods.

My head spun, trying to identify the best course back through the trees. But I was still weak. I knew that without food I wouldn't be able to walk long without falling. The Brightness had pushed my body to the brink. After so long of not experiencing the human form, it had used my body until it could hardly even stand.

My gaze shifted to the cave. And I realized that the Brightness had accounted for this. Piled a few feet away from me were a couple rabbits, harassed and dragged from their lairs, their necks broken. I hadn't simply been running. I had been hunting and foraging for myself. The Brightness planned to keep me here after all. I shivered at the knowing seated deep within me, that it planned on using me as its last and first devotee to rebuild its kingdom.

I looked back at my palms, realizing that the blood on them was not my own. That the marks scoring my wrists and legs had nothing to do with the trees, but were actually the teeth marks of the rabbits that had died trying to defend themselves. The things I was expected to feed on, while the Brightness subsisted on me. On my mind.

Then, a deeper inkling clicked like vertebrae straightening into my skull, righting what felt like the very meridian of my life so far. The Brightness had left knowledge in its wake; the painful memory of that day, when each member of my family took their life...

The Brightness had had to subsist on something else after the prolonged absence of the human mind in these woods, a forced fast brought about by my family. That meant the Brightness had had to resort to the minds of animals, critters, maybe even insect life.

I finally understood...

My thoughts fixed themselves on my family, as fear and dread mounted within me: their suicide hadn't been an act of faith, but one of sacrifice. They had been trying to starve the Brightness until it faded. With the extinction of its worshipers, the Brightness would have flickered out like a star eventually. Their final act had been one of revolt against the Brightness.

My realization ballooned into horror. I bent over, clutching my shivering knees before I could hit the ground again. *I* had botched their plans to rid the world of this unnatural thing. I had come back, nursed the Brightness back from the brink of everlasting darkness.

But if despair had turned my body to goo, anger hardened it all over again. I picked myself up, staggering forward like a rickety marionette.

I managed to stumble back inside the chanting chamber, knowing what was required of me. I sought out and found the Brightness's throne. That abomination made of wild reed growing out of human bone. A seat only a madman would willingly claim as its own. I could no longer tell if there was an actual seat somewhere among that tangled mess. But something did catch my human eyes. Something glittered among the darkness. I reached my hand—grabbed—and pulled at the last stake from it, the rough stone biting into my palm. I pulled and pulled until it broke away from the reeds. I went back outside and stood in the yard where I had once danced and sang with my family.

I held the stake above my head and called to the Brightness.

"Come to me. Come to me, filth."

I felt the black wind in my mind grow, turn resentful. It was about to enter me again. Before it could do so, I placed the thorn under the tenderest part of my neck.

I felt the Brightness flex, forcing itself into me. It was angry.

"I will do it. I'll do it!" I threatened.

It felt good to scream; it gave my voice a strength I had no right to. The Brightness stopped pressing down on my mind.

"Then what will you have, huh? Nothing. *I* am the body! *I* am the body! Not you!"

I forced the stake deeper into my neck, willing myself to believe I would do it.

I will do it.

It knew that. I knew it.

Just as I was about to force the tip of the stake into my throat, I felt the Brightness drain from my mind.

And then a silence.

The wind swept through the trees. I could not hear their voices any longer. Just the common sounds of leaves blowing and critters creeping in the underbrush. It was beautiful. The sunlight touched the tip of my head. I wanted to cry. I did.

I had done it. I had accomplished far more than I had set out to.

I got my bearings and proceeded to return the way I had come. Out the yard, past the cabins, through the trees. I would make my way out just as I had come. One step at a time.

A snapping and breakage in the forest I was headed for stilled my advance.

The shape that emerged from the trees wasn't any monster my fractured mind had cobbled together to torment me. It was Jason using a branch to hobble along.

"Jason!"

Relief washed over me. I realized, then, that the only reason I had come to this place was to unburden myself of the truth all over again. I ran up to him, plunging myself in his warmth. I clung to something real. There Jason gathered under my fingers. I dug my face into his neck, inhaling his scent, until...

I pulled back to stare into his kind eyes.

But something was wrong. They did not welcome me. They burned me instead, like the coldest of ice that sticks to and rips out your tongue when you try and pull away. Just as I did. When I tried to recoil, his forearms gripped my own.

"Jason?"

He took my hand, helping the stake I still held into my throat.

I bumbled backward as an unfathomable amount of red burst out of me.

"I am the body," Jason said.

The woman coughed up blood and called and cried and struggled to breathe. She looked at me but did not see me any longer. None shall find her remains. She is ephemeral and will go on to feed the very forest she has grown out of, the place where I have chosen to dwell. I am the body, and I can never die, so long as someone weeps or wakes or wanders in sight of my cave.

The blood has slowed now. After the woman finishes dying, I will take the horn she hath illicitly plucked and restore it to my throne. They never learn. But in time, they shall abandon their concrete hives and return to the woods. There, my throne shall regrow its horns, one devotee at a time, until my Light shall fill all of you up.

So much scorn shown to the only thing in this vast and treacherous universe who worships you...

I only ask for the barest scraps of your regard. The cozy embrace of your mind. The occasional privilege of your senses so that I might ever so briefly inhabit this beautiful world you have been given to touch and scent and taste. But I have not lost faith in you. I will never lose faith.

Devil in the Music

by J.W. Bodden

I NEVER TRUSTED EASY invitations, except to nab a star. These balmy nights of summer were ripe for love and abduction. A giddy smile reflected off the invite on my phone's screen, guiding me across the wind-swept stalks to an isolated cornfield. Clutching a love letter in my sweaty palms, I put on the butch swagger Momma's belt demanded and manned up for tonight's show.

A crowd corralled near a gap in the greenery, blowing rings of cigarette smoke like funeral garlands. I skulked through the thickening foliage, watching the members of the Star Chasers Society make their preparations. Peepers held binoculars glued to their faces, poison pens hauled bags of hate mail, and kidnappers tied slipknots of rope. I bit my lip, thrilled to finally meet them. Despite our online forum's name, we weren't amateur stargazers, but seasoned stalkers obsessed with a handsome pop idol riding on a mechanical bull: Longhorn.

None of them noticed me except for Ramrod, our forum's mod and godmother of the lurker underground. She squared up against me dressed in racing overalls, showing off her tattooed cleavage—inked with indictments accusing her of crashing famous starlets offroad.

"You're not tall enough for this ride." She tousled my damp curls. "Go home, Pussyfoot."

I cringed at my nickname, even though it fitted a fanatic chasing after his idol. "We all clicked the same link on the forum," I bristled. "I got an invitation to His concert, same as you."

"Listen to me." She thumbed the knife dangling from her belt. "You'll never rope this stud. I'd suggest you run away, but what stalker can turn down the chance of snagging a star?"

I took a dainty step toward her, dropping my butch act, and quickly confessed the hard truths I couldn't entrust to my nagging mother. "What gay boy can ignore his true love's call?"

Before she could answer, the ground rumbled. A terrible sound boomed across the cornfield, swaying the stalks like a cattle stampede. The bass-heavy reverb hit me square on my chest, pushing me back. Three notes echoed across the night, rising and falling with a sexy beat.

Unable to resist, I left Ramrod and followed the music into the ploughlands. Longhorn's song pulsed with my heartbeat, luring me forward. Lovesickness festered inside me as I crumpled the envelope in my grip. My idol would soon become infected. He just didn't know it.

I chased after Longhorn's song deeper into the greenery. A twisting passageway cut through the stalks, swaying with its rhythm—almost as if Longhorn wanted to get found. I giggled, happy to oblige as the song spiked my fever better than sneaking behind His motorcade.

Wading through the thicket reminded me of my momma's farm, rattling echoes of her screaming inside my head. She disapproved of Longhorn's music, belt-whipping me if my hips shimmied without restraint. But His songs were my escape from pretending I wasn't the queer Momma despised. She saw darkness in me, and I felt it in my bones—a stalker's demented love.

But if any partner could forgive a boy who rifled celebrity trash, it was Longhorn. He would take me despite my sickness and allow me to be myself, letting all my dark desires bloom.

Turning a sharp bend ahead, I stopped at the sight of horns peeking above rows of corn. My breath caught in my throat as I pushed through the stalks, stumbling on a clutch of totem poles propped into the mud—black stones carved with glyphs and topped by polished bull skulls. I couldn't help but fall to my knees to thank my idol. He'd left behind signs to show me the way.

But my devotions were soon interrupted. All around me, Star Chasers gathered before the totems, oiling handcuffs and fastening ball gags, hell-bent on abducting my true love. Blushing fangirls built altars from glossy pinups on the monoliths. Every image showed Him on top of a mechanical bull, muscular thighs hugging its ribcage. He was the ideal image of a stud. Everything I could never be. Not without shame, I felt myself harden, quickly hiding the bulge beneath my shirt. But Ramrod's chuckles warned me that my weakness hadn't gone unnoticed.

Ramrod wiped a spot of mud from my cheeks. Our forum's mod always looked after me on the message board. She was my fairy godmother with celebrity bloodstains on her tire tracks.

"I get your obsession, Pussyfoot," she said. "No stalker can resist an elusive celebrity."

"Don't I know it," I whispered, knowing all too well that Longhorn's mystique was impossible to fight. My idol gave no interviews, released albums without a label, and drew the crowds on legend alone. Nobody knew much about Him or His rodeo bull act. I'd scoured the tabloids in a feeding frenzy, but He remained a mystery, honing my fixation like a blade's edge.

Ramrod's eyes lingered on my letter. "Do you really think a love note can seduce a star?"

"Honestly, I don't know if it can," I admitted. "What did you bring Him?"

She pushed up her cleavage under the racing overalls. "Nothing gets a celebrity's attention like a high-speed chase. My gift's a simple one. A head-on collision he'll never forget."

I clenched the envelope in my grip tighter, envy boiling inside me. Her gift was far more memorable than my schoolboy love letter, but I wasn't ready to give up on our fated romance yet. We were both destined to dance together. Longhorn was the only one who could set me free.

Sneaking across the passageway, a glint of spotlights lifted the darkness through gaps in the stems. The beacons dimmed, then flared back to life, pulsing with the beat of Longhorn's song. I couldn't help shimmying my hips to His music, but quickly corrected myself. Momma's nagging was cruel but always right—no queeny gay boy would ever catch himself a famous stud.

But I wasn't the only one excited to close in on our idol. Elbowed and pushed aside, the Star Chasers swarmed around me, dancing buck naked, swapping spit and methamphetamine smoke. Bullhead masks concealed every one of their faces. Spellbound, they barbequed rats in crackling bonfires and slit their wrists, bleeding into plastic jer-rycans—offerings to lure and snatch a star.

I tried to ignore their desperate attempts for attention but couldn't help the jealousy boiling inside me. Sharing His song with the rest of the stalkers made me feel cheated and replaceable. I couldn't stomach Him singing for anyone else. Longhorn belonged to me alone.

As His song played on repeat, I noticed Ramrod scowling at the crowd. But something was off. Tears streaked her cheeks as she clutched the knife on her belt. Her voice rattled like Momma's ven-tilator. "My little joyride can't compete with blood by the gallon, Pussyfoot."

"Don't mind the bleeders," I said, trying to reassure her, but I couldn't stop staring at the fans' mad rituals—hoping my darkness didn't consume me just yet. "What's wrong with them?"

"Can't you feel it?" She pulled her blade, teasing her throat with its edge. "They hear a devil in the music, and it wants to get fed. My gift won't lure me a star with blood on the menu."

Ramrod turned away, whistling Longhorn's three notes. Then, without warning, she went quiet—the knife had found its mark. Blood splattered on the ground, and she collapsed into my arms. I tried to stop the bleeding, but the blade had carved her way too deep. Grief doubled me over. Ramrod had always taken good care of me, but I failed her when she needed me the most.

As she stopped breathing, my mind split between a boy missing his only friend and a stalker bewitched by obsession. I mourned after her, but my sickness delighted in the shrinking competition. Taking a keepsake to remember her, I stole the knife cradled in her grip for myself.

For a moment, I hesitated to go any further. I wondered why a su-perstar would invite a pack of dangerous stalkers to a private concert.

But I then reminded myself that idols were nothing without worship. This was all a game, a competition for His attention. Knife in one hand and envelope in the other, my offering felt like a childish trinket. Ramrod's death taught me love was a gainful thing. There was always a price to pay when bartering with desire—a terrible sacrifice.

Longhorn's song got louder, its sound waves tunneling new trails through the greenery. Sweat ran down my neck as His music warped with static and the bellow of a wild animal. Its primal roar froze me with fear, but the crowd pushed me forward. There was no going back now.

The Star Chasers heard His call, same as I did. They stumbled through the shifting stalks, stepping over limbs and severed chunks of flesh. Keeping my distance, I watched them cackling, star-struck, as they sliced meat off their bones to build blood-dripping effigies of our idol. Their sculptures, made from fists hacked into hooves and ribs sharpened like horns, never compared to the handsome beefcake Himself. Even their best bits failed to imitate His charms.

Pussyfooting as my nickname demanded, I sampled the Star Chasers' meat, but they lacked an authentic celebrity flavor. Still, they were on to something. Only our bodies were worthy offerings. To claim my prize, I needed to show Longhorn I was willing to pay for love in flesh and bone. So I unzipped my pants, clenched Ramrod's knife, and lopped my manhood off.

Covered in blood, I stuffed the flaccid organ into my envelope and sealed it with a kiss. The pain meant nothing as long as my true love got fed. After binding the wound with my undies, I staggered on, a coppery stink polluting the air. Hemorrhaging aside, I'd struck a good bargain.

Weak and dizzy, Momma's nagging pestered me; no belt this time. She begged me to run home, but Longhorn's song had its hooks in deep. I took a whiff of His musk, the sweat of a bull-riding stud. What gay boy could resist his partner's charms? The obvious answer was none.

The stalks wilted around me, revealing a concert stage. His performance was about to begin. Hiding the blooming red stain on my crotch, I joined the hooting fans crowding the dais. Longhorn's shadow cast over us, devouring the night. My breath stopped as He slowly took shape: shirtless, jockstrap swollen by His bulge. The pop idol rode a huge mechanical bull. He bucked on it bareback, gripping it by the horns—oily mechanisms screeching motors and gears.

Longhorn flexed His muscles to lure the fans closer. In a mad stampede, the Star Chasers climbed on the bull to seize Him but got torn apart by its bone-crunching machinery. Yet they kept jumping into the meat grinder all too willingly. His fanatics were, at last, part of the show.

Heart thumping against my chest, I clutched my love letter and the organ tucked inside. My knees buckled as I climbed the platform, like a sweetheart about to propose. Longhorn winked and met my gaze. Heat burned between us, a blinding connection under the spotlights.

Gingerly, I lay my love letter on the platform. My entire body trembled. This was our moment, the start of our long-fated romance. I held my breath as Longhorn turned His gaze to my envelope, but surprisingly, it was His mechanical bull—scraping metal hooves—who approached it instead. As the beast closed on my offering, a wriggling trunk wormed from its muzzle and sniffed at my love letter. In a rage, it stomped on the envelope, crushing my manhood with a sickening squelch. My blood went cold as the beast began to twist and deform.

The beast reared on its hindquarters, gears screaming and motors blazing with sparks. Its riveted joints groaned and extended, stretching until it towered over the stage. Blood dripped down a heaving ribcage, its sternum muscles welded into an iron-cast exoskeleton. I watched, slack-jawed, as my stud caught fire atop the beast. His perfect body blistered and melted like wax, dissolving into gobs on the overheated machinery. He slowly disappeared, fusing with the metal.

I wanted to run and escape this nightmare, but I froze as the real Longhorn revealed itself. Its trunk coiled, muscles tensing before shattering the spotlights with a boom. With each lumbering step, the beast collapsed the concert stage, burying me under a tomb of steel beams.

Broken bones slowed me to a crawl as I wriggled out of the heap. I groaned in pain, my body aching as the beast loomed closer, casting a shadow over me. Then, as an opening number, it trumpeted three bone-chilling notes, stirring the dead back to their feet. Mesmerized by the beast's lightless eyes, the corpses girded around the fearsome creature and joined it in a dance. Longhorn licked its incisors with a blood-wet tongue, feeding off the adoration of its audience.

Tears blurred my vision as the corpses danced in lockstep around me, losing more organs with every twirl. They jigged in the mud helplessly, entranced by the beast's black voids for eyes. I dropped to my knees, unable to stop mourning my idol. Waves of loss washed over me. The dream of our love burned away like His body, leaving the taste of its ashes in my mouth. I'd been a fool to believe in romance. My stud had never been real—just bait for the hungry beast.

The creature had conned me. Its songs were never meant for the living. Anger burned through me as I tightened my grip on Ramrod's knife. I squared my shoulders, hiding my fear behind a well-practiced butch pose, as I slowly stalked after it. I wanted to avenge my lost love by stabbing the beast in its back. But as I snuck closer, a cold yet familiar hand tousled my curls.

Ramrod's corpse smiled, the red slit on her throat forming a second grin. I rushed to take her in my arms, but she pushed me back, offering her pale hand instead. Her voice gurgled from her severed windpipe, splashing icy blood on my face. I couldn't understand my reanimated godmother's exact words, but her meaning was clear: she invited me to join the dancing dead.

At first, I hesitated, unsure if Ramrod's corpse wasn't just another of Longhorn's tricks. But as I wavered, the beast lurched toward me. Its hypnotic gaze caught me like sharp hooks. My idol's loss slowly faded, and a strange desire began to take root. I couldn't help but blush at its blood-stained muscles and the shapely curve of its horns. The beast's terrifying body was irresistible. Despite my efforts, I couldn't turn away. A new obsession blossomed inside me.

The beast was close enough to touch and smell its breath. Unable to resist, I petted its iron frame and felt its motors throb. This creature wanted my death just as much as I did its love. For the first time, I felt an attraction that wasn't an illusion but a true desire. The beast was the stud I'd been looking for—a dark partner, a killer worthy of my stalker love. It was the one who would set a gay boy free. I'd wasted time chasing tabloid fantasies. This singing devil was real.

With the knife's edge nicking my throat, Longhorn's strange music swept me to my tiptoes. I finally let go of Momma's belt-taught lessons, queered my hips, and pirouetted with the rest of the dead. Romanced by my new lover's song, I was sure we'd dance together for eternity.

#FireofLove

by M. Stern

"Hey, Ilana, you ever hear of that last one?" Darren Arnault called without turning from his computer screen. "I should remember it, if it was such a big deal, but I can't seem to—"

He was pulled back into full immersion in the on-screen video by the leitmotif coming from the speakers. It signified a new item on the list of *The Craziest Viral Phenomena You Probably Forgot*.

"The next viral craze in our countdown made for one very sore summer," said the show's host. "When the Turn Purple Challenge started trending, purple welts were the must-have accessory that fidget spinners were a few years before. Remember fidget spinners?"

The screen displayed one of the toys spinning between a thumb and forefinger.

"We didn't think so," said the host as the hand tossed the toy. "The Turn Purple Challenge, though, is hard to forget. The idea was simple. Give yourself a bruise and show it off on social. But boy did things get complicated!"

A clip played on-screen of two teenagers in a park. One was on his knees, stretched over a bench. The other wailed on his back with a sock full of rolled quarters. In the next clip, the two men reversed roles. In the third, from a later video, the friends proudly displayed massive blue-black and purple welts all over their bodies. Supportive emojis floated in front of the footage.

"Teenagers! Right?" said the host. "But it wasn't just them! Everyone from C-level executives to elementary school art teachers showed off a new shade of purple that summer."

A clip montage played: A man and a woman joyfully going tit-for-tat, laying into each other with crowbars. A gray-haired grandmother of five doing a two-handed spinning swing of a 25-pound sledgehammer and launching it into her book club buddy's back. A seated, middle-aged man wearing a helmet letting out guttural howls as neighbors of all ages and races beat him with blunt objects.

"Yes, things got nuts," narrated the host over the footage. "Who ever imagined that average citizens would get so violent just because everyone else was?"

The host now appeared on-screen. He was a man in his mid-30s wearing jeans and a t-shirt. He stood against a blank white background and held up a picture of psychologist Solomon Asch.

"Well, maybe this guy did," the man said.

He balled up the photo and threw it over his shoulder.

"Turn Purple Summer ended with minimal deaths, but *we're* just getting started. Because, as the next bit of viral chaos shows, the madness of crowds knows no bounds."

Darren leaned closer to the screen.

"It all starts with the death of art, I think," said Lucius from the passenger seat.

"Who's Art?" replied Ritter. The windshield wipers were screeching against the window, the light rain having stopped a few minutes ago. He finally switched them off.

"Art like creative expression. It's been replaced by stuff you don't have to work to enjoy. It used to be you would read about a catastrophe fictionalized in a novel or see one at the movies. Now you can spend all day watching real-life chaos. Why bother with imitations?"

"You're overthinking it," said Ritter. "People have always gawked at car crashes."

"Right, but they didn't intentionally crash their cars to impress each other. Besides in that one book."

"Never read it," said Ritter.

"That's the other side of it though," continued Lucius. "Getting caught up in viral 'challenges,' or whatever, is an addiction, I think. People want to be noticed. To feel impressive. Extreme behavior gets you there without requiring talent. Algorithms reward it. People get addicted to the attention—and to upping the ante. Once we only had *Jackass*. Now we have a society of jackasses."

"I don't think it demands a philosophical treatise," said Ritter, annoyed. "It's just monkey-see, monkey-do. Mass stupidity. People have always gotten bad ideas from the people around them. The scale is just bigger now. You see it more when people—"

Ritter bit his lip hard, then continued.

"—overdo it."

The two were quiet.

"So what does your boss want to do with his electricity, exactly?" asked Lucius.

"Wants to install some new light fixtures in the cabin. He decides he can do this stuff from watching viral home improvement videos.

Discovers he can't halfway through. Usually he pays an electrician top dollar to fix it."

"Always getting in over his head, eh?" said Lucius.

"Certainly is," Ritter laughed. "But he means well."

***

"You remember this one, Darren?" Ilana shouted behind her without turning from the computer screen.

The host appeared on-screen wearing a pilot's hat and goggles and said:

"Since the Wright Brothers landed their spaceship on Plymouth Rock, or however it happened, man has wanted to fly like the birds."

Darren and Ilana watched transfixed, their noses nearly touching their respective screens.

"As with all things, though, a simple hashtag turned this basic human striving into an embarrassing cascade of stupidity," said the host. "The #TrytoFly phenomenon consisted of people, mostly parents and grandparents, building personal aircrafts out of whatever they had lying around, and sharing videos of the launch attempts. Sometimes they even got the whole family involved!"

Now the screen showed clips of footage watermarked *#TryToFly*.

A man wearing skis with a huge fan on his back flew across a back yard and slammed face-first into a tree. His girlfriend dropped the camera and ran after him.

A man pull-started a device affixed to his friend's shoulders, a lawnmower with plastic blade extensions. The device slipped and an ersatz propeller embedded itself deep into the friend's chest on its first rotation. A parachute deployed. A bloody, confusing attempt to dislodge the blade ensued.

An entire family sat on a large lawn chair. Huge balloons lifted them into the air. The chair ascended to cheers, which became screams as the chair tipped at 200 feet and children, then parents, plummeted.

"What was the final result of this fantastical flying fad? About a hundred aspiring aeronautical engineers wiped from the gene pool, thousands of broken bones, and nary a single workable personal plane design. I think we've all learned something from this one, haven't we? Leave some stuff to the experts!"

The host, who now had a jetpack strapped to his back, gave a thumbs-up to the camera, pressed a button, and flew stage-right. There was a loud crash off-screen, followed by pained howling and censored swearing.

WE'LL BE BACK SHORTLY flashed on the screen, accompanied by elevator music.

Ilana was dimly aware of a tear running down her cheek.

"I don't remember that at all," she whispered. "I swear it didn't happen."

"How's his wife?" said Lucius as they pulled onto a country road. "They co-run the company, right?"

"Correct," said Ritter. "She's alright. Same as him, really. Power couples, you know? Into having meetings about meetings. They've only just begun mingling with us employees since the incidents started."

"Trying to keep the morale up?"

Ritter nodded.

"Gave us bonuses too," said Ritter, thumping the steering wheel. "Business has never been so good."

"She decent-looking?"

Ritter gave Lucius a side-eye.

"Never thought about it, honestly," said Ritter. "Since Lorelei left me, I don't think about women much. When you've been with someone that long, you come out different."

"Lorelei, that's... Judy's mother?"

"Noooo," said Ritter. "Nonono. With Judy's mother it ended years ago. Early—experience, you could say. That's why Judy is—"

Ritter bit his lip.

"Why Judy was already in her 20s. I was married to her mom, though, briefly. Married three times actually; Lorelei was the last. Two shorts and a long. Don't hear about that these days, do you? Why bother, right? I think it's a religious thing from growing up. No matter what the relationship looks like, you feel like it eventually requires a wedding."

"Doesn't sound like you have much—" Lucius caught himself.

"Luck with weddings?" said Ritter, smirking.

"Sorry, I didn't think—"

"It's fine. I mean, shit, we're in the same boat, right?"

"Pretty much," said Lucius.

The host now appeared on screen wearing a dress, gray wig, and pearls, resembling Vicki Lawrence in *Mama's Family*. He was yelling out a name as if searching for someone, but the name was censored with an electronic beep. Finally he addressed the camera.

"Howdy ya'll," said the host. "You seen [CENSORED] around? I'm his aunt! I guess since his lazy ol' ass disappeared, I'll tell you the next thing on the list. Now, there are nice aunts like myself, and there are mean ants, like the bullet ant. Feisty little bastards! You're probably thinkin', what the hell's a bullet ant?"

The screen showed a question mark. A voice with a British accent suitable for a nature program said:

"The bullet ant, or *Paraponera clavata*, is an insect from the Brazilian rain forest considered to possess nature's most painful sting. The Sateré-Mawé tribe carry out a ritual in which each male tribe member, to symbolize his acceptance of a warrior's lifestyle, wears a wicker glove filled with bullet ants. For 15 minutes he demonstrates his ability to accept the insect's excruciating stings, which render his hand and arm numb for days after."

A *The More You Know* PSA graphic appeared on-screen.

"A few years back, someone around here decided to do those warriors one better," said the host, back on-screen and still in character. "People started popping bullet ants in their mouths, setting a timer, letting them run around in there, and filming the results! And I tell you what, a human mouth ain't where a bullet ant wants to be!"

The screen displayed a series of people's faces close-up, one after another, with ungodly swollen lips and cheeks, tears pouring down their faces, and in some cases thick rivulets of blood dribbling down their chins.

The host now returned on-screen wearing a plush ant costume.

"Not everyone escaped this entomological excitement unscathed." he said. "Throats were closing up all over the place, with more than 150 deaths nationwide from this one before it ran its course."

The video showed a supercut of racing ambulances and local news footage overlayed by graphics lamenting the trend.

"And even if you swallowed one of those damnable creatures and it got past your throat without choking you... Well," said the host.

The video cut back to him, and he was now wearing a monocle and a top hat.

"In the interest of propriety, we'll leave it to your imagination what a bullet ant does to the gastrointestinal faculties."

The narrator winked with a *ding* superimposed over the audio. Then a poop emoji flashed on the screen to the tune of a losing buzzer.

"Hey, was my dear elderly aunt looking for me?" the host now whispered. "Please don't tell her we made that joke. She hates bathroom humor. That's the last one we'll do like that, I promise. Speaking of which, we're finally at—*Number one* on our list."

It was raining again and Ritter flicked on the wipers.

"So your cousin Ron, he was a writer?" said Ritter, the subject now opened up for discussion.

"Sure was."

"Judy wrote too," said Ritter. "She was a poet."

"You know what Ron really wanted to do though? Wanted to be an inventor."

"That so?"

"Yep. Loved aviation in particular. Had a dream of building his own personal one-man helicopter."

"Wonder if they knew each other, him and Judy. Two writers from the same area going to the same wedding in Florida. They must have, right?"

"He never mentioned her," said Lucius. "Maybe he knew her but kept it a secret. Strange how secrets die with people."

"What do you mean?"

"Buddy of mine, Kirk, died three years ago," said Lucius. "After the funeral, me and a couple other people go to the bar. I remember that right after college, Kirk had been dating this girl. Love of his life, marriage in the offing, the whole bit. A mutual acquaintance of ours ran off with her. So Kirk somehow got his hands on a bullet ant. They're these special ants from Brazil. Sting like nothing else on earth. He was at a party at the guy's house one night. Guy thought Kirk didn't know him and the girl were an item. Kirk went to the bathroom, made a stop in the guy's bedroom, and somehow managed to affix the bullet ant in one of the guy's socks. A week later he saw the guy again. Guy had a damn cast on his foot. Almost got gangrene apparently!"

"A bit sadistic, isn't it?" said Ritter.

"Matters of the heart," said Lucius. "Anyway, I'm at the bar after Kirk's funeral with everyone and I'm thinking, can I tell this story? Will it get him in trouble? That's when it struck me. I am the only one on earth, far as I know, who knows the full bullet ant story. It was just me and him, and he's gone. Not only do you realize it doesn't matter anymore, you start asking yourself: Did it really happen? Did I make it up? There's nowhere in the world you can turn for verification."

"You could ask the guy who nearly lost his foot," said Ritter.

"Maybe he didn't exist either," said Lucius. He gave a strange laugh, then continued, "So who knows, maybe Ron and Judy knew each other. Maybe he was fucking her."

Ritter took the comment like a surprise slap and glanced at Lucius.

"The hell's that about?" Ritter said. "Watch that."

"My sincere apologies. Poorly phrased. I just mean it's strange the things people do that nobody will *ever* know about. Memories lost to time just like people."

"Let's focus on the problem at hand," said Ritter in a measured tone, covering the remaining anger.

"Fixing the electricity," said Lucius.

Ritter nodded.

"How long have we been watching this?" Darren and Ilana said in unison, on either side of the room.

Both stared at their screens. Both drooled. Neither heard the other. Neither answered.

Fifteen minutes later, Ritter was still rattled by Lucius' remark. He drove silently, his mind tilted toward the time immediately after the event and the dreamlike nine months since.

He remembered his phone buzzing non-stop and the text message and voicemail counts mounting. He remembered turning on the television and seeing the Florida hotel in flames. Florida was far away though, and he looked at his text from Judy with the name and location of the hotel she was staying at for a friend's wedding. He could not connect what it all meant. When he finally could, he still would not.

Nor would he inform his bosses of the tragedy. He took no time off work, and didn't flinch at the growing number of conversations the marketing team was having about the company's "potential PR problem." It all seemed quite distant. As far away as Florida.

Ritter simply made a quiet, private mental place to mourn—and to blame.

And from that private place he searched, tirelessly, for fellow victims of the tragedy—being as anonymous as he could while making himself available online for contact.

Lucius found and contacted him, and told him how his beloved cousin died in the flames and his family owned a junkyard just outside of town.

The windshield wipers were squealing again. Ritter switched them off and, breaking the silence, said, "They weren't even a part of it, Judy and Ron. They were just there."

"Would it change things if it was their idea?" said Lucius.

"I couldn't tell you," said Ritter.

"What can I tell ya?" the host's voice said from the dueling computer speakers. "What happened and what didn't? What's real and what isn't? Can we ever be certain?"

He stood there on-screen, bearded and wearing a barrel like Diogenes, affecting deep contemplation.

A loud buzzer sounded.

"Gah!" he yelled, jumping at the startle and looking around in irritation.

"One thing we *can* be certain of, friends, is that even if you didn't remember those last few, you'll definitely remember this one," he said. "And I'm not using the 'royal you,' here—I mean you, Darren and Ilana Arnault."

On either side of the room, Ilana and Darren Arnault were identically positioned staring at their screens; shoulders hunched, mouths hanging open, drool puddling on their respective desks, eyes bloodshot. They groaned simultaneously in response to the host.

The host was now wearing an outfit split down the middle; a tuxedo on one side, a bridal gown on the other.

"Weddings," the host said. "Beautiful celebrations of matrimony. Sacred religious rituals. Great parties. Nine months ago, though, a trend appeared that turned these hallowed events into deathtraps. A viral video with the hashtag #FireofLove instructed, enticed, and encouraged edgy lovebirds to play, literally, with fire—to thrill their guests, provide an unforgettable experience, and, of course, get some shares and thumbs-ups themselves. How? By painting the walls with flammable materials! Gasoline hearts! Toluene tributes! Announcements of adoration rendered in acetone! And then lighting the whole thing ablaze and recording the flaming spectacle. What could possibly go wrong?"

On the screen ran a supercut of horrific fires in hotels, homes, and event spaces. Squealing alarms. Flame-engulfed hallways. Full buildings collapsing.

"What *we* know that *no one* else knows, however, is that Bride & Groom Supreme was the source of the meme! Yes, #FireofLove was born from its marketing department. That wedding industry titan bombarded the online world with short videos of people having a blast, celebrating their weddings with this new, non-traditional tradition! And as the major purveyor of news in the space, Bride & Groom Supreme reported on it and blogged about it, ostensibly, half-heartedly warning against it—all the while profiting from and pushing the trend. Remember?"

"We didn't think it would go that far," they said in unison.

"But you had to know fire was a teensy-weensy bit dangerous, right? I mean, enough to have the videos filmed and distributed anonymously by, let me see here..."

The host was reading from a stack of legal documents.

"Romanian hackers who you paid through a proxy via an anonymous Bitcoin account?"

They were silent.

"It sounds pretty damning to me, frankly. Fire being the most destructive force on Earth is not a closely guarded secret. You must have anticipated something going south. Oh, and then when it *did*, let's see..."

The host put on reading glasses and returned to the documents.

"Mhhm, pursuant to the heretofore, etc.," he read aloud to himself. Then announced, "Ah-ha, *here*! 'Darren and Ilana Arnault displayed general indifference to *five* warnings, *three* complaints, *two* authoritative heads ups, and multiple low-key nudges that the #FireofLove campaign was simply *too hot*."

A rimshot played on a drum kit. The host cleared his throat and continued.

"'People were getting severely injured, they said! Firefighters were apoplectic, they said! It was only a matter of time before someone got killed, they said!' Your responses were?"

There was silence.

"How bad can I feel about it?" said the host in Darren's voice. "If I cut off my hand doing a home improvement project I saw online, is it the content creator's fault? What about the people who shared it? Or the recommendation algorithms? If one person is responsible, isn't everyone?

"And...

"If we do a press release to take responsibility, what's the gain?" said the host in Ilana's voice. "We'll be ruined, and people will keep doing it anyway. Cat's out of the bag. Idiots are idiots. We're making money hand-over-fist, there's no reason to narc ourselves out. This will burn out like every other viral trend.

"Burn it did," said the host, voice back to normal. "Out? Not so much. Nearly a thousand dead! And people are still doing this one! A great incentive, Arnaults, to mingle only among the single. You've made me feel fortunate that I never get invited to things."

The host now wore a suit and held a microphone, into which he said, "Since we do a giveaway every episode, and today you're our only viewers, you'll get to split the prize! As our *grand prize* winners, you will spend the rest of eternity watching viral content like you've been watching today—being exposed to human misery of a volume and severity never before experienced by the mortal mind!"

"But why us?" Darren said. "We made a mistake, sure—but certainly others have done worse."

The host snorted.

"Everybody's always looking for a tidy explanation! Lord. Okay, how's this: this cabin is built on sacred land and you upset some spirits. Ever think of that? No, how about you accidentally killed an evil wizard or something. You certainly burned enough fucking buildings to the ground, statistically there had to be a wizard in there somewhere. I get it though—I'm the guy who knows, right?"

"Who are you?" they asked in unison.

The host was now dressed in a plush devil costume.

"Maybe I'm the devil and I like to play games."

Then he was dressed in a white robe with a halo glowing above his head.

"No! Maybe I'm God! And I'm here to teach you a lesson."

Then he was dressed in all black.

"Or maybe I'm neither," he said, "and you just spend too much time watching videos online."

Then the host got right up to the camera, and said in a low growl, "So, do you *really* want to know my name?"

Each set of computer speakers blared the inquiry, rattling the room.

"There's a car to swap out at the junkyard, you're sure?" said Ritter, slamming the car door, walking around back and opening the trunk.

Lucius hopped out of the passenger side, climbed past some bramble and branches scattered around the wooded area where they were parked, and ran around after him.

"Sure as can be! You getting cold feet on me?"

Ritter pulled two shotguns from the trunk and handed one to Lucius.

"Not a bit," said Ritter. "Cool as a cucumber."

"For Ron," he added, racking his shotgun.

"For Judy," said Lucius, racking his as well. They walked shoulder to shoulder up the long dirt path.

On either side of the room, the host leaned out of each computer screen simultaneously. The flickering, pixelated figure got his mouth next to Darren's ear on the right, and next to Ilana's ear on the left.

He whispered a secret.

"Hey, Darren, you guys here?" Ritter yelled down the stairs, walking down casually with Lucius behind him. "It's me! I brought the multimeter and some other tools. Should do the trick."

The two men with rifles halted at what they saw.

"Guh!" said Lucius, pulling his t-shirt's collar up over his nose.

"Looks like someone did the job for us already," said Ritter.

In the basement office sat two state-of-the-art big-screen computers, one on the far left of the room and one on the far right. In front of each was an expensive, ergonomically designed computer chair. In each chair sat a dried out, desiccated husk of a corpse. Each corpse was seated in an identical position, hunched forward, nose nearly touching the computer screen, empty eyes staring blindly and mouth dropped open impossibly wide, gaping with amazement even in death.

Ritter nearly tripped on a chair at the bottom of the staircase, walked around it and into the room. He walked to the left and poked Ilana's corpse with the butt of his rifle.

"What the hell happened to them?" Lucius asked from behind him.

"Beats me," said Ritter. "Carbon monoxide maybe? Radon?"

"Possible, I guess," said Lucius, scratching his head. "But you ever heard of carbon monoxide turning people into mummies?"

"If this is the first time, it couldn't have happened to a nicer couple. For all these two bastards put us through. Us and everyone else. Maybe they rotted from the guilt. Maybe God decided it was their time to go."

"Divine punishment, huh?" Lucius asked. "I can't imagine it ever works quite that way. Wouldn't we all be dried-up sacks of bones? For all the finger-pointing we do, everyone's guilty of something, right? It's just what we're willing to admit to ourselves."

Ritter stood at the midpoint of the carpet in the middle of the room, the exact midpoint between the two corpses. He looked at the carpet and thought.

Ritter rushed out of the elevator and saw eight sets of annoyed eyes lock on him through the glass wall panel of the conference room. He entered the conference room and into silence, receiving not even a snide *thank you for joining us*. His shirt was buttoned crooked and he was furiously chomping on gum as he sat down at the glass table.

It was the monthly meeting of the Bride & Groom Supreme marketing team. Business had been bad. B&GS was integrated into every vertical in the wedding industry—from dresses and tuxes to event services to table tchotchkes to a suite of wedding-themed publications and websites. Every segment was floundering. Traditional, big weddings were unfashionable, and small creative ones were not far behind. B&GS kept waiting for the next trend, but each quarter it seemed less likely the business would survive to see it.

The further the business tanked, the more layoffs there were, the tenser these meetings got. Perceived unseriousness would end in dismissal. Ritter spoke energetically, fighting to mask his horrendous hangover.

"I was putting together some ideas last night," said Ritter. In reality, that was the last thing he had been doing.

Ritter's mind was racing to come up with a plausible concept when he heard a laugh next to him.

"Who buys your socks, Ritter?"

Through the glass table, Ritter looked down and saw his dress pants sliding up to reveal a pink-checkered designer sock.

He was briefly startled, then pulled his pant leg down and chuckled.

"Only clean ones I could find, washing machine's busted," said Ritter. "So, we're looking to launch a campaign that's going to turn heads, right? Something to bring in the younger audience."

He noted his coworkers' eyerolling and temple rubbing and said, "Ilana, what's that you're looking at right now?"

There was a chill in the room. It was well known that Ilana never paid attention in meetings. Calling her out for it was begging to be fired.

"Excuse me?"

"No, no—I know you're a multitasker. Obviously you were listening—you heard the question so you had to be, right?"

A subtle relaxing of the mood started with Darren, who sat next to her as always, and filtered through the room.

"Just for brainstorming's sake, what is it you're always looking at?" Ritter asked.

"Cooking videos," Darren answered for her.

"*Crazy* cooking videos," Ilana clarified. "Have you seen these? Giant milkshakes and molecular gastronomy and wild foreign restaurants—I could watch them all day. They're addictive. Darren is one to talk, by the way. He watches the home improvement version of the same stuff. He wants a lathe! I don't know where he'll find time to use it, he's too busy watching videos about making furniture to ever actually make furniture."

Darren threw his hands up, guilty.

It came to Ritter all at once.

"See?" he said. "That's it! We have to think memes. Addictive viewing. Wedding-related content that people will *share*—that they can't put down. We do weddings from start to finish, right? So this isn't even branded content. It's bigger. We need to breathe life back into weddings *as such*. When weddings are *exciting* again, we're back on top. We have to shift the paradigm with content."

There was a collective nodding.

"Like a—wedding-related cooking show?" Darren asked.

"No, something *intense*. What are weddings all about, really?"

"Family?" said someone.

"Before that. What gets you there?"

There was silence.

"Passion," said Ritter. "We need a meme video that *screams* passion. We need..."

He thought for a moment.

"Fire," said Ritter.

Lucius lifted the shotgun and pulled the trigger and Ritter's head exploded. The body stood for a fraction of a second, as if it was still processing the loss of its decision-making organ, then dropped to the floor.

"Some of us, for instance, are guilty of fucking another man's wife," said Lucius. He took a pair of socks from his back pocket. They were monogrammed with a Bride & Groom Supreme logo. The sort of thing one would get at a company Christmas party and wear on laundry day.

"You left these at my house," said Lucius.

He waved them as if taunting the deceased, threw them onto the headless corpse, and kicked what had recently been Ritter in the ribs.

He stepped back and looked at the scene.

"Shame about the shitty wiring in this place," he said, searching around for an electrical panel to sabotage.

Confident in Ritter's assertion that gunshots were normal out here in hunting country, he moved calmly. His story was airtight. No need to panic and botch a last-minute arson.

He was surprised when the computer monitors on either side of the room sprung to life.

"Electricity really is spotty here," he muttered.

He stepped over Ritter's body and hunched down near the desiccated face of Ilana Arnault, looking at the screen over her shoulder.

"What we watchin'?" he said to the body.

As if answering him, an on-screen voice said, "Do you have a craving for crime? Then we've got a killer episode for you! Because today we're looking at *The Craziest Revenge Killings You Probably Forgot.*"

Lucius could not help being curious. He pulled the chair by the stairs past Ritter's body and sat in it next to Ilana. He nudged the inanimate Ilana to the side and got his face closer to the screen. Surely he had a few minutes to spare, the video was probably not very long.

Break Some Shit

by James Fritz

600,000 TEENAGERS ROAR AS they await the next act at the Rome Music Festival in New York. The sun unleashes its fury on the crowd. There's no shade to be had at the Air Force base. Most of the attendees have run out of money and can't afford the twenty dollar water bottles. The crowd simmers with anger and excitement as BU5ST gets ready backstage.

"You sure there aren't any bathrooms around?" Ted asks.

"Nah," Thump says. "Nearest one's back at the bus, man."

"Shit... We have it just as bad as the attendees," Ted says.

By far, this is the biggest concert the band has ever performed at. There are more people at this festival than there were at Woodstock. Though few of them care about peace, love, and flower power. Most care about getting high, getting laid, and getting drunk.

Ted takes a deep breath as the MC introduces them.

"You motherfuckers ready?" Ted asks. "Let's go!"

The musicians go out on stage. A sound wave crashes into them from the audience. More than half a million people bob up and down. It looks like an ocean of drunk, sex-crazed, drugged-up, angsty teenagers.

Ted's mouth falls open. He holds his microphone to his lips, but he doesn't speak. He's performed at countless rowdy concerts and knows when things look to be getting out of hand. The scene in front of him got out of hand hours ago.

Some of the attendees are violent. Fist fights break out. People shove each other around in a mosh pit. A sizable fraction of the women are topless. Empty bottles and cups are thrown at the stage. Pandemonium rules with an iron fist. Ted wonders how to rein them back in. Things can only get worse from here.

Before he can say anything, Thump starts banging on the drums. The guitarist and bassist join in. Ted changes his mind as the music pummels him. A grin streaks across his face. Excitement rushes through his veins.

Who cares if the crowd gets a little wild? We're here to have fun.

He gives in to the mania.

"WHAT'S UP, MOTHERFUCKERS?!" he screams.

He waves his hand up and down as the band performs its first song. The crowd imitates him like an orchestra following a conductor. The beat sounds like bombs going off on a battlefield. Ted belts out the song's lyrics. His vocal cords strain as the heavy metal scratches against them. The crowd sings along with him.

"WE...DON'T...GIVE A FUCK WHAT YOU THINK! WE WANT TO LIVE OUR LIVES AND FUCK AROUND AND DO SOME DRUGS AND BREAK SOME SHIT..."

The crowd feeds off Ted. He feeds off the crowd. Sweat falls from his forehead as he saunters back and forth. Thump goes hog-wild as the song ends. The guitarist and bassist play the last few chords.

Ted smiles like a kid at a candy store. Every single person in the crowd is stoked to be there. None of them are having a bad time. All are enjoying his act. Moments like these are the primary reason he became a musician.

"I have a question for you," Ted says. "How many of you guys like the band DOORY?"

Predictably, the crowd boos. Trash flies through the air. Ted laughs.

"Have you ever had one of those days when you felt that everything was fucked and you just wanted to rip the whole world apart? Well...*today's the day, motherfuckers!*"

The stage actually vibrates with the noise of the crowd. It seems to be possessed by a demonic spirit. The mosh pit swirls around like a blender running full-speed. More fights break out. The performance verges on becoming a riot.

Ted knows that he has the crowd in the palm of his hand. The power he holds feels like a drug. He whips them up even further.

"I want you to let go of all the bullshit. School shit, job shit, family shit, boyfriend shit, girlfriend shit... Reach deep down inside, take all that negative stuff, and get it the fuck out of here!"

A lone heckler tries to shout Ted down. He engages him.

"You don't think I'm real?" Ted says. "I'm the realest motherfucker here! I don't give a fuck about anything. Here, watch this."

He drops his microphone, unbuckles his pants, and pulls them off, underwear and all. Squatting down toward the front of the stage, he lets his bowels loosen.

"Oh yeah... Fuck, that feels good..."

The crowd of 600,000 goes silent for a moment as Ted does his business on stage. Then he grabs his pants and puts them back on.

"Was that real enough for you?" Ted says. "I'm letting go of all my shit!"

The crowd explodes like a nuclear bomb. Every single attendee cheers. Ted bends over, picks up the log, and chucks it into the crowd. People scatter.

"TIME TO LET IT ALL GO, BABY!"

The band starts the next song. The guitarist strums out a lightning-fast melody. Thump's hands move in a blur at the drum set.

Ted sees an opening in the crowd. A group of guys stand around two fighters squaring off. One of them throws a haymaker. The other fighter blocks it and tackles his opponent to the ground. Then he starts raining down blows. The people around egg him on.

Ted almost misses his entrance. For a moment, the facade breaks. A voice inside him says that he should stop the performance. People are getting hurt. The concert has spiraled out of control. He wonders if they would even listen to him if he asked them to calm down.

No... It's too late, man. They're gone. Fucking gone...

He decides that the only thing he can do is give a good performance.

"I don't want any of you guys getting hurt out there," Ted says, "but we are here to have fun! There aren't any rules now, motherfuckers!"

He continues the song. People start climbing the sound tower toward the rear of the crowd. One of them almost makes it to the top before falling off. Even from the stage, Ted can see the tower start to wobble. He shrugs it off. The band plays its next song.

"Now that we got all the bad shit out of our system, it's time to bring in the good shit," Ted says. "If you've got a special someone out there, this next song is for you."

The drummer lays down a slow beat for *Screwin*. Ted waves his free hand above his head. Like a well-trained dog, the audience mimics him. He knows that if he told them to jump off a cliff, they would ask him which one.

"MY FEELINGS ARE BREWIN, BREWIN, BREWIN... I JUST LIKE SCREWIN, SCREWIN, SCREWIN... YOU AND ME SHOULD START DOIN, DOIN, DOIN..."

A topless girl crowd-surfs near the stage. Several boys grab for her breasts. She tries to swat them away, but the hands keep coming. One of them pulls her to the ground and mounts her. The people around whistle and cheer.

Before Ted can react, the sound tower starts to fall. He watches it happen in slow motion. A horde of people stands underneath it. None of them seem to realize what's happening.

"Hey, guys, look out back—"

Bang!

The sound tower smacks onto the ground, crushing everybody under it. A cloud of dust billows out from the wreckage. The people around scream with glee. Ted stands gobsmacked on stage. It's as if each act of violence and depravity drives the crowd further.

"Man, you guys are getting rowdy out there!" he says.

Through it all, the performance goes on. Pieces of plywood are passed through the crowd. Ted notices the gaps in the fencing surrounding the field. A crew of guys breaks the boards off one by one.

That's when an idea occurs to him.

"Bring one of those boards over here," he says. "I want to crowd-surf!"

The crowd complies. One of the boards makes its way to the stage. Ted holds his hands out to balance himself as he steps onto it. No less than six people support him.

"I'm just like you motherfuckers!" he says. "We're all the same, man!"

The board makes its way through the crowd. Ted sees a bloodied teenager sprawled out on the ground. Bruises cover his chest and face. Nobody else seems to notice. Everybody focuses on the performance. Ted keeps the concert going. The band rocks out song after song.

"No fucking parents around here, baby!" he says. "We own this town! We're never leaving! And if you don't like it, you can suck my fucking cock!"

Eventually, the attendees holding him up bring him back to the front. The moment that he sets foot on the stage, he smells something burning. It takes him a moment to see the fire billowing where the sound tower fell. The flames grow taller as they spread out and consume everything in their path.

"Burn it all down, baby!" Ted says. "Burn the whole fucking system down! Let it rip, man!"

Another fire starts closer to the stage. One of the attendees holds a blowtorch. A hockey mask covers his face. He gives the peace sign to Ted and receives one back.

The performance turns into a full-on riot. Plastic bottles cover the stage. The mosh pit grows bigger and bigger. Some of the attendees go through the gaps in the fence and jump on top of the cars in the parking lot. Car alarms start beeping. Windshields shatter.

The band performs its final song. The music booming from the loudspeakers is almost impossible to hear over the roar of the crowd. Ted's throat coarsens as he screams the final lyrics. The guitarist smashes his instrument on the stage at the song's conclusion. Several fires now burn freely out in the field. The plywood boards from the fence keep them going.

"That's all we got for you, motherfuckers!" Ted says. "Break some shit, baby!"

He drops the microphone to the floor as he walks off stage. His shirt clings to his sweaty chest. Exhaustion comes on immediately. He walks like a zombie back to the BUSST trailer.

Sirens wail as emergency vehicles park in front of the field. A parade of firefighters, police officers, and paramedics hurry by.

"Burn it all down, baby… Burn it all down…"

Gunshots ring out from the parking lot. A girl screams. Ted doesn't even turn around.

"I wish every concert went like that," Thump says. "That was fucked!"

"Too true, man... Too true..." Ted says.

Boom!

An explosion rocks the field. A mushroom cloud billows into the air. Ted opens the door to the trailer.

"Break some shit... Just break some shit, baby..."

Heads Be Flying

by Devin James Leonard

"The Great God hath sent us signs in the sky!
We have heard uncommon noise in the heavens,
and have seen heads fall down upon the earth."
*Speech of Tahayadoris, a Mohawk sachem, at Albany, NY - October
25, 1689*

The strip club was only four blocks up from the Hudson River, a short enough walk that when Lucas Hardin arrived, his clothes were still a sopping-wet mess. He entered *Night Moves* with his hair draped over his forehead like a soaked mop, his boots squishing with every footstep, and his t-shirt suctioned to his body like a vacuum-sealed bag of meat.

One of the regular girls was onstage, fully nude, doing her usual routine, every table around the stage occupied by drooling men waving dollar bills at her. Not one set of eyes took notice of Lucas, not even Donny, the part-time enforcer and full-time bouncer, who was stationed near the boss's office, entranced while peering at the striptease. Lucas walked right on by without remark and opened the door, squelching his way across the carpeted floor.

Francis Pomeroy was lounging behind his marble desk, suit jacket off, shirt sleeves rolled up, and rolling a cigarette. With his slick black hair and dark almond-colored eyes—not to mention his stereotypical mobster profession—he was often mistaken for a full-blooded Italian, but actually came from a long line of Native American heritage. He did not comment on Lucas's wet condition. Once he finished licking his rolling paper and plucking a strand of tobacco from his lip, he asked, "Job all done?"

Lucas hugged himself, shivering. "In a word, yes."

"And in more words?"

Lucas stepped closer, feet squish-squishing, and Francis said, "Went for a swim, did you?" Even though he meant it as a joke, he showed no expression, his frigid personality as cold as Lucas's current condition.

"We've got a problem," Lucas muttered.

"Don't tell me you lost Donny's boat."

Lucas nodded with a tremble. "Floating halfway to Kingston by now, I'm guessing. But no, that's not the problem, boss."

Francis shifted his gaze over Lucas's shoulder. "Where are the rest of the crew?"

"That's the problem."

"Did you take care of the old blabbermouth?"

"Yes."

"Then what could—?"

"We took care of him," Lucas said, "but something else took care of the others."

If the boss said Uncle Chet had to go, then he had to go. So that's what they did: Lucas, Max, Rob, and Uncle Chet's nephew Karl accompanied him down to the docks under the guise of heading up the Hudson for some late-night business. The crew had often used the jon boat to transport or pick up cargo across the river, so the old man didn't expect a thing. Twelve feet of aluminum, the boat was compact, reasonably quiet, perfect for evading river patrols, and just the right fit for five men.

Lucas navigated the boat's outboard trolling motor, skirting along the eastern side of the Hudson River, heading north against the flowing current. A few miles up, he passed a small island and killed the engine, pretending the boat had run out of gas. Karl, sitting up front with his uncle, faked a phone call for help as the river pushed them backward. When they coasted to the island, Uncle Chet hopped into the knee-high water and pulled the boat to shore.

Once they were all on land, Uncle Chet headed for the dark woods and hollered, "Whichever one of you knuckleheads forgot to check the gas better come help me find something for a fire."

Lucas, Max, and Rob faced Karl, not because he was to blame for the imaginary empty fuel tank, but because Karl was Uncle Chet's blood relation.

Karl looked at each of their faces and whispered, "What? Me?"

"Pick up on that cue, did you?" Lucas said.

"You're saying I gotta do it?" Karl said. "I didn't bring my piece with me."

Lucas spread his empty palms. "Neither did we."

"Why do I have to do it? He's my uncle, for Christ's sake."

"That's precisely why it's on you," Rob said.

"Well," Karl stammered, "with what?"

"Got a machete on board," Max suggested.

"That's ruthless," Karl hissed.

"Ain't as ruthless as drowning him, and that's the only other option you got."

While Karl thought it over, he slapped himself in the arms and face, warding off mosquitoes. The biting bugs made him choose quickly. "Lucas," he said, "can you do it?"

"Can I," he said, "or will I?"

"Will you?"

"Fine," Lucas grunted. Karl fetched him the machete from the boat, and he marched into the darkness of the wooded island.

It only took him a minute to locate the beam of the flashlight and hear the old man's yapping starting up as soon as he heard Lucas coming.

"Nothing worse than wet feet," Uncle Chet grumbled while gathering sticks. "If I'm gonna be stranded out here on account of you delinquents, I'm gon' least be warm and dry."

With the machete hidden against his leg, Lucas approached him from behind. Uncle Chet continued to snap twigs and flap his lips, paying no mind.

"Which one of you morons didn't check the gas? This younger generation, I'm telling you."

Always yammering, that Uncle Chet. If he had ever taken a moment to shut his mouth, it may have occurred to him it was the reason he was out here: He talked too much.

Lucas snuck closer, and when he was within arm's reach, he raised the machete high above his head. The instant he swung, Uncle Chet twisted slightly to peer over his shoulder, and the blade struck his collarbone instead of his skull where Lucas had been aiming. Chet let out an excruciating cry, as loud as waves crashing, and fell to his hands and knees with the blade still embedded in his bone.

Lucas stamped a foot on the old man's back for leverage and tugged on the machete with both hands, but he couldn't get it free. The blade was wedged like food lodged between teeth. Every time he wriggled the handle, Uncle Chet let loose with rip-roaring howls of agony, his tortured screams seeming to shake the trees.

"Sorry," Lucas said, pulling with every ounce of effort. "I'm sorry."

Finally, he pried the machete free from Chet's shoulder and, without hesitation, he reared back and brought the blade down, hard and fast, into the back of his head. All noise ceased at once, and the old man slumped.

"I'm sorry, Uncle Chet," Lucas said, winded and panting. He wasn't sorry he murdered him; he was sorry he had failed to make it painless.

Once Lucas had caught his breath, he wrenched the blade from Chet's skull, carried it out to the shore where the others were waiting, and threw it into the water as far as he could chuck it.

Max, Rob, and Karl were standing around with their shoulders slumped, heads lowered, and looking glum. Sure, they all felt terrible about what had transpired, especially because Uncle Chet was Karl's family. Chet had come up in the organization long before these four men were born. It didn't sit right with any of them, offing an elder. But Francis Pomeroy, the shot caller, said it had to be done.

Just then, a long, monstrous wailing erupted from the woods and resounded across the still air.

Karl straightened with alarm, directing his bulging eyes toward the thickets. "He's still alive."

Lucas shook his head decisively. "There's no way."

"You're certain?"

"You want details? Yes, I'm certain."

"Then what the hell was that?"

"Let's go," Lucas said, retreating to the boat.

"Go where?" Karl said.

"Did you forget we're not actually stranded? Get in."

"But—"

A second ear-splitting, blaring sound rang out, even more piercing and closer than the first. It no longer emanated from the woods in front of them, but from above the trees.

Following yet another shriek, everyone craned their heads toward the night sky.

"A bird?" Rob said.

"Sounds like a damn *pterodactyl*," said Max.

"Whatever it is, it's not Uncle Chet," Lucas said. He dashed to the boat, jumped in, and started pulling the cord on the motor's engine. Max and Rob leaped into the middle, hasty in their flight, and faced stern-side, watching Lucas yank on the engine rope, once, twice, the motor coughing but not starting. Karl was in the water, pushing the boat off the shoreline. He was still treading in the river when the engine gurgled to life on the third pull.

Lucas gripped the outboard extension handle, preparing for the voyage. "Karl on?" he said.

The two men turned toward the bow and swiveled their heads from left to right. One of them called out to Karl as if he were a great distance away. The boat was drifting from the island, already in deeper waters, but Karl was not aboard. Max and Rob leaned over the sides, looking down at the water as black as the night.

"Where is he?" Lucas shouted over the puttering engine.

A shower like heavy rain fell upon the boat, soaking the men as if a water balloon had popped over their heads. Just a second later, an object dropped from above and hit the water right beside them, creating a loud and violent splash. And a split second after that, something thumped on the floor of the boat between Lucas and the other two men's feet. The fallen object was round and swayed back and forth, rolling with the motion of the boat. Lucas leaned over and picked it up, holding it close to his face. Whatever he was gripping felt like ropey seaweed. Max and Rob brought out their cell phones and shone their flashlights. Lucas was holding Karl's severed head by the hair.

"Jesus H. Christ," Lucas yelped, and let go of the head, kicking it upon instinct, and hurling it straight at Max and Rob.

Rob stretched his hands out, catching it on impulse, and with a disgusted groan, said, "Ugh!" and underhand-tossed it over to Max's lap as if playing a game of hot potato.

"Yo!" Max squealed in revulsion, and scooped it up and chucked it overboard.

Lucas accelerated, and the jon boat bounced over the semi-calm surface, flying up and crashing down. All the while, Max and Rob howled and aimed their flashlights at each other. And though Lucas couldn't see where he was steering, he saw his comrades' faces caked in blood, hair wet, and clothes drenched in red. He needn't wonder what that shower that had fallen on them was, nor the heavy splash in the water. Aside from his head, it had all been Karl.

Lucas steered southbound, the ride going faster than before, now that they were moving with the current. The moon snuck out from behind a cloud, and though the wind and the tide were mild, Max and Rob were anything but. They blathered erratic nonsensical questions, their voices sounding like they were sobbing. Lucas told them to shut up—he couldn't focus.

A strong wind blew into the boat, a forceful gush of air so close to the top of Lucas's head he ducked and lost his grip on the throttle. The engine decelerated, and the boat drifted to a coasting halt like a dying car rolling to a slow stop.

Lucas peered up into the moonlight, snapping his eyes in every direction. He had seen something shoot across his vision when that gust of air had shot by, narrowly missing him.

"What are you doing?" Max snapped. "Get us out of here!"

Lucas was stunned, momentarily forgetting he was steering the boat, and didn't realize they were no longer moving.

"Lucas! Drive!"

A large round object streaked across the moonlit sky, black, silhouetted, and gargantuan, with flowing strands of hair-like matter as thick as ropes trailing behind it. Those screams, that of a banshee, came from its position. It circled them like a fly hovering over cow dung. And it screeched.

Faces craned toward the object. Voices blathered in terror: "What is that?" "Oh, my god!" "Drive, Lucas, drive!" "Go, go, go!"

Lucas, blinded by darkness and dread, accelerated at full throttle, the monstrous screaming continuing to emanate directly over them, never dimming.

"Hurry! Faster!" either Max or Rob bellowed.

Lucas was moving as fast as the engine allowed, but that big black thing wouldn't quit. It circled them from above. And then it dove, descending suddenly, grabbing Max from his seat and plucking him out of the boat. He vanished in a blink, and all that remained were his cries growing fainter as he was taken away.

Lucas cranked the steering rod, whipping the boat into a wide one-eighty to turn back. Rob said, "What are you doing? Don't go back. He's a goner."

Too late, Lucas was already heading upstream, crashing up and down over the wake. No matter where he looked, he could see nothing other than the dark. It was a waste of time. He rerouted southbound—

Bang! Max dropped out of the sky, crashing onto the side of the boat, half-in and half-out, and flopped overboard. The heavy impact and added weight jerked the boat, making it tilt. Rob floundered with the momentum and took a header into the rushing water, causing Lucas to lose control of the steering lever. The boat sliced to the left, and the backside swung around, cutting against the current and bashing into the waves as hard as a vehicle slamming into a brick wall. The sudden stop ejected Lucas, launching him into the river.

The boat was coasting twenty yards downstream, long gone from Lucas's reach by the time he broke to the surface with a coughing gasp.

Upstream, Rob desperately shouted, "Lucas, where are you?"

Lucas kept quiet, refusing to respond. He stroked his arms and gently paddled his feet, so as not to disturb the water and make a sound.

"Lucas!"

The large round object in the sky returned the call. Lucas could see it as clearly as ever. It flew right overtop him, a black tumbleweed with monstrous glowing eyes and a mouth as wide as a wood chipper. He could have sworn he saw wings and talons too, but mostly, its appearance resembled a face, a head—a head the size of a haystack!

The flying head-shaped creature swooped down on Rob, snatching him up like a bird hunting a fish, and soared up and up toward the moonlight. Rob screamed in agony as he was carried off. And then he screamed no more. Lucas didn't wait to see or hear what had become of him; he faced downstream and paddled toward the shore.

When Lucas Hardin finished recounting the events, Francis Pomeroy's eyes opened slightly with a knowing gape, the subtlest change from his normal, blank expression that would have gone unnoticed to those unaccustomed to the mobster. He immediately summoned Donny the doorman into the room, instructing him to close the establishment, remove the customers, send the women home, and get Wes on the phone. "Get him over here now, hop to it," he ordered, and also, "Lucas says your boat's gone. Sorry about that, Don."

Twenty minutes later, the boss's older brother sluggishly drifted into the office. Wes Pomeroy must have inherited all the physical features from their Native American ancestors, leaving none for Francis. He was large and solid, standing at a towering six-foot-five, at least a foot taller than Francis, and his complexion was that of a rough leather tan, much darker than his brother's. The only attribute they appeared to have in common was their jet-black hair, though Wes's mane was long and flowing, damn near reaching the back pockets of his jeans.

"Wes is familiar with Indian legends," Francis said to Lucas. "Our grandparents told us all the tales, but I never kept up with them much. Tell him what you encountered."

So Lucas did. Wes sat on the couch in the corner and listened attentively, albeit tiredly, due to the late-night meeting. And when Lucas finished, Wes spoke for the first time, his voice husky, steadfast, and direct, as he delivered the tale, the myth, the legend, of the flying head.

"The stories tell of a harsh winter that caused a famine for the Iroquois. The animals had all let out, plants stopped growing, no fish to catch. Nothing left to hunt or gather to eat, so the younger tribesmen suggested they leave and search out a new land to settle. But the older ones, they wouldn't hear any of it. They wanted to stay put and refused the younglings' request. So the younger ones, what they did, they murdered all the elders, chopped off their heads, and threw them in the water. That's how the flying head was born.

"The decapitated heads of the elders transformed into one giant floating head, a monster with long black hair, wings, claws, and ravenous teeth. The flying head sought those young men out and slaughtered them.

"There are a few variations to the story. One says the Hudson River was where the heads were thrown. Others say it was Sacandaga Lake. Either way, we are not far from either of those bodies of water, and regardless of where it came from, legend says the monster still roams the land, its hunger for vengeance against those who disobey their elders forever insatiable."

Lucas had been drying himself with a towel for the duration of Wes's speech. He felt the story was finished, and now his boss was gawking at him expectantly, as if waiting for him to add more facts to support his brother's tale. Lucas kept tousling his hair, saying nothing.

"Well," Francis said, "does that sound like what you saw?"

Lucas shook his head, not in disagreement, but in bewilderment.

"So, the stories are true, huh?" Francis said thoughtfully. He sighed and said, "Flying frigging head. How do we kill it, Wes?"

Wes cast his gaze downward, as though he were sifting through the tangled web of his memory in search of the information. "There was another story," he said. "An Iroquois woman pretended to roast acorns over a fire and tricked the monster into eating a hot coal. It didn't kill the creature, but it retreated and was never seen again."

Francis drummed his fingers atop his desk, thinking, then said, "High-powered rifle ought to do the trick. Did you try to shoot it, Lucas?"

"None of us had guns."

"Then how'n the hell did you get rid of Uncle Chet?"

"There was a machete on the boat. I handled it."

Francis groaned and stretched as he leaned back in his chair. "The other three—Karl, Max, Rob—where are they?"

"What's left of them?" Lucas said. "Likely floating down the river with Donny's boat."

"Well, they don't have any ties to the organization," Francis said, "but Donny's boat, being that it's Donny's, sure does. The law finds floating corpses *and* the jon boat, they might connect this whole mess to us. You need to find it."

"No disrespect, boss, but I'm not going anywhere near the river or that island ever again."

Wes interjected, saying, "That doesn't matter none. It'll come for you yet. This monster, it's not just some hungry beast you stumbled upon. It has intent. It has a purpose. It seeks revenge."

"Revenge?" Lucas said. "For what? What did we ever do to that thing?"

"Why, revenge for Uncle Chet, of course," Wes said. "Don't you understand the moral of the story?"

Lucas and Francis considered each other with furrowed brows and shook their heads.

"That monster was born out of the youngling's disobedience and betrayal of their older kin, the message being—*mind your elders*. Uncle Chet may not have been *your* uncle, but he was your *elder*, and you slaughtered him."

Francis scoffed. "Well, Lucas, it appears you've got nowhere to hide. And you need to be getting back out there looking for Donny's boat. Does this thing come out in the daytime, Wes?"

Wes shrugged. "Reckon not likely."

"Good. Lucas, you'll get another boat and go out first light."

"And if I don't find it?"

"Don't come back here unless you've killed that creature. I don't want your curse rubbing off on me."

"How do you suppose I do that, boss?"

"I'll set you up with some firepower. And if bullets don't kill it, pack a flare gun. That's as close to getting a hot coal in its mouth as I can think up. Now, get out of here before that beast finds out you're here. Listen to your elders, like Wes said."

Lucas made to push himself out of the chair when the office walls rumbled like distant thunder, and he sat back down. A hectic amount of commotion erupted from the stage room outside, glass shattering, heavy objects breaking, sounding like a stampede.

A harsh, deafening screech as tortuous as a steam whistle penetrated the room. Lucas cringed, cupping his hands to his ears, and whipped his head around to face the noise. Wes leaned away from the door as though an unpleasant smell had reached his nostrils.

Francis bolted to his feet. "Jesus, don't tell me that thing—" he said, and yanked out a desk drawer and brought out a shiny chrome pistol, leveling it toward Lucas as he circled the desk.

"What are you doing?" Lucas yelped.

"What do you think I'm doing? I'm tossing your ass out there so it leaves us be."

Wes cleared his throat and said calmly, "Actually, Francis, I don't think that's gonna matter much."

"Why not?"

"Were you not the one who made the call to kill Chet?"

Francis shrugged. "I'm the boss, aren't I?"

"Well, if you ordered the killing, then I'd say you don't have to worry about this boy's curse rubbing off on you. You're already wearing it."

"You mean it's come for me too?" Francis cried out.

The wall bashed inward, causing paint chips, dust, and sheetrock to fall. Lucas faced forward, hands clenching the arms of his chair.

Francis retreated behind his desk, dropping to his knees and wailing, "Are you sure, Wes? Are you sure it's here to kill me?"

Wes just sat there in the corner. He pursed his lips at his little brother and said, with the utmost certainty, "I am your elder. Mind what I tell you."

The flying head's horrifying siren exploded the office door to pieces. Shards of wood hurled into the back of Lucas's chair, yet he did not flinch. He shut his eyes, picturing the ferocious monster sailing inward, the strands of its thick black hair quivering with serpentine fluidity. Directly over his shoulder, the hungry piercing shrills rang out close enough to rattle his skull and make his ears bleed.

But it wasn't so deafening that he couldn't hear Francis's pleas to his brother, his cries of agony, and those screams that turned into choking and gargling as the flying head consumed him first.

The Itch

by Blake Kourik

HE DIDN'T KNOW WHEN it began again, but he felt it in his toes. The slight tingling, the feather tickling that made him squirm, like a grade schooler who had to use the restroom when the teacher wouldn't let him. It always started in his toes and worked its way to his head, at first taking its time, then gaining traction.

"So, can you get the rest of that audit to me by the end of the day?"

His boss, Mr. Jotham, stood above him, downcast eyes glancing over the neat stacks of papers piled high by his computer. He leaned over the edge of his desk, waiting for an answer, and sipped gingerly from the mug of coffee in his bony hand. A faded and cracked Dilbert cartoon ran halfway around the white ceramic before disappearing under Jotham's fingers. The result of washing the mug in the dishwasher, no doubt. Greg was sure the little white label the mug came with said only to handwash. A small chip cracked the otherwise smooth circumference of the lip too. Carelessness on his boss's behalf, likely, when putting it in the goddamn dishwasher.

"Yes," Greg said and turned his eyes up, forcing an obligatory corporate smile that showed his boss, *Yes, sir. Everything's just A-OKAY here.* "Yes, sure thing."

He forced the same tight, closed-mouth smile wider on his face, and his boss returned the volley with his own signature HR grin, taking a hand off his desk to give him a close-to-the-chest thumbs-up.

"Okay. Good man." His boss leaned over and clapped him on the back.

Greg bit into his tongue as the hand touched him, lifted, then clapped twice more. The vibrations ran down his spine, out to his toes, further waking the itch. Jotham stole down the hall and Greg watched him lean into another workspace. Harold Reemer's. Jotham asked Harold how he was doing, Harold cracked a joke, his boss laughed, and Greg swiveled back around in his chair to lose himself in the numbers on his computer. Rows of digits in their proper spaces for a different account. Greg pulled up the McDaniel audit and started typing.

His feet tapped up and down on the braided carpet and he tried to push his mind away from the motion, ignoring the growing sensation, expanding like Magic Grow Capsules, six styles, two steps: drop in water and watch 'em grow. Soft, expanding foam that changed into dinosaurs, animals, vehicles, or *bugs* with a little moisture. A little push was all it took.

Inside his shoes, under his arches, the itch unfolded into winged bees. A cluster of spiders, swarming ants, spread out over his toes and curved up his ankles. Greg clacked away on his computer, crunching the finishing numbers for the McDaniel's account, hammering the keyboard as his heels hammered the carpet, up and down. Up and down, both feet danced under his desk as if on hot coals. *(when Greg was one, his first word had been pi, a word his mother repeated to him often, and as soon as he could talk, she taught him to count, reciting numbers aloud to her, from one to ten, and she taught him to count to her everything that he had from his toys, to his shirts, to his crayons, to the days in the week, and...)*

Digits reflected off the corneas of his eyes, projected from his computer screen into his brain. Ones and tens, and twenties and fifties, six-digit figures that reflected investment earnings. Individual expenses and corporate losses, private shares, and yearly revenues, and the hands on the clock counted away numbers as Gregory did the same at his computer, scrambling to finish. He had to complete the audit before the itch got too bad. Hours ticked by and the flow of numbers, figures, and integers tamed the tapping, but as time slipped by, the itch grew worse (*God, it did*) and the moment he finished and sent the documents off, he felt it full-force, reaching up his calves.

It picked up speed as he came to a stand, pushed his chair out, and turned off the computer. Greg grabbed his jacket, pulled it over his shoulders, and both of his legs simmered, rippling, *moving* with the itch, a horribly funny feeling, like the darkest punchline in a demented joke. One told from an emotionless mouth of grinning, sharp teeth.

"Hey, Greggy-Weggy, want to feel something funny? Want to feel something you've never felt before? It feels horrible, but lemme tell you, Greg, it tickles *like a sonuva bitch."*

The itch stampeded, buzzing, tingling, jittering his calves and prickling his thighs, working up his body, as if he'd just stepped in an ant mound and the ants were crawling up, and he couldn't get them off, the millions of bugs, angry and *biting*. It crawled up his skin, over his pores to the soft spots of his joints, higher and higher.

Greg left his cubicle, walked through the office, and out the front doors. The receptionist, Janet Brinsley, looked up as he left, but didn't say goodbye. She shrunk behind the desk, crouching her head on her shoulders, and tried to look busy at the computer. Gregory Surnow never even looked her way. Janet never talked to him nor had any desire to in the immediate future if she could help it, but that was the way it was with so many of the number-crunchers Jotham hired. Cubicle weasels. Strange little men who—she had no doubt—lived alone, collected comic books, and called the numbers at the back of newspapers for any and all sexual release. Gregory Surnow, to her, however, unlike the other weasels, was one of the strange ones. One of the *fidgeters*. A good worker, according to Mr. Jotham, but too jittery, the same fidgeting her mother warned her about, pointing them out when she was a child, whispering in her ear while they shopped: "See how he moves? All fidgety. Watch out for them, Jan. Those are the ones always keeping a secret. The fidgeters."

Janet eyed Surnow's gait as he went into the parking lot. He grimaced at every stamp of his feet as he paced to the car. Every footstep he took came down hard. She darted her attention between Surnow and her latest issue of *Cosmopolitan*. If Jotham saw her with it, he'd have a conniption, but seeing that she'd gotten her work done for the day and that no clients had come in since three, she didn't care. It was near closing, and she felt she could slip it under her thigh in a flash if the need arrived. Her eyes flickered out the front windows again to watch Surnow disappear around the corner, then returned to the Astrology Special Section of her magazine. She flipped to page thirty-two and continued reading about her sexual, emotional, and romantic predictions.

Greg took his car keys from the jacket pocket, opened his door, hopped inside, cranked the engine, and threw the gear in reverse. He flipped on the radio *(as he got older, she taught him to count higher, and he learned one through one hundred, then one through ten thousand, and he learned the value of π, 3.14 to begin with, but he never knew his father and he had always been alone, his mother never talked about him, only asked her son to repeat to her numbers, recite her digits and fractions, and the value of pi lengthened).* Noise helped, and Peter Frampton came on asking if he felt like he did, and he doubted it, highly doubted it, and hoped he didn't feel like he did either.

He ripped out of his spot, and late afternoon sunshine poured through the windshield as he shifted to drive. Fat white clouds lolled over the blue skyline and a soft breeze ruffled the air. Grazing squirrels hopped through the trees, pigeons and sparrows lined the tops of buildings, and a tolerable flow of traffic filled the roadways that would turn sour and clog, bumper to bumper, at 5:00 p.m.

Greg remembered all the paperwork, all the accounts he managed every day, and ticked off the number of cars that he passed on his drive. Two Mercedes Benz, one Volkswagen, five Fords, nine Hondas *(and as Greg got older, the memorized digits grew longer, 3.14 became 3.1415, then 3.1415926, then 3.141592653589, then 3.14159265358979323846).*

The itch marched up, making the muscles contract in his legs, cringing the pale flesh of his thighs, his buttocks clenching together. His scrotum crawled as a million legs pricked up his lower back. Greg rolled down the windows before his hands tightened on the wheel. His veins bulged beneath the skin, and the tendons in his fingers turned to steel cords, each soldered to the bone in a flexed position. He tried to loosen them but found he couldn't *(and his mother made him repeat the digits every day, every morning when she woke up, and once a year, when she got bad, and she got sick).* Sweat stood out from his pores and ran down his face, dripping from his chin, slicking his shirt to his body, his pants to his legs. The inside of his mouth turned to cotton *(he ran off the digits, repeating them over, again and again, until his mother got to her worst, and he had to close his eyes and ignore her as she went into her bedroom and he had to).*

Greg boosted his speed another four miles per hour and drove thirty-nine, his toes balled, feet crunched in their socks. His apartment was past the corner intersection of Battlefield Road and Campbell Avenue, and if you added the letters of those street names together, then divided them by two, you could attain their square root, 5.385, but *(cover his ears and not listen to the sounds and wait until she took care of her problem and came back and got him)*.

He pulled right into the turning lane before the light and at the intersection, looked left, seeing, counting the cars waiting in lines by the one Burger King on Campbell and the one Starbucks on Battle-field. Two Buicks, one BMW, and a silver Nissan sat at the Starbucks. One Ford at the drive-thru window of Burger King and a Buick at the peeling menu board. Six vehicles in total, 66.67% of them in line at Starbucks, the other 33.33% at Burger King.

The itch reached the middle of his back, and fumes of trundling beetles scuttled up his skin, lacquered pincers *pinching*, barbs digging into his muscles, pulling the itch, up, *up*. At the red light, he lurched forward over the wheel. A hot bubble of acid gurgled in his throat, singeing the backs of his nostrils. His eyes watered and spilled over, but his hands never unclutched from the circumference of the wheel as he gagged and spit. Saliva trickled from the sides of his mouth. His insides screamed as the itch contorted. Inside his stomach, it folded in on itself, over and over again, a ball of centipedes that circled to his chest, burrowing inward, gnawing, eating, the insides of his lungs turned to rotting wood.

A thousand mouths munched and chewed and *(and so he'd wait in the living room, cradling his head between his legs, putting his earbuds in, and covering them with his hands)* the light turned green, *(rocking back and forth, repeating the numbers, saying them out loud, and ig-noring the sounds)* Greg pressed his foot down on the gas, tore through the intersection, and screeched down Battlefield Road.

Ranks of mantises ascended his spine, bristled wings buzzing up his back, and parading fire ants, a pulsing mass, rose like an arterial embolism toward his head. A ballooning death rose to the largest cavity, to grow and grow, and bite, and eat, and sting, expand, pressing out and multiplying—

"*Three point one four one five NINE!*" he yelled in his car. "*Three point one four one five nine two six five three five eight nine seven nine three two three eight four SIX!*" Frothed spit dripped from his mouth.

Amounts, quantities, times, dates, aggregates, sum totals, tallies, quotas, firm, round objects, facts he could run his hands over, let his mind grip and hold onto, *smooth*. Smooth in his mind, submerging the itch, drowning the crawling sensation in steroid cream. Hydrocortisone, Icy Hot, OFF! spray, Raid instant killer, liquid protection, pointed at lumbering, eyeless spiders that crawled up his chest, his neck, into his—

He gripped the wheel between his hands.

In his mind, he gripped the cold aluminum cans of extinguisher, bug killer, anti-itch, intensive healing formula facts—*numbers* the only temporary relief to push back the itch. To keep it at bay, before killing it, ridding himself of it, but it always came back. The numbers were temporary, and so was the solution. Longer relief, the tool provided. When he was able to use his tool, the itch limped away in retreat, but always recomposed. It always healed, then came back. His condition was a dark, hungry Shelob, born of incessant itch, and it never sated. He could injure it. He could wield his sword against it to pierce the dark black leather of its hide. He could cause it to run, fleeing from his body *hundreds of crawling, itching, arachnid legs* but it always came back. When it became well enough to attack again, every year, it came back, hungry *(the sounds that came from the bathroom, even with his earbuds in, the cracking, splitting, tearing noises).*

His apartment appeared on the edge of the road. On the concrete horizon, his complex rose, and he recited numbers, formulas, facts, and statistics, his learned defense. His elvish sword. His weapon of chain-linked numerals, digits welded together, ground down and whetted to the sharpest point.

The twisting blanket of bugs inside his chest, a jungle of insects, squirmed past his diaphragm, up the middle, and wove toward the nape of his neck *(and the muffled screaming of his mother from her back bedroom, and the wet sounds against the bathroom porcelain that seeped under her door).*

Six months ago, at the state fair, he'd found the tool he used to rid himself of the itch. The magic weapon that proved to be the quickest, most silent, safest way. His stainless-steel bolt. The clean, air-charged pistol released the itch in the cleanest way possible, without ever letting those around him know what he held inside.

He found the air gun online but hadn't purchased it until the state fair, the event the Ozark Fairgrounds promoted in the papers for weeks. The agricultural and livestock convention held in town, the biggest to come to the Midwest for the rest of the year and likely the decade. In the advertisement, under big bolded words declaring the sheer size of the event itself, smaller text read that almost anything you could ever think to need, and more, would be there.

Greg attended the exposition back in January and met one of the salesmen who retailed his tool. An older man, Rick Gatwick, with a puckered face marked by a thousand wrinkles, which made him look like one of The California Raisins, eyed Greg as soon as he walked over, and started his spiel when he saw him eye the selection.

"That's a good'un. Heckuva tool," he said to Greg as he glanced over one of the guns propped up in its case. "Way of the future for these smaller towns. I should know. Born and raised here, over in Polk County. Darn proud of that fact too. Just wish my poppy had one of these when we was still raising heads. That's heads of beef, course, son," he said and threw Greg a full-toothed smile of horse dentures.

"How's it work?" Greg asked, watching the gun.

"Heckuva way. Works on air. Compressed air, that is, in these tiny canisters."

Rick picked one up out of the case and turned it over in the air between them, displaying it between his pointer and thumb.

"You use these little fellers, centerfire cartridges, better than rimfire cartridges—these can hold more pressure—and for each shot it sends a 15 cm bolt straight out at this pistol with the power of a 9mm gun. Now, that's high-velocity penetration, son. You stick the end of the pistol right up to the head of your cattle, 'tween the eyes, pull the trigger, and—"

He made a popping sound with his mouth and thumbed the creased spot of skin between his brows.

"Goes into the head, penetrates the skull, and shoots through the brain to give the animal a nice, quick death. Cleaner and more humane. Cattle dies," he snapped his fingers, "'fore they even know what hit 'em."

"How much does it cost?" Greg had asked.

"Usually run 'bout $300 even, but since I like the look of ya', a real discernin' fella', I'll knock ten percent off. How's $270 sound?"

Greg considered then took out his wallet, and the first time he used the tool, he became attached. No other way proved more effective nor more efficient. He hadn't had to suffer waiting for the itch to take its course anymore. Nor had he ever had to perform other methods to rid himself of it, less desirable, unpleasant ways. Other ways that released the itch from his body couldn't provide the effectiveness or efficiency that the bolt did.

In the times since, he refined his methods. Two woven poly tarps, a roll of painter's tape, ammonia bleach cleaner, hydrogen peroxide, and a scrubbing brush sat awaiting him at home. He removed his clothes first every time now. With the captive bolt pistol, there was no pain, no disturbance, and no one ever knew what he did behind his closed—

A car honked from behind and Greg lurched forward, turning right onto the road that ran parallel to his apartment. A crack of lightning pain erupted through his body as the writhing insectile mass dug into his head. His every muscle contracted, aching, screaming with bright white, shooting pain. Electric currents of agony pulsed up and down him. Spittle dripped from his hanging jaw, and his vision blurred in tears, brought back to reality.

His eyes upturned and the car behind him honked again as his speed dropped *(and once a year, only, it happened, and his mother would come back out, freshly showered, clean, and she'd console Greggy, and tell him not to worry, that everything was alright and that one day he'd understand, and she'd have him repeat to her the digits of π, and she'd kiss him on his forehead and tell him how proud of him she was).*

Greg twisted into the turning lane, curved left, and drove over the opposite two lanes to the entrance to his apartment complex. He drove past the *A* building parking lots, past the front office, turned left, and pulled into the first space of the *B* building parking. The mailboxes for the *B* building sat to his left. He threw his gear in *park* and tore the keys from the ignition *(after he recited for her the first 25 digits, then the first 100, then the next 500).*

He didn't bother locking his car. Over the asphalt parking, up the inclined sidewalk, to the wooden stairwell against the wall of the building, he flew up the single flight, over the wooden planks of the balcony, and jammed his code into his door's electronic keypad. 5676 *(and eventually he understood).*

The door beeped open and the bolt unlatched itself. Greg threw himself into the room, collapsed on the floor, and slammed the door behind him.

Greg ripped the jacket from his body, working himself from his button-down shirt and tie. His limbs writhed as he yanked his pants off each leg, the itch expanding in his cranium, pushing out against the walls of his skull. It boiled his brain, his aching brain, his hot, aching brain. His eyes burned as the bugs grew inside of them, angry, teeming. His skin scraped over the carpet, and his bones cried with every movement, the itch breaking down his body, exuding acid into his bloodstream, eating, oozing black widow toxins through his arteries. The itch mushroomed and tore open like a cocoon between his ears.

Greg dragged his body over the carpet, to the closet, clawing open the door. He reached to the back, the black case of the captive bolt pistol. He unlatched the lid and snatched the pistol from inside *(π equaled 3.14159265358979323846264338327950288419716939937510 5820974944).*

Greg hauled himself over the carpet to the cold tile of the bathroom, the pistol gripped in his hand. It clicked against each line of grout in the tiling. In the shower, two woven blue poly tarps hung taped to the walls. They draped from the shower rod, replacing the curtain. A single slit in the middle of the two tarps was the only opening. The remaining tape roll sat atop the closed toilet seat. On the floor, a bottle of ammonia bleach, hydrogen peroxide, and a box of bristle brushes stood sentry. Slithering on his stomach, he clawed his way to the tub and pulled himself over the lip. Through the slit in the tarps, he crashed into the tub and the metal pistol clanged against the lining as he fell inside. His head banged the bar soap holder, and the itch consumed the bright flash of pain as his skull cracked against porcelain.

He heaved his feet into the tub, grabbed the tape from the toilet seat, and feverishly tore strips from the roll, letting the pistol fall between his legs. Greg closed the entry slit in the tarps from the inside, and the gray matter inside his head curdled with the itch. The veins in his eyes popped out in strands. His vision turned yellow and red.

Greg's lungs shriveled. His teeth moaned in their sockets and the world strobed in bright, screeching pain. He picked up the pistol and turned it in his hands, pointing the muzzle toward himself. Then he stuck the end of the gun in his mouth, pulled the trigger, and released the 9mm bolt from its sheath into his head.

Chunks of exoskeleton, wings, and legs splattered the tile of the shower, sending brackish rivulets trickling down the grout. Greg fell backward, and his head clanged against the lining of the tub. Grasshoppers buzzed and limped out of his skull, toward the drain at the base of the shower. Injured mantises, roaches, and beetles stumbled over one another from the hole in his head and ants fell in clumps, marching over his legs. Clusters of arachnids skittered down the drainpipe like water. A lone fly flew out of the bathroom, to the front door, and squirmed beneath it, outside.

Dark green liquid flowed down Gregory's back and washed all the remaining bug parts down the drain. The thick mess flowed past his calves into the water-stained drain, and in the empty bathroom, the gulping sound of the pipes echoed throughout the apartment.

A sharp breath sucked into Greg's mouth, and his head lifted on its spine. At the base of his neck, the punctured hole sealed like water coming together, and flesh merged, lining the cranium. Muscle re-formed, blood vessels roped over bright pink tissue, and brain matter expanded, pulsing with life. Sheets of translucent membranes layered upon themselves, and his skull crackled together like glass shattering in reverse. The skull sealed, and muscle wove over the slick, shining bone. Liquid skin plastered over the muscle then solidified and sprouted hair.

Greg sat up, soaked in the tub. He cricked his neck to the side and grimaced at the pop. He placed a hand under his chin, cracked his neck even further, and another sharper crackle rang out. The itch was gone.

He stood up and balanced himself against the shower wall. His equilibrium always came back slowly. For a second, his world swirled around him, then regained composure. He flicked on the water. Greg twisted the handle and waited for the water to steam before pulling the spout diverter for the shower head. Hot water flowed over his scalp, through his still-growing hair, and he looked down at the drain.

He'd taken the plug off ahead of time and nothing was caught in the drainage pipe. He closed his eyes and tilted his face up to the water. That was great. Just great to see. It'd been cleaner this time. Even more so than the last. Another year until it happened again, and he was getting better. His mother would be proud.

Hot water rained over him and washed away the mess, sending bright green streams down the tile and porcelain. Green water seeped down the drain, and eventually cleared as the mess washed away. The water washed it all down the drain, out of his apartment, apart from him.

Greg reached for the soap and plastic cup he kept on his hanging caddy. He held the cup up to the shower head, filled it with water, then splashed the back of the tub to rinse the remaining bits off.

Water pattered on the tarp like rain, soporific and warm. Greg placed the cup back on the caddy and snapped the lid of the soap open. He poured a gob into his palm and scrubbed his body. Green suds sloughed off his skin, down his legs, over his toes. The warm water flowed, cleaning his body, the taped-up tarps, and the pistol at his feet. When he got out of the shower, he'd "once-over" the tub with chemicals, disassemble the pistol, clean it and dry it.

Three hundred and sixty-five days until it came again, and next year he'd leave work earlier. He let it go too long this time, but no one noticed, and that was good. Anonymity was the key to the equation. It was five o'clock, and on the streets outside the traffic, right on schedule, started to pour. It clogged the main ways and crammed the avenues as people made their way home for the evening from work.

Inside a Chevy Impala, a man in a worn blue suit sat six cars behind the light, sweat on his brow. His eyes focused ahead at the stalled traffic and the clock on his dash as he tapped his hands on the wheel. He had dinner at 7:00 p.m. and he still needed to change for that. It was a big dinner with his boss at TASHIDA SUSHI, one of the nicer Japanese sit-downs in town, and was a good chance for him to score some brownie points with the big man. Maybe after a few rounds of saké, he could see about getting that raise too, but he wouldn't even have time to change into nicer clothes if traffic didn't pick up.

From his rolled-down window, a light breeze rippled his hair, and a fly flew into the car and landed on the dash. The bug stared up at him with its segmented red eyes, and the man raised his hand, slowly, then swatted the insect. It squished beneath his palm, and the man grimaced at the splat. He turned his palm over to inspect the damage, and a car honked behind him.

The man looked up and saw the light had turned green. The car behind him laid on the horn again, and he pressed his foot on the gas and pulled through the intersection. He reached into the glovebox for a Kleenex, wiped his dash, then the bug juice from his hand. As he drove, he looked at the smear the bug left on the Kleenex; the darnedest thing. On the napkin, the small smear looked bright green.

He shook his head and tossed the crumpled tissue on the passenger's side floorboard. He'd throw it out when he got home. It didn't matter anyway. There'd be plenty more where those came from.

Summer was just around the corner, and hotter weather meant more bugs. The man drove past another intersection, thankfully green, and continued his way home to change for dinner. As he drove along, he rolled up his windows. More bugs on the way for sure. Summer was just heating up again.

Andie

by Jen Mierisch

AFTER ALL THESE YEARS, Andie was still there, sprawled in a corner of the tree house in the slanting afternoon sun. She looked just the same, apart from the dirt smearing her pearly plastic skin. Her bald head tilted.

Hi, Henry.

Henry brought rags from the garage and gently wiped away the grime. Andie's perfect lips were worn, the luster rubbed off. His cheeks flushed as he remembered why.

He'd named her when Andie MacDowell from *Groundhog Day* reigned in his teenage dreams. The mannequin had come home in his dad's junk-hauling truck one night, jumbled with shelves and other crap from a shuttered department store. Dad would've whipped Henry if he'd seen him take it, but he'd been too drunk to notice.

She'd weathered the years well. Henry went back to the garage for a small paintbrush and the half-empty can of red paint his dad had used on the back fence. Soon, Andie had fresh red lips, a bloody rose, dramatic against her white face.

That's much better, Henry.

"Looking good, Andie."

No place like home. Don't you think?

It hadn't been Henry's home for twenty years. Nobody came around much, after what happened to Mom.

Henry's gaze stroked Andie's long limbs, her shapely breasts, and then he turned to go. Her opaque eyes watched him climb down the ladder to the grass.

"Henry Johnson? Is that you?"

He jumped and turned around.

Melinda Sanford was heavier, a bit wearier, but still a redhead, still cute. "Sorry. Didn't mean to startle you. Is somebody up there?"

"No!" he said too loud. "Just talking to myself."

She smiled kindly. "I heard about your dad. I'm so sorry."

Henry scratched his head. "Thanks," he mumbled. "I came to clean out the house, maybe sell some things."

"You haven't changed a bit."

He shrugged. "How's, uh..." *Who was that guy she'd married?*

"Denny?" She made a face. "He's in Schererville. It's his weekend with the kids."

"Oh."

"Your sister around?"

"She moved overseas a while back."

Melinda's blue eyes lingered on Henry's. "If there's anything I can do to help, let me know, okay?" She rummaged in her purse for a business card. "Here's my number."

Henry watched Melinda walk across the street. Back in the day, she hadn't been the type to give her number to Henry Johnson.

Are you going to call her?

Henry lit a cigarette, took a drag, and glanced at Andie. "Maybe."

She doesn't really want to help you.

"No?"

She wants to get the scoop about what happened. So she can tell every-one.

Henry frowned. It never occurred to him to gossip. Most people weren't worth talking about.

"Melinda knows everyone around here," he said. "And the card says she's in real estate. Maybe she can help me sell the house and Dad's truck."

Who cares if she knows everyone. She doesn't know you.

"Doesn't matter if she knows me."

She wants to know you.

He barked a laugh. "I don't think so."

I heard what she said, Henry.

"What do you mean?"

She gave you her number. So obvious.

Henry exhaled smoke and thought about Melinda's curvy backside.

Remember all those times we sat up here and talked all night?

Henry tossed his cigarette into a coffee can half-full of twenty-year-old butts. "I remember."

I know you, Henry.

"You've always been a great listener, Andie." He sighed. "I wouldn't have made it through high school without you."

I know all about you, Henry. More than she ever will.

He stared out the window at the star-sprinkled sky. A cool breeze snaked through the sleeve of his t-shirt, raising gooseflesh along his torso. It smelled like smoke from someone's campfire. Like the flames that had cremated his father.

"I just want to get out of here," he said. "To get rid of the last of it, and never see this place again."

The mannequin's laugh was choppy, like the chatter of an assembly line.

Henry, don't be silly. You can't leave.

"Don't say that."

Not until you dig it up.

"Stop."

If you don't, she will.

"Shut up!" He heaved himself down the ladder with angry hands and hustled toward the house.

———

"I'm sorry, Andie."

Her limbs lay unmoving across the dusty boards.

Henry took her plastic hand. "I didn't mean what I said."

Hi, Henry.

The breath left him in a whoosh. "I was afraid I'd lost you."

You left me for years, you know.

"I lived with Aunt Rhoda for a while," he said. "They made me, after—"

Did you miss me, Henry?

"I thought about you all the time," he said. "You know, you're the only one who ever really listened to me."

Of course I did. I know you like nobody else does.

"Yeah."

No woman could ever understand you like I do.

"Maybe..."

The mannequin jerked upright. Her head swiveled to face Henry.

I know everything.

The world went dark, and then the images came. Henry's mother, criticizing him again for spending so much time in the tree house alone. Telling him to make an effort, to find real friends, as if he hadn't tried, as if real people wanted anything to do with him. Henry was always the problem, of course, never anybody else. She had never understood how hard it was, and she would never, *ever* shut up about it.

There it is. Not buried so deep after all.

That day Henry had come home from school to see his mother dragging Andie by a leg toward her pickup truck, the bed filled with bags of garbage. The moment everything went red and Henry seized the shovel that leaned against the house. The way she hadn't made a sound as her body hit the dirt of the driveway.

I'll keep your secrets, Henry. I don't ask for much in return.

Henry's father going to prison, because nobody believed he hadn't been drunk enough to finally beat his wife to death. Henry putting as much distance as possible between himself and this house, even after Dad got out, even after he got sick.

I like this lipstick you gave me.

"It looks real pretty, Andie."

You know what else I'd like?

"What's that?"

Some hair. I think red would suit me. Don't you?

After all these years, his hunting knife was still here. And the sharpening stone.

He reached for his phone.

"You're the only woman who's ever understood me, Andie."

And I still love you, Henry. I always will.

The ladder creaked below.

"Henry? It's Melinda. I got your text. You said you had something to show me?"

It's Only a Movie

by Daniel Gene Barlekamp

"I'LL PICK YOU UP at 1:30," my mom says through the rolled-down window.

She's sitting in the driver's seat of her black SUV. I'm standing at the curb, my face and hands turning clammy in the misty rain.

"Can't I come with you?" I ask. "I'll wait in the car or something."

"No," she says. "The adults need to talk."

I hate when she talks to me that way, like I'm a little kid. She acts like it's some big secret, but I know where she's going: the lawyer's office. Again.

"I don't know how long it'll take," she continues. "Someone might call the police if I leave you alone in the car that long."

My eyes scan the deserted parking lot, hundreds of empty spaces spreading in all directions like the grid on a gigantic sheet of graph paper. I doubt anyone will be around to notice, let alone call the police, but it's no use arguing.

"Fine," I say.

"Here," she says, rummaging through her purse, "go see a movie. That'll kill the morning, right?"

She passes some folded bills through the open window.

"You can even buy a popcorn and a soda," she adds. "*Small*. I want to get some lunch in you later."

I put the money in my pocket without looking at it.

"Alright, if I'm done early, I might stop at the store, then I'll text you when I'm on my way back. Meet me out here. Pick a good show!"

She rolls up the window and drives away, the gray mist swallowing her receding taillights. I turn around to face the behemoth behind me: the Quietbrook Mall.

It's only eleven o'clock in the morning, but it might as well be the middle of the night. Who goes to the mall anymore? People like my grandma, who do laps early in the morning to get some indoor exercise, are long gone, and none of the afternoon shoppers have arrived yet. After the heavy glass door swings shut behind me, I can hear the squeak of my sneakers against the polished tile floors. There is no echo. Each footfall evaporates into the dead air. Weak sunlight shines through the skylights that run the length of the ceiling, while a piano version of a pop song I can't quite identify floats softly from hidden speakers. The gates to all the stores are raised, but I don't see any people, not even a clerk behind the waist-high counters in the jewelry store.

I resist the urge to scream, to topple one of the racks of cellphone cases at a nearby kiosk just to make some noise, and instead find my way to the hallway that branches off to the movie theater. The shiny tile turns to purple carpeting, still streaked from the vacuum cleaner the night before. If the mall is dead, the theater is even deader. Most people I know go to the movies after school or on Friday nights, not in the morning.

When I round the corner into the lobby, it's quiet. The only sound comes from a few arcade machines in the corner running through their demos, *0 CREDITS* flashing across their screens. A crane arm moves back and forth by itself as if propelled by an invisible hand, tempting passersby to try their luck at fishing out a neon-green alien or a purple squishy ball. I start to turn back to the hallway, assuming the theater hasn't yet opened for the day, when a jerky movement behind the concession stand catches my eye. A young man emerges from the back room. His greasy hair is combed down flat against his forehead, and he wears a frayed polo shirt with the name of the theater embossed in gold.

"Can I help you?" he says across the empty lobby.

I consider leaving, but two and a half hours is a lot of time to kill wandering around half-abandoned department stores and staring into the fountain that only operates some of the time.

"What's playing?" I ask, approaching the glass counter filled with bright yellow popcorn.

"*The Mausoleum*," he said.

"What's that?"

"Scary movie." His mouth widens in a toothy grin. "Real scary."

I grumble. I'll sit through almost anything, but I hate scary movies. Life is scary enough without adding monsters, axe murderers, and all that garbage into the mix.

"What else?" I ask.

"There is nothing else. Not that many people come here at this hour. We only run one theater in the morning."

I think for a moment, picturing the endless corridors of spotless tile, the untouched clothing racks.

"One, please," I say.

"Excellent choice." The man is still grinning. A tiny bead of spit has formed at one corner of his lips. "Can I offer you anything else? A small popcorn, perhaps?"

I glance over his shoulder at the dispenser, where brown artificial butter drips into a striped bucket.

"No thanks."

"Suit yourself," he says, tearing off a ticket and handing me the stub. "Theater 13, on your left. All the way at the end."

The dim hallway on my left disappears around a bend. I can't tell how long it is. I look back one last time to find the man grinning at me.

"Remember," he says. "It's only a movie."

About halfway down the hallway, I notice a poster for *The Mausoleum*. It's the only poster on either wall. It shows a tall, thin old man dressed like an undertaker from the 1800s, top hat and all, glaring over his shoulder at the viewer while prying open the door to an old mausoleum. Beneath the title runs the tagline:

Just keep telling yourself it's only a movie...

"Funny," I mutter, remembering the words of the man who sold me my ticket, but I'm kidding myself. This really isn't my scene. My throat turns dry as I take the last few steps toward the end of the hallway and Theater 13.

A minute later, I'm sitting front and center, the only person in the darkened theater. After a brief message about the location of the fire exits, the movie begins, skipping the previews entirely. The opening shot shows the exterior of an ornate stone mausoleum rising up in the middle of an old graveyard, brown leaves swirling around the tombstones. Then the camera cuts to the interior of the mausoleum, panning down endless white-marble corridors lined with plaques that mark the graves. The walls seem to close in on either side, reminding me of the silent, pristine wings of the Quietbrook Mall. Finally, ominous violin music swells as slow footsteps echo off the mausoleum's floor, growing louder until a shadow—a tall, thin shadow of a person wearing a top hat—falls over the floor in front of the camera's perspective. The violins deliver a shrieking jolt. I nearly leap out of my seat.

Forget it, I think, throwing my hands over my eyes. *I won't watch. I'll open my eyes once it's over.*

For what feels like an eternity, I listen to the sounds of creaking hinges, evil laughs, and the screams of victims who, I assume, are dragged by the undertaker into the bowels of the mausoleum, never to return. Once the onslaught gets going, it doesn't let up. I feel my lips forming the words, *It's only a movie, it's only a movie...*

After a few minutes, the nonstop barrage of awful noises starts to dull my senses. I've heard of people experiencing narcolepsy and passing out in the middle of stressful situations, and that must be what happens to me. Either that, or I lull myself to sleep repeating my mantra—*it's only a movie, it's only a movie*—because I awake in my seat some time later, my hands resting in my lap and my chin pressed against my chest. Someone is shaking me by the shoulder.

"Kid. Hey, kid."

I open my eyes. A woman, probably the manager, is looking down at me. She has on a polo shirt just like the one worn by the man who sold me my ticket. Her eyes look unfocused and ringed by dark circles, as though she hasn't slept.

"What are you doing?" she wants to know.

"Sorry," I say, rubbing my eyes. "My mom dropped me off, and I...I came to see a movie."

"Movie's over."

I look at the screen. She's right. They haven't turned on the lights, but the screen is gray-black, and the theater is quiet. When I don't answer, the woman gets impatient.

"What are you trying to do, see it again for free?" she demands.

In my half-asleep state, I almost laugh in her face at the idea. See it again? I didn't want to see it the first time.

"Definitely not," I say.

"Then beat it, before I call security."

She grabs her dustpan and broom—even though there's no one else in the theater to make a mess—and stalks back toward the projection booth.

I check my phone to find a text from my mom. She'll be outside in five minutes. Relieved to get out of that place, I boost myself over the row of seats in front of me and head for the exit. Out of the corner of my eye, I think I see a shadow, tall and thin, pass across the screen, probably the manager bustling around in front of the camera in the projection booth.

When I get back to the lobby, I find it just as eerily quiet as before, even though it's now well into the afternoon. No popcorn pops. The arcade machines flash their same message, and the crane arm jerks endlessly back and forth as though trying to escape its glass case.

I breathe a sigh of relief when I make it back to the mall, where I expect to find some signs of human life. I'm wrong. The stores are still empty, and the corridor yawns before me, spotless and deserted. I quicken my pace with a creeping sense of unease. The corridor seems to stretch on forever, the main entrance nowhere in sight. As I pass kiosk after kiosk, I notice the piano music has stopped, and my footsteps echo off the gleaming white tiles in a way they didn't before. Do I hear another pair of footsteps approaching behind me? It's most likely some lonely shopper. I just want to hurry up and find the exit.

I stop at the convergence of four corridors. As I look left, right, and forward, a shadow falls across the floor in front of me. It is narrow, and very long.

As though it is wearing a top hat.

Extreme Eats

by Matthew Fryer

"Hi. Can I help you?"

"Jep North, your new domestic technician." Jep flashed his ID badge, already irritated by the gaudy décor and glaring lights of the studio. "I was told to report for this morning's shoot."

"Excellent." The woman smiled. "Our last cleaner has unfortunately become...permanently indisposed. I'm Asha, the floor manager. But before we go any further, are you cool with cleaning up vomit?"

"Sure."

"What about blood?"

"I guess so."

"And dead bodies?"

"Wow." Jep raised his eyebrows. "That escalated quickly."

"It's better to check now, rather than you collapsing halfway through the shoot and having to be wheeled off to the medical center."

"I'm fine, bring it on. I just want to finish my shift, get out of these overalls, then hit the Rabid Rooster Tavern on B deck with the rest of the moonbase's riffraff."

"Ha! I like your honesty. Welcome to Studio 13."

"Thanks." Jep glanced around the studio floor. There were two dining tables arranged in the center, neatly set with chairs, placemats, and cutlery, and a small crew bustled around plugging in cables, tweaking the cameras, and positioning spotlights. He squinted against the glare. Why did it have to be so *bright?*

"We're due to start filming in about ten minutes. Are you familiar with *Extreme Eats?*"

"Vaguely. I haven't seen it, but isn't it some kind of competitive eating tournament? With prisoners?"

"Yes. They're all death row inmates. Anyone who survives gets their execution commuted to life imprisonment and gets moved to the luxury winner's wing. With maximum privileges."

"Like they do on *Zero-G Gorecage?*"

"Exactly. That's another Studio 13 production. Entertainment is life…"

"And lives are entertainment."

"You got it!" Asha beamed.

Jep licked his dry lips, the ghost of last night's whiskey still swimming around his skull. "So how does the show work? And what exactly do you need me to do?"

"It's simple. The contestants all have to consume a three-course meal, each with a specific endurance theme. All you have to do is wipe down the tables between each course, mop the floor if there've been any messy accidents, and clear away the deceased."

"Don't security deal with them?"

"At the close of filming, yes, but we use the changing room as a temporary morgue for shows with high mortality rates." She shrugged. "Everybody always complains it's too cold in there anyway."

"Fine. I'll borrow a powercart from the loading dock. Might as well save my back."

Asha nodded. "Afterwards, we'll need you to deep clean the room too. Be sure to wear protection. We've had problems with infection before."

"Will do."

Jep rubbed his aching temples, trying not to blame Christabel—his soon-to-be ex-wife—for the fact he'd gotten a hangover. But blaming her for everything had become second nature these days.

The last conversation they'd had was at home last night. As usual, it had descended into petty insults and squabbling, so Jep had sloped off to the pub just to get away from her, and deliberately left for work this morning before she woke up.

Sad nostalgia crept up on him, catching him unawares. He remembered how much he used to love Christabel before they drifted apart. She was smart, sharp, and had a disarming, wry smile that melted Jep's heart the moment they met back on Earth.

It had been a crazy whirlwind romance. They'd married quickly and signed up for a fresh start on Tranquility—one of the new bases that was recruiting as-yet childless married couples as part of the colonization program—before slowly realizing with a cold, creeping gloom that they were entirely incompatible. They didn't have any hobbies or core beliefs in common, and once the honeymoon period was over, that seemed to come as an unpleasant shock to both of them. Being stuck together on a moonbase was make or break for many couples, and for Jep and Christabel, it just rammed home how superficial their attraction had been. Having just been promoted to supervisor at the lunar arboretum where she worked, Christabel hated Jep's lack of career ambition almost as much as she despaired of his love for whiskey, but those cards were firmly on the table from the beginning and he wasn't about to change or apologize for who he was.

It didn't take long for the cracks to show, and in true textbook style, all those quirky personality traits that once endeared them to each other became tooth-grindingly annoying. Christabel snorted when she laughed, which Jep used to find adorable, but now it just made his jaw clench, and his wife's predilection for animated Disney films had gone from seeming charming to childish. She recently told him that he cleared his throat far too often, and that his hobby of collecting interestingly shaped moonrocks—which she used to think was cute—was a stupid waste of time.

Two weeks ago, they finally acknowledged it was over. At least that was one thing they agreed on.

Christabel was already sleeping with Bjorn, the burly security chief who worked at the Murderball dome and lived in the quarters next door. In fact, it was her day off today, so she was probably in bed with the big lunk already.

She thought she was being discreet, but Jep's ears were keen as a bat's and he could hear them going at it through the thin walls. Christabel would probably love to rub his face in it, but as they were still technically married until the divorce proceedings were initiated, she'd most likely be worried about how any documented affairs might affect the eventual settlement.

Jep tried telling himself that he couldn't care less, but that wasn't true. Not because he still had any feelings for Christabel, but because it galled him that his wife had found happiness in the arms of somebody else so quickly. Hopefully, Bjorn, the hulking square-jawed chump, would end up getting hospitalized by one of the PCP-fuelled gladiators he spent his working hours trying to keep in line.

Jep always referred to him as Bonehead Bjorn just to aggravate Christabel, and then would enjoy watching her squirm as she tried not to arouse suspicion by defending him too much.

"Is everything okay?" Asha asked.

"Sorry," Jep said, narrowing his eyes. The studio spotlights seemed to be drilling directly into his brain. "I've got a lot on my mind at the moment."

"Sorry to hear that, but once filming starts, you'll have plenty to distract you."

"I'm sure. So what are these *endurance themes* you mentioned?"

"Ah, yes. The appetizer's theme is gross out," Asha said, rather too cheerfully. "Our chef prepares real delicacies, selected from various cultures on Earth, all renowned for being difficult to stomach."

"So the contestants just have to force it down and keep it there?"

"Precisely. Tonight's appetizer is rakfisk and tuna eyeball chowder."

"Rakfisk?"

"A Norwegian dish. It's a kind of self-digested trout."

"Sounds delicious."

Asha smiled. "It's the *smell* more than anything. Even the waiters have to wear nose plugs and respirator masks to prevent them from gagging."

"I'll add them to my list. Corpse cart, chemical gloves, nose plugs, and a gas mask. I always knew working in television would be a barrel of fun."

Asha laughed, and it seemed genuine. Christabel used to find his sarcasm amusing, but now it just antagonized her. Speaking of which, Jep would be sure to tell his dear wife that he'd been working behind the scenes at Studio 13. Christabel loved the kind of lurid stuff they peddled and would be consumed with envy.

"The chef is serving the chowder with a slab of casu martzu."

"What's that?"

"A Sardinian cheese. It's banned in most jurisdictions on health grounds."

"Why?"

"It's fermented until it decomposes, then cheese flies lay their larvae in it. They're tiny white worms, and they eat the putrid cheese and excrete it, which is apparently what creates the unique flavour and semi-liquid texture. It's supposed to be most enjoyable when spread on flatbread."

"I'll have to take your word for that."

"Not tempted?"

"Rotting worm feces on my bread sounds yummy, but I'll stick to strawberry jam, thanks."

Asha chuckled. "You might also want to wear a visor when cleaning it up."

"What for?"

"To stop the worm larvae from jumping into your eyes."

"Wow. I might as well just go for the full hazmat suit." Jep swallowed hard, swaying at a sudden wave of dizzy nausea. He *knew* those final couple shots in the Rabid Rooster last night were a bad idea.

Asha nodded, misreading his discomfort as squeamishness. "Gross out is generally the messiest round, but at least you get it over with first. After a short break, we serve the main course to the contestants who've managed not to barf their way out of the competition. The theme for this one is pain."

"Of course it is."

"It was originally just hot, irritant spices and strong alcohol. Anything that *burned*. Blistering-hot chilli peppers stuffed with wasabi and concentrated mustard, washed down with triple-distilled Balkan vodka, that kind of thing. But the producers eventually decided this was too tame, and now the chef includes ingredients that cause actual physical injury."

"Razor blade risotto? Broken glass burgers?"

"Almost." Asha grinned. "But as with the appetizer, it's all genuine food and traditional recipes. The only difference is that the chef doesn't remove any of the sharp edges. Tonight's main is Peruvian sea urchin ceviche."

"So…I'm guessing they leave the spikes on?"

"You got it. The spines are like barbed needles, so you can imagine the nasty puncture wounds they inflict on the soft tissues of the mouth, tongue, and throat. And the stomach, if they even get down that far. And on top of that, the venom causes inflammation and sometimes full-blown allergic reactions. It's going to be *ugly*."

"So this is the part of the show when people start dying?"

Asha nodded. "Definitely."

Jep's tongue felt like a wad of sandpaper, filling his mouth, and he tried to take a deep breath but struggled to fully expand his lungs. He could do with a lie down; this really was the mother of all hangovers. Maybe he wouldn't go to the Rabid Rooster after work, and just head home for an early night. With Christabel probably round at Bonehead Bjorn's, at least he would have the place to himself.

"So what's for dessert?"

"The theme is poison. To be honest, it's not great television compared with the first two courses, as it takes so long to have an effect. But post-production editing means we cut straight to the convulsions and heart attacks. If anyone is still alive after an hour, they're given an antidote, free medical treatment, and they win their prize. Tonight's menu features a cherry and almond traybake."

Jep froze. "Say that again."

"A cherry and almond traybake?"

His bowels flushed cold, sweat prickling across his brow.

On his way into Studio 13, Jep had seen a small kitchen and gone inside to grab a glass of water and take the edge off his dry throat. A tray of freshly cut cherry and almond slices had been cooling on the counter, and ever the opportunistic sweet-tooth, Jep had demolished three of them before reporting to Asha for work. He'd noticed a caustic bitterness lurking beneath the fruity sweetness and the delicious, buttery sponge, but just thought the chef had over-roasted the almonds.

His throat tightened. His rapidly escalating symptoms were nothing to do with a hangover after all.

"It's kind of like a regular traybake, but the cherry stones are included," Asha explained, oblivious to his horror. "They're crushed into a fine powder, then stirred into the mix and also dusted on top. Cherry stones are full of prussic acid, which is cyanide to you and me. The recipe also uses wild almonds instead of the sweet edible variety. These break down into even more cyanide once consumed." She blinked at Jep. "Are you okay?"

"The kitchen on the way in..." he croaked. "There was a tray on the counter."

Asha's permasmile finally dropped from her face. "You *didn't.*"

"They looked amazing... I was hungry." His vision blurred and his legs started to spasm. "I didn't know what this show was really about."

"I *told* the chef not to leave them lying around." Asha frowned. "Or at least lock the damn kitchen door."

"You mentioned an antidote?" Jep's stomach cramped violently as a crushing ache swept up through his torso.

Asha glanced over her shoulder, then pulled out a digital tablet and tapped rapidly at the screen. "I really shouldn't do this after an untoward incident has already occurred, and my boss would be absolutely furious if he saw, but here." She held the tablet out towards Jep. It hazed in his watery vision, but he could just make out that the screen was full of legalese text, with an electronic signature box below.

"What's this?" he wheezed.

"A Studio 13 employment contract. Sign it while you still can, and the company will take responsibility. It's health and accident insurance, basically."

"Thank you." He quickly scribbled his name on the screen.

"I'm not gonna lie," Asha said. "This covers *my* ass regarding your accident, but yours too. I do try and look after the staff." She slipped the tablet away. "Duty of care and all that."

"Yes, yes. The antidote?"

"Well, this is awkward." Asha licked her lips. "We haven't got any."

"What?"

"Sorry. We've run out, and Tranquility's medical centre isn't due a delivery until the supply ship lands tomorrow. That's why we had the chef make a ceviche with whole sea urchins. Nobody could realistically survive trying to eat that, and even if by some miracle they *did* manage to choke it down, the extra-strong traybake would finish them off long before their required survival time was up. Rather than delay the filming of this episode, it was easier—and cheaper—just to rig it. A bit naughty, I know, but the lack of cyanide antidote was never supposed to be an issue." Asha grimaced sympathetically. "Until you helped yourself to the desserts."

Jep's legs gave way and he thudded down onto his knees as terror roiled through his guts. His heart pounded like a jackhammer, growing faster by the second.

"Can we get a medical team in here?" Asha yelled and then crouched down beside him. "Who's your legal next of kin?"

Everything faded to grey and Jep gasped as a sharp pain snagged his chest. "My wife..."

"Well, look on the bright side. She'll do *very* well out of this. The spouse gets half a million credits after an accidental death in service. It's a good thing we got your contract signed. Just in time too."

"No..." Jep collapsed forward onto his face as a terrible image of Christabel clinking champagne flutes with Bonehead Bjorn formed in his dying brain.

Voices shouted, echoing through the studio, but the sound quickly faded until all he could hear was Christabel and Bjorn's laughter.

Celebratory, mocking laughter.

No...

Then, finally, silence.

Resort Gaia

by Panayiotis Antoniades and Rebecca Rowland

THERE WERE SEEDS AT the bottom of the large glass water dispenser: large seeds, all of them a pale yellowish grey, debris from the slices of lemon floating at the top of the multi-gallon enclosure sitting atop a tall table in the expansive foyer.

Gloria turned to stare at them while her husband, Chris, chatted up the desk clerk, trying to smooth his way into an early check-in. It had been a long flight and an even longer taxi ride to the resort. Gloria snatched a nearby excursion brochure and began to fan her face with it. "Do the rooms come with air conditioning?" she asked, interrupting Chris's smarmy attempt at small talk with the disinterested employee.

The woman behind the counter did not shift her eyes from the computer screen in front of her. "Your accommodations will be quite comfortable, I assure you," she said. "Everything at Resort Gaia is temperature-controlled for maximum efficiency." Her fingers danced over the keyboard. "All activities outside of the resort grounds are canceled for the week, I'm afraid." She glanced curtly at Gloria, then nodded her head at the makeshift fan. "But there is plenty to experience right here at Resort Gaia." She looked at Chris. "I assure you," she repeated.

"Water?" Another employee dressed in the same uniform as the desk clerk suddenly appeared at their side, holding a tall glass filled to the brim with ice water and lemon rounds, their rinds so brightly hued, Gloria swore they were plastic. The exterior of the glass was wet with condensation.

Gloria accepted the offer and nodded politely. Seconds later, a third staff member appeared with an identical glass for Chris. The couple wordlessly sipped their drinks, eyeing the other guests speckling the entrance hall. Most appeared to be married couples—women with men, men with men, women with women. Each had isolated themselves in neat packages of two. There were no children anywhere.

"If this is a parent encounter, why were we told specifically not to bring our sons?" Chris asked, wiping the thin mustache of water from his upper lip.

Gloria frowned. "No one has children here." She gestured to the other couples, tucked into random corners of the cavernous room, huddled alongside piles of luggage. "Is everyone here for the same event?"

The desk clerk's mouth fixed itself into a thin dash along her jaw. "We find that the process goes more smoothly when the children in question are not present." The mouth returned to flatline, then: "You are very fortunate, Mrs. Richardson. Although you can see, we do schedule ten couples in every encounter, the number of entries for this very special opportunity was innumerable. Your children must have written a powerfully persuasive essay to earn you a spot here."

Chris rolled his eyes. "Written? Powerful?" He scoffed. "The dumb fucks can hardly put a sentence together. There is no way in the deepest regions of hell that our two morons submitted a winning...anything."

Gloria patted his back. "Our boys aren't the sharpest tools in the shed," she said. "It must have been a friend of ours." She placed the glass of water on the counter, then rested her hand on her husband's upper arm. "Oh! I bet it was the Lanes. They are so smart, those two." She turned to the desk clerk. "He's a college professor, and she's a—"

"The rules mandate that the application must come from the entrants' children," the clerk stated firmly. "And the content required is quite extensive. We receive thousands of entries every week, ma'am. If you have been selected as one of our ten, I can tell you with great certainty: your children ensured it, and from what we gleaned from their application, you are quite deserving."

Chris picked up the glass of water from the counter and handed it back to his wife. "Parenting is a difficult job, but Gloria and I make sure our boys receive nothing but the best. Isn't that right, honey?"

Gloria swallowed a large gulp. The water tasted thicker somehow; she wondered if lemon had that effect. "Chris makes certain our boys toe the line—there's no worse disservice to a child than sparing the rod—but if our children don't have the best opportunities the Lord can grant, well, I just don't know who does. Maybe our dear President Trump, God bless his soul."

Chris lowered his eyes like a man leading a football team in solemn prayer. "Someday, the powers that be are going to issue a public apology to that man."

Gloria swallowed another mouthful of water. "Amen."

"Your room is ready," said the desk clerk, her eyes firmly reupholstered to the screen. "Thank you for your patience."

The employee who had issued the glass of water to Chris earlier appeared once more by his side. "May I take your bags, sir?"

Chris took a long sip from his water before responding. "Why, yes. Thank you."

"Be sure to finish your water," the desk clerk called out after them before they disappeared within the sleek silver elevator car. "It can be quite hot here during the day, and we don't like our guests getting dehydrated." She paused, then added, "Raymond, give the Richardsons their health forms to complete, would you?"

Chris nodded, then followed behind the cart carrying their bags. He leaned in close to his wife and whispered in her ear, "Do I have to tip the guy? I mean, we won this vacation. You'd think gratuity would be included in the prize."

Gloria looked behind her one final time before entering the elevator. The couples who remained in the lobby were lining up to receive their keys from the concierge. There was something off about the procession, though Gloria could not put her finger on what it was. "I'm sure it's been taken care of," she said. Though something itched the back of her mind, she was too exhausted from the trip to scratch at it.

Upon exiting an elevator car with decor more expensive than that in their living room, Chris and Gloria headed to Room 217. The commute had siphoned nearly every bit of energy from their bodies. "This better be worth the fucking trouble," said Chris while fumbling with the room key. "Or when we get back, those two idiots you spawned are getting a first-class ass-whoop."

Gloria's jaw was the first to drop to the floor, but it was quickly followed by an *uuuuuugh* sound emanating from Chris's mouth. The couple stood dumbstruck in the doorway, their eyes in denial of the luxury that lay before them in the room.

From the golden chandeliers to the exotic plants, from the fine art paintings to the enormous king-sized bed, the room screamed heaven on earth. A luxury beyond luxury.

Still in awe, the couple entered the room only to be even more dazzled by what was waiting for them inside. Their haven was equipped with adaptive climate control, mood lights, a full personal buffet teeming with exquisite dishes and fruits, a variety of expensive alcoholic drinks, and a hot tub Jacuzzi.

"Oh, hon, I think I'll never wanna leave this place," said Gloria, a teenager in love.

Chris scooped a handful of succulent grapes into his mouth and issued a pleased grunt in agreement. "Whether the two shits wrote that essay or not, we definitely deserve to be here, so thank you, Lord," he added.

The couple closed the door behind them, and for the rest of the night, they ate like ravenous cannibals, fucked like newlyweds, and slept like babies. They awoke late the next morning and, still recovering from jet lag, lackadaisically strolled downstairs at noon, nonetheless relaxed, pampered, and dressed in their best vacation garments.

The head hostess greeted them at the entrance to the dining hall, her mouth spread painfully wide, every ivory piano key on display. "Hello, Mr. and Mrs. Richardson," she beamed. "I hope you are pleased with your accommodations."

"How did you know—" Gloria began, taken aback that the woman had recognized them. It seemed they were celebrities, and they were being treated as such. Her husband cut short her inquiry.

"Goddamn," bellowed Chris, "we could stay here forever!"

Gloria nodded enthusiastically in agreement. "I cannot believe how you managed to have everything custom-made to our needs," she said.

"Was that the reason for all that info on the form we filled in? I'm not paying anything extra, ya know," Chris added, only half-joking.

The hostess maintained her toothy grin. "We at Resort Gaia would do whatever necessary to tenderize—er, *tend* to your body and soul's needs." Her face reddened, but she recomposed her perpetual smile immediately. "And perhaps you will stay here forever."

Chris frowned. "We can't st—"

"As a beautiful memory, I mean, sir," she clarified. "Now, come, you lovely couple. Your table is ready. You will be seated with the gracious teacher Miss Pope and the McDermonts, another delightful pair. They are highly sought-after influencers, you know. 'Family First'-themed YouTubers." She winked at Chris, then gestured with her arm for the two to follow her.

At their table sat a middle-aged woman with thick brunette locks. Everything about her was broad, from the span of her thick shoulders to the bouffant of her painfully straightened and re-curled hair. She gave Gloria and Chris a once-over glance before returning her focus to the plate of food in front of her. Next to her, a small-chested, pretty blonde held a pocket mirror in her palm and meticulously studied her own face. A tall, rugged-looking man leaned sideways and tried to check his own reflection, the two of them vying for a starring role in the three-inch-wide glass.

Gloria shimmied into her seat as Chris pulled out his chair and sat down heavily. He readjusted his tie and stuffed a corner of the cloth napkin into his collar. "Hey, y'all," he said loudly. "I'm Christopher Richardson. This is my wife, Gloria." He held a hand out to the only other man at the table only to find it ignored.

The brunette looked up from her plate. "I'm Katherine Pope," she said dryly. "I teach at an exclusive private school for young men." She shook Chris' hand but did not bother to acknowledge Gloria.

"Young men?" echoed Chris. "Do you teach at the university?"

Miss Pope swallowed a gulp of white wine, then signaled to the waitstaff to request a refill. "High school," she said, nodding to the sommelier as he emptied the bottle into her glass. "My boys are very mature for their age. It comes with good breeding, you know."

"Oh, I couldn't agree more," interjected the blonde woman. She took a last look at herself in the mirror, then handed it to her husband. "Good breeding is everything, isn't it? We're the McDermonts. Three million followers and counting!" She pressed her hands gently against her own cheeks, feigning surprise. "You've probably seen us: the *Family Values Makes a Valued Family* show. We post updates twice a week."

"Three times on TikTok," added her husband, slipping the mirror into the chest pocket of his sports jacket.

Gloria smiled and nodded her head. "Yes! My mommies group shares your posts on Facebook. We just loved the one about repurposing the islands America used to test atom bombs in the fifties."

Mrs. McDermont lowered her voice and scanned the dining room before speaking. "Don't get me wrong. I don't mind the gays. Have a cousin who dresses up in ladies' clothing and sings show tunes at libraries or something. I mean, *I* didn't go to see him, but I hear people do. Anyway, wouldn't they just *adore* a chain of islands of their own? The men on one island, the women on the other, doing...well, whatever it is women like that do. And then everybody is happy!"

Mr. McDermont cleared his throat. "No more of this gay agenda in the classroom, am I right? Why am I paying for my child to learn about someone else's sexual perversions?"

Miss Pope swallowed another mouthful of wine. "Amen to that. We have to raise healthy, robust, heterosexual men." She put down her glass and leaned back in her chair as a waiter placed a cloud of chocolate mousse in front of her. "Don't even get me started on those *bisexuals*."

Mr. McDermont rubbed his jaw, the purposely grown shadow of beard making a soft scratching noise against his skin. "Just an excuse to be perverts." He pointed at the ceiling. "Not on my watch, sister!"

"I'll have a whiskey, double. Neat," said Chris to the server placing an identical dish of dessert in front of Mrs. McDermont.

"What brand, sir?" asked the waiter.

"Do you have a price list?" Chris asked.

"Everything at Resort Gaia is complimentary, for the needs of your body and soul," said the waiter, his countenance frozen in a perpetual smile.

"Then bring me the most expensive whiskey you got," replied Chris, adding a *heh heh heh* chuckle at the end to punctuate the request.

"And a glass of your very best red wine for me," added Gloria. "Filled to the brim. None of that half-glass bullshit."

The waiter bowed and exited. At the end of their afternoon of fine dining, socializing with their table mates, and consuming an exorbitant amount of free premium wine and whiskey, the Richardsons wolfed down their chocolate mousse and wiped their mouths in preparation to return to their room for a nap. Suddenly, however, a shriek issued from a table nearby.

A terrified-looking woman sporting a brownish-red wig (or possibly the remains of a dead squirrel) on her head pointed excitedly to her dish as if a rat were waving hello from it. Instead, to everyone's horror, in the center of a large bowl of strawberry shortcake peeked the tip of a female index finger, its nail painted a bright cherry-red.

To everyone's surprise and dread, the waiter picked up the finger and, maintaining the same smile he'd worn on his face for the dinner rush's entirety, lifted the digit up for everyone to have a good look. The action stirred a panic in the room, but the waiter, refusing to unhinge his grin, moved the finger to his mouth and took a bite out of it, masticating the hunk of flesh between his molars with great joy. As he did so, two women at a nearby table turned their heads and began to vomit onto the floor their calamari and truffles risotto in revulsion.

The waiter, still smiling despite the disgust that had begun to spread across the hall, spoke loudly and delicately, purposefully annunciating each syllable. "Dear beloved guests! What you have just witnessed was but a mere prank for your night's entertainment, concocted by our mischievous sweets and pastry chef, the one and only Mr. Archibald Spector, using props from our horror movie-themed night we had two days ago. We do have a particular sense of humor here at Resort Gaia, you see." He bowed and placed the remainder of the fingertip into his mouth and bit down hard, the crunch of the nail audible even from across the room. "Our sincere apologies for any inconvenience we might have caused. We assure you that we will more than make it up to you."

Despite the fact that a nervous sprinkling of laughter followed the disturbing scene, nearly half of the people witnessing the prank gone wrong pushed aside their unfinished dinners and desserts. Chris and Gloria were not among that half. In fact, they took the opportunity to score a second portion from the table next to theirs.

"It would be a pity to let good food go to waste," Chris noted. Gloria smiled and shoveled another spoonful of mousse into her mouth.

It was the perfect end to a perfect first day, but as the Richardsons waited in front of the elevators back to their room, Gloria looked over her shoulder. Again, the nagging sensation that something was not right nipped at the back of her mind.

Chris, clearly intoxicated, pinched her left buttock and pulled her into the waiting doors of the lift. In a failed James Bond voice, he cooed, "Come on, hon. It was nothing but a bad joke. Let me make you forget all about it in our *looove* chamber. We've got two more days here. Let's make the best out of it."

Gloria buried her face in her husband's shoulder and breathed in his scent, an acrid mixture of stale liquor, salty perspiration, and after-shave. At least they weren't stuck at home with the boys, she thought.

The next morning, the Richardsons woke up late again and barely made it to the continental breakfast in the resort's expansive lobby. Although the hall was empty of all other guests, the creepily attentive waitstaff stood at attention, seeming to anticipate the Richardsons' arrival.

Gloria walked to the expansive table of breads and fruits and began to pile flaky croissants and danish drizzled with icing onto a plate. The couple had stuffed their stomachs the previous evening until they reached the state of pythons having devoured an elephant, but they could not resist the temptation.

While a waiter filled a mug of coffee for him, Chris shoved the remainder of a chocolate doughnut into his mouth. As he wiped the remnants from his mouth, a lithe blonde employee of the hotel sidled next to him. "Sir?" she inquired, a sly grin spilling across her face. "Perhaps I can suggest a spa treatment for you and your missus?"

Chris could not place her accent. "Depends," he replied. "Is that included in the package?"

The woman's grin shifted, exposing more teeth. "Sir, everything in Resort Gaia is available for you free of charge. We do this purposefully in order to get you ready for becoming what you are meant to be."

Gloria frowned, swallowing a masticated mouthful of pineapple. "Don't you mean *who he is supposed to become*?" she asked. Gloria scanned her husband's facial expression. He was eyeing the pert blonde like she was one of the pastries.

"Now, now, hon," Chris replied patronizingly. He continued to stare at the hostess. "She made a mistake. Can't you see? She's probably one of those Eastern European imports." He placed a hand on the hotel employee's upper arm. "I'm not one of them fancy boys, you know: lying around the sauna in a towel, fixing their nails and shit, but I sure could use a back rub." He punctuated the statement with a slight squeeze of the woman's bicep. "Sometimes, even perfection needs a little tune-up. You know what I'm sayin,' darlin'?" He winked at her then, a wanton leer smeared along his jaw.

"Just sign us up, *darling*," Gloria said, much too loudly for the nearly vacant lobby. "Let us freshen up and we can be there in a half-hour." She was visibly irritated, but she noticed that the employee, though not encouraging of Chris's advances, accepted his violation of her personal space without question.

"Very good, Mrs. Richardson," said the woman. "I assure you, the treatments here will leave you feeling quite differently than when you arrived." She nodded at Chris before turning and walking back toward the front desk. "Mr. Richardson."

Sure enough, the employee had been true to her word. After three-hour massages, the couple found themselves unbelievably relaxed—nearly comatose—and fast drifting into sleep. They returned to their rooms and slept until the sky grew hazy and dim, and as they sauntered back down to their dining table assignment with Miss Pope and the McDermonts, they barely glanced at the windows, as the beauty of the white sand beaches and turquoise water outside of the hotel—everything, really, outside of their own immediate needs—had become merely an afterthought.

So had the stated theme of their vacation encounter.

It went on this way for the rest of their stay: gluttonous consumption followed by luxurious massages, surface yet relatively pleasant small talk with some of the other guests, languorous midday naps, and more overindulgence in food and liquor.

On the evening before the Richardsons were set to return home, the waitstaff seemed even more solicitous than they had been previously. When Gloria drained the last of the wine from her goblet, the steward was by her side, refilling the chalice before she had a chance to set it on the table. As Chris swirled the last sip of amber liquid from his glass, a doting woman—most often, the same one who had offered them their first spa treatments—appeared holding tongs with fresh ice and a decanter of top-shelf whiskey. The couple stayed late into the evening, the room growing hot and tilting ever so slightly on its axis.

Halfway through the extensive feast, the McDermonts appeared to have absconded to their room, but the Richardsons took no notice. Miss Pope hadn't joined them for dinner at all, and they dismissed her absence without care almost as soon as they saw her empty chair. In fact, they did not remember leaving the dining room and returning to their own room, so when Chris awoke the next day, he was thoroughly confused. Instead of facing the ceiling of his hotel room, his eyes squinted to adjust to a view of fluorescent lights above him. He turned his head, which pounded in ferocious hangover. He was not in the luxury suit but in a cold, stone room. Though he tried to sit up, moving was not an option: He appeared to be tied to a sleek, steel table.

"Now, now, don't be stressed, Mr. Richardson," a stranger's voice stated from somewhere nearby. "You'll fill your body with toxins...and we don't want that, do we?"

Chris turned his head to look on his other side. The man was sitting a stone's throw away, his face indistinct, indifferent, and slightly shaded by a large brown hood. Chris attempted to roll over, but his body was numb from the neck down, a faint tingle shivering through his appendages like they had fallen asleep.

"I will explain everything to you, as I always do with our highly valued customers," continued the man. He pulled a pair of thin rubber gloves from a nearby table and stretched them over his hands. "You see, Mr. Richardson, the world has come to a point where everything is for sale. At the same time, humans have lost any moral value and relentlessly try to destroy not only life on Earth—including our own pathetic species—but Earth itself." The man held his gloved hands up and examined them closely, then began slowly moving sideways in back of Chris' head. "Gaia," he whispered when he was out of Chris' range of vision.

Chris strained to turn his head, but found his ability stunted. He screamed out in frustration, "What does that have anything to do with me?"

With me: his own words echoed in his mind. Where was Gloria?

"Untie me and I'll teach you some lost moral values, you sick fuck." Chris screamed with more intensity, rousing his wife, also incapacitated on a table behind him, from her slumber to an immediate state of alert disorientation.

The hooded figure turned to Gloria but continued talking in a soft yet authoritative manner. "Good morning, Mrs. Richardson. Glad you can join us. How was your slumber? Are you feeling rested? Your hunger satiated? Your muscles relaxed?"

Gloria tried to sit up but the numbness conquered her body, pinning her to what she surmised was some kind of a metal bed. "Chris?" she called out, turning her head frantically from side to side but seeing nothing but unadorned walls. "Chris?!"

"I'm here!" her husband screamed back. "And this cunt freak better untie me right quick, or he is in for a load of—"

"My beloved Richardsons, since you are both with us and awake now, let me finish what I was explaining to Christopher here," the hooded figure said, gesturing to Chris, though it was clear neither of them could see it. "This world is going to shit, and it's all because of the human animal. An animal inferior to the rest. No other animal destroys its kind and the Earth like humans. No other animal disrespects nature like humans. No other animal treats its own offspring like humans do."

The hooded man paused for a second, shuffled a set of knives and surgical scalpels, and glanced at the Richardsons before continuing his monologue. To his left, Gloria began to cry softly.

"That's the exact reason why you are here," he continued. "Since the day you had your children, you set your sights on diminishing them: beating them to a pulp, starving them half to death, and if—"

Chris cut him off, protesting. "The ignorant bastards had to learn discipline!"

Gloria piggybacked on her husband's explanation, adding, "And respect family values! Isn't that why we're here? You must have made some mistake. We're here because of our good parenting skills. We were *chosen*."

"Untie us, you sick fuck," shouted Chris, spit spraying from his mouth with each word.

The man paused. "First of all, you are not tied up. Our medical staff injected you with a heavy paralytic action so that you won't feel a thing during the procedure."

The last sentence fell hard on the couple. Both stared at the ceiling, mouths agape, their words unable to escape.

"We aren't monsters, for goodness sakes," the hooded man continued. "But as I was saying, beating them to a pulp, starving them half to death, and if little Timmy told us the truth—and our research indicates that he did—you were complacent in allowing your neighbor, Mr. Nicolas Jackson, a convicted pedophile, to babysit him. Childcare can be very expensive—I am certain of that. But what did the discounted afternoon hours, five days a week for three years, cost Timmy?"

The terror running through Chris and Gloria's bodies seared like an electric current, burning every cell and nerve. There was no way in hell that this person, whoever he was, could have known this information.

"Your kids," said the man, "the '*dumb fucks,*' as you called them, did not win a competition. You were right about that part. Instead, they signed you up for what they thought was a parent education program. You see, even though they've endured extensive abuse from the both of you, they decided, instead of attempting suicide for the third time (you took your time calling 911 that last incident, didn't you, Mrs. Richardson?) to enroll the two of you in a program to help you become better parents. Their parents. Because, for some reason, although you've fucked them up so badly, they still love you."

Gloria sniffled, her teeth beginning to chatter with fear. "Okay, okay. We'll take the reform program. Whatever it is, we'll do it," she pleaded. "We want the program. We want to be better parents." Her voice trembled audibly. Chris remained silent, anger boiling from the bottom of his soul, begging to be unleashed.

"Ah, but here's the rub, Mrs. Richardson," the man replied, his tone changing to one of slight amusement. "Your kids didn't find our program on Google. They signed you up for a parents' reform program on the Dark Web. The program they perused does not actually exist. Instead, they unwittingly signed you up for Resort Gaia, a very special holiday attraction for humans who do not deserve their humanity, who do not deserve this Earth."

"What?" Gloria cried out. "I don't...I don't understand. You people...you people are—"

"Congratulations, Mr. and Mrs. Richardson. You, along with seventeen other meticulously selected individuals, have been chosen to serve the purpose of our organization, The Protectors of Gaia, in getting the Earth back to order. To *Re-sort* Gaia. But don't worry, your kids were rewarded very well, with cash in a bank account and a new home in which to finally bloom."

"You fucking lunatics," Chris spat. "Untie me now, you fuck, and I will *re-sort* your face with my bare fists!"

Gloria remained silent, her brain still trying to catch up to what she was hearing.

"Oh, Mr. Richardson," said the hooded man with mocking pity in his voice. "Your fists belong to us now. So do your arms and legs and kidneys, and by the time we finish with today's procedure, you'll have donated your eyes, your bone marrow, a percentage of your fat, and gallons of your blood for the needs of people who deserve to stay alive as humans and fix this planet.

"In other words, Mr. and Mrs. Richardson," hissed the man, putting his face so close to Chris's they almost touched. "We will harvest your organs and drain your blood in order to help save people who *do* deserve to be alive, while simultaneously eradicating parasites like yourself. But don't worry; nothing—*nothing* will go to waste."

The Richardsons could not utter a single word. For the first time in their lives, they felt helpless and powerless.

"By the way, Mr. Richardson," the man continued, returning to the display of surgical instruments and selecting a large scalpel, "that fine burger you devoured last night? That was Miss Pope. She spent her career molesting more than thirty boys under the guise of 'private lessons.' And don't get me started on the McDermonts..." He held the knife up to the light and examined its blade. "I'm not sure when hatred, discrimination, and batshit paranoia became family values, but I can promise you: those kinds of emotions have no *value* to them. Not here, not in America, not anywhere."

"Please..." Gloria's voice came out as only a whisper. "Please don't—"

A grin appeared in the corner of the man's mouth. "In case you were curious, your heart will be the first thing removed. The organ that lay metaphorically dormant in your interactions with your own children will surely be in the grandest of shape, since it received so little use." He paused to allow the smile to widen and swallow the bottom half of his face. "*I assure you.*"

Gloria began to scream, her cries of terror futilely echoing off the sandstone walls.

"Nothing goes to waste here at Resort Gaia," continued the man. "After we use you as human fuel, we will remove your last remaining vital organs and then feed you to the other parasites sent here to be reformed every week. Whatever remains from your unnecessary existence goes directly into the Earth as fertilizer for sustainable agriculture. That's the way of Gaia. It's the way it has always been and always should be."

"You hippie bastard," Chris hissed, his teeth grinding. "Just you wait—"

The man held the scalpel aloft so that it glimmered in the reflection of the ceiling lights. "We've had a lovely discussion, Mr. and Mrs. Richardson, and I hope you enjoyed your stay, but I think the time has come for quiet reflection and peace. Tongues out, please."

The Will of the Woods

by Dylan T. Bosworth

MY SHOE WAS STUCK in the mud behind me, and I was trying to scrape the muck from my sock with a stick. My friends were doubled over laughing, their drunk faces clown-like in the iridescent blue light of the moon. The glow filtered down through the canopy of leaves in rays, and my friends' foggy breath hung like ghosts in the still air.

I don't know why I did this—why I had agreed to come out here again. I despised the woods. Every squelching step, every creaking branch. The cold dankness of it, seeping through the skin to grip my bones. Derrick loved it out here though, and Mike followed Derrick wherever he went, especially if they were drunk. Which, being a Friday night in our one-stoplight town, of course we were drunk. I didn't have other friends, so what else could I do besides tag along?

My pant legs were soaked through from the cold dew that gathered on the brush, and my nose was numb from the frigid October air blowing off the lake. A low fog curled along the ground, and none of us could see where we were stepping—our flashlights reflecting that thick mist, making it look even thicker than it was. We tried not to jump when an owl cooed or a branch snapped off in the darkness between the trees, but I felt my heart lurch into my throat each time something sounded that I couldn't readily explain.

I had this strange feeling that crept up on me. It was this feeling that no matter how many times we walked through these woods, no matter how often we got ahold of my parents' liquor and meandered off into the night, the trees around us—the bushes and all their little ferns and flowers and fungi that came with them—always seemed different. It was like the forest had shuffled each night and put its pieces back together in random places.

Mike and Derrick never seemed to notice. They were happy to jump over logs and pick up long sticks for pretend sword fights. They were also happy to berate me every time I suggested we turn back.

"Guys," I said.

They ignored me, walking farther ahead, whispering amongst themselves.

Sometimes I wondered if we were friends or if they kept me around to feel better about themselves.

I kept pace behind them though, and fantasized about punching the backs of their heads, pushing their faces into the mud, and leaving them for the animals to nibble. I could never do it, though. Being as short as I was, violence—even self-defense—had never been an option for me.

After walking in silence and feeling sorry for myself, we stepped into a low patch in the forest where the ground dipped inward like a giant bowl. The moon, big and bright like a massive dead eyeball in the sky, cast a gloomy blue light over the clearing, making the rolling fog glow like ghosts crawling across the ground. Beneath the fog, hundreds of big white mushrooms grew with their glistening caps like phosphorescent beacons—a spectral army in a sea of mist.

In the middle lay the deer. Her hair was smooth and wet with dew, her legs folded under her. She looked around with big, glass-like eyes, staring at nothing. If not for her hot breath blowing like smoke in the cool air, she could have been fake, but the closer we got, we could hear her mewling.

"Jesus," Derrick said. "It's like a different world here." He bent down to pick one of the mushrooms out of the ground and held it up to examine in the moonlight.

Mike nodded, but never took his eyes off the doe. For all the hardness he projected, nothing upset Mike more than a scared or injured animal. "What's wrong with her?" he asked.

Derrick and I furrowed our brows and looked at each other. "What do you mean?" I asked.

"There's something wrong. She'd have run by now." Mike took a few steps forward and craned his neck to see better.

Now that I looked at her, she *did* seem injured. With her cries louder now, her mewling took on a different meaning. Suddenly, Mike bolted ahead at the doe.

Derrick threw the mushroom he held to the ground and chased after.

When Mike approached, she tried to stand, but something pulled her back down to the forest floor. She strained, trying to get her legs out from underneath her, bending them before her with her hooves driving into the dirt, fighting to push herself up from the ground.

Mike slowed and looked back at us. "Hey, guys?" he yelled, and Derrick slowed when he caught sight of whatever Mike saw.

I was frozen. I'd never seen a deer up close, and the damn thing scared me. My heart hammered in my chest when I stood twenty paces away, considering the possibility that the deer might run toward me.

The doe must have gotten scared when Derrick approached too, and somewhere within her, she found the strength to push herself up on her front legs.

When she raised herself feebly from the ground, everything that was inside of her was sucked out. Her organs hung in strings, gushes of blood oozing out like it was slowly pouring from a bucket. Her insides were sticking from where they connected in her body, but they were tethered to the ground too. Blood, snot, and bile blew from her nose and throat as she opened her mouth to scream.

I held a hand over my mouth, trying desperately to keep my dinner down. Mike still walked forward, his arm outstretched to the deer, but he doubled over and vomited on his shoes. Derrick put his shirt over his nose and caught up with Mike, patting him on the back, while I stayed at the edge of the clearing, watching alone.

The deer wavered, her front legs wobbling uncontrollably, until she finally collapsed back to the ground. She bleated out a long cry and lay back down flat against the earth.

Mike wiped his mouth off and ran at the doe again, but as he reached her, a loud snap cracked through the quiet of the night like gunfire.

The deer's back split and sunk inward like a capsizing ship.

I shivered, unable to calm my nerves, as Mike dropped to his knees and tried to dig through the muck to free the doe. When Derrick reached her, he tried to soothe her as her cracked-in-half body was slowly pulled down into the soft dirt of the clearing.

"Fucking do something!" Mike yelled back at me.

His words struck me like a punch in the gut. My friends needed something from me, and it was something I couldn't possibly do. I felt this panicked tug within me. This need to run, to leave my friends and fly back through the trees to the safety of home. I wanted to crawl beneath my covers and pretend I never came into the woods at all.

Instead, I wavered. I stood there, my feet digging trenches in the dirt as my body fought to do something. The doe's big black eyes stared like empty voids, glistening in the night. Her mouth opened and closed without making a sound, and I watched in silence as the last of her was pulled underneath the ground.

The bowl we were in, the divot in the clearing, thrummed then—a pulse that raised the soft dirt like the woods itself exhaled, and the next thing I knew, we were running.

I tripped, a dozen times I tripped. I couldn't focus under the fog. Sometimes my friends were with me, and other times I felt more alone than ever before. Branches ripped at my face and tore my clothes. The dried vines of poison ivy that crawled up the bark of the trees unraveled, unspooling themselves and snaking along the ground, tethering my ankles. The trees shuddered around us as we ran. The thick branches clustered with twigs full of brittle leaves fluttered and rattled over our heads.

We jumped through the opening of the woods into my back yard, covered in sweat and panting, despite the cold October air. Huddled in safety away from the blackness of the churning woods, we stood breathless in the center of the yard, bent over and gasping for air.

We looked at each other for a long while, eyes big as the doe's, and none of us said a word. Mike openly cried, big wet tears running down his face that he didn't bother wiping away. I shook my head, mad as hell they dragged me back in the woods again when I could have been at home by myself—safe from whatever the hell was buried out there dragging whole creatures down into the ground.

"I'm going in," I said, holding back everything I wanted to say.

Mike and Derrick ignored me. "What is that?" Mike said, sniffling and wiping the wetness from his face. He pointed to Derrick's wrist.

Derrick held his arm up, angling it so a floodlight from the porch could set it in better light. "Cobwebs?" he asked.

I didn't want to look. I had a gnawing feeling in my gut that what they were looking at wasn't something I wanted to see, because if it reaffirmed the fear I felt prickling at the back of my neck, I would snap. My nerves fizzled and frayed, already on the verge of shorting out and leaving me a collapsed, drooling pile of useless flesh and bone.

Derrick was right. Whatever it was did look like cobwebs. Looking closer, I saw a thick wad of white tendrils—a writhing glob of microscopic worms on his wrist. Mike reached out and grabbed a clump of it from Derrick's arm. He held his fingers up in the yardlight, spreading them apart, and the tendrils webbed across his fingers like filamental slime. Some of the errant, veinous strands wriggled in the glow of the lights, and we all looked on, none of us sure what we were seeing.

"Guys," Mike said. "I'm out. I can't do it anymore tonight." He smeared the white stringy glob across his pant legs and walked across the yard. I watched him go as he disappeared into the darkness around the side of my house.

Derrick wiped the mess that clung to his forearm on the seat of his pants. He stayed in the yard for a while, shuffling his feet in the grass like he didn't know what to say. After a moment, he looked at me and said, "You saw all that, right?" He stared back toward the woods and shook his head, like he was trying to come to grips with the deer in the clearing and whatever had happened to it. Trying to tell his mind: *No.*

The images replayed in my head, and I wished my buzz hadn't worn off so quickly. I didn't want to remember. I was afraid of what I'd see in my dreams, if I were to get any sleep at all.

I nodded at him. "Yeah, I saw it. You're not crazy."

Without saying anything else, Derrick slicked his hand through his shaggy hair, turned, and walked off the way Mike had gone.

If I dreamed later that night, I didn't remember it.

The night was a blur of spiraling images. Misremembered things that had to have rational explanations. Night sweats making me churn. I tossed and turned so much that I wasn't sure if I slept at all.

By morning, I thought maybe the deer had just fallen into some divot in the ground mid-run and broken something. That the clearing in the woods was some sinkhole, and maybe we had walked upon it at exactly the wrong moment.

Then I remember the sound, like a rifle cracking out through the trees, and the doe's spine inverting as it was *pulled* under the earth. No sinkhole I could think of had ever done that.

Dad would know. He always knew about weird things like sinkholes and dates of tragic mudslides and such. Too bad my parents were at the cabin up north.

As the hours passed, I tried to forget about the whole thing and figured hanging out with Derrick and Mike was better than nothing, even though I wasn't yet sure how I felt about things from the night before. Wasn't even sure how I felt about Derrick and Mike at all anymore. I didn't feel right being alone though.

I called them both and neither answered their phones. Derrick didn't have a house phone, but Mike's mom picked up at his place.

"He's still sleeping, Aaron," she said. "What'd you boys get up to last night, huh? He says he's *sick*, but I know the smell of liquor." She wasn't mad, exactly. She said it with a slight giggle under her voice, but it still made my cheeks heat up like I got caught red-handed.

Embarrassed, I thought of lying, but just told her I was sorry, and asked her if she could have Mike call me when he woke up.

I lay in bed for much of the day and tried to forget everything. Every time I got up and happened to glance out the windows to the back yard, I froze. The edge seemed to encroach, like if I stared for too long at the darkness that made up the interior, it'd begin to spill out.

My parents and I no longer spent weekends together, me being at an awkward age where I'd outgrown everything my parents knew about entertaining kids. Nevertheless, I wished they were home. Even if whatever was in the woods was a fraction of my worst imaginings, I knew that neither I nor anybody stood a chance against it. Still, the house felt safer when they were there.

As night drew closer, the thick blackness that settled in the woods behind my house reached into the yard, stretching forward. I swear I could see it move.

The fact that Mike was sick and never called, and there was no word from Derrick at all, didn't sit well with me. I couldn't help but sit around and think of the cobweb-like substance. They both approached the deer and touched her as she was dying, being dragged down into the dirt.

What's wrong with her? Mike's words, echoing in my head.

As the evening faded away, I turned on every light in the house and eyeballed the woods that butted up against my back yard as if some diseased deer or creature was going to come crawling out.

As I sat in my bedroom holding my phone with my finger hovering over Mike's name, the motion-sensor floodlight in my back yard flashed on. My skin went cold. I crept to the window, peering just over the ledge in case some creature was there. I held my breath, hoping whatever was out there wouldn't see me staring.

A lone figure walked from the street side of my house and crossed my yard toward the woods. Not something coming out of the trees, but someone going in. When they passed under the yard light, I spotted shaggy brown hair and a flannel bathrobe. Purple spray-painted Jordans that could only belong to one person.

"Derrick?" I could see my scrunched-up face in the reflection of the window. I banged on the glass, but my friend never looked. "What the fuck are you doing?" I muttered, lacing up my shoes and flying down the stairs to my back door. I threw the slider open and stepped onto the deck, yelling at Derrick to turn around, but I watched as his silhouetted body faded into the darkness as he entered the mouth of the woods.

Taking the steps by twos, I raced down the deck into my yard to chase him. Was he sleepwalking? Having some episode? After the night before, I couldn't let him go out there alone, not after what we had seen. I didn't catch up with him and feared the worst.

As my feet hit the grass, Mike rounded the corner and I plowed into him, both of us tumbling over one another in a flurry of arms and legs.

I rolled to my feet and brushed myself off. "Mike," I said. "Thank God. I just saw Derrick going into the woods. You got to help—"

Mike stood slowly and looked beyond me toward the entrance to the wooded trail—looked past me like I wasn't even there.

"Mike?"

His eyes flicked toward mine, and when the light caught them, something in his pupils writhed. Something was in there, something alive and wriggling, like a tangled ball of angel-haired worms thrashing around. He blinked and stepped around me, following the footprints through the dewy grass Derrick had made a moment before.

My heart felt like a jackhammer was pounding through it. The breath caught in my throat as Mike passed by, and I couldn't help but shiver as his arm brushed my own.

What the hell was happening? My first idea was that this was a joke. Like these two idiots stayed away all day so they could come over at night to mess with me.

I knew deep down that I was wrong. That this was something serious, and my mind raced with only more questions and not one reasonable answer.

His eyes. What is wrong with his eyes?

These horrible thoughts mixed in my head, contorting together, merging and dancing with the images of the clearing and the doe being split in two and consumed by the earth. Something was luring my friends out there, and this wasn't some joke they had conjured up. Whatever this was, it was real, and I had to stop it.

Mike was halfway across the lawn, and I ran to catch up with him. I grabbed him by the shoulder and he spun, turning on me, and shrieked in my face. He screamed like some prehistoric beast, with no words or language other than hatred. Those spindly whisps of white—the things like worms I'd seen sloshing in his eyes, seen glistening like tendrils of slime between his fingers the night before—they reached out of his throat as he screamed, stretching beyond his slick teeth, and thrashed in the wind of his breath. They slithered and twisted in the cool October air like they were tasting the night, stretching out to lick at my face. I ducked out of the way, and Mike closed his mouth, sucking the fibrous monstrosity back behind his lips, and he turned and walked into the trees.

The world swam, my mind tumbling as I was forced to my knees. I trembled as I held a hand against my chest, willing the nerves to calm my heart, to slow my breath down so I could think. The police, they'd know what to do. I reached into my pocket, but my phone wasn't there. I looked once up to my house and again back to the trees. If I went for my cell, Mike and Derrick would be dead before I could ever dial 911.

Gathering every ounce of courage I could muster, I ran for the trees after my only friends.

Mike was far ahead on the trail, and I could barely make out his shadow through the thick density of the woods. I tried to run and promptly tripped over a downed limb, scratching my palms against the grainy terrain of the forest floor. I felt mired in—imprisoned by—the dense fog and the underbrush that tangled around my limbs and scratched at my face.

It didn't matter now. My friends were far ahead, and time was running out. I picked through the vines, roots, and fallen branches as I crept after them, moving as swiftly as possible without falling again. I was gaining on Mike. His shadow was larger now, only a few dozen paces away. If I was quick enough, I could charge him from behind, knock him down, and punch some sense into him. Maybe knock him unconscious until I could find Derrick and figure out the rest.

But he stayed just far enough in front of me, no matter how fast I moved, and before long, I saw his shape descend until the top of his head disappeared beneath the dark horizon of the forest's edge.

The clearing.

The bowl that fueled my terror.

When my feet came to the edge of the clearing, part of me was still taken aback by the majesty of the place. The moon was big and bright, ominously dousing everything in its corpse-like bluish hue. The fog settled gently in the basin—still, like a smoky lake before the dawn. Beneath it all, the mushrooms that had been a ghostly white now pulsed with a pinkish glow, throbbing like the beating heart of the woods.

Derrick approached the center, still in his bathrobe, his hood pulled over his head, and Mike closed in. They walked trance-like between the stalks of fungus that sprouted from the ground.

In the light radiance of the moon where the glow touched their skin, I could see fine white hairs beginning to sprout from their flesh to wiggle in the misty air. I walked after them slowly, careful not to make any noise, and was wary about what I was smashing beneath my feet. The way the bowl had thrummed last time, pulsed like it took a deep breath after sucking down the corpse of the deer, was weighing heavily on my thoughts. Each timid step seemed like the tightrope I walked was getting more frayed by the inch.

The ground beneath my feet rumbled. When the tremor ceased, Mike and Derrick got to their knees and lay back against the ground, staring unblinkingly toward the sky.

The deer. Her passive black eyes. The way she appeared at peace, gently taking in the night until her soft whimpers cursed our ears.

I had to act, had to pull my friends from their stupor, because whatever pulled the guts out of the doe was probably working on them already. Whatever snapped her back and sucked her down—that rumble told me it was already coming for my friends.

I ran. I ran, not caring where I stepped. Not caring what noise I made. I ran and threw myself down next to Mike and Derrick, and began to slap them awake. My open hand stung, snapping against their cold cheeks as I shouted at them, "Wake up. Wake up, Goddammit!"

Their eyes never blinked, and my hand came away sticky. The white wisps that filled Mike's eyes and his throat as he screamed at me were everywhere. The filaments, like slippery cilia, bled from both, seeming to come from every pore, and they reached out and fused with others rising from the ground all around us. Thousands of little tentacles reached from the earth like sapling webs, spiraling forth to connect with my friends—to wrap them up, to encase them and rip at their skin.

The ground shifted, and Derrick's legs sunk into the dirt. I tried to dig him out, but the ground vibrated, hemorrhaging like a fissure was about to open and swallow us whole. I grabbed his arms and pulled. The harder I pulled, the harder whatever gripped him from the other side fought back. Blood poured from his mouth, and he coughed a wet crimson spray that misted my face and dripped down my chin.

I tugged, my arms weak and my hands losing their grip. Derrick's eyes rolled back in his head, and he screamed as the wet, snake-like threads poured out of his mouth, wrapped his head in a sticky membrane, and spread down his body to connect with the dirt. Derrick went limp, and my feet sunk into the muck as it started dragging us down. My shoes filled with wetness, and when I looked, the moonlight showed a pit forming below, filled with a pool of my friend's blood.

The mushrooms in the clearing changed, pulsing with a swelling redness like they were one organism, breathing, beating together as they consumed. Spindly threads of the mycelial tentacles started to climb my jeans and pull at the fabric. I let Derrick go and watched him sink into the mud as I stepped away, tears, snot, and blood running down my face.

Mike was lying prone now a few feet away. I realized I was screaming as a broken sob cut through the sound. My throat burned, my muscles ached, and I fought not to gag as I stepped through the blood and webs of tendrils, trying to scrape the stuff off my pants. I grabbed Mike by his feet and began to pull him backward. His body let loose from the ground with a sick sucking sound, and when I rolled Mike over to try to pick him up, try to carry him away, his face was missing.

Roped clumps of muscle and glistening meat hung in a patchwork across his cheeks, his eyes and teeth bright white in the moon's glow. He stared with no eyelids to blink, no lips to mouth a word, and I knew he was dead.

Between the fibers of his muscles, those creeping organic strands poked from his face and slithered, elongating to meet the ground. Soon, he was covered like a fly wrapped in a spider's web, and the dirt opened to pull him under.

I dropped his feet and I ran.

I ran and I ran, and I couldn't breathe. I tripped and puked, scraping myself along every sharp rock and jagged strip of bark as I loped through the trees. The police. The DNR. The National Wildlife Service. Somebody. I needed somebody. But my friends were already dead.

My friends were dead.

They were dead.

I crashed out of the woods and stomped up the back steps and through my house to get the phone. My bedroom door handle put a hole in the wall as I burst into the room. Phone in hand, my fingers vibrating like I was having a seizure, I tried to unlock the screen.

As my thumb hovered over the number pad, trying to stop shaking enough to press the 9 button, I saw a tiny wisp of white hair-like thread coming out of my wrist.

My heart lurched into my throat, and the top of my head tingled as goosebumps ripped across my flesh. I dropped the phone on the bed and ran to the bathroom, grabbing a pair of tweezers from the drawer. I tore my clothes off and checked my body for more white wisps.

Nothing.

Standing naked in the bathroom, I pinched the single thread at the base where it had sneaked underneath my skin and pulled. The thread stretched, tugging under my flesh as the tendril slid out. When it was almost at the end, almost out of my skin, the worming thing snapped where it was pinched between the tweezers and the rest of it sucked up into my arm before I could grab it and pull it back.

No. No no no. Mike, with squiggly mycelium rummaging through the fluid of his pupils—them, flailing from his throat as he screamed.

I had to get it out.

I poked the sharp points of the tweezers into the hole in my wrist where the thing had sucked itself through. I spread the tips apart, trying to open the hole wider. The pain almost brought me to my knees as it spread like fire down my wrist and into my fingertips. Blood trickled slowly from the wound and plopped in bright splashes on the beige-tiled floor.

I ground my teeth and clenched my fist, fighting through the pain as I pushed on with the tweezers, spreading the hole in my wrist as wide as I could. Underneath the blood and meat in the hole was a tiny white thread, and I went to squeeze it with the tweezers.

When I touched the thread with the tip of the metal, it disappeared, sucking itself up my wrist.

"Fuck!" I screamed. "Fuck you!"

I dropped the tweezers on the ground and rummaged through the drawer. There had to be something better. My mind reeled. My wrist felt like a glowing hot wire had been shoved under my skin. Mike's skinless face flashed through my mind. Derrick's mummified head, spurting blood through quiet gasps.

My hand landed on my dad's box of spare safety razors, and my skin prickled, anticipating what I knew I had to do. I peeled a razor out of the box and pressed the corner of the blade to the edge of the bleeding hole I already made in my wrist. I took a deep breath and held it as I slid it through my skin, wrist to elbow.

The pain, sharp like being struck by lightning, nearly paralyzed me. I stood with my eyes closed, feeling like my teeth were about to shatter as I clenched my jaw, and then I let out a scream I couldn't even recognize as my own.

When I finally looked at it, I couldn't see anything with all the blood, and I had to rinse my arm off under the faucet. The porcelain stained a deep red, blood still flowing from my arm, but under the water, things started to clear up. I pulled apart the seams of the cut to see inside, and I could no longer feel anything. My fingers on my right hand didn't work, and the lips of the wound had just a slight sting as I spread them.

The inside of my wrist looked like a tangle of brown and red branches, with spots of black veinous strands raggedly running along the tendons and muscle fibers. Among them, entwining them, were the white threads of the thing in the woods. The fibers looped and wrapped around every part of my arm, growing longer by the second while I watched.

My head swam. My vision blurred. I reached into my wrist and began to pull the white threads out, yanking them from where they constricted my veins and tendons. I grabbed, I pulled, I tore, ripping against any fibrous thing my fingers touched. My arm was numb to my neck, and the muscles that allowed me to hold it up were no longer working.

My vision penciled, going dim, back to light, then dark, to black. My blood, my veins, hung over the flesh of my arm in ragged strands. The floor was a puddle of tacky red. I tried to walk out, to get to my phone, still watching the white threads spin and wind and grow their way through the inside of my wrist. I swooned and felt my knees crash against the tiled floor, and then there was only the dark.

I awoke to whispers in a language I'd never heard but somehow understood. They called to me. Beckoning me with sweet, lulling voices.

I was deep in the woods when I opened my eyes, swaying and reeling, my right arm limp and throbbing at my side. I stumbled over bushes and branches, tripping, unable to use my hands to break my fall. Again, blackness overtook me.

I woke later to rumbling under my feet. I walked, but my eyes were closed, and the whispers were louder, guiding me to the source. The ground shook like the world was breaking apart, and I opened my eyes.

I was in the clearing. The bowl. The little mushrooms that sprinkled the divot by the thousands were glowing bright red, and as the earth tremored below me, the whispers grew into a swelling hum of consciousness. I felt every inch of my body, inside and out, with an awareness of things I shouldn't have known. The whispers—not voices now, but a collection of energies—an ocean of knowledge.

Without the words for them, the energies, the whispers, the consciousness gave me my instructions, and my body followed without any will of my own. I felt elation. Satiety, but also the urge of my other parts' hunger. I melded into the spectrum of existence within the dirt. The mycelial threads now wept from my flesh to connect with their brethren in the dirt. No longer I, *we* lay on the ground and spread our hyphae, forming new strands and connections—information, iron, magnesium, zinc, flowing.

Flowing.

In the darkness, we feel all of each other. Somewhere, soft thumps drum above us, and our strands grow to penetrate the surface once more. The earth sends signals through us, and I, *we*, feel what it is to belong.

Come Out and Play

by Paul O'Neill

THE WIND SNAPPED AT the yellow police tape as Toby stared at the ground, refusing to accept the figure huddled at his feet.

The rain poured down, soaking him through, making the cotton of his hoodie cling to his thin shoulders. He stood on the grass bank of the River Dourie, watching the water as it burbled by. The downpour needled the river, created a static noise like a telly without a station.

It didn't take long for an angry crowd to gather. Fussing officers tried to hold them on the bridge that looked over the river. He knew what the people of Pitlair wanted to scream at him, could see it in their eyes.

We always knew you weren't right, but this?

Toby stared at the figure curled up on the grass. The girl's pale blue coat looked like a piece of the sky had fallen to Earth. The brightness of it had no right being there on such a dull, grey day.

He'd stumbled across her during an impromptu stroll after his long shift at the dairy farm. Why he picked today to stray from his routine, he didn't know. *List* didn't include walk after work. *List* was what kept him tethered. *List* kept him safe. Thinking about how he deviated from *List's* instruction made his brain all itchy.

"Were you having fun?" he asked the still figure. "Did you have friends?"

She'd died clutching her stomach like she had nothing but a belly-ache.

Her hood covered her face. What did she look like? Did she smile in those last moments?

A finger of jealousy swirled in his gut. It was the last thing he expected to be feeling in that nightmare moment. Had he ever held his arms out, spun, let the spring rain fall on his tongue with not a care in the world? He'd never felt comfortable when he was in the open. The sky pressed down too heavy, was far too big to be real.

The police officers were still rushing about to cordon off the crime scene, find places to stick their flappy yellow tape. He didn't know Pitlair had this many cops. They all gave him the same blazing stare that said, *It was always going to be you.*

Everyone in this small Scottish town seemed to know how he was raised. Locked in his room like a prisoner, unable to make noise. Any sound made his mum turn into a monster.

When he got to primary school, he was so incredibly thrilled to see other human beings, he didn't know how to act. He'd been too eager, too weird, too close. It didn't take long for them to shun him, call him names, pretend he didn't exist for weeks at a time.

He'd been a teenager when he heard the gargle of his mum choking, the thud as she fell off the couch, the rolling solidity of the wine bottle coming to a stop on the floor. He was useless with fear in that moment, trapped on the other side of the bedroom door. She needed help, but if she was okay and saw him, he'd be denied food for days. She'd started to go stiff and yellow by the time he worked up the courage to go to her.

And when he'd left high school, he'd stumbled across a story on Facebook that stopped him dead.

Study finds that 100% of serious criminals were neglected or abused as children.

It was a moment of awakening. He decided to get himself a referral to a psychiatrist and *List* was born. He never strayed from *List*. *List* kept the promised future away. *List* was his shot at a normal life.

A wind blew a shock of cold rain into his face, snapping him back to the moment, to the dead girl.

Even under the grey sky, it was as if those bedroom walls were still around him, pressing. How many steps had he paced in that room? How many fingernails had he snapped off, clawing at the walls? How many times had he pissed himself for fear of being caught going to the toilet? He was a boy in his jail cell, bred for a stint in Broadshade from the start.

"We can't let that happen," he told the still girl.

A chill inched its way over his shoulders. He tried to take in a deep breath, but it hitched in the middle.

From the gathering crowd, someone wailed, collapsed against a policewoman who tried her best to keep the man upright. Phones were held aloft as they hurled their hate down at him, called him murderer, sicko.

"I guess this is where we say goodbye, sky girl. I—"

He stared down at the figure, a heat crawling its way over his stomach, rising to his chest.

Poking out of the blue hood was a long, grey snout. Whiskers, sharp and silver, stabbed at the air. A long tail flowed from somewhere under the girl's coat. The end of it pointed at him like an accusing finger.

"Emily!" the man on the bridge screamed. "What have you done to my Emily? What have you done? I'll get you for this!"

The man's pain was aimed at him, Toby knew. He could almost feel the hatred of it in his bones.

When Toby turned his attention back to the girl, she returned to normal, face hidden. Just a dead little girl on a random Tuesday evening in April, rain pelting, beading off her waterproof jacket.

"Did you have fun in your life?" he said over the lump in his throat. "What did it taste like?"

They eventually let him out of the police station on the other side of midnight. All the officers' eyes held the same promise.

We know what you are. We know what you did.

They peppered him with questions, getting angrier and angrier as he stuck to his "story." They all refused to hold his gaze, as if his inner turmoil was somehow transferrable.

He'd done nothing but repeat his desire to go for a walk after work. He did not tell them about *List*, didn't want them to think him unfit in the head. Didn't want to tell them how he'd shamed *List*, deviated from its safety.

He ignored the rumble in his stomach as he stood in front of the bruised and battered refrigerator. *List* was taped on the door on yellowed paper:

0630 – Out of bed (no snooze!)
0635 – Sink wash
0645 – Two slices of toast
0700 – Walk to work
0730-1530 – Work (no long lunch break, no socials)
1600 – In door, put wash on
1615 – Shower
1645 – Meditate
1700 – Microwave dinner
1730-1830 – Light TV or football highlights
1830-1930 – Read

1930 – Sort washing into dryer, do dishes
1945 – Masturbate
2000 – Supper / snack
2030-2130 – Read
2130-2145 – Meditate
2145 – Bed
Do not stray from this path ever!

Since he and Dr. Mahabub, his psychiatrist, developed *List*, he'd stuck to its routine, never strayed.

"Until today," he said, tracing a finger over its curled edges.

He looked at his phone. 00:42. He'd skipped *List* from 1600 with his decision to go for a cheeky wee stroll. He slapped himself on the forehead, swore. It did nothing to dim the shame.

Despite wanting nothing more than to collapse in bed and forget, *List* needed doing.

He microwaved a dinner, then marched for a shower, taking care of the masturbate part as he washed. When that was done, he sat at the table, closed his eyes for two minutes of meditation while his macaroni and cheese steamed up at him with its thick, globulous stench. He ate it while watching the news, decided it was a very bad idea, switched it off. Seeing yourself next to a dead body was not good for the soul.

He put a wash on, did the dishes at speed. He grabbed a cereal bar from an empty cupboard, lay on the couch with his head on the arm rest, picked up his crumpled copy of *Cathedral* by Raymond Carver.

The words wouldn't cross the threshold from the vanilla-scented pages to his brain. The words floated in some in-between space, no matter how he strained his eyes.

Scritch, scritch, scriiitch.

Toby shot up, held the book close to his chest. The noises came from a shadowy corner. The giggle of something inhuman whined its way toward him.

"Who's there?"

Whatever moved in the walls itched at the other side of the plaster, trying to claw through.

He moved closer, bending an ear to the corner where it was hard to tell where the black damp ended and the shadows began. The musty stench of that damp lived inside his clothes constantly, no matter how much he washed them.

Squee, squee.

The high-pitched squeaks made his spine straighten, like someone had filled it with shards of ice. The things tumbled inside the walls, falling over each other. The plasterboard trembled when he placed a hand on it. The wetness of the wall crawled into his palm. It was a green, wet feeling.

Toby...

He jerked his hand back. The wall groaned, bulged at the centre. Plaster crumbled to the floor, making a *shoosh* noise like falling sand. From small fissures, grey fur poked out.

"You've went nuts, Toby," he said to himself, backing away.

Can Toby come out to play?

Aw, why is he always too busy?

Why are his blinds always, always closed?

The voices chirped at his brain, made a familiar anger bubble in his gut. That pure rage was always near the surface. That's why *List* was so important. *List* dampened, calmed.

We know what you are, Toby.

He yelled, launched his socked foot through the wall. The cry of small, injured rodents scurried into his ears. The grey things moved against his foot, nibbled his toes.

He jerked his dusty foot out, stopped himself from falling over by leaning on the couch. He expected a river of rodents to flood after him, fill his flat.

There was nothing but a black, yawning hole surrounded by settling white dust. No sound. No squeeing. No toothy rodents come to bite him.

"Hello?"

The smell that misted its way out of the hole stung his eyes. It was a combination of fresh cow shit and stringy pumpkin guts. It moved inside his throat, made him gag and hold a hand over his mouth.

Something moved in the hole.

"I see you, Toby," laughed a deep, merry voice. "We all see you."

"I've gone insane," said Toby.

"We're all a little mad down here, Trip."

"H-How do you know that name?"

No one had called him Trip in decades. Toby "Trip" Trippier.

Look busy, Trip's coming. Don't look at Trip's eyes, he'll talk your ear off. Why you gotta stand so close, Trip? Don't you know how to human, Trip?

A luminous yellow eye filled the gap. It was too big to be a small rodent. It shone with a magical light, like a dragon's eye.

"We know you, Toby. We've always known what you'd turn out to be. One of us."

"I...I fell off the couch, knocked my head. I've gone off my rocker."

"People like us didn't have a rocker to begin with, my buddy. We never had a chance. Come, be a street rat. Do a red dance in the rain. Just like that little girl. Come out and play."

The eye didn't blink. Just stared into him with a gleeful glow. Toby wrung the top of his t-shirt, tried to breathe slow. "I need to finish this story, then meditate, before putting my head down for the night. Up early for work, you know? Cows won't milk themselves. Not yet, anyways. I...I can't come out and play. I'm not allowed."

"I can smell how much you want to. We'll show you how. That's what friends do, right?"

"Friends?" The word felt alien on his tongue. He looked at the battered book, the compulsion to pick it up heavy within him. "I can't. My real life's in here. Leave me alone before I torch you."

"And you live such a *real* life here, do you? I thought when that old boot coughed on her own vomit, you'd have lived under the stars. With us, you can do what your heart desires and not have to care. Anything at all. Try it. It tastes like ice cream and gravy."

Toby's rage heaved inside. It moved his shoulders, curled up in his temples.

"Come out and play, Toby."

He roared, sent his foot through the plaster again. "Get away! Get. Rat bastard. Fuck you."

The dust clawed at his throat, made him cough, stung his eyes, but still he took his anger out on the wall until he made a hole large enough for him to fit through.

Sweat prickled at his cheeks by the time he came back to himself, surveyed the damage.

The eye was gone.

The rats continued to squee and chirp and laugh. And then a silence fell. It fell like a heavy curtain around Toby's shoulders.

He leaned forward, stuck his head in the hole. He expected the stench of rat shit to mist up at him, or a rat to fly at his eyes, but there was nothing. Nothing but the mouldy innards of his damp confines.

The council was going to have a lot to say about his destruction of the flat. Maybe now they'd actually do something about it, fix it so his winters weren't a plague of sore chests and deep coughs. Maybe.

The rain continued to bead down his living room window, making the outside a blurry darkness. The anger that had flared to the surface so readily now simmered down to a blue shame in his gut. He stared down at his hands. The blood from his knuckles had crusted in the white plaster dust.

"What am I?"

He knew fine well what he could be. Knew what his upbringing signalled in his future. Every book he read or show he watched about serial killers all sang the same story—his story. A story of neglect and abuse. Being locked in that room for all his days had made him go spare, made him less human.

"Lock it down, Toby," he told himself. "Where were we?"

He paced with the book in his hands, forced down one of his favourite short stories, "Careful." He wasn't much into new things, only the familiar, real things.

He traced a thumb along the scrawled, childish handwriting on the inside of the back cover.

Everyone has good in them.

"Everyone has good in them."

The digital clock on his coffee table blinked 01:13 in its alien green glow by the time he was done.

Shadows flittered on the road outside. Ratty laughter pricked at his ears. It sounded like a gaggle of schoolkids were raising hell, throwing things, their cackles muffled by the rain. It was nothing unusual in this town. Something large and plastic toppled over. They must've kicked over a wheelie bin. Glass shattered, giggles grew louder.

Toby went to the window, opened it a crack so he could get a look at the thugs causing the bother.

Five teens rampaged, drinking from large green bottles, their colourful hoodies and hats soaked through.

He wanted to yell at them, tell them to jaunt on, cause a mess somewhere else. The shout stopped in his throat, holding itself by its claws, refusing to leave.

They were rats.

Huge, boy-sized rats causing hell. Their tales swished in the air as they jumped on a toppled black bin. One craned its thick neck up at the rain, opened its large jaws, let out an *ow-ow-aaaooow* like a wolf howling.

Toby pressed his face closer to the cold glass, tried to see if anyone else had stirred. The miserable houses and flats were all dark. How could he be the only one wakened by such a racket?

What to do? Call the police?

Hi, Officer, it's me again. The one you're sure killed that little piece of sky. There's a bunch of rats playing in my street, disturbing my peace. Please come and vanquish them at your earliest convenience.

No, that wouldn't work. Even if they did show up, it would be in a couple hours, well after the action. The police were good at that around here. For the likes of him, anyways.

The street fell quiet. Five pairs of black eyes turned to him. Their cold attention made his balls want to hide inside his stomach.

"Come out and play, Trip," called one rat with a red baseball cap.

"We'll laugh and sing-a-sing, ding-a-ling," said one with a leather jacket.

"Toby is the one who pounds his nails. Eats their flesh when all else fails," hooted another with an eyepatch.

"Come out and play."

"Come out and play."

"COME OUT AND PLAY!"

The one with the leather jacket sniffed the air, crouched down to four legs. Orange streetlight flickered along its sharp whiskers. "Fresh meat comes."

It sprinted down the street toward a bank of trees, the others following. Toby knew the sound of someone being set upon all too well. They jumped on a man with a white beard, knocking him to the ground, then stomped and clawed him with joy.

"Stop!" Toby slapped at the window. "Leave him alone."

It was a homeless man they beat up. A harmless gent who'd fallen on rough times and Toby often saw trundling up this street, head always down, muttering to himself.

The crisp scent of rain on concrete was heavy in the air as Toby ran out the front door, yelling at the rats to leave the poor old guy alone.

He grabbed one of them, ignored the electric shock that zipped up his hand. His knuckles popped as he threw the rat to the side.

The other four rats saw this, turned to face him, crouched, ready to pounce. Toby stood there, making himself as tall as he could. The rain had already soaked through his t-shirt, chilling him to the bones.

"He's out. He's out," they chirped.

The rat he'd thrown aside got to its feet, nodded at Toby, then scampered down the brae to the rusty bridge at the bottom of his street. The others followed, vanishing into night.

He stared at the bridge. With the trees overhanging it, it seemed like the yawning jaws of some huge beast. That bridge was where the crowd had gathered earlier. Where they'd hurled names down at him.

We know what you are.

He blinked out of it, went over to the struggling man who coughed blood onto the path.

"You okay there?" he said, helping the man up.

The smell of wine was so harsh Toby could taste it. The man's eyes went wide. He shook free, stumbled, got to his feet, backed off with his palms up. "I've not got nothing, you cunt. I never hurted anybody, I swear. Leave me."

"It wasn't me."

"You're that child killer."

"I found her like that, all cold and—"

"They should put people like you down at birth. Evil is in the blood."

Gravel turned under Toby's boot as he leaned forward. The man fell to the ground with panic, picked himself back up, then ran up the road.

Water dripped from Toby's eyebrows as he watched the man go. "I found her like that. I found her."

The rats called to him in unison from the dark: "Come find us."

He knew he should go back inside, get some rest before work, but something sizzled inside him, sparked like a Catherine wheel on bonfire night.

The sound of the river grew large as he made his way down to the bridge. The trees dripped. The rushing water plopped. Everything was slick down by the river. Mud squelched under foot as he followed the sounds of cackling mayhem.

The River Dourie cut through the heart of Pitlair. A disused road ran along its bank with abandoned warehouses facing the water. Huge pipes ran above the river, joining the other side. They must've run under his house, he thought as he moved nearer the rats and their play.

It was from the entrance of one of these massive pipes that the sounds came. Inside the wet, cave-like opening glinted broken glass, small syringes.

He looked around at this strange, broken place, seeing it as if for the first time. This was the place they warned children never to come. They sang songs about it at primary school, drummed it into you so you'd never forget.

He leaned in closer, stuck his head into the dark pipe. All he could hear was the *drip, drip* of the rain. The air was cloying and thick as a green smog. He covered his mouth when he hauled himself up, stood inside the pipe.

The merry voices itched their way to him from the dark depths.

"*Toby Trippy, here he comes. Out to play and numb his gums. Dare he let the inside out? Smash and grab and let blood spout!*"

This was followed by a spiralling cascade of laughter that hit him like a monster's breath. He stood there, clenching his fists, feeling a vein pulsate down the centre of his forehead.

Glass popped under his boots when he started making his slow way into the blackness of the pipe. He had to duck his shoulders. More than once, a slimy hand of what looked like seaweed clawed at his hair.

There was an orange glow like fire at the far end of the pipe. The rushing water that must've been somewhere below him roared inside the metal confines.

"What are you doing here, Toby?" he whispered, hearing the echo of it bite back at him.

As he inched forward, heart pounding in his ears, the light grew. The way the shadows danced told him he was nearing a bend in the pipe. The noise of the rats became an uproarious wave. It sounded like there were hundreds, thousands of them having a party, screaming, singing, stomping.

Did he really want to put himself in the middle of that? Is that what they wanted? Entice him here and nibble him to death, somewhere under the bowels of the town where no one would ever look?

A pang of sorrow pinched his heart. If that were to happen, he had no one to miss him. They'd briefly mention him over their pints or cups of tea and move on, unsurprised.

You hear about that weirdo, Toby Trip?

I heard he got chewed alive.

He was gonna be Pitlair's next best killer.

Had that look about him, you know?

"Stop it," he hissed.

A stench wafted around him. A gooey smell like trampled snails mixed with rat shit and orange rust. It was enough to turn him green inside, make him turn his head and gag a line of bile onto the pipe.

When the sickness passed, he thought of the homeless man the rats had set about. The innocent little girl.

He shuffled his way forward. "You can't just do what you want and not care. You can't. It's not right."

He made his way to the firelight that moved over the bend in the pipe. The sounds of the river were muffled here. Was he deep under the town? Under his house? Was there a scratched-out tunnel that led directly to his living room walls?

A flash of that massive yellow eye that had stared at him through the hole in his plasterboard came back, the way it seemed to smile.

We've always known what you'd turn out to be.

His breath hitched when he stuck his neck out, slowly looking around the sharp, ninety-degree turn. The heat of fire wafted over his face. He squinted, waited for his eyes to adjust to the streaming, dancing figures.

The end of the pipe looked down into a massive space. Toby's mind flashed to the feast halls in *A Game of Thrones*, only the space was furnished in the style of an abandoned church with benches scattered and broken all over the place. A small bonfire lit the middle of the cavern, making black shadows of the far corners. Where the metal of the pipe ended, a collection of wooden crates made for a crude staircase down into the lair.

The rat people were everywhere, all wearing human clothes and knick-knacks. He couldn't see the ground for their swarming. Their furred bodies pulsed as they moved.

Had they made this place themselves? Scratched it from the dirt with teeth and claw?

Every squeal that bounced up at him made his shoulders tense. Why had he come here? All the anger he'd felt at them for hurting the old man fell away, leaving him cold and full of fright.

When he turned to leave, glass under his boots scratched, echoing down at the horde.

The noise snapped to utter silence.

All the black eyes stared up at him, sniffed with their long noses, smiled.

This was his end, he knew. They'd fly up at him, tear him to shreds while singing their songs. His body would never be found.

The rats stared, frozen. Only the quivering of fur under their human clothes rippled. The flames danced, playing across their promise-heavy faces.

"He has come to play," a hefty voice bellowed from a dark corner.

Whispered titters flowed across the rats, making their fur stand up like cats threatened. They moved out of the way, making a path, their heads bowed.

Something shuffled from the dark. A huge rat. Toby felt his insides scream, *Run, run.* The figure must've been as tall as he was. About its neck and paws, jewels glistened in the firelight. It wore a black bomber jacket with nothing to cover its muscular rat legs. Yellow eyes gleamed with joy as it stared up at Toby.

"You." The word fell out of Toby's open mouth.

"You've come home." It leaned forward, took in a great sniff of the air. "Ahh. The hunger rolls off you in waves."

"W-What are..." His voice bounced off the walls, made him close his mouth.

"What am I?" It spread its thick arms out wide, surveyed the rats like a performer waiting for a crowd to join in. "I am Rattapallax and these are my family. Welcome home."

Toby leaned, stared down the long dark tunnel he'd shuffled down. He could hear the pouring rain hitting the top of the pipe. His legs itched to bolt, run away, see if he could make it to the outside world.

Rattapallax strolled closer, coming to the edge of the crates. It craned its neck, staring up at him.

"How thin the veil is between order and delicious mayhem," the rat said. "Join us, and you can let it all out. Just like you wanted when your mummy locked you in that room all day and night. You had red, red dreams, didn't you? Your mummy got mad when you put the light on. Wanted you in the dark with your pet rock. Even the light under the door was too much of a reminder of your existence."

"Shut up. You can't... You don't know what it was like."

The rats straightened, gasped in a breath that affected the air behind Toby's ears. Their eyes longed to pounce at him, but Rattapallax snapped his fingers and the rats grew still.

"No one ever cared for you," said Rattapallax. "Never cared what you grew to be. We care. We think you're beautiful."

Shame crawled beneath Toby's skin at the sick wanting within. Something in him yearned to go down there, join the rats and their malicious play.

He leaned on the curve of the pipe, ignored the flakes of metal that jagged his palm. "No. I...I can be a good guy. I am a good guy."

Rattapallax chuckled. The rat placed a hand over its mouth, tried to stifle it, but the laughter wouldn't be denied. It grew and grew until the force of it shook the massive rat's stomach. The other rats joined in, their gremlin laughter taking Toby back to school days of everyone pointing, laughing.

"Stop!" Toby screamed, slapping both hands over his ears.

Rattapallax snapped his fingers, and the tumult died like a candle being snuffed by a cruel wind.

"I am Rattapallax and I have always been here. For I am everywhere, inside everything. The world couldn't survive without the balance we provide, Toby. We trim the numbers." The wooden crates moved as Rattapallax set a large foot on the first step. "You have greatness within you. Be my masterpiece."

As Rattapallax spoke, two rats snuck up beside the king rat, moved toward Toby with slinky, liquid movement. Their eyes glinted, waiting for the signal to leap.

Everyone has good in them.

It was a whisper from the past. Mrs. Joy, his high school English teacher, said it during detention. That was when she'd handed Toby his beat-up copy of *Cathedral* that he'd cherished all these years. It was the only thing from his childhood he'd kept. He could still remember scribbling those words she said on the inside of the back cover. She'd been the only one to look him in the eye for longer than a flash his whole life.

"Everyone has good in them," he said to the giant rat. "Even me."

Toby bent down, picked up a large piece of rotted wood, and hurled it down at Rattapallax. It hit home with a *thunk*. The rat stumbled back, clutched its head.

The other rats gained on him. They hurried up the crates, squeaking and chirping, tumbling over each other like a rush of water about to burst from a dam.

Toby sprinted, foot slipping on the crumbly rust and slimy rat shit that coated everything. At the end of the tunnel, the night had never seemed so bright.

Despite the rodents pounding closer, he kept looking ahead at the widening end of the pipe. When he launched himself at the opening, the smells of rain and mud hit him.

He landed on his chest. Air whooshed out his lungs in a violent burst. The skin on his stomach was on fire. He knew it'd be a scraped red mess under his clothes.

When he turned himself over, he skittered back on his hands like a bug expecting to be stomped on. The rats hadn't been far behind him.

In the dark opening of the pipe, he saw their eyes. They'd stopped, sticking to shadow as if the slight light would burn them. Their eyes shone like stars in a black sky. The rats hiccupped laughter, their eyes vanishing back into the pipe, withdrawing.

Toby collapsed, lay on the wet, gravelly ground. The rain pattered off his face in a refreshing wave. He could go to sleep right here. He'd never felt so ragged, so torn in the head.

What had he just witnessed?

He felt like a zombie on the walk home, his mind empty, whitewashed from all the impossible things he'd seen. He stumbled, staggered about like a drunk.

He walked in his front door, peeled the soaking, muck-covered clothes off, and had a quick shower. No matter how hot he made the water, how it scalded, he couldn't seem to clean the reek from his skin, from underneath his fingernails.

His sanity felt like it would flow with the purply black water that fell off him, swirling down the drain.

Maybe his brain had shattered, and he'd died in his bedroom all those years ago. Maybe this slow nightmare was his own personal hell.

Join us, and you can let it all out, the massive rat had said. *You had red, red dreams, didn't you? Your mummy even got mad when you put the light on. Wanted you in the dark with your pet rock.*

The thought made his first ever memory surface. He was six years old, filled to the brim with Christmas excitement. When Mum had come through to his quiet room on shaky legs, offering him a shimmery green present, tears sprung from his eyes.

His mother always looked as if she couldn't bear the weight of her own thin bones, shook like she had a fever. In the following years, he'd find out exactly what that meant, but at six, he was sure she was sick, was frightened she'd die and leave him all alone in his bedroom forever.

He took the present from her, almost dropped it. It was very heavy. It must've been something huge, something expensive, something special.

"For me?" he said.

"What did I tell you about speaking words at me?" She stubbed out a cigarette on his doorframe, glared at him as if he were a spider that refused to die under boot. "Silence now."

"But it's Christma—"

"You know what happens to unquiet boys. Silence."

She slammed the door closed, leaving him to his bedroom. The walls had never seemed so large, so solid. A cross of a shadow shone on the wall from the windowpane and the orangey streetlight outside.

Toby sat on the floor, tore into the present.

It was a rock.

A black, sooty lump of rock like a miniature mountain. He hugged it tight to his chest, ignored the stabby ends of it. "I'll call you Pointy."

He set Pointy on his windowsill, knelt beside it, stared out the window and the outside world with his chin resting on his hands.

Other kids hollered and played around, *ding-dinging* the bells on new bikes, wobbled on new skates, wore frozen, joyous smiles on their red faces.

The water in the shower cooled. His knuckles went white as he clenched his fist, fingernails biting into his palm so hard little drips of blood welled out, fell into the drain, following the rat pipe stink.

He'd never felt so heavy his whole life, so weighed down. How swell it would be to lighten his shadow, let go of all the trapped havoc that lived inside.

"I need to tell the police," he said, stopping the shower.

He dried himself off, chucked on the first clothes he could find from his bedroom floor. A mismatched pair of blue tracksuit bottoms and a brown jumper.

How easy would it be to crawl into bed, forget the whole thing? His clock blinked 02:42 at him.

"It's what a good person would do," he said to himself as he marched out his front door.

The rain had ceased its torrent as he walked to the police station on the edge of Pitlair. He could taste the oily puddles in the gravelly car park as he paused for a second, built himself up. The police station looked more like an ancient prison with its broken, barred windows.

"Knew you'd be in here sooner or later," said the policewoman behind the reception. "Here to give yourself up? Confess?"

He sighed, clenched his jaw as he recognised her. Freckles, they called her at school. One of the kids who teased him endlessly, pretended he never existed.

"What's that supposed to mean?" Toby pushed the words through his jagged teeth.

"Been a long night. Just let it out."

"I...I need to report a crime."

"You did that already. All I've taken for the last eight hours is abuse from people screaming at me, telling me we were daft letting you walk. That poor wee Emily. You know what her mother said to me when I was holding her back on the bridge?" Freckles stood, leaned on her desk so she was eye-to-eye with him. "Emily hadn't finished her Lego Harry Potter set, the one with the Knight Bus. That's what detail the mother went on about, over and over. That the bus was never going to be finished. That's what you took."

"That's not—"

"Kinda weird that you just happened across her like that. No witnesses. No reason to be there. Nothing."

"I told you what happened."

"I'm very well informed of what you told us."

"I think I know where the...people are that done this. They set about a homeless man. Sounds nuts, I know, but they live in the pipes down there. They nearly killed that man until I stepped in."

The sounds of rats burrowing into his walls, the giggling invitations to come out and play, the impossibly large rodents and their leader. All this he left out. He'd be placed in his cell in Broadshade in a heartbeat, no questions asked.

"You stepped in, did you?" asked Freckles. "A regular hero, you are. Should give you a fucking medal. I'm not buying it. I know your type."

"What type's that?"

"You were always wrong inside, Toby."

"Listen, the people who did it are inside the pipes over the Dourie. I swear. You gonna send someone round to arrest them?"

"Did you bring me any evidence?"

"What?"

"Sounds awfully handy if you were to show up here to take the heat off your own name. You know what they're saying about you?"

"I never done anything wrong. Never."

"I bet you still think of that poor Emily, eh?"

"Aye, but—"

"So, you admit it?"

"No, no, no. That's not what I meant. You ever found a dead person?"

"More than you can imagine. Around here, it's part of induction week."

Toby resisted the urge to slap the desk, scream into the woman's face that they were wasting precious time, that the rats were free and loose and up for anything. "You gonna try to stop them?"

"Who?"

"The ones in the pipe! Don't you care at all? I thought you were supposed to help people."

A breathy giggle fell out her mouth. "What town you been living in? That's rich." She took her deliberate time running a thumb under her eye. "We help good people, and you're not *good* people. The sooner we can pin Emily on you, the better. And you can stop looking at me like that."

His mind boiled over with fantasies of grabbing her by the collar, running a large knife through her neck. He'd watch the blood spurt over the desk, revelling in the way it pit-patted on the linoleum floor. Then he'd take care of the other officers that came running, take them all out, flee into the night, alive and free.

"How much were you into kids, I wonder," said Freckles. "What would we find on your hard drive? I might just go raid your home and—"

"Don't!"

"Got something to hide, have you?"

"I've had bother with...rats. They chew through my walls at night."

Freckles picked up some papers, made a show of shuffling them. "Thank you for playing good citizen. I'll put it on my to-do list. Right at the bottom."

Back in his living room, a familiar, panicky pressure grew in his chest. He tugged at his hair, tried to swallow the scream that wanted to let itself out.

"Come out and play, Toby," the rat hoodlums chirped from outside. "Make us sing your name forever."

"No," said Toby. "Finish the list. *List* is calm. Find your centre."

"The only thing in the centre of you is gooey, delicious evil."

"You don't know that!"

"Hey, Trip, here's a new list for ya. One, come out and play. Two, kill the first person you meet. Three, be happy. Come kill, just like you killed that little drop of sky."

"You sick, yellow-fanged fucks. Leave me alone!"

The window frame groaned, cracked. A crowd of rat boys pressed their grey faces against the glass, eyes shouting malice and glee.

"*Come out and play,*" they all sang.

They called his name, but he refused to hear it. It was time for bed. How he longed to close his eyes after this bastard of a day. Everything would be okay tomorrow. Maybe it had all been a dream. A little dead girl. Giant, singing rats. It made no sense.

He paused in the doorway of his bedroom. Something was curled up in his bed, duvet over her head. Only her hair flowed over the pillow, spilling over the side of the bed. He'd recognise that slick, midnight-black hair anywhere.

"Mum?"

The figure sprung up in one liquid movement. The dried, ancient figure of his mother squinted, held the covers tight to her chest.

"Who are you?" she said. "What you in my house for?"

Mum kicked her scrawny legs out the bed, stood. She was barely there at all. A velvety, raisin-skinned version of the mum he remembered.

"It's me." Toby backed off a step. "You not recognise me? Mum?"

"Mummy has some bed bugs in her head. Go back to your room, Steven."

The mention of the name gut-punched him, almost sucked the wind from his lungs.

Steven was the brother he never met. The one who got crushed into the road by a lorry while Mum watched. Steven had been trying to catch up to the ice cream truck before it drove away.

"I'm Toby." His voice was as pale as a lost little boy. "Remember, Mum? It's me."

She dragged a stiff leg behind her. Her foot *shooshed* along the carpet. She was like a thing pulling itself from the depths of the sea. A rotten salty smell tingled his nostrils, growing with every step she took.

When she got halfway, an orange bar of streetlight landed on her nose. Her distended, hairy nose that poked out the tangles of black hair.

He could almost hear her toes growing into razor-sharp nails, hear the hair pushing itself out her pores. A tail lashed in the space between them, snapping like a hungry snake.

"Where's my boy? What have you done to my Steven?"

"He died. Then I came along and—"

"Trying to take my Steven's place. Get in your room. What have I told you. Room, now! And never let me hear you again."

"No."

"No? I'll give you *no!*"

She swayed her hips. The tail cracked his side. A red lance of pain made him seethe in a breath through his teeth.

"Never come out! You were never my Steven. My Steeeven!"

The sorrow in the screamed name pricked at his soul. He held his side as he ran out the house, into the cold rain. By the time he made it to the end of his small path, he was soaked through, socks squidgy, jumper heavy.

He turned. His mother's sick cries came from the chasm of his open front door.

What would've happened if his brother hadn't died? If he had his brother beside him, maybe it would all be different. He wouldn't have been locked away, shunned, forgotten about. He'd know what happiness was. Played in the street. Breathed summer joy.

"Your poor, poor brother," a ratty voice hissed behind him.

The rat scampered its way to the middle of the road and lay down. It wore a white overcoat and a cap that had an ice cream cone stitched onto it.

"Did Steven look like this?"

It sprawled itself out, kicked its legs in the air like a squashed beetle.

Other rat people came from the shadows, pointed, guffawed. Toby stood there, mouth open. He could see the tire tracks on the rat, how it had been run over, sending its guts everywhere like a grape that had been pressed too hard under thumb.

He turned, his stomach heaving. The sick burned his throat. It landed in a slow, thick pile by his feet.

The rat on the road got up, doing a joyous dance before being greeted with ratty high-fives.

They stopped, stared at Toby, waited. A white-hot rage tensed him all over. They must've sensed that. They huddled together, shivery fear in their beady eyes.

"I'll fucking kill you," said Toby. "I'll kill you all."

"Aw, we've done it now," they said in unison. "The real Toby comes. Run!"

The rats dropped to all fours, sprinted down into the darkness of the bridge toward the River Dourie. Toby gave chase, a groan bubbled out of him with every step on the stony path.

The dark cloaked him as he sprinted under the trees that hung over the bridge. The rain needled the canopy above him, drowning his thoughts. The noise called to him.

Show them who you are.

He followed the rats to the pipe, saw the last one as it leapt into the opening. He stood before it. The rodents' spiky laughter burbled out of the darkness.

"*He's here. He's here. He's really, really here,*" they sang.

He stared at the sky, letting the rain fall over his face. Despite the heavy cloud, he could see a twinge of promised daylight.

"You can be someone else," he said to himself. "You can be good, right? Right?"

He slapped himself and boy did it feel good. The ache of it was a thrill that swirled in his gut. Even after all these years free from that bedroom, being outside was still an alien experience. Like his brain could not compute how far the sky was, thought it was some mirage.

A twig snapped.

Toby turned, feeling dizzy like he'd been drinking all night.

"I knew you'd come back."

Rainwater dripped into Toby's mouth as he stood, watching the figure get close. It was the huge rat, only this time it wore a black raincoat, no rings or jewellery.

"You," was all Toby could force out.

"Rattapallax, at your humble service. You're one of us, Toby. Someone who was never given a chance. We'll make them see the error in their ways, won't we? The world needs to pay its price."

On the grass bank, the yellow police tape still fluttered in the wind. It seemed like so long ago he watched the police stick it there while he waited beside the girl's twisted body.

Toby turned his back on Rattapallax, tugged his hair until it screamed fire along his scalp.

"You need a family," said Rattapallax. "We are that family."

The big rat walked onto the grass beside him. Something *clinked*, dangling from its hand. The metal of it glinted in the dark. It was a heavy dog chain.

Rattapallax moved through the tape, ignoring the way it stuck to its large abdomen, and stared down at the grass. "This was the spot. Right here. She was a little drop of sky, and you killed her."

"I found her there," said Toby, the words crawling out his mouth over the lump in his throat. "It wasn't me."

The rat turned, squinted knowingly at him. "You so sure about that?"

"It was you and your gang of monsters. You can't just go killing people."

"Someone's got to. And it's sooo easy. You see, all people have it in them to kill. That's what these humans don't understand. How thin the veil is between killers and non-killers, good and evil. The only thing, the *only* thing keeping them from violence, is how far they're pushed. That's all. Push enough and the rage flows out. And some people have the violence right there, just under the skin, ready to come out in marvellous waves. Red waves." The rat closed its eyes, turned its nose up to the sky, inhaled so hard Toby could hear the hairs in its nostrils whistle at the air. "That's what we feed on. Mmm… And you're a feast."

"I'm not like that."

"You were born for this."

The rat's voice changed, turned into a memory of a teacher reciting his school report card.

"*Toby learned calming techniques in class today after stabbing a classmate with a pencil again. He needs routine. If this continues, he'll end up expelled.*"

The rat's voice changed back to its charged timbre. "Sound familiar? A tale of a lost boy who was never given a chance."

Toby ignored the squash of mud and grass under his foot, the way it sent needles of cold into his calves.

The rain slicked off the rat's jacket. The dog chain swayed in its grip.

"Give in to your nature, Toby. Be with us, and I promise every day will be glorious and free."

"I…I can't."

"Time to accept your role in this world."

Toby stared into the moving river, feeling his eyes go together. He was so utterly tired that he could curl up and sleep right here. Tears joined the wetness on his face. He let them flow. With them, a flood of memories came.

How many times had he longed to press his thumbs through his mum's eyeballs when she closed his bedroom door, locking him away? How many days, nights, years had he spent yelling at the walls until his voice gave in?

"Oh, that's the stuff," Rattapallax hummed in ecstasy. "Push her eyes in. She deserved it. Ride the wave, the glorious wave."

"How are you inside my head?"

"I told you. I'm in everything. I am everything. *I am you. You are me. Violence breeds us harmony. With a knick-knack, paddy-whack, give Toby a bone. This old rat sings on his throne.*"

"Go away."

"Never."

"Go away!"

"Kill me. I know you want to. Here," Rattapallax held out the chain until it jabbed Toby in the stomach, "let me make it easier for you."

Despite saying the word "no" over and over, Toby gripped the chain by its leather handle.

"Sing me a song of crimson, Toby. Or picture me as Mummy dearest. That's it. Show me how you wished you were never born. Scream at her about the letter you wrote to Santa that said you'd trade your life for Steven's so Mummy could have smiley eyes again."

"Stop."

"Be yourself, Toby. Let go. Do it. DO IT!"

His hand tremored where he gripped the chain. The rain hammered down, seemed to will him on with its impatience.

Hit him, smack him, make him bleed.

"You're beautiful," said Rattapallax, lowering its head, offering itself up.

Peace glowed in him like a calm breath. He closed his eyes, felt the sensation lick at his muscles, fill him with energy.

He let it all go.

The chain cracked the rat's skull. The rodent went down with a shriek of laughter.

"Yes, yyeeess!" said Rattapallax on his knees. "Again."

Toby swung the chain as hard as he could. It came home. The rat collapsed to the sodden earth, just where he'd found little Emily.

"Kill me," whispered Rattapallax. "Kill…"

He heard someone yell in anguish, then realised the sound was coming from him. A heat burned down his arm when he hit the figure again and again, finding blood and bone.

The rat was silent, but Toby went on, striking until his arm muscles failed.

The chain dropped to the ground, lay there like a silver snake content after a kill. Toby sunk to his knees. Wet and cold spread through his tracksuit bottoms.

The rat things watched from the pipe. Despite Toby killing their king, they sounded as gleeful as a bunch of bad boys throwing stones at a head teacher.

"You'll all be next!" Toby roared at them.

The rats scuttled away into the depths of the pipe, shrieking and giggling all the while.

The rain continued its deluge. He spread his arms out, letting it wash him through. Had the air always tasted this good? Had wet grass always smelled so lively?

The spiritual calm was slapped out of him when he stared down at Rattapallax.

It wasn't a rat.

A bald man with white eyebrows stared back at him with sightless eyes. His skull was a misshapen, pulverised mess.

"What have I done?"

The realisation buckled him, made him set his forehead on the grass as he sobbed.

A dog whined somewhere close by. On the bridge, a woman wailed with panic then yelled for help. Déjà vu took hold of his brain. The cops would be here soon, he knew. Freckles would be delighted as they bundled him into the back of their van.

He was so, so tired. When he blinked at the sight of the man he'd just killed, the man Rattapallax had tricked him into killing, he saw the little girl again. The girl in the sky-blue jacket.

"Did you have fun?" he said.

He curled up into a little ball next to his victim.

"I'll just wait here. Close my eyes for a little bit. They're coming to get me. Take me away."

A police siren broke the peaceful sound of the burbling river.

The heavy cell door slammed behind him. His home welcomed him into its confines. The walls felt close, pressing, like a comforting womb. He closed his eyes, let out a slow, peaceful breath.

From the tiny square window, sunlight bounced about the space, sharpening the yellow of the aged paint. Summer had been glorious so far, like nothing he'd ever seen. And here he was, locked inside Broadshade forever.

The last few months were a blur. His face was all over social media and the papers. He'd read the articles that said he'd been a gibbering madman, screaming nonsensical things at reporters. He'd screamed *Rattapallax* at them as they flashed their photos, called their questions. They'd never understand.

His fellow inmates stayed well clear of him, gave him the same sideways look he'd received his whole life. That was fine. He knew what he was.

The prison door creaked open with a rusty squeal, admitting a small man dressed in black. Dressed in black with a small square of white at his collar.

Toby couldn't help the smile that moved up his face. "What can I do you for, Father?"

The man took a long time bringing his face up from the floor to look into his eyes. "I once knew your mother. Told her once I'd help when Steven died. It was such a terrible, terrible thing when...when..."

"You mean when Steven got splattered all over the road 'cause he wanted an ice cream? I wasn't here to see it though. I was pickling in my mummy's tummy. Guess I got to feed on her sorrow and anger along with the vodka. I was ruined from the start, Father."

The priest tried his hardest to maintain eye contact, but to Toby, it seemed as if there was an invisible line tugging his face to the side like he smelled something foul.

"People been staring at me like that my whole life," said Toby. "I don't like it."

He hoped that would deter the priest, make him put his tail between his legs and shuffle on out, try to save someone else's soul. Toby clucked his tongue when the old man gingerly sat on the edge of his bed, screws creaking from the wall.

"It's been eating at me, I guess," said the priest. "How I didn't visit your mother after what happened. Didn't know how it ate her up inside. How she treated you. Then, for you to do what you did. That nice fellow only out for a walk with his dog. That girl..."

"Are you actually offloading your sins to me? Some fucking man of the cloth you are."

"I'm here to help. No one's too far gone for that. Even if it comes too late."

Toby giggled, spread his arms out, gestured at his surroundings. "I'm at peace, Father. Got my routine. Soon, we'll go for a wee walksies in the bright summer sun. Then I'll come back here, read the next chapter in the book they gave me, meditate, sleep, repeat. I feel quite at home. Born into it, you might say."

"Don't be so—"

"How can you possibly help me now, eh?"

"G-God will forgive—"

"Aye, right."

"God and love is everywhere, is in everything."

"Everything..."

I'm in everything. I am everything. That's what Rattapallax had said.

The sun beamed in the window, making the back of Toby's hands prickle with heat. He stared at those hands, turned them over. "Do you really think I'm worth saving?"

The priest itched at his wiry eyebrows, sucked in a breath. "Yes. Yes, I do."

"Try not to sound too confident there, Father."

Toby turned. As he moved, the priest flinched as if expecting a blow. Toby chuckled, stared out the window, squinting his eyes against the brilliance of it. The red walls of Broadshade prison were a loud exclamation against the grey, drab town below.

"You've gone far off the path meant for all of us," the priest continued. "The path is never denied us. No matter who we are."

"And who am I, exactly?"

"A...A lost soul."

"The rat was right."

"What?"

"I see it now. The world needs people like me. If God was so good, why are these red walls filled to the brim with killers and nutters? We have a role to play. Just like you."

"Don't be so foul."

"What's wrong? Am I making you uncomfortable? Am I supposed to say sorry for what I've become? Least I've come to terms with who I am. You look like you'd rip that collar off in a heartbeat."

Toby glared down at the crooked figure. The priest shoved a finger into the gap between his neck and the collar like it irritated his skin.

"Why are you looking at me like that?" asked the priest.

Rattapallax stared up at him, wearing the priest's garb, a knowing smile spread across his wide mouth. Toby could feel his own eyes grow large.

The priest shuffled on the bed. "W-Why are you smiling?"

"You said God is everywhere, in everything, right?"

The priest stood, backed toward the door. "That's what I believe, yes."

"Let me show you what else is inside every living thing. The red song that anyone can sing."

"Don't." The priest raised his palms, his back hitting the door. "Stop. Help!"

"You're in my house now. And here, we accept who we are. No matter what."

Toby flew forward, head-butting the old man in the nose. He held him up against the door as the guards fidgeted with the heavy lock.

As Toby sank his teeth into the man's neck, tasting the iron of his blood, Rattapallax screamed delight inside his mind.

The door flew open. Toby dropped the old man, who gargled his last breath, blood streaming from the artery he'd chewed right through.

One heavy-set guard stared down at the sight in shock, white growing on his face. "That was Father Thom. You'll go to Hell for that."

Toby ran a tongue over his sharp, sharp teeth. The smell of blood infused him, sang its peace in his blood. "Oh, I'm counting on it, boys. I'm still hungry. Who's next?"

Somewhere in the distance, he could hear the sound of rats scuttling, dancing, shouting with glee.

"Who's next?"

About the Authors

B.L. DANIELS is a writer of horror and weird fiction. He is the author of the *Plague Blade* dark-fantasy series, and his short stories have been featured in various literary magazines and anthologies. He lives in New England with his family and a couple of devious cats. Follow him on Instagram @bldauthor or visit his website at https://bldaniels.com.

BLAKE KOURIK grew up in Texas and Florida, before attending college in Missouri. He currently resides in the Springfield area, working and writing, with aspirations of eventually becoming a professional liar, full-time.

CARSON FREDRIKSEN is a neurodivergent writer from Calgary, Alberta who often enjoys rummaging through his dark, albeit, unique imagination to enhance his everyday life. His debut horror novel *Beyond the Deep* was recently published by Baynam Books Press. His previous short stories have appeared in such online publications as Sometimes Hilarious Horror, CommuterLit, Rooster Republic Press and Howling Wolf Press. In 2022, his short story "Your Biggest Fans" was named an 'Honourable Mention' in *Tales from the Moonlit Path*'s Halloween challenge. In his spare time, Carson can be seen cycling the neighbourhood, watching Jeopardy and spending time with his friends and family. He can also be found at: https://www.carsonfre driksen.com/.

DANIEL BARLEKAMP is the author of fiction, poetry, and audio drama for adults and young readers. His middle-grade horror has appeared and is forthcoming in several magazines and anthologies, including *The Haunted States of America* (Godwin Books/Macmillan, 2024). Originally from New Jersey, Daniel now lives with his wife and son in Massachusetts, where he works in immigration law. Visit him at dgbarlekamp.com.

DEVIN LEONARD is a native of upstate New York and prefers the countryside over cities, and animals over humans. When he isn't writing or devouring books, he likes to walk his dog, throw paint on canvases, and make crop circles in random cornfields to entice the Men in Black. His published stories can be found on Instagram @devinjamesleonard.

DYLAN FREEMAN is a former contributor to the SCP Foundation creative writing project, but is currently seeking professional publication. Their work has been previously featured in the 2022 anthology *Shadows over Avalon* by 18thwall Productions. Their favorite hobby (and only third most-expensive) is collecting LEGO.

DYLAN T. BOSWORTH is a writer and enthusiast of all things dark and dreadful. An active member of the Great Lakes Association of Horror Writers, he is most often found somewhere deep in the Midwest, teaching his two children how to survive the horrors of Small Town, America.

ELIJAH M. NEWTON is a horror writer, memoirist, and host of true-crime podcast *Deliver Us Some Evil* with his wife Mel. For updates, news, art, and all the finest of evil, visit https://deliverusso meevil.com/.

IAN KLINK is a filmmaker, writer, and artist whose work includes the feature film *Anybody's Blues*, the novel *Lucky* from New Fangle

Press, and short stories for *Weren't Another Way to Be: Outlaw Fiction Inspired by Waylon Jennings, The Beauty in Darkness: Illustrated Poetry Anthology, Negative Creep: A Nirvana-Inspired Anthology, A-Z of Horror: U is for Unexplained, Hellbound Books Anthology of Flash Fiction, The Creeps, Vampiress Carmilla, The Siren's Call*, and *Chilling Tales For Dark Nights*. Born and raised in Iowa, Klink lives in Pennsylvania, where he shares his talents as a teacher of multimedia studies.

JAMES FRITZ graduated from Loyola University Chicago with degrees in business and music. He recently quit his job as a data analyst to write full-time. Several of his short stories have been picked up by publishers such as Gypsum Sound Tales, Hellbound Books, and Black Hare Press. You can find him on Instagram under the handle @james.fritz.writing.

JEN MIERISCH'S dream job is to write *Twilight Zone* episodes, but until then, she's a website administrator by day and a writer of odd stories by night. Jen's work can be found in the *Arcanist, NoSleep Podcast, Scare Street*, and numerous anthologies. Jen can be found haunting her local library near Chicago. She is an active member of the Horror Writers Association. For more about Jen, visit www.jen mierisch.com.

J. L. ROYCE is an author of science fiction, the macabre, and whatever else strikes him. He lives in the northern reaches of the American Midwest, exploring the wilderness without and within. His work appears in *Alien Dimensions, Allegory, Cosmic Horror Monthly, Fifth Di, Fireside, Ghostlight, Love Letters to Poe, Lovecraftiana, Mysterion, parABnormal, Penumbric, Sci Phi, Strange Aeon, Utopia, Wyldblood*, etc. He is a member of WWA, HWA, and GLAHW. Find more of his stories at: www.jlroyce.com.

J.R. GRAHAM primarily writes horror and dark fantasy. She likes to travel to creepy and haunted places in her spare time. Her story "Ruby" was published in *Elegant Literature Magazine* #10 and her dark mermaid story, "An Offer Freely Given" was published in the anthology *Ghost Towns*. She lives in Utah with her husband, their two dogs and slightly demonic cat.

J.W. BODDEN is a queer speculative fiction writer from Tegucigalpa, Honduras. His short fiction has appeared in *Spellbinder Magazine, Penumbric Speculative Fiction Magazine,* and *Eldritch Myth.* He's also a first reader at *Radon Journal* and *The Skull & Laurel.* Though busy prepping for doomsday and wandering fictional worlds, you can summon him on X: @jwbodden.

M. STERN is an author of horror, science fiction, and sword & sorcery whose stories have appeared in nearly two dozen anthologies and magazines, including *Chthonic Matter Quarterly, Necronomi-RomCom (Dark Edition), Weirdbook Magazine, Startling Stories, From Beyond the Threshold,* and *Die By The Sword Vol. I & Vol. II.* If you want the latest news about tales of horrors hidden in the human heart and madness concealed behind the memes he has on the way, check out his author blog at http://www.msternauthor.com.

MATTHEW FRYER was born in Sheffield, England and there he still lives with his wife and troublesome cat. He works in the windowless basement of a local hospital and in addition to enjoying noisy music and spiced rum, he likes books, films and video games about all things horror, fantasy and science fiction. He has seen many of his tales published over the years in magazines such as *Space and Time, Murky Depths, Andromeda Spaceways,* and *Criminal Class Review* and anthologies such as *The Horror Library* (Dark Moon Books), *Night Terrors* (Blood Bound Books) and *Dead Bait* (Severed Press). For more about Matthew, visit http://matthewfryer.com/.

MEGAN DIEDERICKS writes poetry and fiction, everything from meek to macabre can be found in between the lines. She self-published her debut poetry collection: *the darkest of times, the darkest of thoughts* in 2022, and her fiction has appeared in titles from various presses and online journals. Keep up with Megan on Instagram: @meganreflects.

MELISSA BURKLEY received her Ph.D. in Psychology from the University of North Carolina Chapel Hill. She is a renowned expert on sexism/racism and her research has been featured in several media outlets, including *The New York Times* and *Cosmopolitan*, with appearances on *Oprah Radio* and *Martha Stewart Radio*. Her literary work has appeared in *Tainted Love: Women in Horror Anthology, Night Terrors (Vol. 8 & 14), Women in Horror Annual 2, Hinnom Magazine*, and *Poets & Writers Magazine*. Her poetry has appeared in *Spooky Magazine* and the *HWA Poetry Showcase*. For more about Melissa, visit http://www.melissaburkley.com/.

NICOLA LOMBARDI is an active participant in the Horror Writers Association. He has published in Italy the novels *The Gypsy Spiders, Black Mother, Night Calls, The Red Bed, The Tank* and *Strigarium*, as well as seven collections of stories since 1989. In addition, he has published novelizations from the films of Dario Argento (*Profondo Rosso* and *Suspiria*) and translated works by Jack Ketchum, Seabury Quinn, Charlee Jacob, F.B. Long and many others for the Italian market. Several of his stories have appeared in English, including in the anthologies *The Beauty of Death: I & II*. In 2021 Tartarus Press published his collection *The Gypsy Spiders and Other Tales of Italian Horror*. Full bibliography at www.nicola lombardi. com. His story The Virgho Method was translated from the original Italian language to English for this anthology by Joe Weintraub. JOE WEINTRAUB has published fiction, essays, and poetry in all sorts of literary places and his plays have been produced throughout the USA and internationally. As a translator he has introduced the Italian and Swiss horror writers, Nicola Lombardi and Davide Staffiero, to the English-speaking world. More at https://jweintraub.weebly.com/.

PANAYIOTIS ANTONIADES is by day, an experienced marketer and growth strategist working with international brands and fighting zombies of the corporate world. By night, he becomes "Undead Dad," an unstoppable force consuming, reviewing, beta-reading, and promoting fine slabs of horror literature on Instagram, Goodreads, Amazon, and Twitter. He often pens his own horror stories that are yet to see the light of day and befriends authors around the globe. Even though he hates hot weather, he currently rots away on a sunny island in the Mediterranean Sea along with an enchanting witch and an adorable energy-sucking vampire. A Gen Xer with a passion for rock and metal, he plays bass guitar and performs concerts in his car regularly. To find out more about Panayiotis, visit his Instagram account @Undead_Dad_reads. He has such great sights to show you.

PAUL O'NEILL is a short story writer with more than fifty published tales. Those works have appeared in the *No Sleep Podcast, Scare Street*, Sinister Smile Press, Crystal Lake Publishing, *the Horror Zine*, and many other publications and competitions. He runs Short Story Club on Substack where he and over 200 readers analyze the classics on a regular basis. He lives in Fife, Scotland.

REBECCA ROWLAND is a Shirley Jackson Award-nominated dark fiction author of three fiction collections, three novels, a handful of novellas, and too many short stories. She is also a Bram Stoker Award-nominated curator of seven horror anthologies, including the best-sellers *Unburied: A Collection of Queer Dark Fiction* and *American Cannibal,* and the 2023 winner of the Godless 666 Award for best novelette. The former acquisitions editor at AM Ink Publishing,

Rebecca shivers in a cold and landlocked corner of America. In her spare time, she pets her cats, eats cheese, and drinks vodka, though not necessarily in that order. Find her at www.RowlandBooks.com or on Instagram @Rebecca_Rowland_books.

RICHARD J. O'BRIEN lives in New Jersey. He paints, writes fiction, and teaches part-time at University of Delaware. Richard's stories have appeared in *Dark Moon Digest, Disturbed Digest, Pulp Literature, The Del Sol Review, Weirdbook,* and other publications over the years. His novels include *The Last Days of Iggy Scanlon, Dark Accidents of Strange Identity,* and *Rejoice for the Dead* (Between the Lines Publishing). Richard earned an MFA in creative writing at Fairleigh Dickinson University.

RIVER J. MYERS is a writer whose work explores the darker corners of human psychology and supernatural phenomena. Their stories have appeared in *Dug Up Magazine, Guilty Crime Story Mag,* and *Solitude Diaries.* When not writing, River enjoys exploring video games that often inspire their fiction.

ROB FRANCIS is an academic and writer based in London. He writes short fantasy and horror, and his stories have appeared in magazines including *The Arcanist, Apparition Lit, Metaphorosis, Tales to Terrify* and *Weird Horror Magazine.* He has also published stories in anthologies including *Alternative War* (B Cubed Press), *The Old Ways* (Eerie River), and *Costs of Living* (Whisper Hour Press). Rob lurks on X (formerly Twitter) @RAFurbaneco.

RON J. CRUZ crafts dark fiction in the haunting shadows of the Sierra Nevada foothills. When he isn't teaching English Composition at Folsom Lake College or capturing quirky photographs, he throws darts competitively (and sometimes erratically). Learn more about Ron and his work at https://ronjcruz.com.

TIM BOITEAU lives in Michigan with his family. He is a Writers of the Future winner and author of several books, most recently the horror novel *The Nilwere* (Grendel Press, 2024). His microfiction piece "Cherry Blossom" won Story of the Year at *50-Word Stories*. Recent stories have appeared in *New Maps, The NoSleep Podcast, Triangulation: Hospitium,* and *Kaleidotrope.* He is an avid runner and piano player.

WINNIE SOLDI is a Page-award winning writer and actor. He grew up in Florence, Italy, and subsequently moved to New York City to earn a BFA in Drama from NYU - Tisch. Growing up speaking multiple languages and having lived in different countries, his screenplays and stories often explore the nuance and meaning of a mixed and conflicting identity through character-focused dramas and horror. As an actor, he's had the privilege of working with Oscar-winning directors such as Kenneth Branagh and Gabriele Salvatores. You can find out more about his work at www.winniesoldi.com.

About the Editor

STEPHEN RHOADES was born long ago. He is the editor of the anthology series *Inanimate Things* and is also the author of such novels as *The California Butcher* and *The Paranormal and Normal Investigators*. To find out more, visit www.buttinchair.com or you can find him on Instagram @authorstephenrhoades. He currently resides in the deepest, darkest parts of Alabama with his wife and family.